Cast of Characters

Lawton (Lawty) Lawrence. The victim. A da: bit of a cad. He exits early but remains on everyone's minds.

Mrs. Anabel Adams. The owner of Beechlands. Her bosom is far more impressive than her bank account. She also has a secret.

Miss Killigrew. The tiny, good-hearted, elderly receptionist.

Paul Livingston. A short, fat Londoner who comes to Beechlands as a potential investor but has nothing good to say about the hotel.

Julian Frake. A wealthy middle-aged Londoner who is also a potential investor, as well as a great admirer of female beauty.

Marigold Trent. A tall, graceful platinum blonde given to wearing very naughty clothing. She collects both men and jewelry.

Jim Bridges. A bitter young architect whose war injuries left him with scars both visible and invisible. His wife left him for Lawty.

Cintra Norton. A 44-year-old film star whose mouth is perpetually open and whose life is totally chaotic.

Christie Layne. Quite unremarkable in dress and demeanor, she's called a "braown maouse" by one and all. But these still waters run deep.

"Gaston Leroux." The head waiter, aka Albert Cummings, who is a not-so-reformed thief and an old acquaintance of Inspector Parry's.

Robert Lord. Every good hotel needs a French chef, which is why he is addressed as Robère Lore.

Sir Eric Hammerton. A pickled baronet. He arrives late and leaves early.

Inspector Lane Parry. A handsome, fortyish, Oxbridge-educated copper who is forced to take refuge at Beechlands during a raging snow storm.

Lilly Baker, Ethel Wills, and Marion Wood. The maids.

Books by Maureen Sarsfield

Green December Fills the Graveyard
which is now published as
Murder at Shots Hall
1945

Gloriana
1946

A Party for Lawty
which has also been published as
A Dinner for None
and is now reprinted as
Murder at Beechlands
1948

Murder at Beechlands

by
Maureen Sarsfield

The Rue Morgue Press
Boulder / Lyons

The Rue Morgue Press
P.O. Box 4119
Boulder, CO 80306

Printed by
Johnson Printing

PRINTED IN THE UNITED STATES OF AMERICA

The Mystery of Maureen Sarsfield

British writer Maureen Sarsfield had all the tools necessary to make it as a major mystery writer, but after publishing just three novels—two of which were mysteries—between 1945 and 1948, she completely disappeared from the literary landscape. Whether she died young, commenced her short career at an advanced age or simply grew tired of the writing life is unknown. The biographical copy on the dust jacket of the American edition of *Green December Fills the Graveyard* (reprinted as *Murder at Shots Hall*) merely identifies her as a new writer, making no comment on her age. Many of the characters in her three novels are in their thirties or forties, and she writes so believably about the sensibilities and attitudes of that age group that she herself probably either belonged to it or had recently entered the early stages of middle age.

Although other mystery writers had been known to give up the form after gaining financial independence (Anthony Berkeley and Ernest Bramah in Britain and Phoebe Atwood Taylor in the United States spring immediately to mind), it seems odd that Sarsfield would have retired after only two mysteries, especially since she began publishing at a time when it was somewhat unusual for an unknown British writer to be picked up so quickly by a U.S. publisher. There is no evidence that her books, although widely reviewed, made much of a splash in the U.S. Other than an appearance in 1950 in *Two Complete Detective Novels* (a pulp magazine) by *Green December Fills the Graveyard*, her books seem not to have been reprinted. Her one mainstream book, the very British *Gloriana*, a look at the bickering inhabitants of a neighborhood in London awaiting the arrival of the young woman title character, failed to attract an American publisher.

Her choice of titles for her mystery books may have been partly to blame for what we assume were unimpressive sales. *Green December Fills the Graveyard* is not only a mouthful but perhaps a bit too literary. Her second and final mystery was published under equally nondescript titles on either side of the Atlantic: in Britain as *A Dinner for None* and in the U.S. as *A Party for Lawty*. It is here reprinted under yet another title, *Mur-*

der at Beechlands. We make no apologies for giving both mysteries somewhat more genre-driven titles. However, while dull titles and mediocre sales
would immediately condemn a mystery author to literary oblivion in today's
cutthroat publishing world, in the 1940s publishers gave their writers more
time to develop an audience, which makes it all the more puzzling why
there were no further books from an author who achieved the critical success that Sarsfield did. This is, of course, pure speculation. All our efforts,
going back several years, to discover anything at all about Sarsfield have
failed. Hopefully, the republication of her two mysteries will rectify this
situation.

Those two mysteries are gems of the British school. Both feature the
fortyish Lane Parry, a Scotland Yard detective who twice finds evil deeds
in the backwaters of Sussex. Parry is a complex and well-drawn character,
yet it is Flikka Ashley, a 36-year-old sculptor, who dominates the action
and the minds—at least of the male characters—in *Murder at Shots Hall*.
You would be hard pressed to find another non-series character in the crime
fiction of that era who so completely steals the stage from the investigating
sleuth. What is even more remarkable is that she manages to do so in a
book that is filled with so many fully realized subordinate players. Adding
to the virtuosity of Sarsfield's debut is her ability to move smoothly and
efficiently from one point of view to another.

Eccentric characters also abound in *Murder at Beechlands*, whose plot
and setting are very much in the Agatha Christie tradition. When Parry's
car fails him during a raging snowstorm, he seeks shelter at a private country hotel, where the murdered body of one of the guests has been ejected
from the premises via an upstairs window. Cut off from his usual police
assistants by the blizzard, Parry functions almost more like an amateur sleuth
than a Scotland Yard detective. In addition to the Christie-like setting, the
characters trapped in the hotel may remind you of the inhabitants of *Gosford
Park*, the recent Oscar-nominated period mystery film from Robert Altman.

One can only speculate where Sarsfield's career would have gone had
she continued in the vein of these two books. Even so, she made her mark
on the field. If the brevity of her career prevented her from becoming one
of the masters of the field, she stands, as W. Somerset Maugham so honestly described himself, in the front rank of the second raters.

Tom & Enid Schantz
Lyons, Colorado
July 2003

CHAPTER 1

UP in her private suite on the first floor, Mrs. Anabel Adams paced the deep red pile carpet of her sitting room, backward and forward and round and round. She hadn't paid for the carpet yet, a fact that the London furnishing house that had supplied her with it had been reminding her of for twelve months. Their reminders were becoming less and less polite.

Down in a corner of the lounge, peered at by a sightless gilt cupid holding a gilt torch from which sprouted a frosted electric candle, Mr. Livingston and Mr. Frake discussed Mrs. Anabel Adams with such concern that anyone listening to them might have thought they wanted to do her a good turn. From time to time they glanced over their shoulders, however, to make quite sure no one was listening. They had both arrived by the same train at Watching station, and, in separate taxis, had reached the porticoed entrance of the Beechlands Hotel at almost the same moment. Neither knew the other had left London for their goal on the crowded 2:45, nor had they noticed each other on the dark, snow-enwrapped platform. Hence the two taxis. For although they were rivals, they were far too businesslike to waste their money on two taxis when one would have done quite as well. Especially as they had each had to bribe their drivers heavily to take them the five miles to Beechlands, for it had been snowing heavily all day. By five o'clock (the train was late) the roads were very nearly impassable.

In the front hall, sneered at by a very large but very bad reproduction of "The Laughing Cavalier," one rather bony shoulder propped against the uncomfortably granulated dark brown and gilt-speckled paneling, Jim Bridges stared absently at the curtain of snowflakes framed in the plate-glass windows of the main door. Anabel, as she so frequently did when she was worried and wished for sympathetic instead of amusing and profitable company, had rung him late in the afternoon, begging him to come and see her. He had now been there for over an hour and hadn't seen her yet. She appeared to be either permanently engaged or had forgotten she had summoned him. This was not unusual, but he was beginning to wonder, if he waited much longer, whether he would be able to get home through all this snow. He looked up at the hall clock. It was past half past five. Through the open doors of the dining room he could see that one of the tables had been festively decorated, as if in someone's honor, with a lot of pink roses mixed up with the leftover Christmas holly.

Behind him, he could hear Miss Killigrew, the receptionist, telephoning in her office. A quarter to six struck, and she left the office and appeared behind the desk, patting her stringy gray hair. She was so short that only her head and shoulders showed above the desk. As usual, she was out of breath, as if she had been running.

"Who's the honored guest?" Jim asked her.

"Didn't you know?" Miss Killigrew breathed. "I've never met him before, of course, but we've all heard about him. Such a surprise for Mrs. Adams. I'm so glad. He's just back from South America—Mr.—at least, he's a wing commander—Lawton Lawrence."

Jim's plain and colorless face registered polite interest. The back of his neck felt as though a rat were gnawing it. The insides of his hands turned very cold.

"Did he—is his wife with him?" he asked Miss Killigrew.

"She's still in South America, I believe."

When he'd come in, he'd thrown his snowy coat on one of the radiators. As he picked it up and started to put it on, he noticed that the melted snow had made puddles on the carpet. So Lawty was back, was he? Returned in triumph to his old haunt, and the table was decorated in his honor with pink roses mixed up with holly.

"Oh! Mr. Bridges?"

"Yes, Miss Killigrew?" Jim liked saying her name, it suited her so ridiculously well.

"Oh, you aren't going, are you? Madam said she particularly wanted to see you. I think she must be changing early for dinner."

He slithered his shoulders out of his coat, put it back on the radiator, and wandered toward the shallow steps that led to the cocktail bar. Was that why Anabel wanted to see him?

In No. 3, a large room at the opposite end of the corridor to Anabel Adams's suite, Cintra Norton tore off her slacks and violently began to tear a very tight dinner frock over her head. Half in and half out of the garment, she muttered to herself, tore it off again, and threw it on the floor, which was already cluttered with various bits and pieces of clothing, shoes, sandals, and squashed lipstick. Then she clutched her gingery golden hair, and opening her mouth very wide, groaned like an animal in pain. After that she reached her hands out in front of her, clawed at the air so that her gold-varnished nails flashed, and scrambled back into her slacks. The hotel seemed unnaturally still, muffled, dead. Swaying slightly, she toppled to the door, opened it, listened, heard nothing, crept down the corridor and up the stairs that led to the top floor.

"Lawty?" she whispered, and turned the handle of the door she had come to a stop at. "Lawty? Lawty?" She opened the door. The lights were all on, but the room was empty.

For a moment she hesitated, one hand on her throat as if she were about to choke herself. The writing table seemed a hundred miles away, separated from her by an unnavigable sea of royal blue pile carpet. On the writing table Lawty's dispatch case was wide open.

"Oh, my God, oh, my God," Cintra whispered, and groped across the blue pile sea.

From the kitchen quarters came noises and smells. The clatter of cooking pots and dishes, and smells of expensive food, were wafted under the door on a current of hot air. One of the kitchenmaids was giggling. In the pantry, Gaston, the headwaiter, silently polished some silver pepper pots. Now and then he looked round, but there was nobody there. Just to make sure, he shut the pantry door and put a chair in such a position that anyone opening the door would bump into it and make a noise as he came in.

In the cocktail bar, which was very hot, Marigold Trent played darts by herself, stopping occasionally to take a sip of her brandy and soda. On one of the bar stools, her back against the wall at the farthest end of the bar, her very straight legs in their white, hand-knitted skiing stockings dangling inertly, her mouse-colored hair as usual rolled in its neat bun at the nape of her neck, Christie Layne twisted the stem of her almost empty glass round and round in her fingers. At the other end of the bar, lolling on it, Wing Commander Lawton Lawrence, D.S.O., D.F.C. (retired), watched Marigold's graceful antics at the dart board. She was very tall, always beautifully dressed, and her hair was natural platinum blonde. At frequent intervals he detached himself from the bar, strolled behind it, and refilled his and Marigold's glasses, pouring out very large tots. The barmaid had left two days before in a tremendous hurry, saying she wouldn't never enter the doors of Beechlands Hotel ever again.

Christie had put the appropriate amount of money in the till when she poured herself out a whisky and orange. Lawty never put anything in the till, nor did he chalk up his and Marigold's drinks on a bar chit. Anabel had said, "All your drinks on the house, Lawty darling, it's your party." So Lawty was having his party. Every time he went behind the bar he stumbled over Christie. Occasionally he apologized without looking at her.

"A double, and another double—oh! And a treble twenty," lovely Marigold exclaimed.

"How marvelous," Christie said.

"Dear little braown maouse, I didn't realize you were abaout the 'aouse,"

Marigold laughed, patting Christie on the arm.

Whenever Christie turned up on an occasion when everybody or any-one felt festive, she was greeted with the same remark: "Look aout, there's a braown maouse abaout the 'aouse." Further than that, people just tripped over her, bumped into her, and said they were so sorry, but they'd forgotten her name. Except when Anabel rang her up and said to her that for God's sake, darling, would she come along straightaway as she felt so depressed, or worried, or both. Anabel had rung her up that evening, much earlier, and Christie had been waiting since five o'clock for a further invitation to go upstairs and listen to the worry, whatever it was this time.

Marigold launched another attack on the dart board, Lawty's eyes still on her. He had, thought Christie, had plenty to drink. But his two years in South America seemed to have made him even better-looking than ever. He was the best looking man she had ever seen. About his grim and rather dissipated face there was something fascinating.

"Well, Lawty?" she said. "Glad to be back?"

He dragged his eyes away from Marigold's hair and looked at her.

"Hullo?" he said. "I've met you before, haven't I?"

"Two years ago, before you went civil-aviating abroad."

"Yes, of course. Have a drink?"

He didn't remember her in the least, Christie thought. But she said she would have a drink, and said, "Cheers," pleasantly, when he poured her out one.

"Cheers," Lawty said. "Is everyone changing tonight, Marigold?"

"Darling? What? Yes, of course." Marigold smiled at him, turning her back on the dart board. "Haven't you brought your natty little tuxedo with you?"

"Where's Cintra?"

"Oh, God, how should I know? Redyeing her hair again, I suppose. Why?"

Lawty didn't answer. Marigold's eyes hardened; then she was smiling again. Christie sat in her corner, once more forgotten. She never did, she never said, she never wore anything remarkable. She simply faded into the background. The bar clock pinged six, and she looked down into her drink and wondered what would happen if she did do something really remark-able, such as giving someone a tap behind the ear with the sharp little gilt-plated ice hammer that lived on the bar. Snick, just behind the ear, and down they'd go. She picked up the ice hammer and tapped it on the bar.

"What's that?" Marigold's eyes opened wide in sudden anxiety. "Lawty, what was that?"

"What d'you mean?"

"I heard three knocks. You know, three knocks." Marigold's voice rose.

"Three knocks, you know, Lawty. Before Grant was killed Anabel told me she heard them, and before . . ."

"I'm so sorry," Christie said penitently. "It was only me."

Lawty turned his eyes on her, then turned them away. Evidently he had suddenly remembered who she was.

CHAPTER 2

THE sky still spewed its fleecy snowflakes, blotting out everything. Fortunately there was no wind to make matters worse. But they were too bad for the various people Anabel had asked to Lawty's party to amuse Lawty and suitably impress Paul Livingston and Julian Frake. To amuse Lawty she had asked three young women who lived in the Watching direction. One of them had a husband in tow, but he wasn't very particular. The principal thing was that the three young women all had plenty of money, which they didn't mind spending, and were the type Lawty liked. And Lawty liked them well perfumed, well made up, slickly dressed, and with as few morals as possible. As well as the three young women and the one husband, Anabel had asked a sprightly countess and a permanently pickled (but pickled in the nicest possible way, of course) baronet for the edification of Paul Livingston and Julian Frake. Paul Livingston, particularly, went into raptures over titles. It was only too bad the hotel itself was so empty, but she could lay the blame on the weather for that.

But after one look at the weather, the three young women and the one husband, the sprightly countess, and even the pickled baronet had decided that no party in the world was worth the risk of getting stuck in a snowdrift. So instead of a stream of expensive-looking cars converging on Beechlands, the roads were quite empty except for one solitary car that nosed its way slowly through the white-spotted darkness, its driver lost, though not in the least bewildered.

"Oh, hell," he said suddenly, and pulled the wheel over too late.

With a silent, comfortable wallowing motion, the car bogged itself in a drift by the side of the road, its wheels revolving fruitlessly, except to dig the car farther into the deep, snow-hidden ditch. So that was that. Good old sunny Sussex. If it wasn't blowing a gale, or raining, or befogged, it was feet deep in snow.

"Well, my little one, you've had it . . . ."

Over six feet of the little one got out of the car, with some difficulty, as it was almost on its side, and reviewed the situation. A charming end to a week of duck shooting on a bleak marsh. He switched off the engine and was glad he was alone in his misfortune. There was nothing to be seen but snow. No house, not even a cow shed; no convenient A.A. telephone box. No wayfarers struggling home who might send a message for a breakdown gang to tow the car out of its present position—not that any breakdown gang would turn out on such an evening. There wasn't even a signpost pointing to some uncivilized Sussex village where there might be a pub that couldn't give anyone a bed because they didn't let rooms, or a double whisky because they had no whisky. And no gin. Sorry, no spirits of any sort.

There was, however, one sign that, if not now, at one time the bleak spot had been inhabited. On the other side of the road an enormously high, forbidding stone wall, snow-capped, reared itself. Unfortunately it was too high to climb. But walls weren't built for nothing. They existed either to keep people out or to keep them in. This wall was more of a fortification than anything else. On its far side might be a derelict mansion, a prison, a hospital, or an institution of some sort.

"Lane Parry, you were a fool to start back on an evening like this," Lane Parry told himself.

He dug in his overcoat pocket and unearthed his small silver flask. It was half full, and when he took a gulp of whisky it felt comfortingly warm as it trickled down inside him. He had vaguely noticed the wall about a quarter of a mile back, but he couldn't remember if he had passed any sort of entrance. But somewhere or other there must be one. The wall couldn't go on forever. He decided to walk on in the hope of finding either an inhabited lodge or, if there was no lodge, a gate. The snow was nearly up to his knees, and for once he wished he wore a hat. The snowflakes melted on his hair and trickled down the back of his neck and clung to his eyelashes with the persistence of ticks. But although he faced being benighted, he found something fascinating in the silence, the loneliness, the untracked snow. Waiting for him behind the curtain of moving flakes, anything might lurk. He shone his torch on his watch. It was just six o'clock. At the same moment, muffled, very far away, but distinct, a clock struck six. A church clock? A village hall clock? The clock of someone's ancestral stable yard?

Parry was right first guess. It was the clock in the squat tower of Ditchit church, the nearest village to Beechlands.

Anabel vaguely heard the six strokes as she paced her red pile carpet. Six o'clock, and she hadn't seen either Julian Frake or Paul Livingston yet. She stopped her interminable pacing and picked up the receiver of the house telephone.

"Miss Killigrew? Please ask Mr. Frake if he'll come up and have a drink."

She waited for the usual "Yes, Mrs. Adams," but no Miss Killigrew answered.

"Damn the woman," Anabel said, and banged the receiver down. Evidently Miss Killigrew had deserted her post in the office. So now what? Anabel felt that to go downstairs, search out Julian Frake—or even Paul Livingston—and ask him to come upstairs with her would be undignified. And at all costs she must preserve her dignity. Anabel's dignity was one of her assets. It made the hotel less of a hotel than a country mansion, she had long ago decided. It also had the most petrifying effect on tradesmen who wanted her to pay the bills she owed them. Towered over by her large, firm, and outstanding bosom, they visibly wilted, and, with any luck, took their departure.

Anabel's morale not being too good, she had a quick gin, powdered her face, and pressed her hair into place in front of her bedroom mirror. Her bedroom was done in off-white brocades, tinged with black, to match her hair, or rather, to tone with it. Her hair was dyed jet-black, but she had left one white streak untouched. The effect was almost as striking as her bosom. When she had had her sitting room decorated with deep red brocade curtains to match the Knole settee and the unpaid-for carpet, her idea had been that deep red had a mellowing influence on her favored visitors. The only trouble was that none of her clothes matched the background, so she had had to get a lot of new ones that didn't clash.

"Damn," Anabel said to her reflection.

The best thing to do would be to go down to the bar, where, no doubt, Julian and Paul were now having drinks together as if they loved each other like blood brothers, and hope that one of them would have the sense to draw her tactfully to one side and suggest a private chat before dinner. She'd have to go down soon, anyway. There was Lawty's party to reorganize. And the magnificence, the gaiety, the smartness of Lawty's party was to have been one of the baits to tempt Julian and Paul. And now it had come unstuck. Anabel mentally upbraided the three young women, the one husband, the sprightly countess, and the permanently pickled baronet for having been so weak-gutted as to cry off because of the snow.

Now there were only herself, Lawty, Marigold, and Cintra to impress the two rivals. Then she suddenly remembered about Christie and Jim. Poor, kindly darlings, but such bores, and so terribly unsmart and ordinary. Still, if she asked them to join the party, they could sit next each other and swell the table by their presence, even if they didn't grace it.

Anabel sailed downstairs. Half an hour for plenty of drinks before dinner, then they would go up and change. From the kitchen still came the usual noises, the usual smells. But, all of a sudden, a feeling of terrifying unreality came over her. The pantry door was shut. Why? She turned the handle, flung it open, and nearly fell over a chair.

"What is that chair doing there?" she demanded, feeling normal again.

"A booby trap? I don't want any of your nonsense, Gaston."

"But, madame, I'm so sorry!" Gaston whipped the chair to the side of the room, his long, greenish-white face full of concern. "I wanted to stand on it to reach the top shelf."

"Why?"

"To get the little pink coffee cup the countess likes so much, madame."

"They aren't coming," Anabel said. "None of them. Relay the table for eight."

Fortunately the bar was small. The seven people in it seemed almost a crowd, and the effect was heightened by the immense amount of cigarette smoke and the way Cintra was flinging herself from one corner of the room to the other, creating the impression that she was quads. Anabel's practiced eye took in the scene, weighing up everyone's mood, and for a moment the charming smile on her large face froze. Good God, she'd forgotten all about the Lawty-Jim Bridges business when she had summoned Jim to come and see her. Should she try to get rid of Jim instead of asking him to dine? Or should she ignore the embarrassing situation, as though she took it for granted the affair of over two years ago had been forgotten by everybody? On the whole, she thought that the best bet, for Lawty was getting on for drunk and didn't appear to even notice Jim, while Jim was sitting quietly over a beer at the other end of the bar, not looking in Lawty's direction or, for that matter, anyone's.

"Ah!" Paul Livingston exclaimed, and inserting himself between Julian Frake and Anabel, greeted her with outstretched hands. He was a short fat man, and his head nearly came into collision with Anabel's bust. "Anabel dear, how well you look!"

"So lovely to see you, dear!" She reached over him and clasped Julian's hand warmly. "So awfully rude of me not to've put in an appearance earlier. Old Lord Whatsisname came to tea and simply wouldn't go. Such an old bore, otherwise I'd have asked you both to come up."

No Lord Whatsisname had been to tea with her, but as she had to make some sort of excuse, she might as well make an impressive one.

"Lawty darling, have you got a drink? Marigold? Do have another. Cintra, what're you drinking, dear?" Anabel then smiled benevolently at Christie and Jim, and sailed behind the bar.

"No barmaid tonight?" Julian asked, raising his voice, because Cintra was making a sort of yowling noise over a solitary dice game, and Lawty and Marigold were talking into each other's faces.

"I had to send her away," Anabel said calmly.

Cintra dug her gold nails into her hair. "Don't talk about it, for God's sake," she wailed. "She simply terrified me, saying this place gave her the willies. Anabel darling, it isn't haunted, is it? She said she heard noises."

"Cintra, don't be silly." Anabel smiled, but inwardly she seethed with rage. Once Cintra got started, nothing would stop her.

"I told you—" Paul Livingston gave Julian Frake a jab in the ribs with a pudgy forefinger, the sweat breaking out on his face. "It must be something unlucky with this place. First Grant killed like that, then that other man getting killed—"

Anabel took firm hold of a large bottle of champagne and let the cork fly. A lot of the champagne flowed over the bar, but at least it created a diversion.

Jim unglued his gaze from his beer glass and looked up. Christie still sat in the same position with her legs dangling, but the expression in her eyes startled him. He knew everyone thought he was a harmless bore, just as he, in common with everyone who knew her, thought Christie Layne was a harmless, ordinary little bore without any particular intelligence and no wit. So it was a shock to find that apparently they were all quite wrong. For he had caught her in the act of lapping up every word that was being said, every action; lapping up the atmosphere, quietly amused at everybody's antics and obviously seeing through every pretense. Mentally, she was stripping the whole lot of them of their veneer, and, with her calm gray eyes, seeing them as they in reality were. Then, to his dismay, he met her eye, and knew she knew he had surprised her with her guard down.

He buried his face in his beer glass. He didn't want to share Christie's secret with her. He scarcely knew her, to begin with, and there was something indecent in finding her out like this. An intimacy he didn't want forced on him against his will, as if, at the point of a gun, he had been made to pull all her clothes off, throw her into a bed, and get in beside her. He felt, somehow, shameful, and bitterly resentful. The gabble of talk rose round him in waves, and, like waves, suddenly and unaccountably subsided.

"What's that?" Marigold said. "Listen."

Cintra swayed and put her hands round her throat, her eyes staring. "The three knocks—" Her voice rasped as if she were in mortal agony.

"Oh, really, don't be so ridiculous." Anabel frowned, wishing Cintra would really choke herself and that Marigold hadn't drunk so much that she was aping Cintra's hysteria. "It's the chef chopping up the chickens in the kitchen."

"Something awful's going to happen," Paul gasped. "Julian, like I told you, this place wouldn't bring no luck to anyone. Don't you touch it with a broom handle."

"I haven't got a broom handle on me," Julian said pleasantly. "And if I had, I wouldn't start knocking Anabel's house about with it. Marigold, sweet, another drink?"

"I think we'd all better go and change," Anabel said firmly. "Lawty darling, take a drink up with you?" At all costs, she must put a stop to this nonsense. If she didn't, it wouldn't be only Lawty's party that would come unstuck. "Lawty?" she repeated, as he didn't seem to hear her. "I think we'll all go up and change, don't you?"

Lawty swayed away from the bar, showing his perfect white teeth. "I'll go up and bloody well throw myself out of the window. A nice prize packet you handed on to me, didn't you, Jim? You must be as bucked as hell."

Like a battleship going into action, Anabel weighed anchor, and maneuvering herself from behind the bar, swept everyone out of the room before her as if they were a flock of sheep, Paul, Julian, Cintra, Marigold, Lawty, Jim, Christie.

Bedroom, bathroom, lavatory doors banged in various parts of the house, some of them loudly, some of them softly. There were noises of baths being turned on, bedroom hot and cold taps running. Footsteps went up and down corridors, thumping footsteps, light ones, softly hesitant ones. But all the noises were dimmed and muffled by the fuggy atmosphere, the many curtains and heavy furnishings.

In the kitchen the chef finished dismembering chickens and laid the chopper aside.

"I'll need some cracked ice to put round the grapefruit," he told Lilly, the junior of the two kitchenmaids. "Go and get the ice hammer out of the bar, and don't drink up all the booze when you're doing it."

"I can't go in the bar, not like this," Lilly objected.

"They'll all have gone to doll themselves up."

"Oh, O.K. And don't blame me if I get caught with a dirty apron on. Where'll I find the hammer, anyhow?"

"In the bar, I told you." The chef rested his hands on his hips and shook his head. "What're your eyes for? If it isn't on the bar itself, then it'll be on one of the shelves. Where else d'you suppose? Hidden under one of the rugs?"

Five minutes later Lilly returned.

"I can't find the hammer nowhere. I looked under the rugs and all. It's gone. And there was a queer noise, like as if someone'd threw a sack of coals out of one of the upstairs windows onto the terrace. I don't like this place. I'm going to give notice tomorrow. That barmaid was right, there's ghosts here. She said she heard noises, and now I've just heard one. Nasty, it was. Gave me the creeps, it did. And now someone's took the ice hammer, so how'm I going to crack the ice up?"

CHAPTER 3

"EXCELSIOR, excelsior," Parry remarked. "Pick 'em up and put 'em down."

It had stopped snowing for the time being, but he was sick to death of wading along the apparently endless snow-buried road. He had been walking for nearly an hour, but reckoned he could have left the car only about a mile and a half behind him; the going was slow, even with his long legs. On his right, the wall still reared itself, unbroken. He turned another corner, then another, and to his relief his torch shone on a large, imposing gate. Best of all, the gate was open, not bolted and barred.

He went in what he supposed must be a drive, and saw the snow was unblemished by car tracks or footprints. Here and there tall trees and stiff, formal groups of evergreen bushes broke the whiteness, themselves laden with snow. Between the trees lights shone, and leaving the drive, Parry headed straight for them. So far as he could make out, the house was large, very high, and probably old. There was nothing to indicate what sort of people lived in it, except that there must be quite a lot of them. More than half the windows were lit up, and over the pillared portico a miniature searchlight threw a silver circle on the snow. He stumbled up the steps, looked for a bell, failed to find one, and tried the double doors. Like the gate, they were unlocked.

Blinking in the lights, Parry thought the hall, or whatever it was, singularly hideous. Why cover up respectable paneling with dark brown and gold-speckled granular paint? Why the awful reproduction of "The Laughing Cavalier"? Why so much gilt? And what the hell was the appalling noise? It sounded like a herd of buffaloes stampeding, accompanied by throaty howlings that were scarcely human. He stepped aside just in time to avoid being run down by a human avalanche, headed by a female maniac with gingery gold hair, wearing the tightest dress he'd ever seen and very high-heeled gold sandals. At the same time he was aware that a small, elderly female was bobbing about behind a kind of gilded redout saying something to him. But whatever it was she was saying was drowned by the hubbub outside.

Parry opened one half of the swing door and took a look at the inmates at play. He thought it rather tough that he had landed at a private lunatic asylum, but he supposed it was the sort of thing that was bound to happen on a night like this. Having drunk the rest of his whisky, he felt warmed within and pleasantly light in the head.

The lunatic in the dangerously tight frock was staggering about with her mouth wide open, scrabbling up handfuls of snow and throwing them wildly at nothing. Every now and then she fell over her skirt, when she gave tongue, her arms stretched out in front of her. As if this were a signal, a fat little man with a hooked nose pounced at her with, apparently, intentions to devour her. Parry thought it much more likely she'd devour him first. A tall, very decorative female lunatic in a silver garment that almost matched her hair tried feverishly to cram snow down the neck of a middle-aged, well-set-up man, who bawled, "Ow! Ow! Ow-ow-ow!"

The lanky youngish man in flannel trousers and the mousy-haired girl in the white knitted stockings Parry took to be keepers, as they stood perfectly still and did nothing at all. Then the girl suddenly began to make the hardest snowballs he'd ever seen and aim them with deadly precision backed by so much strength she might have had steel springs in her arms. The man in the flannel bags, after watching her covertly, did the same, and Parry changed his mind. Evidently they were nuts too.

The chief lunatic seemed a base case. Despite the awful noises she made when she fell over her skirt, she appeared able to utter only one word, and it was meaningless.

"Lawty! Lawty! Lawty!" And, as a variation, "Lawty? Lawty? Lawty?"

"Aren't they babies?"

"I beg your pardon?"

Parry turned, bumped into a mountain of black and white brocade, and received a charming though dignified smile. Here, in person, was the matron, he presumed.

"So sorry to butt in," he said, smiling with equal charm, but not so much dignity, "only my car's stuck in a drift along the road."

"Stuck? Too bad for you. Such a night! Miss Killigrew? You'll stay, of course? Miss Killigrew? Give this gentleman number fourteen."

"I've not come to stay yet," Parry said. "Though I admit no one in his senses would've tried to drive back to town on a night like this. Maybe in a few years I'll turn up in a plain van. Though very likely not. One of the free government institutions would be more in my line. I'd hate my wife to waste unnecessary money. Did you know your gate's open? I suppose it's O.K., but a couple of them do seem to be definitely homicidal. They come in voluntarily, of course, as the two sexes are allowed to frolic together?"

The matron and the one called Miss Killigrew looked at him very strangely indeed, as if he were nuts himself. Or were they nuts too? He glanced furtively out the door, wondering if he'd better make a bolt for it. If the black and white brocade attacked him, he wouldn't have a hope in hell. On the other hand, he might be playfully attacked in full force if he tried to escape via the drive. The silver lunatic was doing her best to throw the middle-aged, well-set-up man into a drift; the one in the tight frock flung the fat little man away from her, and shrieking, "Lawty? Lawty? Lawty?" rushed away from the others, gaped upward, then down, and stood transfixed, pointing at something Parry couldn't see, directly under the wall of the house; and out of her thin, angular body came the most bloodcurdling screams he'd ever heard.

"I think something should be done about that one," he said, and grasping his torch firmly, as a possible weapon of defense, dodged past the girl in the white knitted stockings and made off across the now trampled snow.

"You're getting your pretty sandals all spoiled," he said soothingly. "Don't you think you'd better go in before you catch a cold?"

But the creature took no notice. She went on screaming and pointing at something black and white that lay in a streak of light that shone from one of the ground-floor windows. And the black and white thing had a face, and out of the face's mouth blood trickled, and there was more blood on the snow.

"Cintra, be quiet!"

The black and white lady loomed beside Parry, looking very cross indeed. "Cintra, stop it. Oh, my God! Oh, my God!"

"Get them all inside at once," Parry ordered. "And make them stay in. One of your inmates seems to've jumped, or fallen, out of that window up there, poor devil."

"He said he would!" Cintra cried. "He said he was going to bloody well jump out of the window!"

"Lawty, oh, God, Lawty—"

So Lawty wasn't just a made-up lunatic word. It was a name, and this bloody mess was its owner, or erstwhile owner. Parry turned his torch on. White, horror-stricken faces crowded behind him. The little fat man was making horrible gurgling noises.

"Madam, please get all these people inside at once, now," Parry addressed the brocaded bosom with authority, and it took effect.

He didn't watch them go into the house, but swiveled his torch over the ground. The snow all round Lawty was smooth. Not even a bird had hopped across it. High above, on the top floor, light streamed from an open window, the parted curtains hanging limp and still. Why the hell weren't the windows barred? This was a nice finale to his week's holiday, which had anyway been rather dreary. For a base moment he pondered whether, now the coast was clear, he'd hook it. But the coast wasn't clear. The youngish man in the flannel trousers had come silently up behind him, and stood with his hands in his pockets, staring at Lawty. Under his breath he hummed, "Oh, the bold aviator lay dying," then suddenly shut his mouth very tightly.

"May I ask," Parry said, "if you're one of the—if you live here?"

"No, I don't live here."

"I see."

"He couldn't've fallen out of the window. The sill's too high from the floor."

"Oh? You might help me carry him in, will you? Just stay where you are for the moment, though."

Parry despoiled the snow with his footprints, and, kneeling down, shone his torch on the crumpled body.

"Good God, he's still alive—just. He oughtn't to be moved except on a stretcher, but we can't let him freeze. Give me a hand. By the way, what's your name?"

"Bridges. Jim Bridges. Which end'll I take, head or heels?"

Cool customer, Parry thought. Rather too cool. "Get him under the knees. I'll take the top part of him."

As they picked Lawty up and carried him toward the door, Parry could feel the broken bones under his hands and hear them grating together. More blood trickled out of the open mouth. With some difficulty they got up the steps. Lawty was over six feet and heavy with muscle.

"Put him down for a moment and hook the doors open," Parry said. So the sill of the room with the open window was too high from the floor for anyone to fall out? Then he must have jumped. "And if any of the boys and girls are hanging around, tell them to clear out, will you, Bridges? That's to say if they're capable of understanding a simple suggestion like that."

Apparently they were. He could hear some sobbings and moanings and exclamations, but the hall was empty when they staggered in with the unlovely burden. Parry steered for the nearest door and found he had chosen the dining room.

"Hell. We'll have to put him on the floor. Kick that chair out of the way if you can."

They put Lawty on the floor. Another trickle of blood ran out, of his mouth. He sighed a bubbling sigh. The blood stopped running.

"He's dead." Parry crouched down on one knee. "He must've been damn tough not to've been killed outright, if, of course, it was that top-floor window he fell from, or jumped out of."

"He always had that room. He liked the view. And he wasn't the kind of chap to try to do himself in, even when he was tight."

"Tight or sober," Parry patiently pointed out, "people of even slightly unsound mind are quite apt to jump out of windows."

"What the devil d'you mean, slightly unsound mind?"

Parry took out his cigarette case, offered it to Jim, and laughed suddenly.

"Kee-riste. Isn't this a private mental home or what have you?"

Jim stared at Parry, and for the first time showed some emotion, and it was amusement.

"It's a hotel. Beechlands Hotel. Still, you aren't far out. It's a bit like a madhouse sometimes."

"Good God," Parry said, "I thought the monument in the black and white brocade was the matron, and the small, bobbing female the second in command. No wonder they looked at me rather old-fashioned. The monument asked me if I'd come to stay, and I said no, not yet, but perhaps I'd turn up in a plain van in a few years. I appear to've put my foot in it."

"Anabel'll have forgotten by now," Jim shrugged. "Things slip out of her head very easily when there's something else to think of. She'll be in such a God-awful state about Lawty nothing else will register for a hit."

"Is Anabel the monument? Manageress, or what"

"Mrs. Anabel Adams. She owns the place, more or less."

Parry pulled at his lower lip. This Jim Bridges gave a first impression of being dull and ordinary; but somehow, Parry felt, he wasn't nearly so dull or ordinary as he seemed.

"Why choose 'Oh, the bold aviator lay dying'?" he asked.

Jim reddened. "It was damn bad taste. I didn't realize what I was doing. Association of ideas, I suppose. He was a bold aviator, if you see what I mean?"

"I do," Parry said, not quite truthfully.

"Wing Commander Lawton Lawrence, D.S.O., D.F.C., retired."

Parry whistled softly. "He was a hell of a swell during the war, when he was young, wasn't he? A tough chap. A bit too tough in the end, if I remember. Rather a nasty reputation for chuck 'em on the bed, love 'em, and leave 'em. Poor devil, he did it once too often, didn't he, and had to clear out?"

"Yes."

"Took someone else's wife while her husband was all mashed up in hospital?"

"Yes."

"I hope the woman isn't around now, else we'll have more hysterics. Is she?"

"No."

"You aren't very communicative, are you?" Parry said.

"No." Jim's voice was flat. "I'd rather not rake up the subject of my erstwhile wife, if you don't mind. It's not tasty. Lawty got me to divorce her. Funny, because he didn't usually marry them."

Parry had an unpleasant foreboding that he'd walked into something exceedingly nasty.

"Sorry," he said, meaning it. "I think I'll be off now. Will you ring up a doctor and get him to come along and see about the body and so on?"

He avoided looking at Jim, knelt down again, and tried to straighten the shattered arms and legs before he went. For going he was. He'd walked into something nasty, the suicide—presumably—of someone who'd decided to make amends in the worst possible taste. But he could walk out of it again. Not his business. This wasn't his bailiwick. All the same, it seemed only decent to do something for all that remained of a man who'd once been very gallant.

Lawty couldn't have moved after he'd hit the ground. He was too smashed up. His ribs must have pierced his lungs. From the way he'd been lying, he had obviously landed on his front, his head twisted to the side so that his right cheek was upward. All that soft snow, and yet he was so pulped. Then Parry remembered that the snow where the poor devil had landed was only a thin surface. Why? Had the heat from the overheated house melted it as it fell? Or was .there some sort of cellar underneath the place with a central heating plant in it, which warmed the ground above? He tried to prop Lawty's head straight, but it flopped sideways.

He looked up. Jim stood by the door, as if he waited for further orders.

"I think you'd better ring the local police, too," Parry said slowly. "Then come back in here. And it'd be just as well if no one left the house. No one at all, if you'll tell the inmates—or rather, the guests and staff and so on."

Jim half opened the door, then stopped.

"By the way," he said, "the doctor and the local police might like to know who it is that's ordering them about."

I'm for it now, Parry inwardly groaned. Now they'll get their hooks on me. Never again would he come to Sussex. Too many things happened in Sussex.

"Smith," he said pleasantly, and waited without any hope at all for Jim to depart, which of course he didn't. "I had an idea you wouldn't believe me, even though the London phone book has about six pages of Smiths in it, any of which might be me. My name's Parry. Lane Parry. If you must have the whole mouthful, then Inspector Lane Parry, Criminal Investigation Department, Scotland Yard, London, and, as the Americans would add, Eng."

"I see. A policeman." Jim shut the door after him, and left Parry alone with Lawty and the neat, fresh bruise behind Lawty's ear.

CHAPTER 4

PARRY locked the dining-room door. When the doctor and the local police arrived, he would hand the business over to them and go. Only where to, he had no idea. He should have asked Jim Bridges where he was. The name of Beechlands Hotel conveyed nothing to him. He supposed that he'd be called as a witness at the inquest, but in the meantime all he wished for was to get out of this, somehow extricate his car from its burial place, and get back to London.

Instinctively he began to tick things off in his mind. The screeching Cintra female had screeched out something to the effect that Lawty'd said he'd do it, that he'd said he was bloody well going to jump out of the window. According to Jim Bridges, the sill was too high from the floor for anyone to fall out of the window. According to Jim Bridges, Lawty always had that room when he stayed there. He had also implied that Lawty was half tight, but that even when half tight he wasn't the sort of chap to jump out of windows. And Lawty had pinched Jim Bridges' wife off him when he was all mashed up in hospital. So, unless Jim Bridges had been glad to get rid of his wife, he must pretty well have hated Lawty like hell.

Parry half closed his eyes, looking backward. The snow where Lawty had landed was flat and smooth. No knob or spike had stuck up out of it that might have made that round bruise just behind Lawty's ear. Nor, so far as he had been able to see, was there any projection sticking out of the side of the house that Lawty might have hit when he made his last flight.

So what? Parry asked himself. He didn't like this at all. Was there anyone else in this grotesque hotel, besides Jim Bridges, who bore Lawty a grudge? Probably all of them, in some way or another, if, that was to say, they had all known him before. Except, perhaps, the mountain-breasted Anabel. It would hardly do her hotel any good if she bumped off one of her guests. Or hadn't he been bumped off at all? Parry hoped not. He disliked murder.

But that small, tidy, round bruise—Parry switched on his torch and had another look at it. Right on the spot, the mastoid process. And the bruise had something odd about it. Very faintly, it showed a kind of hobnail pattern, as if it had been made by some metal instrument crisscrossed with deep lines. Sneak up behind Lawty, then tap, just as Lawty was turning his head to see who it was, and as he staggered, take him up under the knees and tip him out of the window. If the tap behind the ear had been a bit harder, it would have probably killed him, except that he was so damn tough. People read too many thrillers. Nearly everyone who gorged himself on them must know several different and equally easy ways of killing or stunning his fellow humans, and a crack on that particular place was one of them.

A tidy reconstruction, or wasn't it? He hoped he hadn't caught screeching Cintra's hysteria. Who was Cintra, anyway? Her face was vaguely familiar to him; but try as he would, he couldn't place her. The handle of the dining-room door turned, then rattled.

"Who's that?" Parry asked.

"Bridges."

Parry unlocked the door and shut it behind Jim.

"Everything in order?" he said. "Doctor and police and so on?"

"Nothing's in order," Jim said. "Not even the phone. There isn't a kick out of it."

"Damn," Parry said. "How long's it been out of order, d'you know?"

"Miss Killigrew said it was O.K. just before six when some people rang up to say they weren't coming to Lawty's party, or rather, the party Anabel was giving for Lawty."

"Was that the party?" Parry jerked his head at the decorated table.

"Yes. Hothouse roses and leftover Christmas holly."

"And bits of tinsel. Very tasty." Parry smiled.

The door opened quietly, and he turned round. It was the girl in the white knitted stockings. She left the door open and walked very deliberately across the room to where Lawty lay on the floor. Jim muttered something and sidled out into the hall. Parry waited for whatever was going to happen now. Nothing much did. With what appeared to be a great effort, the girl bent over Lawty, looked at his face, put out one hand and touched it, and walked out of the room again, shutting the door behind her. Her face was the color of chalk, which made her calm gray eyes seem overlarge.

Curious, Parry thought. She didn't look the type to have been one of Lawty's girlfriends, or, indeed, anyone's girlfriend at all. And Jim had glanced at her almost resentfully when he had taken himself off, as if he didn't want to be in the room with her.

"High-ho," Parry said, and went in search of Miss Killigrew.

The hall was empty. From a passage that led off it came smells of food and sounds of females being temperamental, punctuated by male voices talking nineteen to the dozen. Upstairs, muffled by distance, someone was sobbing. Parry leaned over the gilded redout, which he supposed was the reception desk.

"Miss Killigrew?" he called, enjoying the saying of her name.

Miss Killigrew bobbed out of her office, trying unsuccessfully to pat her hair into place.

"Mr. Bridges said," she panted, "you're from Scotland Yard. I don't understand about the phone being out of order. Isn't it terrible about poor Wing Commander Lawrence? Poor Mrs. Adams will feel it terribly. He only arrived this morning, and she was so delighted. She looked on him as a son, you know."

Parry couldn't imagine anything female, whatever her age, looking on Lawty Lawrence as a son, but he made sympathetic and encouraging noises in his throat.

"Of course, as I've only been here a year, I'd never met him before. But all through the war, and afterward till he went to South America, he made this his second home, of course."

Why of course? Parry wondered.

"And there's never been any trouble about the phone since I've been here, and we've had some bad storms."

Parry thought it time to interrupt.

"Is the line underground or overground?" he asked.

"It goes from here—from the exchange in my office, at least—through the wall, then round the hall to the gentlemen's cloakroom, and out of the wall of the gentlemen's cloakroom to the outside of the house, and from there by poles to the gate, and from there to the main underground cable."

It suddenly occurred to Parry that he would like to locate the gentlemen's cloakroom, and asked Miss Killigrew where it was. Its door was in the far corner of the hall, hidden by a gold and red lacquer screen. Unlike what he'd seen of the rest of the hotel, it was neat but not gaudy. Plain white tiles and chromium plating. At first he couldn't see where the telephone line ran through. Then he saw, and his eyebrows nearly rose into his hair. For someone had cut the line; and not only cut it, but removed a good two feet of the line itself, so that nothing was left but two forlorn ends sprouting from the walls. Somewhere, however, must be the instrument used to cut the line, and the two feet of line that had vanished. Find them, anti he might find out whodunit. In the lavatory there was no hiding place for a pin.

You fool, Parry told himself. Of course there was a hiding place. The lid of the white enameled cistern wasn't fixed. He lifted it and felt in its watery depths. Cut into neat two-inch lengths, so that it couldn't possibly be joined together again, was the missing piece of telephone line, and a pair of sharp garden scissors with a loop of string attached to them. Parry carefully wrapped the lot up in his handkerchief and pocketed it. Then he took the key from the lavatory door, locked the door from the outside, and put the key in his pocket as well.

Miss Killigrew had gone back into her office. The hall was still empty, the house still full of the same muffled noises. Parry shut himself in the dining room. What had seemed none of his business now became his business.

When Lawty, either voluntarily or by force, had gone out of his window, he must have been in the middle of changing for dinner. He had on nothing but his bloodstained evening shirt, with a thin vest under it, evening trousers, a pair of very fine black silk socks, but no shoes. His trouser pockets were empty. Nothing sinister or suggestive was hidden inside his shirt. He wasn't even wearing a wrist watch.

Parry arranged some chairs in such a position that they would have to be moved to get at Lawty's body and examined the three long windows hidden behind sham tapestry curtains. They were latched. He unlatched the middle window. The dining room was at the side, on the end of the house. He had no idea what the windows looked out on, or how far they were from the ground. He began cautiously to raise the window, then pulled it down again and hurriedly latched it.

"God almighty," he said.

An ear-splitting clamor of bells nearly deafened him. It stopped when he shut the window again, much to his relief. Pulling the curtains back in place, he let himself out of the dining room, locked the door, and stuffed the key in his pocket, which was beginning to bulge. Miss Killigrew bolted out of her office, her hand over her heart.

"Was that you?" she gasped. "Or was it burglars?"

"Me. I'm so sorry," Parry apologized. "I didn't know the window had a burglar alarm on it."

"They all have," Miss Killigrew explained breathlessly, "and all the doors that lead to the outside too. That is—are—is the main door in the hall here, and the side door, and the tradesmen's and servants' entrance at the back. When you and Mr. Bridges were in the dining room with poor Wing Commander Lawrence, I went round the house, made sure everyone was in it that ought to be, and set the alarms to go off. I locked all the doors—I mean, the outside ones—and latched all the windows I could. Then I locked the door keys in the safe, along with the key that locks and unlocks the box where the burglar-alarm bells are, and the switch that turns them on and off. So no one can get in or out without the alarms going, or get the keys. What's more," Miss Killigrew added, "I didn't tell any of the guests or the staff that I'd done it."

Parry gazed on Miss Killigrew with respect, admiration, and not a little curiosity.

"How very enterprising of you, Miss Killigrew."

"I asked madam first."

"And madam agreed it would be a good idea, I take it?"

"Yes, Inspector."

"Why?"

Miss Killigrew looked at him as if he were a fool. And perhaps I am, Parry thought.

"We had the alarms fitted six months ago, after a burglar got in and stole a lot of jewelry while madam and the guests were at dinner."

"But why should you expect burglars tonight?" Parry asked. "Because Lawty—Wing Commander Lawrence fell out of his window doesn't mean someone's going to break in. Or out."

"Madam's very nervous," Miss Killigrew said with an air of finality mixed with nosiness. "Especially with the telephone not working. Madam's very highly strung, and she's very upset, naturally."

"Naturally. Have you got a pair of garden scissors, by the way?"

Rather to his surprise, Miss Killigrew said they had. "Hanging on a hook by the main door. The guests often like to pick greenery to take back to London, or flowers." She peered over the desk, straining her short, wrinkled neck forward. "That's queer. They've gone. That's very queer. Really, Inspector, I sometimes think there's an Elemental here, the way things vanish."

"Really?" Parry encouraged. "How interesting."

"One of the kitchenmaids told me just now she went into the bar to get the little ice hammer, and it wasn't there. Now the scissors."

"I shouldn't worry."

So an Elemental had taken the little ice hammer too, had it? Presumably one of those little ice hammers commonly found in cocktail bars, the flat pane on one side of its head cut into a sharp hobnailed pattern, the other end tapering to a sharp conical point. Parry's soul sighed deeply within him. Someone had damn well murdered Lawty Lawrence, then made sure the police, the doctor, couldn't be rung up to verify the fact. Premeditated? Done on the spur of the moment?

"Miss Killigrew?" Parry's manner was naturally charming and reassuring. He turned the reassurance full blast on little Miss Killigrew, together with a smile. "The loss of an ice hammer from the bar and a pair of scissors isn't very important, but still, I'm sure it's a nuisance. Have any strangers been in and out today? People dropping in for drinks, then going?"

"No one at all." A watery smile lit up Miss Killigrew's face, and she thought how handsome, how very handsome the inspector from Scotland Yard was. "Only Miss Layne and Mr. Bridges came in, as madam wanted to see them. And of course Mr. Frake and Mr. Livingston arrived from London. But nobody's been out. Even the outside staff haven't come tonight. The two maids and waitresses that sleep out, you know. One drop of rain is enough excuse for them to stay away."

Parry began to weary of Miss Killigrew's information. It might be informative, but it was damn negative. He'd have to face madam in her lair, wherever it was. There was just one more thing, though.

"Have you been in your office all the time? What I mean is, have you heard or seen anyone going, say, to the men's lavatory since the phone was last working?"

Miss Killigrew bridled. "The gentlemen's cloakroom? I wouldn't know when I'm in my office."

"And you've been in your office all the time?"

"No, Inspector, I haven't." Miss Killigrew recovered from the shock of hearing cloakroom called lavatory. "Round about six I went to see if the lounge fire was all right, and the dining-room fire, and if the radiator in the writing room was working properly, and later I went into the kitchen because Lilly, the kitchenmaid, was making such a noise, which was when she told me about the ice hammer—that was about half past six, perhaps later. I didn't look at the time."

Good sign, Parry thought. People who wanted to make themselves nice alibis always knew what the time was when they did this or that, or went here or there. In any case, he couldn't see Miss Killigrew cracking Lawty behind the ear with an ice hammer, then pitching him out of the window. For one thing, she was so very small.

"I think perhaps I'd better have a word with Mrs. Adams," he said.

"Madam's suite is on the first floor. The door opposite the top of the stairs."

"Thanks. And Miss Killigrew, will you stay at the desk? Just in case someone wants to get in the main door?"

"Yes, Inspector. You will try not to upset madam, won't you? She's feeling very bad."

Parry nodded and smiled. As he went up the stairs he thought that very shortly madam would be feeling a damn sight worse. If death, as she no doubt presumed, by accident upset her, she'd hardly take kindly to the probability of death by murder. He'd have broken the news to Miss Killigrew before he bearded her employer, except that if he had, she might be afraid to stay there in the hall alone.

CHAPTER 5

ANABEL was not alone in her red brocade sitting room. Perched on the arm of a chair, Christie pulled at a cigarette and consoled Anabel as best she could with soothing, sensible sympathy. Parry, knocking, and first being told he couldn't come in, then told he could come in, went in before permission to enter was withdrawn.

Christie stood up. She had nice manners. When anyone noticed her, they always said so. "Such nice manners—almost olde worlde."

"I'm so sorry to intrude," Parry apologized, feeling that was rather the sort of remark the undertaker would make when he called to take the measurements of the deceased.

Anabel's bosom heaved. She looked upset, all right, he thought.

"You're a policeman," she accused him in a voice clogged with emotion and, by the smell, a great deal of gin. "Miss Killigrew told me."

"I'll go, shall I?" Christie said, making for the door.

"Don't go, dear," Anabel implored. "You're the only person who isn't having hysterics. Damn Cintra, flinging herself about and making such a row, just as if she'd lost one who was as a son to her. He was as my own flesh and blood, Inspector Parry."

Wonderful. And she'd got his name right.

"If you don't mind, Mrs. Adams, I'd rather like a few words with you by yourself."

"I'll be around whenever you want me, Anabel."

"Yes, dear." Anabel's mind had already wandered from Christie and transferred itself to Parry.

And Parry thought, I'd like a word with that girl too, and followed her into the corridor, shutting Anabel's door behind him. Christie looked at him over her shoulder and stopped. She was much smaller than he had at first imagined. But though she was slight, she didn't seem frail. No one who threw snowballs like that could possibly be frail.

"I'm lost in admiration of your stockings," he smiled at her.

"Old skiing ones."

"Mrs. Adams didn't introduce us, but you know who I am."

"I'm so sorry." Christie smiled a small, pleasant smile. "My name's Christie Layne. Spinster," she added.

"You don't live here, do you?" Parry asked, knowing very well she didn't. But he had to set the ball rolling somehow.

"I live about two miles away, between here and Ditchit. I live by myself now."

"Didn't you always?"

Christie shook her head. "I used to live with an old uncle. Looked after him, you know. He died a couple of years ago and left me the house. At least, it's more like a cottage."

This wasn't getting him very far. But Parry was patient, and he could find out more about the girl from Anabel Adams.

"If you don't mind my asking, Miss Layne, why did you come into the dining room to look at, and touch, Wing Commander Lawrence when he was dead?"

If Parry'd thought that would rattle her, he was disappointed. She didn't turn a hair, though it was some time before she answered.

"I suppose it must've seemed odd to you," she said slowly. "The fact of the matter is I've always been an awful coward about dead people. I managed things so's I wouldn't have to look at my father and mother after they were dead, and when my uncle died in the hospital at Watching, I pretended I couldn't get a taxi in time to go and look at him before the undertaker took him away. So I thought this evening that here was a chance to pull myself together and get over being afraid of something there's nothing to be afraid of. So I went and looked at Lawty, and touched him."

"I hope you feel better about dead people now?" Parry asked, really hoping that she did. He'd once had that fear himself, long before he had to mess about with far too many corpses.

"Yes, I feel quite all right about them now. Though I didn't realize that a dead person looked so completely dead."

"Which just goes to prove," Parry said cheerfully, "that there's something in the idea that bodies don't count a damn, it's the soul that's inside them that's the real person."

Well, that was a sententious little speech. He caught Christie's eye, and realized, rather to his discomfort, that she thought so too.

"Did you know Wing Commander Lawrence well?"

"I met him several times here before he went to South America."

"You didn't know him intimately?"

"Only once. I mean—"

"You mean," Parry said, tactfully giving her a loophole, "that one time you suddenly got to know him much better than you ever did before? Discovered what sort of books he read, and what was his favorite food?"

Christie's eyes roamed the floor, then she raised them.

"I don't think it's much good trying to fool you, is it?" she asked.

"I don't suppose it is," Parry agreed. "But you can have a damn good shot at it if you want to."

Her mouth broadened. "I think it'd be more dignified if I didn't. It was my own fault for letting it slip out. And that's the first time it ever has. I won't say I hope you aren't too shocked, because I'm sure you're not."

"He was exceedingly good-looking, and—" Parry didn't finish what he was going to say, which was, "and no doubt he got a lot of amusement out of seducing you." "Did you see much of him after that?" he asked instead.

"No. Not till today. I didn't see him again before he went abroad. Anabel rang me up today and asked me to come and see her. She didn't say he was back, so I didn't know he was here till I went into the bar and saw him there." Christie smoothed back a lock of hair that had come unstuck from her bun, and smiled quickly, almost, Parry thought, secretively, as if she was trying to hide that quick smile that came and went. "He didn't recognize me for about an hour, and even then I don't suppose he remembered my name. Poor Lawty."

"Must be a shock for you, this mess?" Parry suggested.

"It's a shock for everyone, isn't it?" Christie said.

Now she was fencing. I've got, simply got, to find out if she was in love with him, Parry told himself. And if she resented his having loved her, left her, and then forgotten her.

Unexpectedly, as if she had read his thoughts, she answered the question before he asked it.

"I was in love with him that once. As you say, he was exceedingly good-looking, the best-looking man I've ever met. But when he pinched Jim Bridges' wife, I realized he wasn't worth loving, so I didn't any more. I just liked him, because he was the sort most people couldn't help liking, except the chaps whose girlfriends or wives he'd pinched." And she gave him a friendly nod and walked down the corridor away from him.

Parry watched her, swaying from his heels to his toes. At the far end of the corridor she stopped outside a door, knocked, and went into whoever's room it was. So, as well as Jim Bridges, here was another one who might very well like to revenge herself on Lawty. For he couldn't believe she didn't resent Lawty's casual treatment of her. If she'd been smart, attractive, or the same type as the girl in the silver frock, she probably wouldn't have minded. She'd have been justifiably annoyed, then found a new boyfriend, or several. But she wasn't that type. He was damned if he knew what type she was, and it suddenly occurred to him that in some odd way she was attractive. That inside her she belied her outside appearance of quiet mousiness, and this discovery rather alarmed him.

From behind Anabel's door came noises. A chair being impatiently moved, the clink of a glass being smacked down on something. Evidently Anabel was getting impatient at being kept waiting, neglected, all by herself.

Parry, resigning himself to the inevitable, which, he decided, would be a fine old show of temperament, accompanied by a lot of bosom-heaving, tapped on the door and went in.

Sitting halfway up the stairs that led to the top floor, in semidarkness, Jim stubbed out the cigarette he had been smoking. He'd parked himself on the stairs because he'd wanted to get away from the others. He'd have gone and sat with Anabel, but Anabel had sent for Christie, and he didn't want to help Christie in the consoling of Anabel. He still could not shake off the feeling of intimacy that had been pushed on him when he'd caught her eye down in the bar, that bloody awful feeling that he alone, and no one else, shared her secret, that he was the only person who knew she wasn't a dumb little braown maouse. And then, all unwittingly, he'd had another of her secrets thrust on him, only this time he had to share it with Parry as well. He hadn't realized they were standing just below him talking till it was too late to make his escape. If he'd tried to make a bolt for it to the top floor, they'd have heard him and thought he'd been trying to snoop.

He supposed he ought to feel sorry for her because Lawty had once slept with her only to forget all about her. But what he felt, instead, was a sort of disgusted resentment that she'd let him. Women were utter hell.

You never knew what they were secretly getting up to. He'd had no idea, when he was in hospital all that time, being laboriously, painfully, and dreadfully slowly patched up after floating about in a sea of burning oil after his ship had struck a mine right at the end of the war, that his wife had been living with Lawty. And she'd always been so sweet to him when she'd come to see him and sat by his bed.

"I always had the jimjams when you went to sea as an ordinary seaman," she used to say. "Though it was terribly gutty of you, darling."

Jimjams like hell. She'd kissed him and gone off, back to Lawty. Well, Lawty'd had his at last. He'd had it. And of course, in common with everyone else, Christie knew about the affair of Lawty and his wife. She knew all about him, and now he knew all about her, secretly.

On the landing halfway up the stairs was a bathroom. Jim floundered into it, shut the door, and began violently to wash his hands.

The clock in the bar struck the quarter past eight. Marigold crouched on her bar stool, her hands clenched in her lap. Why had everyone drifted off and left her all alone? She could smell the smell of the South American cigarettes Lawty'd been smoking. The smell was still quite fresh, as if he were sitting there, invisible, looking at her under his dark, heavy lids. Where'd they put him? Where'd they put Lawty?

Marigold dug her long, pointed red nails into the palms of her hands, and shivered.

CHAPTER 6

PARRY was more than thankful for the whisky and soda Anabel pressed on him. The warming and cheering effects of the couple of pulls from his flask had worn off some time ago. Anabel's whisky was good. He rolled it round his mouth before swallowing it, wondering from what angle he should proceed to the attack on his involuntary hostess. Although she was obviously dramatizing the horrible situation so far as it concerned herself, she was just as obviously very genuinely upset. And the poor old trout'd been crying, Parry could see. He hoped she couldn't read his thoughts. She wouldn't like the idea of anyone even mentally dubbing her an old trout.

"It's hard to say if my unheralded arrival was opportune or inopportune," he said.

"I'm thankful you're here." Anabel treated him to a wan but heroic smile. After all, even a policeman might have money, and if she was nice to him, he might come back again and spend it in the cocktail bar. "Do have another drink, won't you, Inspector?"

"I've not finished this one yet, thanks very much," he pointed out. "I suppose you've known Wing Commander Lawrence a long time?"

Anabel quivered and pressed a large chiffon handkerchief to her face, which badly needed another coat of powder.

"Years," she answered into the handkerchief, so that her voice were muffled. "I bought Beechlands before the war. Lawty and the rest of the boys used to come here when the war started. Lawty made it his home, if you see what I mean?"

Parry nodded, though he wasn't quite sure if he did see what she meant.

"He was a bomber pilot," Anabel went on. "There was a big bomber station near Watching. He spent all his leaves here, and was always in and out. He was like my own son, Inspector." Anabel's eyes filled again, and a large tear rolled down her cheek.

Parry felt very sorry for her. It was nasty enough to see any woman cry, but a middle-aged, fat one crying was pathetic. She got up and leaned on the ornate mantelpiece, looking like a prima donna posing in some opera.

"He was very well off, but people said such unkind things about him sometimes. Jealousy, of course. I must say, it was very naughty of him to run off with Jim's wife, but after all, he did marry her. If only he hadn't!" Anabel wrung her hands. "She turned out to be a perfect bitch. What d'you think? He took her with him to South America and she started in on an affair with some bloody dago a week after they got there!"

Anabel wasn't posing now. She was being perfectly naturally furious, almost dropping her aitches, though not quite. Once, Parry was sure, she'd been a barmaid.

"Only Lawty was such a fool, he forgave her. I can't understand it, because he wasn't ever faithful to any of his girlfriends—everyone knew that. But he simply adored this bitch. Can you imagine it? And he put up with her for two years."

"I take it," Parry interrupted, "that after two years he gave her up as a bad job?"

"That's it," Anabel agreed. "And threw over his job out there and came home. And now—and now—"

And now he was dead. Evidently Anabel had made up her mind that he'd done himself in because of the wife.

"But, Mrs. Adams," he said, "was he the type to commit suicide? He didn't appear to've been that sort at all."

"That's what's so queer," Anabel puzzled. "Of course, he'd had a few, but he was having a lovely time with Marigold, and when he'd had a few he often said the most silly things."

"Such as?"

"Like this evening. Not that it was anything. Only silly," Anabel said hurriedly. "Nothing, only silly."

"The girl in silver—I take it she's Marigold, by the way?—said—no it wasn't her, it was the other one, the screaming one you called Cintra—said that Lawty'd said he was going to bloody well jump out of the window."

Anabel's dignity returned. "I can't remember Cintra saying anything of the sort, Inspector."

"But I can. Did he?"

"Well—yes, but he often said wild things like that when he was pick-led."

"Then you don't think he committed suicide at all?"

Anabel's eyes stared at him over the handkerchief.

"I— But he must've committed suicide. Otherwise how else—I mean, no, he must've fallen out of his bedroom window."

Tying herself up in knots. Good.

"I'm told the sill of that particular window's too high from the floor for anyone to fall out by mistake," Parry said pleasantly.

Anabel still clung to her dignity and made a pretty good job of it. She might easily have been an Edwardian duchess.

"I don't think I quite understand you, Mr. Parry?"

"Very likely you don't," he agreed, putting his glass down. "I think there's every likelihood he was murdered."

"Oh, my Gawd!" cried the duchess, and collapsed into her chair.

Parry got up and appropriated her place at the mantelpiece. Seen from this new angle, below him, her bust looked like some sort of large pouf cushion.

"I'm afraid this must be an appalling shock for you," he said sooth-ingly.

"Shock? Shock? But he can't possibly've been murdered! If a mur-derer had been seen wandering about the house someone'd have noticed—not even any strangers've been in—"

Parry thought it best not to say that the most likely candidate for the role of murderer was right in their midst. For there was truth in what Ana-bel had said. If an unknown man or woman had got into the hotel with the intentions of making his way up to the top floor, to Lawty's room, he'd almost surely have been spotted. Besides, Lawty had arrived only that morn-ing, and whoever had intended to murder him would have to find out which his room was, also when he would be in it. The whole thing smacked of fantasy. But for the cutting of the telephone line, he would have thought he was imagining a crime where no crime existed.

"If you feel you can bear it, would you tell me a little about the people who're actually living in the house?" Parry asked, treading delicately. "After all, if it turns out Lawty really was murdered, we don't want them to get implicated, do we?"

Evidently we didn't. Anabel exclaimed, "My God, no!" and laid a hand over her heart.

"Now, first of all, is there anything else you can tell me about Lawty?" Wing Commander Lawrence was really too much of a mouthful, and Parry guessed that everyone in the hotel called everyone else by his Christian name after they'd known each other for five minutes. "Had he any parents, for instance?"

"The most disagreeable people," Anabel said, drawing herself up. "They had the nerve to write to me and ask me not to let Lawty drink so much. As if I'd encouraged him. So he hardly ever went to see them. He made this his second home."

That's what Miss Killigrew had said, omitting reference to the disagreeable parents.

"I see," Parry went on. "And was he popular? Had he any enemies, d'you think?"

"Popular?" Anabel repeated. "My dear, everyone adored him. He hadn't an enemy in the world."

Except, of course, the chaps whose girlfriends or wives he'd pinched, and maybe some of the girlfriends and wives he'd pinched and then got sick of. However, Parry thought he'd better not put that idea into Anabel's head.

"He wasn't in debt, or anything like that?"

"All men have a few debts," said Anabel, as if she were pointing out some remarkable truth. "But he was very well off. Some old uncle left him money, and his note case was stuffed, simply stuffed, with bank notes when he arrived this morning. He showed them to me—he said, 'There you are, Anabel darling, we'll have a great party.' Oh, poor Lawty! He was one of our national heroes."

"Of course he was," Parry agreed, still soothing. "Everyone's heard of him." And so he had. Lawty had done things in a big way, with plenty of publicity, which, to give him his due, he hadn't asked for. With his war record and good looks, he was God's gift to the press.

Parry studied the carpet. The color of it rather unpleasantly reminded him of drying blood. Evidently Anabel looked on money as something of the greatest importance, a passport to fame and popularity, more desirable than respectability, than moral integrity. Was that because money could buy so much, and she wanted a lot of things? Or because people with money were necessary to her business? Or did she need money herself? The last idea made him feel uncomfortable. Lawty's note case, according to Anabel, was stuffed with bank notes. Was Lawty lying dead in the locked dining room because someone had coveted his money? Had needed it so badly that he'd killed him to get it? He'd have to find the note case.

"By the way, Mrs. Adams, did anyone else know Lawty had a lot of money on him when he arrived this morning?"

"I suppose so," Anabel shrugged. "My God, and he was only thirty-seven."

"When did he arrive in England?"

"Yesterday, he said. He flew, of course." Anabel produced a large, fluffy powder puff from some mysterious hiding place and dabbed it over her face. She was getting restive, one foot tapping.

"This Jim Bridges," Parry went on. "Does he live near here?"

"Such a charming man," Anabel said. "Really charming. So kind, but rather dull, if you see what I mean? Ordinary. But a dear, really a dear. Not well off, poor boy, but so good-natured. His wife, at least Lawty's wife, lived near Watching. I could never imagine why she married him. She was so pretty and so smart. I knew it wouldn't work out well. I said so to everyone. I forget where she met him—in town, I think, and after they were married Jim bought Sloes Farm about a mile from here and did it up. It must have been so dull for her, but of course she came here a lot. What induced him to go to sea as an ordinary sailor in the war I can't imagine, but naturally he was away a lot, and Yvonne—that was his and Lawty's wife—was alone a great deal."

"And she met Lawty here?" Parry prompted, as Anabel showed signs of getting sick of the subject of Jim.

"Yes," she said, almost aggressively, as if she expected Parry to blame her for having let Jim's wife and Lawty become friends. "If I'd known what was really going on, I'd have stopped it. Poor Jim. And then at the end of the war his ship got blown up, by a mine or something like that, and he was burned to bits by the oil. I suppose the oil caught fire. At any rate, he was in hospital for God knows how long after the war was over, having bits grafted onto him and his face patched up. You'd never know it, would you? Fortunately he was very plain, so it didn't matter."

Parry wondered why it didn't matter. A face was a face, however plain it was.

"They made a good job of it," he said. "One can't see any scars at all."

"No. Except sometimes. Poor Jim. He was very good about it when Yvonne ran off with Lawty, though I think it was rather unwise of him to go back and live all alone at Sloes Farm. Such an out-of-the-way place, and he hasn't a car."

"What's he do?" Parry asked.

"He does some kind of designs. Architecture."

"I see. And why'd he come here today?"

"I rang him up."

"Did you tell him Lawty was here?"

"Of course I didn't." Anabel looked shocked. "To tell you the truth, my dear, when I realized that he and Lawty were both here at the same time, I nearly had a fit, but I thought the best thing to do was ignore the whole thing. I was quite right, they didn't have a row or anything like that. I don't think they noticed each other."

Liar, Parry thought, but he left it.

"And what about Miss Layne?"

Anabel showed signs of increasing boredom. Evidently Christie Layne hadn't much money either.

"A very nice, sweet girl. Rather badly off, but so good-hearted. It's such a pity she dresses so dully and does her hair like that, and doesn't use more makeup. But we're very fond of her. Such a quiet little mouse, and most sympathetic."

Parry tried not to laugh. Anabel was a shockingly bad judge of people. He supposed Christie supplied the role of sympathetic audience when Anabel had woes or complaints to unburden, and that willingly or unwillingly, Jim shared the same role.

"Miss Layne knew Lawty before he went to South America?"

"Christie? She may have met him once or twice. She's not his type at all, now is she?"

"Was she," Parry corrected, and wished he hadn't. Anabel began to heave again, and undid the small improvement made by the powder puff by letting some tears run out of her eyes. "Are she and Jim Bridges friends?" he said hurriedly, hoping to stem the flow.

Anabel pressed her hands together. "I really don't know. They're so quiet. Christie lives in the opposite direction, quite a distance away. They'd be a good match for each other."

"How long've you known Christie?" Parry asked, and thought, There I go, I've caught it too. Christian names all round. Soon I'll be calling her Anabel dear, and she'll be calling me Lane darling.

"Years," Anabel answered vaguely. "Her old uncle used to come and lunch here sometimes. He liked good food."

"Everyone in Sussex seems to live with old aunts or uncles at one time or another," Parry said.

"Do they?" Anabel's mind appeared to be elsewhere. "Isn't Marigold Trent a lovely girl? Her hair's naturally platinum blonde. Really, the first time she walked in in that silver-fox coat of hers I thought I'd never seen anyone more lovely. That was before Christmas, and she's been here ever since. The Pantons sent her down, the cigarette people, you know. She and Lawty just took one look at each other this morning—they'd never met before. Poor Marigold, she must be heartbroken. The friendship between them quite platonic, naturally."

"Plenty of money, I suppose?" Parry said unmaliciously.

"Marigold? Oh, yes."

"It must be useful to have people here who pay their bills and don't land you with dud checks."

Anabel turned her large, round black eyes on him, and something flickered back of them, a sudden, awful stab of anxiety. Parry lit a cigarette, realized he should have offered her one first, and apologized. She took one and he lit it for her. Her face looked taut. So lovely Marigold hadn't paid her bill yet? Enchanted by the natural platinum-blonde hair, the silver foxes, the silver dresses, Anabel must has assumed that lovely Marigold's pockets were lined with gold. He guessed that if he poked about in the bar he'd find a pile of Marigold's bar chits, so far unpaid.

"The Pantons're old friends, Mrs. Adams?"

"Oh, yes, they spent a week here last summer."

Just one week. Very old friends indeed. What on earth was Anabel's idea of an old friend? Parry made another mental note that he must locate Lawty's pocketbook, full or empty.

"And Cintra who?" he asked, inadvertently speaking his thoughts out loud.

Anabel brightened. "Cintra Norton, of course. Surely you know Cintra? You must do. She's the greatest film star we ever sent to Hollywood—or rather, Hollywood ever took away from us. She's one of my oldest friends."

"I don't go to the films much," Parry said, feeling he ought to apologize. But now he came to think of it, he'd heard of Cintra, seen her picture in the papers, and that accounted for the feeling he'd had of having seen her before.

"She's the most marvelous actress," Anabel glowed, "and so simple and natural. She's going back to Hollywood soon to make another film. I'll miss her terribly, terribly."

Marigold had fallen from grace. Cintra had taken her place as Anabel's favorite of the moment.

"She knew Lawty before he went abroad, didn't she?"

"Very well. They were such friends," Anabel agreed.

"I rather thought so," Parry said. "She was running round and round in circles in the snow screaming his name over and over again, and she seemed far more upset than anyone else. Is she married?"

Anabel clothed herself in dignity as if it had been an expensive silver-fox coat.

"Her husband, Max Elliot, is charming," she informed Parry. Then she added, with what seemed to him perfectly righteous indignation, "It was really absurd the way she went on. Being jealous of Marigold as if she was a girl of eighteen. Cintra's forty-four if she's a day. Trying to annex Lawty like she always used to, when she was younger. Naturally Lawty'd prefer a girl like Marigold to someone like Cintra, with a husband in tow. She made a perfect fool of herself all today. Not that I'm not fond of Cintra."

All the idols were falling, one by one. Parry began to feel rather bewildered.

"She must've made a packet in Hollywood?" he suggested.

"Cintra's so rich it's nobody's business," Anabel said with such firmness that he took it Cintra paid her bills on the dot. "She came down a week ago, and she brought me the most really beautiful gold and platinum compact. She's so generous, you can't imagine. She'd give anybody anything."

Cintra was ace-high again. But whether she was generous or spendthrift, Parry didn't know. Hunger for a square, hot meal gnawed at his stomach. Was there going to be nothing to eat because Lawty was dead? He groaned inwardly, not only with hunger, but with exasperation. These people weren't real. It was as if he'd got mixed up in some damn silly play. He dropped Cintra like a hot brick and got on the scent of the rest of the outfit.

"Those two men, are they guests? The fat little one and the good-looking chap with the gray hair? Are they old friends of yours? Are they friends of anyone else here? When did they arrive here?" He shot out all his questions at once, in the hope that Anabel would give brief answers, unpunctuated by adjectives.

She dabbed her handkerchief against her lips, still alarmingly dignified.

"I've known Julian Frake and Paul Livingston for years. They both arrived this evening. Actually, I expected Julian to get here before Paul, by an early train. So tiresome."

"Oh?"

"It's too bad of Paul to go on like this, trying to put Julian off," Anabel complained, just as though he knew what in hell she was talking about. "I've never heard such nonsense as he talked. After all, Julian has the most money, so it's not fair on me."

Parry's patience, which was phenomenal, very nearly gave way.

"My dear Mrs. Adams," he said, "do remember this is the first time I've been here, and that I've never met any of these people before. What nonsense was Livingston talking? Why should he try to put Frake off? And off what? Do forgive me," he added, because Anabel was pursing her lips like an oyster shell closing, "for being so inquisitive. But even if Lawty fell out of his bedroom window by accident, or jumped out because he felt depressed, your local police will still have to be called in, and there'll be an inquest. So it might be less disagreeable for you to talk to a complete stranger, who'll be departing any moment now."

"Don't go," Anabel beseeched, half shutting her eyes. "It's so— The shock— The fact of the matter is that Julian and Paul both want to invest money in Beechlands."

"I see." At last he was getting somewhere. "Business partners?"

Anabel hesitated. "Well, no. No, they aren't partners. That's why it's so tiresome Julian didn't get down earlier than Paul. I wanted to have a talk with him first. This place is a gold mine, naturally. A gold mine," she repeated, as if she wanted to convince not only Parry but herself.

Parry wasn't convinced. The place might be a potential gold mine, but to judge from the very few guests staying there, the size of the house, and the probable expenses of its upkeep, it was more than likely that Anabel was drifting onto the rocks. And that was why money loomed so large on her horizon, which, he guessed, was a pretty limited one.

"Julian's quite charming," Anabel went on, "though of course Paul has the better business head. You should have heard the rubbish he talked— telling Julian this place's unlucky, and that he wouldn't touch it with a broom handle, doing his best to put Julian against it—simply because a year or two ago John Grant had a gun accident here and shot himself by mistake, and then young Stainer's plane crashed in the grounds. How could I help it? I admit it was silly of me to have mentioned that before each accident I heard the three knocks, and that set Marigold and Cintra off tonight. Too absurd, when it was only Chef cutting up the chickens in the kitchen."

The gin was suddenly working in Anabel's head, and Parry had some difficulty in disentangling her ramblings.

"You were going to give a party for Lawty tonight?" he asked.

"I rang some people up when he arrived this evening, the sort of people who'd amuse him, and another couple I knew Julian and Paul would like. And then they ratted because of the snow."

"Perhaps just as well?" Parry suggested, and taking out his pipe, looked at it with longing and put it back in his pocket. "Had Julian Frake and Livingston met Lawty before this evening?"

"Paul had." Anabel was getting bored with his questions and showed it.

"And the girl in silver? Marigold Trent?" Parry prompted. "Of course, you told me she met him for the first time today. Has she met Frake and Livingston before?"

"In London." Anabel was now almost too brief where she'd been too chatty, and Parry saw her eye on the gin bottle.

"Don't you think, after this shock, you ought to have something to drink?" he said.

She bowed her head and murmured, "Yes, dear," in a broken voice.

Much more gin, and she'd call him darling, he supposed. He poured her out a large tot, and his stomach gurgled complainingly. So all the guests had met before, except Marigold, who hadn't known Lawty till this morning, and Frake, who hadn't known Lawty in the old days, unless, of course, Anabel was lying, or Marigold and Frake were pulling wool over her eyes.

"Tell me, Mrs. Adams," he said, "what were you all doing before the snowballing party?"

The gin had loosened Anabel's tongue again.

"We were all in the bar, all of us," she answered brokenly. "Just like a happy family. Then we all went up to change rather earlier than usual, because of—because of the party. You know the rest."

Oh, I do, do I? Parry thought. I damn well don't. And they hadn't all changed for dinner. Christie and Jim Bridges still wore the clothes they'd presumably arrived in.

"Miss Layne and Bridges changed too?" he asked innocently.

"What?" Anabel stared up at him. "Of course they didn't. They hadn't anything to change into. I suppose they washed. They went out of the bar with the others."

"Has anyone been up to Lawty's room since he left it by the window?"

Anabel gave a quite genuine and audible shudder.

"I couldn't bear to, not yet. My God, poor Lawty!"

Parry felt he couldn't face another outbreak of emotion, and made for the door.

"I won't bother you any more now," he said. "I'm so extremely sorry your party's had such a tragic ending."

"Send Christie to me, will you, my dear?" Anabel said in a clogged voice. "And Jim?"

"Certainly," Parry agreed, closing the door. He had no intention of sending Christie, Jim, or anyone else to her to hold a council of war behind his back in that dark red crowded room, its overheated air heavy with the smell of some sort of perfume, gin, and cigarette smoke.

The house was very quiet. There was something almost sticky about the silence. It was like being inside a large treacle tin, the lid firmly clamped down so that there was no means of escape. Sensitive always to the atmosphere of other people's houses, Parry decided there was something unpleasantly sinister about the atmosphere of Beechlands. As he went quietly down the stairs in search of Miss Killigrew, a small, thin wail of wind swept round a corner of the house. By the sound of it, there would presently be more snow.

CHAPTER 7

BEHIND the reception desk, Miss Killigrew nibbled a tongue sandwich, from time to time glancing up at the hall clock. A quarter to nine, and no dinner had been served. And anyway, how could a proper dinner be served when poor Wing Commander Lawrence was locked up in the dining room?

"All right, Miss Killigrew?"

Miss Killigrew bobbed her head forward and was delighted to see the nice Inspector Parry coming across the hall. So good-looking, almost as good-looking as poor Wing Commander Lawrence, only thinner. She patted her hair and smiled.

"Quite all right, thank you, Inspector," she told Parry. "I hope it was all right, but really I was so hungry I rang through to the kitchen and got them to make me some sandwiches."

"Aren't you lucky?" Parry sighed enviously.

"Oh, dear!" Miss Killigrew exclaimed. "You must be so hungry too! Please do have the rest of these, I can get some more."

"Miss Killigrew, you're an angel."

Miss Killigrew wriggled with pleasure, and Parry heartlessly devoured the remains of her snack.

"Sure you can get some more for yourself?" he asked with his mouth full.

"Quite, quite sure," she bobbed.

"Seen anyone since I went upstairs?"

"After I rang through to the kitchen, Gaston brought me the sandwiches and then took himself off. Oh, and Miss Trent came and asked me if there were any letters for her. That was about a quarter of an hour ago. So silly. As if there'd be any letters. She ought to know we only have the one post in the morning, and anyhow, if we did have a late post as well, how could any postman get here through the snow?"

"Of course not. Where'd she go then?"

"I couldn't tell you, Inspector," Miss Killigrew said apologetically. "It's so tiresome, I'm too short to look properly over the top of the desk. She might've gone upstairs, or down to the bar, or anywhere. I tried putting a footstool behind the desk once, to stand on, but I fell off it and nearly broke my ankle."

Parry laughed, and Miss Killigrew giggled. Hell, he thought, he'd have to tell her now that probably Lawty'd been murdered. He hoped she wouldn't have hysterics.

He leaned on the desk and looked down at her. "Miss Killigrew, I'm afraid I've got something unpleasant to tell you. It looks to me as if Wing Commander Lawrence neither committed suicide nor fell out of his window by mistake."

Miss Killigrew blinked. "I wondered," she whispered. "I did wonder."

"Why?" Parry lowered his voice.

Miss Killigrew shook her head. "I don't know. At least, you looked as if you thought something wasn't quite right."

"Oh, Lord," Parry said wryly. "I'm not much of a policeman, am I? However, now that you know, will you help me by telling me everything you can about the people here? First of all, has anyone tried to get into the house while I was upstairs?"

Miss Killigrew assumed the air of a conspirator.

"Not by the main door here," she whispered. "And Gaston said none of the outside staff had rung the servants' doorbell."

"What about the staff itself—the indoor staff?"

"There's Chef. He's supposed to be French. The visitors like that. But he's English, and a very nice person. Most respectable, with excellent references. Robert Lord's his name—we call him Robert pronounced in the French way, Ro*bère.* Then there're the two kitchenmaids, Lilly Baker and Ethel Wills. Silly girls, but quite respectable too. Then there's the housemaid that lives in, Marion Wood, who's a nice girl except for her catarrh, and then there's Gaston, the headwaiter. The rest of the staff lives out. And Inspector, I don't like Gaston at all. He's supposed to be Belgian, but he might be anything. He's got a most unpleasant way of creeping about, and suddenly popping out of odd corners, or popping into them. Gaston Leroux. Not that the copies of his references weren't excellent."

"Copies? I see. Have you anything definite against him?"

"I just don't *like* him, Inspector."

"Feminine intuition?" Parry smiled. "There's a lot in it. And the actual guests, staying here?"

Miss Killigrew was able to add nothing to the information Anabel had already given him about the guests, except the interesting fact that Marigold Trent hadn't paid her bill since she arrived, and that she, Miss Killigrew, had suggested to madam that madam should suggest to Miss Trent that she should at any rate pay something on account. Cintra owed nothing except a not very large bar bill.

"Thank you," Parry said. "So that's them—or is it they?" He pulled at his lower lip. "Hotel often as empty as this?" he went on cautiously.

"Oh, well, not always, Inspector."

"I understand from Mrs. Adams that both Mr. Frake and Mr. Livingston have an idea of putting money in the business. Or rather, not both of them but one of them. Whichever one pulls it off with Mrs. Adams."

"Mr. Frake, I do hope," Miss Killigrew said confidentially. "Mr. Frake is a gentleman. So very nice."

Evidently Miss Killigrew didn't approve of Paul Livingston. He wished he could ask her if Anabel was in a bad way financially, but he felt sure, if he did, she wouldn't tell him. She seemed the loyal sort.

He changed the subject.

"Where's the nearest telephone, Miss Killigrew? Also the nearest police I can contact."

"Oh, dear." Miss Killigrew frowned. "The nearest policeman is at Ditchit, and that's two miles from here, down a side road, and he's worse than useless. The nearest police station is Watching, four miles away."

"And the nearest phone?" Parry inquired, feeling rather hopeless.

"That'd be at Mr. Bridges' house. Only—"

"Only what?"

"You'd never find your way there, Inspector. It's in the middle of fields, and unless you knew the way before, you'd get lost." Miss Killigrew gazed at Parry, looking like a small worried owl.

And he couldn't send Jim Bridges off to use his own phone. Jim was a suspect. He couldn't send any of them, for that matter. Except, perhaps, Miss Killigrew, because she was far too tiny to have tipped even an unconscious Lawty out of his window. Only Miss Killigrew would fall into a snowdrift and be lost forever.

Hell and damnation, he swore silently. What a bloody mess!

"And the next nearest phone? Isn't there an A.A. phone box near? Or a village?"

"Ditchit's two miles away. There's Miss Layne's telephone, and her house is two miles away. Of course, there's Toleham Mill, where there is a post office, but it hasn't got a telephone."

"In God's name," Parry said in despair, "where's your local phone exchange?"

"Ditchit, Inspector."

Two miles there, two miles back. That would mean leaving all these people (and Lawty's body) by themselves, to get up to their own devices and occasions, lawful or unlawful, for at least two hours, by the time he'd done explaining everything to the Ditchit policeman, who was worse than useless, according to Miss Killigrew.

"Of course," Miss Killigrew cheered him, "I expect there are places with telephones quite close, only I don't know which they are. There's a farmer called Everard near here, but I don't know if he has a telephone or not. If he has, then he isn't in the book. Lots of people aren't in the book who ought to be."

"What else can you expect," Parry inquired, "if you plant yourself in such a God-forgotten spot?"

"Beautiful glimpses of the sea may be had," Miss Killigrew said reproachfully, "from the Southern Drive, with the rolling downland spreading to the west. There is an excellent cinema in Watching, and horses can be hired from Ditchit—" She broke off, blinked, and smiled. "It's lovely in summer," she added. "Really it is."

"I'm sure it is. But unfortunately this is the eighteenth of January, a dark night, with the roads all snowed up. So what?"

Miss Killigrew glanced behind her and leaned against the desk.

"There's something I forgot to tell you. About Mr. Livingston. They were the last—he and Mr. Frake—to go upstairs, if they did go upstairs, when you and Mr. Bridges brought poor Wing Commander Lawton's body in. I thought it was too bad, really I did. Of course Mr. Frake has much more money to invest than Mr. Livingston, but I thought it was a nasty way to try to put Mr. Frake off."

"Yes?" Parry encouraged, very interested indeed to hear her version of Livingston's odd behavior.

"He, that is, Mr. Livingston, grabbed hold of Mr. Frake's arm and said the most dreadful things. He said directly he came into Beechlands this evening, he knew something awful was going to happen again, that Mr. Frake didn't know the place as long as he'd known it, and how unlucky it was, and doomed to ill luck and failure, and better have nothing to do with it, if he was wise."

"And what did Frake say?"

"He laughed very good-naturedly, and said that well, after all, it was only an accident, about Mr. Grant, and that Flight Lieutenant Stainer brought it on himself, and that if Wing Commander Lawrence fell out of his window, it was his own fault for not being more careful. Then he said to Mr. Livingston, why did he want to invest money in a place that frightened him?"

"What was Livingston's answer to that one?"

"Very childish, Inspector. He said that he hadn't thought of it before, but that it all came over him with a rush when he'd been here for half an hour after he'd arrived this evening, and not to touch it with a broom handle. I must say," Miss Killigrew mused, "Mr. Livingston did look rather green. In fact, very green."

"And how did Mr. Frake look?"

"He didn't look so jolly as he usually does after Mr. Livingston said that. I do think it's a shame!" Miss Killigrew exploded.

Parry had no need to ask why it was a shame, though hard luck was the right phrase. Hard luck on Anabel to have a dead body lying about when she was trying to bring off a business deal. Very hard luck that one half of the deal was trying to put the richer half of the deal off by hysterically trotting out the misfortunes of Beechlands. Were there any more he hadn't heard about? Jim Bridges had lost his wife because she'd met Lawty at Beechlands. Christie had lost her virtue, if, of course, she'd had any to lose. Parry ran his hand through his hair, a little exasperated.

"Will you stay here, Miss Killigrew?" he said. "Unless, of course, Mrs. Adams wants you, or you've got anything important to see to."

Miss Killigrew said she would.

"Wing Commander Lawrence's bedroom was on the top floor, wasn't it?"

"Number twenty, turn to the left when you get to the top of the stairs."

"D'you know if anyone's been in there since?"

Miss Killigrew gulped. "Not so far as I know, Inspector Parry. Oh, and if you're going up, would you be so kind as to turn the lights out when you've finished? And shut the window? The alarms don't go off when a window's shut, only when it's opened."

Parry gave Miss Killigrew what he hoped was a reassuring smile and started for the stairs. He was vaguely aware that she was saying something else, but didn't wait. He'd waited quite long enough as it was. Long enough for anyone with evidence of a crime to conceal to sneak into Lawty's bedroom and leave evidence of his presence by his endeavors to cover it up.

The stairs were broad and thickly carpeted. Halfway up each flight there was a small landing. Parry stopped on the first one and leaned on the banisters. Someone had once expounded a theory to him that unusual weather had unusual effects on some people. It was certainly a fact that before a thunderstorm headaches and a queer, restless feeling attacked nearly everyone, and that a minute or two before an earthquake or a shock, people sometimes felt sick. Might a particularly heavy snowfall in a country where heavy snowfalls were not the usual rule upset other people? Was that the cause of Paul Livingston's fit of hysteria, of the extraordinary way Anabel's guests were behaving themselves?

Hell, what was the use of such damn silly conjecturing? Parry asked himself. He was a policeman, a crime appeared to have been done, and he was laying the blame on the weather. All the same, he had a sneaking sympathy for Paul's burst of temperament. The atmosphere of the hotel, as well as being too stuffy and too hot, was uncomfortably brooding.

He made the first floor without hearing or seeing anyone, except that from behind Anabel's door came the faint noise of a cigarette lighter being snicked on and off. That, at least, was what it sounded like. As he went up the stairs to the top floor, the light grew dimmer and dimmer; evidently the top-floor corridor was in darkness, which seemed odd. Or had Lawty known his old room so well that he'd had no need to put the corridor lights on to find it? Parry turned to the left and switched on his torch. The battery was beginning to give out, but its pale glimmer reflected on the polished shine of "20" in brass figures on one of the closed doors. For a moment he stood still and listened, then turned his torch out and gently pushed open the door. The room was in pitch-darkness. Someone had been in there already and put the lights out. He swung the door to behind him and felt for the switch. All he could find was blank wall. And he wasn't alone. There were other people in there, standing as still as he was himself, trying to stifle the sounds of their breathing.

Parry smiled, and snipping on his torch again, swung its dim beam in a semicircle. Five pairs of eyes stared out of the darkness, like the eyes of wild animals in the jungle.

"Put the lights on! Put the lights on! I can't stand it—I can't stand it any longer!"

There was a click, and the standard lamp on the dressing table lit the room with a warm yellow glow.

"Well, well, well," Parry said pleasantly. "What a surprise,"

CHAPTER 8

THE open window, its sill chest-high from the floor, framed by the royal-blue curtains; the expanse of blue carpet, a motionless lake of pile; Lawty's clothes strewn on the bed and on chairs—these might have been a stage setting against which Julian Frake, Paul Livingston, Cintra, Christie, and Jim posed for the final curtain of a rather ridiculous play that, to the actors' distress, had been booed instead of applauded.

"What on earth're you all doing up here in the dark?" Parry asked.

Paul Livingston licked his lips as if the inside of his mouth was dry. Cintra swayed perilously, her mouth wide open, a look of horror in her eyes. Christie stared at Parry, her face very white, but otherwise unagitated by any particular emotion. Jim stared at the floor, digging his hands in his trousers pockets. Julian Frake pulled an exquisite white linen handkerchief from his cuff and blew his nose, looking sheepish. Everything about Julian was immaculate, unobtrusively so, and in the best of taste.

"Well?" Parry encouraged.

"I—" Julian began, and then stopped.

The door was opening cautiously. Parry moved aside and waited. Long pointed fingers with long pointed scarlet nails crept round the edge of the door, followed by lovely Marigold.

"O-awp!" she gasped, and swayed backward.

"Come in, Miss Trent," Parry invited her, "and join the party."

She looked wildly round the ring of faces, and Julian said gently, "It's all right, Marigold, my sweet."

"What's happening?" she asked in a strained whisper, eying Cintra, though it was Julian she spoke to.

"Nothing," Parry said, "appears to be happening at all. Why'd you come up here?"

"I couldn't find anyone." Marigold spoke in jerks, and a long silky lock of platinum hair flopped over one cheek. Her eyes were greenish, and she was wearing a diamond and platinum bracelet Parry was sure she hadn't had on when she was snowballing. "I was alone in the bar—all alone. Everyone seemed to've disappeared, so I went in the hall. There wasn't anyone there, either, unless you count Miss Killigrew. So I came up here."

"Why?" Her emotion left Parry's heart untouched. Somehow, he didn't think he much liked lovely Marigold.

"I—I couldn't find anyone in the rest of the house." She shuddered.

"Come to your uncle Julian, Marigold, my sweet." Julian held out his hand as if she were a child. Parry guessed the "uncle" was a courtesy title he had bestowed on himself for her comfort. She almost ran across the room, and he took her hand and patted it. "Look here, Inspector—"

But once more the door was opening.

"May I ask," Anabel demanded, sailing into the room, her dignity very real this time, "what you're all doing here? In Lawty's room? It's an insult to him—poking about—"

"But Anabel—"

"Silence, Paul."

"Anabel?" Cintra moaned.

Parry took a deep breath and grabbed at his slipping patience. "Mrs. Adams?" He raised his voice, hoping someone might take some notice of him. "By that token, what're you doing in Lawty's room?"

Anabel forgot all about being charming to Parry in case he turned out to have money to spend.

"I can do what I like in my own house, can't I? I suppose I can go where I like in it, can't I? My God, Miss Killigrew, now what is it?"

Give me strength, Parry inwardly beseeched. Now Miss Killigrew. Who next? The chef? The housemaid with catarrh?

"I couldn't find you in your room, madam," Miss Killigrew apologized breathlessly. "I thought I heard voices up here, so I came up. Chef wants to know—dinner—"

Anabel waved an imperious hand. Miss Killigrew bobbed away from it, and bumped her head on Parry's elbow.

"Gracious me," she panted, and peered round the circle of faces.

"I came up here," Anabel remarked in a funereal voice, remembering she must be nice to Parry, "to put away—to tidy—Lawty's—his things."

"Quite," Parry said understandingly, feeling, somehow, he ought to have said "Quate," and wished they wouldn't speak in jerks, leaving their sentences in midair, punctuated with invisible dashes.

Julian stroked Marigold's hand. She seemed to enjoy it, like a cat. "I was going to say, I know you're a police inspector, but does that mean we have to stay up here in the cold? Personally, I don't mind for myself, but it's a bit tough on the girls," he pointed out.

"I don't want to stay here," Marigold said quickly. "Julian, sweetie, let's go down to the bar, for God's sake."

Parry was aware that behind him Anabel was registering silent disapproval, and having gleaned a small inkling of Anabel's temperament, he wasn't surprised when she stubbornly went against Marigold.

"If Inspector Parry wishes us to stay up here, we shall stay up here."

Parry hadn't asked anyone to stay in Lawty's cold room, but that was just what he wanted them to do. He wanted to tell them Lawty's death wasn't an accident, now, surrounded by Lawty's clutter, their nerves on edge. One of them might give himself away.

"If you don't all know, then one of you at least's sure to know that when a member of the police force is out of his own district and the home counties, hasn't been officially put in charge or asked to help in some case or emergency, he's got no official authority to force anyone to answer questions, or anything else. He can request, but not demand—unless he apprehends a wrongdoer doing wrong, or someone who's wanted." Oh, very nice, Parry congratulated himself, a pretty little official speech delivered in the true official manner, all according to Hoyle, Queensbury Rules, Judges' Rules, and the rest of it. Why in hell didn't Cintra shut her mouth? It was perpetually open, not, as he'd at first thought, in an idle gape, but as if, for some obscure reason, she were trying not to shut it. "Your local police'll take charge directly I can get hold of them, of course."

"But—but—" Paul stammered, the sweat bursting out on his forehead, "why?"

Parry sprung his mine. "So far's I can make out, Wing Commander Lawrence was murdered."

Marigold pressed herself against Julian Frake, her eyes almost squinting with horror.

"Good God!" Julian held her tightly. "How appalling, Parry! How? Why?"

Paul Livingston made a grab at Cintra and clung to her. For the first time Parry could see the scars on Jim's face, gray lines that throbbed a little. Anabel produced a clean chiffon handkerchief and held it over her eyes for a few moments. Christie moved her head, once, from side to side, a small, odd movement that might have meant incredulous sorrow, "Well, I'm not surprised," perplexity—anything or nothing.

"I wasn't up here hiding with the others," Marigold burst into a babble. "I wasn't, you all know I wasn't. I told you why I came up here."

"Sure," Parry agreed kindly, not feeling in the least kind. "And what were you doing round about the time Lawty was killed? Before we found his body?"

"Changing—what else d'you think I was doing?"

"Marigold, darling, it's all right, my sweet," Julian soothed her. "I'm not surprised, now, Parry, you took rather a gloomy view of us, finding us up here in the dark. This is too shocking."

"Yes," Parry agreed. "Murder always is."

Paul began to whine, like a dog in pain. Cintra pushed him away from her and flopped against Christie.

"Poor, poor Lawty," Cintra said in a quite normal voice, then to belie it, shuddered and shivered, twisting her mouth.

"Mrs. Adams?" Parry turned, and she flipped the handkerchief away from her eyes. "I've just told you, you can't be made to answer my questions, but if you would, it would save your being questioned by your local police," he lied shamelessly.

"I will," she announced, as if she were standing at the altar steps, bedecked in white.

"Thank you," Parry said, feeling really grateful. "Then, just to set the ball rolling, what were you doing during the time everyone was changing for dinner, the time when Lawty must've been pitched out the window?"

Anabel gulped and announced with admirable brevity, "Changing too." What shocking bad taste—"set the ball rolling,"—as if it were a football match.

Marigold suddenly leaned forward from the sheltering hold of Julian's arm, fixed her green eyes on Parry, and smiled a smile that was barbed with needle-sharp spikes, dipped in the honey of her seductiveness. Nasty, nasty, he thought, and waited.

"I went up to change for dinner," she said, "at the same time everyone else went up to change for dinner, and stayed in my room till Cintra hammered on my door and drove me out into the snow, to ruin my sandals, just to amuse her."

"You went like a sheep," Cintra remarked with awful pleasantness. "Baaa-aaa. Not maaa-aaa, like the lambs."

"Cintra!" Anabel exclaimed. "To joke, at a time like this—Mr. Parry, you can ask anybody anything you like. No one has anything to conceal."

Oh? he thought. Hadn't they? He was damn sure they had. "Frake? Would you mind?"

"I can't tell you much. I simply went up to my room and changed. I take it you're talking about the time when Lawty must have been—when he—" Julian looked at Marigold, who'd begun to tremble. "It's all right, my sweet, try not to think about it. Sorry, Parry. I just changed, and then Cintra summoned me to join in the snowballing. Did you think we were a pack of lunatics?"

"As a matter of fact," Parry laughed, "I did. Why'd you come up here, and when?" He snapped the question out, not caring whether he had the right to demand an answer or not.

"I was in the bar after you and Jim brought Lawty in. I drifted out with the others. As a matter of fact, my socks were wet, and I wanted to change them. Then I remembered someone, Lord alone knows who, I can't remember, saying something about this window here being open, and the snow coming in if it snowed again. I thought I'd better shut it."

"In the dark?" Parry asked.

"I found the corridor dark when I got up here." Julian ran one finger round the inside of his collar. "I had my lighter with me, found this door, and came in. I suppose the draft from the window blew my lighter out, and I was just feeling for the switch, and not finding it, groping about, when I heard someone breathing. God, it was the most awful sensation I've ever had. I simply stood here, it felt like hours, a lifetime, perfectly still." He laughed ruefully, and Paul visibly and audibly shuddered. "I suppose I lost my head—I thought I heard dozens of people breathing, and then I heard someone else creep in in the dark, and I thought they were an army corps. And then you came in."

"Julian," Paul wailed, "I said this place's unlucky, and I was right, I tell you, I wouldn't touch it—"

"With a broom handle," Julian said wearily.

Paul held out his hands to Parry, clasped, as if he were praying. "I had one hell of a time, Parry. I thought maybe Lawty left a letter to say why he done it, so I comes up after I've been to the lavatory, and it's all dark, and I gropes around, and I gropes in here, and I bumps into something, the bed, maybe, and I thinks what the hell, and then I hears people breathing and I don't know anything more, and I don't know anything about anything. I had a go of diarrhea, and I'll have another one any moment now—you know how it is with shock?"

"Thank you, Paul." Anabel glared, tight-lipped.

"Well, you know how it is?" he implored Parry. "I thought it was Lawty's ghost."

"Stop it, you pig," Marigold said tigerishly. "You and your foul inside.

Talking in the present, like a dime novel."

"What d'you care? You—Parry, or whatever your name is—who killed Lawty? Who? Who?" For an unhappy moment, Parry thought Cintra was going to jump at him and tear chunks out of his face with her golden talons. "I didn't kill him, nor'd Christie, so who did?"

Parry didn't ask why Christie was to be assumed innocent, and it suddenly struck him that the ill-assorted pair were more than ordinary hotel acquaintances. "I take it that you were changing before dinner, too?" he said to Cintra, and she nodded violently, so that her hair fell over her nose. "All right, then d'you mind very much telling me what you're doing here? Or rather," he corrected himself, "what you were doing here, and why?" He nearly added, you needn't answer if you don't want to, but skipped it.

"What?" she stared at him defiantly. "I got sick of the bar after you and Jim brought Lawty in. I went up and sat in my room with Christie for a bit. Then I suddenly felt if I came up here, to Lawty's room, I might get something."

"Get something?" he repeated in some astonishment.

"Something. Yes. Vibrations from the atmosphere."

"Cintra's got sort of second sight," Christie explained. Oh Lord, Parry thought, were they in for a séance, on top of everything else? Table-turning, holding hands in the dark? To his alarm, Cintra's eyes took on a terrifyingly glazed look.

"I didn't put the lights on." She dug the nails of her right hand into the back of her left, and nearly shut her mouth. "I thought if I were alone in the dark I'd be more likely to get something, some sensing of what Lawty's emotions were. I know every room in the house, I pushed the door open and closed it behind me." She drew in her breath at the remembrance, and suddenly laughed, half hysterically, half in amusement, and stopped with a gasp. "I got vibrations, all right, my own, I've never trembled so much in my life. I wasn't alone in here. Oh, my God, it was horrible. And someone else came in—one, two, I don't know, in the dark."

"I see." Parry was longing for a cigarette, but he felt sure that if he produced his case and handed it round, Anabel would say it was desecrating Lawty's memory to smoke in his room so soon after his death. What a setup this was! He could feel that she was wielding a spiritual whitewash brush, in the hope that her guests and friends would remain unspotted in his eyes. He glanced covertly at Marigold. It was obvious what her and Julian's relationship was, and he pitied Julian, as only a man can pity a man. "I'm sorry?" He hadn't realized somebody was saying something to him. It was Christie. She was saying, "Please, can I get Cintra a warm coat?" like a child saying, "Please, Teacher, can I leave the room?"

"Coat? Oh, I see. Just a minute. How'd you amuse yourself when everyone else was changing, if you don't mind my asking?"

"I washed, and then I tidied."

Parry nodded. "And it was Cintra's room you went into after we'd met in the corridor below?" Now he'd done it. He'd caught the general infection of Christian names all round. Any moment he'd be calling Marigold his sweet, and Cintra his darling. "Was it, Miss Layne?" he said, with emphasis on the Miss.

The beginnings of a smile showed at one corner of her mouth, and vanished again. "Yes, Mr. Parry. And then Miss Norton, oh, quite a long time afterward, went out of the room."

Disconcerting girl, Parry thought. She was laughing at him, though he was the only one who realized it. "Yes, and? Why did you come up here?"

"She didn't come back, so I thought I'd go and look for her, for Mrs. Elliot, I mean."

"Mrs.?"

"For Miss Norton. I thought she'd probably be up here, as she really has this sort of second sight. So I came up. I didn't put any lights on, in case I disturbed Miss Norton, so I sneaked in, and then I realized that there were more people in here than Mrs. Elliot, and I thought she must've got the others together for a sort of séance."

"Well, and then?" I'd like five minutes alone with that girl, Parry decided, for the purpose of wringing her neck.

"Then Jim came in, then you came in. "

"How d'you know it was Bridges? Did he put the light on?"

Christie shook her head. "No, he didn't."

"Then how'd you know it was Bridges?" Parry repeated, and nearly said touché, with considerable satisfaction. "Well, how did you know?"

"Our little braown maouse knows everything," Marigold said with a charming smile, "doesn't she?"

"Marigold, dear," Anabel reproved. "This is neither the time nor the place to joke."

Jim levered himself away from the foot of the bed as if he were reluctant to part with its support, even more reluctant to talk. "You came in directly after me," he said to Parry, "a couple of minutes—maybe only a minute and a half, maybe only a minute."

For a moment Parry didn't answer. He felt sure that Christie hadn't thought there was a sort of séance going on when she'd found herself in the dark room surrounded by invisible people. And how'd she known it was Jim Bridges? Then it dawned on him that a woman in love developed almost supernatural instincts about whoever she was in love with. He felt faintly amused.

"Maybe less than a minute," Jim went on monotonously, "maybe half a minute. And, by the way," he said to Parry, "I suppose you are a police-man?"

"Don't be ridiculous, Jim!" Anabel exclaimed, and Miss Killigrew made ccht-cchting little noises with her tongue.

"It's not in the least a ridiculous question," Parry disagreed. "None of you knows anything about me at all." He unbuttoned his jacket, realizing he'd still got his overcoat on, that it was wet from melted snow, and dug out his note case. "Here're my doings. Sorry I can't whip back the lapel of my coat and flash an imposing silver badge at you."

"I told you so." Anabel frowned at Jim. "Now I hope you're satisfied. I didn't doubt who you were for one moment, d—Mr. Parry."

"Second sight?" he asked pleasantly. "Well, Bridges, d'you mind? Can you give a rough idea of where you were and what you were doing when everyone else was changing, and then after we'd brought Lawty in?"

"Sorry for casting doubts on you," Jim apologized handsomely. "Do-ing? I had a wash, then wandered back into the bar. Then I think I wandered upstairs again and had another wash, and after that Cintra roped me into her games. After that—I don't know. I think I went in the bar with the others. Went in and went out, and came up here after I'd had a wash."

"You seem to've got a passion for cleanliness," Parry said dryly. "Why d'you come up here? I mean, into this room, Lawty's room."

"I don't know." Jim looked at his hands, then rammed them back in his pockets. "I don't know at all. It was dark, so I came up. When I came in I heard people breathing, so I just stood still, wondering what the hell. Then you came in, and that was that."

"And you found your way in the dark?"

Jim smiled faintly at the floor. "My night sight's pretty good after the six years I once did at sea, gazing over the vasty deep, as they say."

"I see," Parry said. "And there we are. The lights were on in this room when we found Lawty below. So who came up here and put them out be-fore you all groped your way in? And who, when you five came in here at intervals, were the other people or person already in the room, and where are they now? Each of the five of you says you heard somebody breathing in the room."

"Stop it, stop it, for God's sake!" Paul lost his balance, staggered back-ward, clutched for support to steady himself, and the lamp on the dressing table crashed to the floor, leaving the room in its former inky blackness.

It was Julian who quelled the riot. "It's all right, Marigold, my sweet, don't choke me. Paul, get off the flex."

"The main switch is just behind you, Mr. Parry," Miss Killigrew's voice said somewhere down by his elbow. "Behind the door, so inconvenient."

He reached behind him, found the switch, and at the same moment

Julian turned on the dressing-table lamp. Everybody looked very shaken and hysterical, except Christie and Jim. Parry glanced at Miss Killigrew, to see how she was taking it. Her small, dun-colored eyes were fixed on the scrimmage by the dressing table, which had been joined by Anabel, who was unsuccessfully and with considerable annoyance trying to shut the window. At which of the huddle Miss Killigrew was staring, he couldn't make out, but she stared and stared in a kind of horrified fascination, as if she'd had a sudden, startling revelation.

"The window won't shut," Anabel fumed. "Come down to the bar. Julian? Marigold?" She crowded them out the door, herding them like sheep, sweeping them along, Miss Killigrew with them, engulfed as if by a tidal wave. The door slammed.

Parry turned the key, locking himself in. Somewhere below he thought he heard a plug pulled, the hiss of running water. Was Jim having another wash? There was the thud of a door banging, very faint and muffled. Then he was swallowed up in the cold silence of Lawty's disorderly chamber, the blazing lights making the night sky outside the window look very black and empty.

CHAPTER 9

AFTER the cold of Lawty's room, the bar, which was always too hot, was like an oven. The red and gold decorations made it seen hotter still. Anabel poured out three brandies. The brandy bottle was the first one among the many bottles she'd pounced on. She didn't care for brandy, but she was in a hurry. She had got Christie and Jim to herself at last, and if she didn't unburden her soul to someone sympathetic very soon, she'd have a nervous breakdown.

"Where're the others?" she asked Christie, wishing she could lock the bar door and keep them out.

"Cintra said she was going to change—I think Julian's helping Marigold to put on another pair of sandals."

"Where's that little fool Paul?"

"Coping with his shocked stomach, one supposes," Jim said.

Anabel glanced at the door.

"I know neither of you'll tell a soul," she whispered. "You two seem the only people I can depend on. The bums'll be on the doorstep any moment now."

"Oh, dear," Christie sympathized. "Poor Anabel. The hotel's not paying, is it?"

"I can't think why it isn't!" Anabel exclaimed, looking outraged. "There isn't another place like it in England."

Jim's eyes roved round the rococo decorations, and decided she was probably right.

"I was putting my shirt on tonight," Anabel went on tragically. "If everything'd gone off properly, either Paul or Julian would've come up to scratch. They wrote me they were coming down to talk things over, but how, or why, they both arrived on the same train, God knows. And now Paul's gone off his head trying to put Julian off, and Julian's got far more capital, far more. You *heard* Paul—even before Lawty was killed, poor darling."

Christie nodded. "I see. The highest bidder would pay off your debts, put the hotel on its feet, and so on?"

"Darling, yes, and give me a good percentage of the profits."

"Turn the place into a limited company, so to speak? And now it's all come unstuck. I'm so sorry, Anabel." Jim was so sorry that he'd forgotten his resentment of Christie for the time being, and his own inward gnawings.

"I can't think why Paul—What's that?" Anabel's eyes popped blackly. "Who's screaming? My nerves won't stand any more."

"I'll see," Christie said efficiently, and opened the bar door.

An ear-splitting voice was shrieking her name from somewhere upstairs.

"It's Cintra," Anabel fumed, and added, rather unkindly, "I wish she'd choke."

"I'll go and see what she wants."

As Christie went out of the bar, Marigold, looking beautifully unruffled, came into it.

"Shall I dispense the drinks, Anabel darling?" she asked. "Do sit down, sweetie, you must be so tired. I must find my bar chits and pay them. I do wish you'd remind me, you know how vague I am."

She wasn't in the least vague, but the news that she was actually going to pay some of her bills warmed Anabel's heart. After all, Marigold wasn't going to be another bad debt. Against the ornate red and gold of the bar, her tall, slender, silver simplicity was like a cool shaft of moonlight. She graced any place where she might be. Anabel stood back and admired her and her long, lovely hands as they sorted through the bar chits looking for her own.

"Don't worry about them now, dear."

But Marigold was putting them neatly together, adding them up, taking five-pound notes out of her flat silver evening bag.

"Five pounds seven and six, and two pounds eleven, and six pounds four—Anabel, am I such a drunk?"

"You're too generous, dear," Anabel said.

Feeling slightly sickened, Jim edged away from the bar. Marigold's exquisite insincerity, Anabel's gullibility and quick changes of heart, didn't seem to him in the least funny. Nor did the thought of Lawty, locked up in the dining room, make him feel any happier. The bar door was opening again. Which of the gang was it now? He hoped it would be Paul, because, he decided, Paul was damn funny.

It wasn't Paul, it was Julian Frake.

"Well, Julian dear?" Anabel greeted him.

"Anabel, I do hope you don't mind," he said, "but I've asked Chef to make some sandwiches for the lot of us. I'm famished, and I'm sure everyone else is, and we can hardly have a dinner party at this hour, and under the circumstances. Hello, Christie?"

Christie slipped in quietly and perched on a stool. Julian was always charming to her on the rare occasions they met. He didn't call her a braown maouse, or walk over her feet without noticing her. She smiled at him, not because she particularly liked him, but out of loyalty to Anabel. Paul, with his shocked stomach, was far more to her liking; but if Anabel was to be saved from the bums, Julian seemed to be the only person who could do it. So everyone should try to be pleasant to him. What, she wondered, ailed Paul? Were his hysterical outbursts really a cute business method of trying to put his rival off financing Anabel? Or, like Cintra, did he suffer from attacks of second sight?

"What was Cintra carrying on about this time?" Anabel asked.

"Oh, Cintra?" Christie began to laugh. "She started unzipping her frock and the zipper caught up a bit of her skin, so she got stuck."

"It's ridiculous," Anabel frowned. "Cintra, at her age, ought to have the sense to know that she's thin enough already without having all her dresses made so terribly tight."

Marigold punched the cash register, put a handful of notes into the till, took out some silver change, reached across the bar, and patted Anabel's hand.

"Now, Anabel," she placated, "don't get a thing about Cintra. She's almost alarmingly intelligent."

"I don't wish to be alarmed, thank you, dear."

I can't stand any more of this, Jim told himself. He'd somehow got wedged up against Christie, and when his arm bumped hers, he had a peculiar sensation as if he'd had an electric shock. As he tried to unwedge himself, Paul bounced in the door and almost flung himself at the bar.

"Who was that screaming?" he asked, dithering. "For God's sake, what's happened now? My nerve's gone. Anabel, can't you get me a taxi so I can go back to town?"

Anabel swallowed her rage and managed to smile at him.

"My dear Paul! At this hour? Don't be too absurd."

"I'm not being absurd, Anabel dear. I knew something was going to happen. This place is fated. For God's sake, who was it screaming?"

"Only Cintra," Christie said. "And no one's murdered her."

"Well? Well, where is she, then?"

"Have a drink, Paul." Julian patted him on the back. "Marigold, give Paul a large whisky, darling. Anabel? What're you drinking? Christie? Jim?"

"Ough," Cintra shivered, flopping into the room and banging the door behind her. She'd changed back into her slacks, and her hair was tousled. She stared fixedly at the cash register. "Who's been buying forty-two-odd pounds' worth of drinks? Or has someone been paying their bar chits? Have they?" She dropped her eyes to where Marigold's silver bag lay open on the bar, a five-pound note half in and half out of it. "I see," she muttered.

"What're you drinking, Cintra?" Anabel's bosom swelled as she took a deep breath. Damn and blast Cintra. Why shouldn't Marigold pay her bills without that skinny bag of bones being rude about it? Anabel pushed her way to the bar and leaned her elbows on it. If only she had the money, she'd enlarge the bar counter. The seven of them took up all the room, like a lot of hens huddled together on a perch. And Cintra had thrown an old sweater down on top of one of the ashtrays; and Paul's handkerchief had escaped from his breast pocket, fallen among the glasses, and was slowly absorbing a small pool of spilled brandy. When he drank, he made lapping noises, like a dog; he still kept bursting into a sweat and looked as if he was working up for another outburst about the ill luck of Beechlands, and that he wouldn't touch the place with a broom handle. Julian, however, Anabel was thankful to see, was at any rate paying for the drinks, counting over ten-shilling notes and handfuls of silver.

"Julian?" Cintra nudged him. "Can you give me a light? I left my lighter in my room. Look and see if the back seam of my slacks is split."

"What, my sweet?" Julian obligingly lit her cigarette and inspected her back view. "I don't think anything has split."

"For a wonder," Marigold said, banging at the cash register. In the mirror behind it she could see Julian bending over Cintra, all attention. Couldn't that woman keep her hands off any man? First Lawty, now she was after Julian. Why didn't she glue herself onto Paul for a change, the little fat slug?

The little fat slug suddenly knocked his glass over. "What's that noise?" he choked.

"What noise?" Cintra turned white. "Did you hear knocks? What'd you hear?"

"I don't hear anything." Marigold, still poised over the cash register, stood perfectly still and listened.

The tick of the bar clock seemed very loud. Nobody spoke. The hot red and gold room felt, to the people in it, as though it had suddenly been isolated from the rest of the house, that outside the door nothing and nobody lived and moved, that everything was dark. And shut away from them, all alone, Lawty lay dead, with the table still waiting for his party to begin, decorated with pink roses mixed up with holly and bits of tinsel.

Anabel licked her lips. She must say something, break the silence before one of the others, Marigold or Cintra or Paul, broke it by having hysterics. Only she couldn't think of anything to say, for once in her life. Her hands fumbled on the bar, and though she knew the ice had melted long ago, she pulled the gilded ice bowl toward her. Something clinked against it. The little ice hammer was back in its place. Only how did she know it'd ever been missing? Had someone told her? Miss Killigrew? Or Gaston? Or was she imagining it? Had she dreamed that the ice hammer had vanished?

"Anabel?" Cintra spoke in a hoarse whisper. "What is it?" She picked up the little hammer and held it between her hands, her eyes half shut. "I can feel violence," she whispered. "Hatred—death—What's this thing?" Her voice rose shrilly. She almost threw the hammer away from her. "That's what killed Lawty," she shouted. "There's blood on it."

"There's no blood on it at all," Anabel raged. "None, none at all."

"There isn't really." Christie stretched across and examined it, then tapped it lightly on the bar.

"Don't do than" Marigold flamed. "You did it before dinner. You're trying to frighten me."

Suddenly the center of everyone's attention, Christie smiled apologetically and put the hammer down.

"I wouldn't frighten even a braown maouse," she said, and Jim was filled with a kind of creeping terror.

CHAPTER 10

CINTRA'S screams did not particularly startle Parry. Even from the top floor, behind the locked door, he could hear her wild demands to Christie to come and unzip her. He was only rather relieved that, apparently, she was going to change her frock. The one she was wearing was bound to split before the night was out, and he didn't relish the idea of her running about with nothing on, just to add to the confusion.

He lit a cigarette and went through the pockets of Lawty's dinner jacket. They were empty. On the dressing table, thrown in a heap, were the various things he must have taken out of the pockets of the suit he was wearing when he arrived: a gold cigarette case, a gold lighter, a flat platinum watch, a white silk handkerchief, a scattered handful of silver. He'd done himself proud, or his admirers had. His tortoiseshell hairbrushes were gold-initialed, L.L.

Parry went through the pockets of every garment he could find and unearthed nothing interesting. It was in a side pocket of the leather dispatch case he found Lawty's wallet. Except for some snapshots, some addresses scribbled down on odd bits of paper, and the return half of his railway ticket from London, it was empty. He sat down on the bed and stared at his feet. So that was the motive, was it? Robbery with violence, all on account of a wad of bank notes. Or was that only part of the motive? What the hell, then, were all those people doing in Lawty's room, lurking in the dark, hoping they would not be discovered by their fellow lurkers, after, not before, Lawty's death? Had they all been up there earlier, and, afraid they might have left behind some signs of their former presence, returned in a panic?

Who'd put the lights out, anyway? They'd still been on when he and Jim had carried Lawty into the house. Either Livingston, Frake, Cintra, Jim, or Christie had been the first to creep into the room, and whoever was the first would have probably put out the light and done what he wanted to do by the light of a torch, a match, or a cigarette lighter. Then, hearing someone sneaking along the corridor, he'd have put it out and stayed there in the darkness hoping not to be discovered. Someone had taken one hell of a risk, unless they were all in it.

Parry's mind snapped back to Miss Killigrew. Which of them had she stared at like that, and why? Had one of them made some revealing movement, some significant gesture, which had meant something to her? He'd have to find her directly he'd done with the room, and not only Miss Killigrew, but the ice hammer.

The dressing-table lamp had a long flex, long enough for him to be able to hold the lamp out of the window. The snow on the window sill outside spoke volumes. It had an oddly smooth, patted-down appearance, as though it had been made all nice and tidy so that the shoeprints that decorated its whiteness could not fail to show up plainly. Parry collected Lawty's evening shoes from where they lay by the bed. They fitted the prints on the sill perfectly.

You God-awful fool, he mentally addressed whoever'd murdered Lawty. How could anyone be so imbecile? Instead of leaving well or ill alone, he'd returned, risking everything, with the intention of making quite sure everyone would think Lawty had jumped out the window of his own free will. Instead of which, he'd proved beyond all doubt that he'd been murdered. Forgetting that he'd landed down below without his shoes on, that the shoes would be found in his room, he'd also forgotten the window was not a casement, and that Lawty couldn't have stepped out onto the sill and stood there before jumping. For the window was of the up-and-down variety, and even with the bottom half wide open, there was only a space of less than two feet six or so through which anyone could climb. And Lawty was a big man. If he'd deliberately got out of the window, there would be knee prints, hand prints, all sorts of prints in the snow.

Parry laid a face towel over the sill, in case it snowed again, and weighted it down at each end with two heavy ashtrays. Whistling under his breath, he lined up the possible suspects in his mind's eye, together with motives other than plain robbery with violence. He hadn't met the staff yet. They sounded harmless enough, except for Gaston, who had a way of creeping about that Miss Killigrew didn't approve of.

First, Miss Killigrew. Unless she'd had an accomplice, she couldn't possibly have pitched Lawty over that high sill. Did she need money, anyway? Very likely. But she could hardly be one of Lawty's castoff girlfriends, with the motive of jealousy to drive her to murdering him. Anabel? Anabel undoubtedly craved money, but to murder a valued guest seemed rather a drastic way of getting hold of it. Did she crave more than money? Lawty himself? And Lawty had flirted with Marigold, and treated old Anabel as his mother, and she didn't like it? Rather farfetched, Parry thought.

What about Marigold? It was quite obvious what she was—an exquisite gold-digger. Had she dug for Lawty's gold in vain and in a fit of pique violently banished him from life, then helped herself to his wealth?

Had Cintra killed Lawty because she was jealous of his fancy for lovely Marigold? The idea of Cintra flinging herself at him while he was in the middle of changing for his party, cracking him behind the ear, snarling, "Take that, you swine!" then hurling him from the window, was grimly and disgustingly funny. She'd have done it in the true dramatic manner, scarcely realizing the drama was reality. And, by the way, did she always go on like this? Parry wondered. Did she invariably clutch at her throat, groan as if she were in awful pain, throw herself about, and gape at the assembled company with her mouth open like a cavern? If she did, she and her husband must find life an exhausting business.

Christie had a motive; two, indeed. She was badly off, and Lawty had played a fairly dirty trick on her. Jim had a very solid motive. Parry lit another cigarette, rather clumsily, as he had his gloves on, and tried to rid himself of the sneaking liking he had for these two victims of Lawty's charms. Jim Bridges had an almost unnatural aversion for the girl. He was probably a mass of complexes, inhibitions, and so forth, because his wife had run away with someone more attractive than himself, therefore ten times more sensitive about his patched-up body, and resenting Christie because he guessed she knew he was sensitive. The braown maouse wasn't the little kind fool nearly everyone thought her.

Livingston next. Had dear Paul, in his anxiety to make sure the immaculate Julian wouldn't outbid him, murdered Lawty for the purpose of convincing his rival that Beechlands was doomed to perpetual ill luck? Had Julian, afraid the changeable Anabel might decide that Paul's business brains were more of an asset to the hotel than the Frake fortune, tried to frighten the little man off by adding yet another tragedy to the record, this novel idea occurring to him when Paul had started getting temperamental earlier in the evening?

What a damned awful mess. He must get hold of Miss Killigrew, then cast an eye over Gaston and the kitchen staff. Then what? Persuade the whole household to allow themselves to be locked into the coal cellar, and tramp off to Ditchit and the worse than useless Ditchit policeman? Or stay on guard in the hope that a stranger might arrive at the gates and take a message to Ditchit or Watching for him?

Hell, Parry cursed, and locked himself out in the corridor, leaving the lights burning in the chilly room. When he, got down to the hall, it was empty. No Miss Killigrew bobbed behind her desk, nor was she in her office. The blab-blah of voices led him to the kitchen. It was occupied by the chef, the two kitchenmaids, the housemaid with catarrh, and Gaston. Robère was piling sandwiches onto a silver tray delicately extended in Gaston's long, pale fingers, which began to tremble when he saw Parry. Chef and the three girls had unshakable alibis. They had all been together since before dinner, with the exception of Lilly, who had gone to look for the ice hammer and failed to find it. Lilly began to get hysterical. She was going to give notice. She was going tomorrow. She'd heard noises, and why not? The barmaid had gone because she'd heard noises too. The place was haunted. And she hadn't taken the ice hammer or the garden scissors, and Miss Killigrew hadn't no right to ask questions like as if she had.

None of them had so much as set eyes on Lawty before today, though they'd heard of him, of course. Gaston, clasping the tray, said he'd been polishing silver in his pantry before dinner. Then he'd come into the kitchen. There he'd stayed till Miss Killigrew had asked for some sandwiches, when he'd taken them to her and gone back to the kitchen. He was vague and shifty, which didn't surprise Parry unduly.

"Might I take the sandwiches in the bar now?" he asked, staring at them with eyes like a dead fish.

"Sure," Parry said agreeably, and followed him, shutting the kitchen door. "So your name's Gaston Leroux now, is it?" he asked. "Dyed your bonny golden locks, haven't you, if my memory isn't failing me?"

Parry's memory seldom, if ever, failed him. He inwardly congratulated

Miss Killigrew on the feminine instinct that had prompted her to mistrust Gaston Leroux, alias George Shepherd, alias John Mills, alias Louis de Ville. His real name was Albert Cummings.

"I'm going straight now, Inspector," he whined.

Parry sighed. "I've lost count of the times you've said those same words to me, Albert, or, for the moment, Gaston. You haven't risen from the depths of larceny to the heights of murder, by any chance, have you?"

"I bloody well haven't." Gaston's polite and obsequious manner temporarily fled. "And you haven't a thing on me, neither. And if you think you can do the dirt on me by splitting to the old girl, you're out of luck. She knows I done a couple of stretches."

"Oh?" Parry raised his eyebrows. "Giving you another chance, is she? And don't call her the old girl, it's rude."

Gaston swallowed. "Madame took up a couple of my references and found out they were phony. I'm a better waiter than you'd ever be, so she's reformed me."

"My God!" Parry began to laugh. "How too touching. Dump that tray in the bar and then go back to the kitchen and damn well stay there."

Gaston fled, reappeared empty-handed, shot past, and vanished. Parry got out his pipe and filled it. Now, to add to the complications, there was an old lag mixed up with the party. Albert, or Gaston, or whatever he chose to call himself, had done plenty of robberies, but never accompanied any of them with violence. The usual criminal of that type was pretty consistent. He had his own line and stuck to it. Parry was fair enough not to take it for granted that a professional thief, because he happened to be in a house where murder had been committed, must necessarily be the murderer. Albert alias Gaston, with his professional knowledge and cunning, could have very easily relieved Lawty of his note case without killing him. Or had Gaston helped himself to the contents of the note case, and someone else done the murdering?

"Blast," Parry muttered under his breath and went in search of Miss Killigrew. Looking cautiously through the crack of the half-open door into the bar, he saw she wasn't there. Her office was still empty. She wasn't in the hall, the lounge, or the writing room that opened off the lounge. He bolted upstairs, filled with sudden concern for her. She wasn't in any of the upstairs rooms. He even looked under beds, in cupboards, in bathrooms and lavatories.

"Miss Killigrew?" he called.

Where the devil had she got to? He tried her office again and the pantry between the office and the bar. She wasn't in the storeroom on the far side of the bar, or in the scullery or the lavatory next the kitchen. There appeared to be only one more place to look. Opposite the scullery a short

passage led to a door on which "No Admittance" was painted in red. Why
no admittance? He snipped down the light switch outside the door, turned
the handle, pushed the door open, and found himself stepping into space.
No wonder the warning "No Admittance." A steep iron stepladder led
straight down into a blazing hot abyss, where an enormous furnace gurgled
and sizzled, surrounded by piles of coke. This, evidently, was the boiler
room, and to judge by its position, it was directly below Lawty's landing
place, which accounted for the moist thinness of the snow where he'd lain.

Parry shut the door quietly and went crabwise down the ladder.

"Miss Killigrew?" he said.

Miss Killigrew didn't answer. She lay in a small, crumpled heap, her
head bashed up against the furnace, what was left of her face congested and
horribly swollen. Someone must have lured her to the boiler-room door, or
come upon her outside it, grabbed her by the throat, probably, to silence
cries for help, and hurled her, like an old sack, straight down at the furnace.
The whole thing could have been done in a matter of seconds.

Parry lifted her away and laid her on the cleanest place he could find on
the stone floor. She was dead. Quite dreadfully dead, for the left side of her
head and her left shoulder had started to roast. Up in Lawty's room, Miss
Killigrew had had a moment of revelation and paid for it with her life.

Silently and with fury, Parry cursed himself. If he'd looked after her
properly this wouldn't have happened. All at once the matter of finding the
killer of Lawty, and now Miss Killigrew, became very personal. Lawty
might have earned what had come to him, but not the unfortunate, harmless
little old woman whose sandwiches she'd so eagerly shared with him. It
was out of the question, now, that he could leave this revolting house till
morning, when a messenger in the form of some tradesman or one of the
outside staff appeared on the scene.

He picked Miss Killigrew up in his arms, and with great difficulty carried her up the iron ladder. It was too hot in the boiler room to leave her
there. Voices yapped in the kitchen. The noises from the bar might have
come from the monkey house at the zoo. Parry locked the door, put the key
in his pocket, and proceeded cautiously to the hall. He hoped Miss Killigrew would not mind sharing the dining room with Lawty. The pink hothouse roses smelled very strong and, suitably, of funerals. When he had
arranged her near one of the windows, he covered Miss Killigrew with a
tablecloth. There was something else he felt he ought to do. Miss Killigrew
would be pleased, he knew, to think someone, even a policeman, would
trouble to place pink roses on her elderly spinster breast. Only it would
have been more to the point, Parry decided, if someone had presented her
with flowers during her lifetime. He took, however, considerable pleasure
in disarranging the vulgarity of the festive table decorations. The roses, all

by themselves, on the plain white of Miss Killigrew's makeshift shroud, looked very much better than mixed up with old holly and glittering tinsel.

CHAPTER 11

ANABEL'S small but, to her, important world seemed to be crashing round her head. After a rather bilious mixture of drinks, her imagination, which generally ran on conventional lines, had run off the rails. She was sure that if all these people would stop talking, she would be able to hear her world coming down in slabs, like when what-was-his-name tore down the pillars of some temple or other (or was it someone who had supported the world and then dropped it?), so that it collapsed in a heap of ruins. No, that was the walls of Jericho, only she couldn't at the moment remember what made them fall to bits. Anabel's education had been a little sketchy.

After a tentative and cunning attempt to draw first Julian, then Paul, into a talk on business, she'd had to give it up. Neither of them wanted to talk business. All Paul could think of was Lawty's dead body, which might turn into a wandering ghost any minute, the ill luck that haunted Beechlands, and, according to him, would forever haunt it. As if that wasn't enough, he kept giving startled jumps, thinking he could hear three knocks. Anabel's story of the three knocks, which at the time had seemed to her so dramatic, and which she had once told in an effort to steal the limelight from Cintra, who was having a fit of second sight over somebody's teacup, had turned sour on her. She had never heard three knocks. She wished to heaven she'd never invented them, though when she had done so, she had really convinced herself she had heard them. If Anabel made up a good story, it immediately became as true to her as it very often seemed untrue to other people.

Now Paul was hearing knocks, and Julian appeared to have entirely forgotten why he had come down to Beechlands. Tomorrow was Sunday. On Sunday tradesmen couldn't demand payment, nor could the firm in London that had redecorated the house either come down in person or install a bum in the hotel. But on Monday anything might happen.

Anabel powdered her face. At any rate, Marigold was in the money, her bar chits paid.

"Darling, you've got a huge bit of fluff on your nose!" Marigold exclaimed, and made a dab at Anabel with one of her scarlet talons. "That's all right now, sweetie."

"No, it isn't" Anabel nearly screamed. "You've scratched me!"

"Darling, I'm so sorry, but I don't see any blood."

"I do," Cintra gabbled, and rushed at Anabel waving a rather dirty man's bandanna handkerchief. Fortunately, before she reached her goal, she tripped over the edge of one of the rugs and landed up with her arms round Paul's neck. At last, though he was being half strangled, he stopped looking terrified and looked quite pleased instead. "Oh, God, did I walk over your feet, Paul?"

"I like it," he said, giving one of her arms a fat, moist, but quite unimpassioned kiss. Then he kissed her other arm, with more warmth, and she deliberately trod on his feet and disentangled herself.

"Cintra, sweetie, you ought to've been born a boy," Marigold said.

"Why?" Cintra demanded. "Why, Marigold? Why? Why should I've been born a boy? Why?"

"Because you've got such nice long straight legs," Julian, the soul of tact, explained. "Like a young colt," he added, and wished he hadn't. Such clichés were not up Cintra's alley. He ought to have reserved that one for Marigold, who adored them.

"I want to know why Marigold thinks—"

"Anabel darling, may I open another magnum?" Julian asked, taking out his note case, which, as usual, was well stocked, and patting Marigold's hand. "There's one in the icebox under the bar, isn't there?"

Anabel pulled herself together. She was the hostess, the lady of the manor. From her they must take their cue. It was up to her to set the pace, slow, fast, middling. She smiled at Julian, looking through him at the red and gilt rococo decorations. Some years ago, dining at the Savoy, the people at the next table to hers had talked about rococo decorations. She had no idea what they were, but they sounded the very thing. When she'd had Beechlands done up for the second time and had been discussing the new decorative scheme, the word had come back to her.

"Entirely in the rococo style," she had told the charming young man who had come down from town. His gulp of astonishment had been most satisfactory. Evidently rococo would be very expensive. Therefore it must be equally smart, original, tasteful, and attractive. It had certainly turned out to be exceedingly expensive. Anabel thought it a perfect background for her dignity, poise, and character.

She smiled again at Julian, nodding. "Of course, Julian dear."

Julian went behind the bar, found the magnum, removed the gold foil, cut the wire, and the cork hit the ceiling to rebound on Paul's head, from where it ricocheted into a row of glasses, breaking one of them.

"Really, Paul dear," Anabel said rather crossly, for the glass was an expensive one, "do be more careful."

"Me?" he exploded. "I didn't do nothing, Anabel. It was Julian. I wasn't buying the champagne, was I? I wasn't opening it, was I? I wasn't popping the cork off like a gun, was I? Was I?"

Anabel pursed her lips.

Cintra suddenly put her arm through Jim's and laughed very loudly in his ear. She was, he thought, the only person he'd ever heard laugh in exactly the way it was written, "Har-har-har," and from disliking her in a vague sort of way, he found himself liking her. She wasn't a beautiful tart like Marigold, whom he detested. Nor was she secret and curious about people like Christie. He turned round and grinned at her, feeling immensely comforted, though he wished she would shut her mouth. He supposed the wide-open-mouth business was some new trick, or had she developed adenoids or tonsils? If so, she had better have them removed as soon as possible, unless, in her next film, she was to play the part of an idiot.

"I know I look like hell," she mouthed at him. "This new muck I did my hair with's made it like straw, or tow, or whatever it is. Ask Marigold, she'll tell you what it looks like."

"I wasn't looking at your hair," Jim said truthfully. "I was wondering if you had a sore throat or something. Your uvula looks very inflamed."

"What? Can you see as far down as that?" Cintra clutched her throat, and her upper lip rose till it nearly touched her nose. She looked more than horrified. For a moment she looked as if she were going quite off her head. "Christie?" she wailed, leaning across Jim and dragging Christie toward her, so that she was jammed against Jim and he was sandwiched between them.

Anabel clicked her tongue and thrust a glass of champagne at Cintra. She didn't want any more hysterics.

Cintra grabbed the glass and lurched away from Jim, so that he was left marooned with Christie beside him, and the same feeling of resentful, indecent intimacy made his flesh creep. Only he couldn't move away from her, nor could he think of anything to say. Even if he did say anything, she wouldn't hear him, because for no apparent reason Paul had started having a row with Julian about the champagne cork.

"Have another sandwich," Christie said and, pushing the tray along the bar, went back to her stool.

"Do be quiet, Paul dear," Anabel commanded, her bosom shaking with rage.

"Paul darling," Marigold laughed, "don't be so wild."

"I like him that way." Cintra's voice rose to a hoarse shout. "He's funny. Go on, Paul. Go on, Julian, get nose to nose."

"But I don't want to," he complained. "Come along, Paul, have another drink and forget it."

"Forget what? I won't forget it. I—" Paul glanced nervously over his shoulder, his flushed face turning a pasty gray.

"Have you forgotten Lawty's lying there dead? Who killed him? Did you? Who did?"

"Now, then," Anabel croaked, her throat contracting, "that's enough, thank you. How can you speak like that about poor Lawty?"

"I wasn't. Don't you want to know who killed him, Anabel?"

Anabel seized the telephone on the bar and pushed in the plug that connected it with the kitchen. "Chef?" she said, somehow controlling her voice and regaining her dignity. "Tell Gaston to come in here and serve at the bar. You heard me. I don't care what the policeman said. This is my house, is it not? Very well, tell Gaston to come here and look after the drinks. Now what? Very well, he can wash his hands first."

That, Christie decided, was wise of Anabel. With Gaston as an audience, they might quiet down. Poor Anabel—It was a pity she'd fortified herself with quite such an unwholesome mixture of drinks, for she was rapidly losing control not only of her temper but of her nerves. Paul, as a financial help in time of trouble, looked like being out for good. He'd never invest one penny in a place where he imagined the ghost of the three who had died so violently there might pop out at him any moment. But what ailed him? The few times she had met him at Beechlands before, he'd never gone on like this. Had he a guilty conscience and couldn't stand its pricks? As for Julian, she imagined that after tonight's performance he'd take his money elsewhere. And wherever that would be, Marigold would follow. In the kitchen, the staff were probably discussing the subject of giving notice in the morning, and then who would be left to stand by Anabel? Cintra— but Cintra was due to go back to Hollywood in a month, and Max would go with her. A hoard of idle curiosity-seekers would come from far and near to see where the famous Lawton Lawrence was murdered. Then they'd go away again and never come back. The only ones left would be Jim and herself to take it in turns to help Anabel keep the bums at bay. Or, if they couldn't be kept at bay, to rescue secretly as many of her valuables as were portable. Or would Jim rat? No, Jim wouldn't rat. His sense of duty was too strong. He had a queer sense of duty toward Anabel, because he felt she must blame herself for his wife's having met Lawty at Beechlands and seen so much of him there.

Christie kept her eyes fixed on her lap, in case Jim noticed she was thinking about him. He didn't want anyone to know that the scars that ate into him weren't the ones on his body, but the ones on his mind. Everyone else thought he'd almost forgotten about the dirty trick his wife had played on him. Until this evening he had thought that that was what everyone thought—if it ever occurred to him that people thought about him at all, which they probably didn't. Then he'd discovered, or his instinct had told him, rather, that she'd not only seen through him but into him.

Well, if it did him any good at all, gave him any satisfaction, let him hate and resent her as much as he liked. If his resentment boiled up inside him till he couldn't stand it any longer, he might even be goaded into having a flaming row. There was nothing like a flaming row for getting rid of inhibitions and inferiority complexes. When people got angry enough, they said and did things they'd never say or do normally, and the best part of it was that when they simmered down, they generally couldn't remember the awful things they'd said and done. They simply felt exhausted and emptied out, as if they'd had a huge dose of castor oil and got rid of the poison.

Christie thought with longing of raucously shouted insults, of knuckle dusters, broken bottles, hurled dinner plates, single sticks, and large clods of stickily slung mud. Unfortunately, she could not picture Jim kissing and making it up afterward.

"Our little braown maouse is very quiet, isn't she?" Marigold said.

Christie looked up and smiled. Gaston had crept silently into the room and installed himself behind the bar without her noticing his entry. He had brought a large silver bowl filled with slabs of ice with him, and was pouring out more drinks. He looked rather pastier than usual, if that were possible.

"Isn't she?" Marigold persisted, exquisitely kind and friendly.

"She generally is, isn't she?" Christie said. "I was just thinking that Inspector Parry hasn't told us how Lawty was murdered."

"What d'you mean?" Paul squeaked. "He fell out the window."

"If he fell," Julian pointed out, "then it was an accident, and he wasn't murdered at all. But Parry said definitely he was murdered. I hope he wasn't robbed as well. I never met him before, of course, but he seemed the type who'd carry a lot of money round with him."

A cut-glass goblet slid out of Gaston's fingers and splintered on the floor.

"You can pay for that!" Anabel fumed at him. "They cost a fortune, and that's the second one tonight."

"Anabel, my sweet?" Julian drew her away from the bar into a corner. "Don't worry. We'll get you some new ones. This is all too maddening for you, and for me too."

Anabel took a deep breath and steadied herself. At last she was going to hear the proposal more desirable, far, than a proposal of marriage from the most eligible bachelor—or, of course, widower. The color came back to her face under its mottled coating of powder. She almost blushed, but not quite.

"Oh, dear?"

"We can't possibly talk business with this racket going on. I can't, at any rate."

"Business?" Anabel repeated, as if she didn't know what he meant, and mercifully unaware she hadn't fooled him with her wide-eyed incomprehension. "Business? My dear, I'd forgotten all about it, with this tragic—with Lawty—"

"I know. It's an appalling shock. You'll feel more up to discussing things tomorrow." Poor old Anabel, Julian thought, forgetting he was getting on himself, she must have been through hell, and he wished he'd said something to her sooner. He felt conscience-stricken for having kept her on tenterhooks like this. "Here's to our combined operations, and their success," he said, and raised his glass.

"He can't—he can't have been pushed—pushed out of the window," Marigold said in breathless, Cintra-like spasms. "He was so strong—there was no sign of a struggle."

"Have some ice in your drink, Marigold dear," Anabel suggested loudly and cheerfully, her world resurrected round her by the miracle that had happened.

"Ice, m'selle?" Gaston took up the ice hammer, raised it, and brought it down with a crack on one of the slabs of ice.

Cintra gasped and swayed perilously backward. "Yes. Like that. Like that, crack. I know now—I read it in some book. Only it was done with a spanner. Crack, behind the ear."

"Now then, Cintra—"

Off again, Christie said to herself. But not even Anabel's insistent orders that this was enough, or Cintra's postdated prophecies, Paul's exclamations, Julian's amused soothing, or lovely Marigold's pleas to her Uncle Julian to shut Cintra up, could drown the wolfish sound of the wind that suddenly attacked the windows of the bar, rattling them as if it wanted to get in.

"It's them," Paul swallowed, hugging his stomach. "They want a drink. They resent being shut out. I've 'ad it." And he bolted out of the room, leaving behind him a thick, suspicious silence punctuated only by the assaults of the rising snowstorm and the tick of the clock.

It had at last dawned on the occupants of Beechlands that one of the human beings at present under its roof was, beyond all doubt, a murderer.

But not one of them was aware that Miss Killigrew, for the first time in her life, was sharing her resting place with a man.

CHAPTER 12

PARRY pressed his nose against the plate-glass doors of the main entrance and viewed what he could see of the weather with disgust. The sibilant whistle of the wind was dreary enough, but the snow it drove before it was calamitous. Even if he could leave the house and the people in it, he doubted that he could find his way anywhere. The snowflakes lighted silently on the glass panes, so that they were spotted in uneven patterns of white on black. The wailing of the blizzard drowned the voices in the kitchen and the bar, so that he might have been all alone in the house except for the company of the two dead bodies in the dining room, and the heat, which was almost alive, like the devouring heat of a tropical jungle. The carpets were so thick that he couldn't hear the sound of his own footsteps, which gave an illusion that he wasn't really there at all.

He frowned at the whirling snow, sorely puzzled. For he had looked everywhere, apologetically searched Miss Killigrew, but nowhere could he find the key to the safe. And in the safe were all the rest of the keys except the ones he had pocketed himself. Not only was everyone locked out, but everyone was locked in, unless somebody opened one of the ground-floor windows and set the alarm bells clamoring. Where in hell was the safe key, then? Either Miss Killigrew had hidden it in some private place, or whoever had killed her had presumably taken it from her. The thing against that was that unless she had voluntarily handed over the key, which was very unlikely, there wouldn't have been time for anyone to have searched her as well as kill her. The risk of discovery was too great.

Parry pulled at his lip. Could a woman have had the strength to hurl Miss Killigrew not just down the iron ladder into the boiler room, but hurl her from the boiler-room door right at the furnace? She couldn't have touched the steps in her flight, for the furnace itself was a good nine feet from the bottom of the ladder, and to judge by the position he had found her in, she obviously hadn't rolled. Was any woman in the house capable of such a feat of strength? And then he remembered a lady called Camilla, who had once precipitated a very large detective sergeant from her doorstep halfway down her garden path by the simple method of placing her foot in the small of his back and heaving. So what could have been easier than to grasp Miss Killigrew by her skinny throat, hang on tight with one hand, hang onto the door jamb for support with the other hand, lift a foot, place it in whatever part of Miss Killigrew's middle presented itself, heave like hell, let go her throat at the same time, and launch her like a rocket into space?

As for Lawty, any of the women in the house, except Miss Killigrew, could have disposed of him. The dressing table was near the window, just to one side of it; Lawty, no doubt, had been fiddling about at the dressing table, and, to make everything easier for his murderer, he wouldn't have suspected, when he or she entered, that he did so with the intention of killing him. It would have been the easiest thing in the world to get Lawty to look out the window, then crack, pick him up under the knees, and pitch him out. But for two things, it would have been as near foolproof as made no difference: the little fresh crisscrossed bruise behind Lawty's ear and the fatal error of the shoeprints on the window sill, which proved beyond doubt that Lawty's death hadn't been an accident, but murder.

It was a riddle without, so far, an answer. The answer lay in Miss Killigrew's dead eyes. My dear Miss Killigrew, Parry mentally addressed her, I do wish you could speak and tell me what it was you spotted up there in Lawty's room. Now—what? Someone in the house was wondering when her body would be discovered. It was unlikely to be found, the killer would have decided, till Anabel gave orders for the central heating furnace to be stoked and sent, presumably, one of the staff to attend to it. That was what the self-appointed executioner was waiting for, all keyed up to show the appropriate emotions of incredulity and horror when the time came. So, when the time did come, Parry thought, he was going to get a nasty shock. Instead of a hysterical servant screaming blue murder on the discovery of the body, nothing would happen at all.

Parry tiptoed along the corridor past the bar, hoping no one would hear him, found his way back to the door of the boiler room, and put the key in the lock just as he had found it. Now for the bar. By the sound of it, things were not going too well. As it was nearly midnight and no one, including himself, had had a square meal, and most of the inmates had, no doubt, had a great deal to drink, tempers and nerves must be getting rather frayed.

The atmosphere when he went in was sultry in more ways than one. The intermittent howling of the wind appeared to be very unpopular, and the heat of the room made him feel he'd walked into a Turkish bath by mistake, except that the company was mixed and also clothed. Parry took one fascinated look at the monstrous decorations, caught Gaston's eye, and nearly laughed out loud. Albert alias Gaston could now have the pleasure of mixing him a drink, no doubt wishing, while he did so, he had some cold poison handy.

"Everyone all right?" Parry asked agreeably, wondering if his presence would ease the tension or strain it even more.

"My dear, of course." Anabel bore down on him, her hands half out-stretched as if in welcome. She seemed to have regained some of her composure and was again the languid Edwardian duchess. "Now you must have a drink, poor man. Gaston? What will you have?"

Everyone started saying he must have a drink, poor man, except Christie and Jim. Thou shalt not, Parry told himself, drink with suspects while on duty. Only he wasn't officially on duty at all, and he was exceedingly thirsty.

"I'll have a whisky, if I may," he said and, leaning on the bar, treated Gaston to a pleasant smile. "So you're Gaston? French?"

To his credit, Gaston didn't blink an eyelid. "Belgian, m'sieur. Soda or water?"

"Soda, please. Belgian? What part of Belgium?"

"I was actually born in London," Gaston said with perfect truth, and a twist on his mouth that was as good as a very rude gesture.

"You must be so tired, aren't you, Parry?" Marigold leaned gracefully over his shoulder. She smelled invitingly of some subtle and very expensive perfume. She moved her head, and a lock of her hair brushed his cheek.

"I think we're all tired," Julian said a little wearily. "Cigarette, my sweet?"

"No, thanks," Parry said, willfully misunderstanding, and wished he had the moral courage to add "duckie." He could feel that Christie was laughing inwardly, and turning his head, he grinned at her. She was a little flushed but otherwise as calm as usual. He was sorry he had to suspect her and Jim along with the rest of them.

"Listen, Parry." Paul pushed Marigold to one side, pounced on his arm, and clung to it. "For God's sake lend me your police car to get me away from here. I'll give your driver a good tip, anything—I can't stand this no longer. I've 'ad it."

"Aitches wild," Jim muttered, fiddling with some poker dice.

"My dear Paul," Anabel exclaimed, in a voice of utter exasperation, "Mr. Parry hasn't got a police car or a driver with him. His own car's somewhere in a ditch. Stop going on in this absurd way."

"Parry, have a sandwich." Cintra flung herself and the tray nearly on top of him. "Do, do, for God's sake do have a sandwich."

Why she should invoke the Almighty to persuade him to a sandwich, he had no idea. But he took two and thanked her. Her hair looked exactly as if she had been dragged through a hedge backward, her lipstick was smudged, there was a streak of dirt down one cheek, and her mouth was still wide open. But somehow, he suddenly found something likable about her. She simply didn't seem to care a damn what she looked like. Lovely Marigold, he was sure, cared all the time.

And then he saw the gilt-plated ice hammer lying on the bar. He picked it up carelessly and looked at it, aware that the already strained atmosphere was now stretched to breaking point. The pane of the hammer was crisscrossed with deep lines, making a neat, very sharp hobnail pattern. He put the hammer back on the bar as carelessly as he'd picked it up. Better leave it where it was. It wasn't much help without the person who had used it on Lawty attached to it. If he left it lying about, there was always the chance that the guilty one would purloin it a second time and try to dispose of it. To have put it back where it belonged after it had served its purpose was a good move and couldn't have been difficult to accomplish. The bar counter itself was small. With that collection of people wedged round it, it would have been easy to slip the hammer back among the confusion of glasses and ashtrays. Any one of the eight people—including Gaston as a possible suspect—could have done it.

The wind snarled ferociously outside the windows, and Paul jumped and shivered. But in the hot, stuffy bar the cigarette smoke hung in a still, heavy cloud.

"It's a terribly cold night, isn't it?" Parry said to Anabel, who immediately became the attentive hostess again. "Is your central heating one of those self-regulating oil affairs, or is it the usual coke furnace that has to be stoked?" To implant an idea in Anabel's head was, he felt sure, as easy as planting a nasturtium seed in a window box. He rubbed his hands together as if they were cold.

"It's a coke furnace," Anabel informed him. "Most economical. It only has to be made up once every morning, and once at night."

"Oh?" Parry smiled encouragingly. "So it won't have to be made up again till tomorrow morning?"

The seed took root. Anabel rounded on Gaston accusingly.

"Has anyone had the sense to stoke the furnace tonight?" she demanded. "Or have you forgotten all about it?"

"It isn't my business, madame," Gaston pointed out.

"It is now," Anabel said. "So go and do it."

Gaston looked at his immaculate hands and in cold disdain sidled out of the bar.

"Are we," Jim remarked to nobody, "to be roasted alive?"

"Grilled bones on toast." Cintra pulled up her sleeves, looked critically at her thin arms, and added, "Ough!"

"What's it?" Paul jumped nervously. "Did you hear anything?"

Parry took the opportunity to get out of the room while Anabel was telling Cintra and Paul not to talk nonsense. He could hear the boiler-room door open, Gaston's feet clattering genteelly down the iron ladder, and then an ill-tempered attack on the furnace. Parry waited. The arguments now raging in the bar were loud enough to drown the noises of stoking that proclaimed Gaston had descended to the depths beneath. Was his unhesitating behavior a sign that he was innocent of adding murder to his other talents? Albert Cummings had a cool nerve, but was it as cool as all that? Surely, if he had expected to find the body of one of his victims where he had flung it, and it had vanished completely, he would have paused on the top of the ladder, made some sound of agitation and astonishment.

But one never knew.

Parry wandered back into the bar, intensely interested.

Miss Killigrew's murderer, unless he or she was made of steel, must surely show some sign that he was waiting for Gaston's horrified yells of discovery. But none of them looked as if they were waiting for anything more untoward than what had already happened, unless you counted Paul, who seemed to be permanently occupied in waiting for the blizzard to break in the windows and manifest itself in the form of some sort of spooklike protoplasm.

Gaston made his reentry without anyone's taking any notice of him and took up his place behind the bar again. The only thing that surprised Parry was that he didn't look unduly annoyed about the coke dust that sullied his carefully manicured fingers.

Hell and damnation, Parry swore to himself, this murderer might have made some insane mistakes, but what kind of monster of self-control and icy nerves was the creature? For now he must know that either Miss Killigrew hadn't died at all, as she was meant to, but had taken up her bed and walked, or that her dead body had been discovered and removed, and the person who had made the discovery and done the removal was, so to speak, keeping her corpse up his sleeve to produce it at some inconvenient moment. The blather of voices rose to a crescendo, hovered like a row of exclamation marks above Parry's defenseless head, and subsided like a tide going down with unnatural rapidity.

Anabel cleared her throat. In some telepathic manner the emotions—if he or she ever had such things—of Lawty's and Miss Killigrew's murderer must have suddenly communicated themselves to everyone in the bar. They were all, every one of them, waiting for some further hell to break lose, waiting for Parry to spring something on them.

"Miss Killigrew gone to bed?" he asked.

"Miss Killigrew?" Anabel stared at him. "Gone to bed?"

"Doesn't she ever go to bed?" he asked. "Or is she a kind of sleepless wonder, forever on guard over her office?"

"She wouldn't go to bed yet, before me." Anabel's eyes were still fixed on him, huge lollipops. "She must be in her office. I suppose I ought to give her a drink. Gaston, take Miss Killigrew a large sherry."

A large sherry at midnight? Parry repressed a shudder.

"Don't you think some champagne would be better for her?" Julian suggested.

"Julian darling, why? Miss Killigrew is the sherry type."

Marigold slipped her arm round Julian darling's elbow, and he smiled at her. "Miss Killigrew probably thinks things like champagne or whisky're immoral."

"Why?" Christie asked, politely inquiring.

"Sweetie, sherry's so refeened."

"My sherry is exceedingly good," Anabel said. "Do you think I sell cooking sherry? Really, Marigold, my dear—" Gaston departed with the sherry. The tension eased a little. Parry looked round at the clock. Two minutes, three minutes, four minutes.

"Madame?" Gaston stood at the door, still holding the sherry on a small tray. "I can't find Miss Killigrew. She's not in her office, so I looked in the lounge and the writing room, but I can't find her."

"What?"

Now the balloon's going up, Parry thought, and waited expectantly.

"Nonsense." Anabel levered Paul on one side and went to the telephone. Like the telephone in her sitting room, it had a miniature switchboard with four plugs. One was marked "Office," another "Mrs. Adams," and another "Kitchen." The fourth was marked "Receptionist's Bedroom." Anabel pushed the office plug in.

"Miss Killigrew? Miss Killigrew, Miss Killigrew? Where's she got to?" She plugged in to the kitchen. "Miss Killigrew? Not you, Chef, Miss Killigrew. Miss Killigrew?" Anabel's voice rose. "She must be making up the fire in my room. She'll hear the bell anyway." She pulled out the second plug and pushed in the third. "Miss Killigrew? Really! Miss Killigrew! Miss *Killigrew?*" Fumbling, she pushed in the last plug. "She must've gone to bed. Miss Killigrew? Miss Killigrew! *Miss Killigrew?*"

Gaston's hands began to shake. He put down the tray, felt in his pocket for a handkerchief, pulled it out, and with it a mixed collection of oddments: a silver cigarette case, a lighter, a half crown, a key with a tab attached to it. He wiped his forehead, scrabbled his belongings up off the floor, and stuffed them back in his pocket again.

"Miss Killigrew!" Anabel shouted into the receiver, and banged the rest up and down.

"She's gone!" Paul howled. "Miss Killigrew?" He stumbled to the door and out into the corridor. "Miss Killigrew! Miss Killigrew!"

It was like a tidal wave let loose. Parry was swept out in Paul's wake, as Anabel drove the others in front of her, ramming them through the door with her bosom. Robert Lord, Lilly, Ethel, and Marion appeared from the kitchen, staring, frightened.

"Miss Killigrew?" Paul's shouts echoed and reechoed in the hall.

"Miss Killigrew!"

They were all shouting now. Anabel surged up the stairs; the crowd split up, and, like a pack of terriers after a lot of rats, the rest of them darted in and out of rooms, up and down stairs, infected by Paul's panic.

"Miss Killigrew? Miss Killigrew?"

The wind beat on the plate-glass doors. The radiators in the hall bubbled, making a gobbling noise. Parry craned his head back. A small, pale face looked down at him from the landing above, looking at him with probing eyes. Christie had given up the hunt. Parry somehow knew she knew that it was useless.

Miss Killigrew's name came from every corner of the house, upstairs and down.

"Miss Killigrew!"

"Miss Killigrew?"

"Miss Killigrew!"

All at once, as if by some prearranged signal, the shouting stopped. The sudden silence was almost as unpleasant as the noise.

CHAPTER 13

THERE was a large but uncomfortable settee halfway along the first-floor corridor, flanked at each end by potted palms which nearly hid it and threw distorted shadows on the brocade-covered cushions. The combination of the palms, the steamy heat, and the patches of light and shade gave any one who chose to take his ease on the settee an illusion that he was sweltering in some primeval forest. Anabel had artfully arranged the settee and the palms with an eye to courting couples. She considered it the duty of members of the opposite sex to court, for the purpose of leading up to either marriage or a romantic affair, especially a romantic affair. She ignored the fact that plenty of affairs were not in the least romantic, for romance, to her way of thinking, covered a multitude of sins. So long as everything that went on under her roof was whitewashed with romance, then it was quite proper. At all costs, Beechlands must preserve its reputation for respectability. Fortunately she didn't go out very much, except when she went to town, so she was blissfully unaware that the reputation of Beechlands stank for miles around. So, whether they wanted to or not, she encouraged unattached couples, even if they were only unattached for the weekend, to court. It was good for business. Couples in the process of courting spent far more money than married couples or even engaged couples.

Christie perched herself on the settee, lit a cigarette, and amused herself for a short while by contemplating Anabel's extraordinary philosophy. It was odd that anyone who could be so businesslike and really capable could, at the same time, live in a world of complete self-delusion. If Anabel said things were so, then they were so, even if they were not. If Anabel decided somebody had said or done something, then he had said or done it, even if he hadn't.

The silence that had descended so suddenly on the house was just as suddenly chipped by a renewal of noises. Marigold and Anabel came down the corridor and went into Anabel's sitting room without noticing Christie at all. Anabel looked awful, drawn and scared and defiant at the same time.

Marigold kept looking behind her, her green eyes wide and furtive. Somebody—it sounded like Cintra—was trying to pacify Paul. It was difficult to tell from their voices whether they were upstairs or down. In a hysterical gaggle, Lilly, Ethel, and Marion fled past on their way to the safety of the kitchen. Feet walked along the corridor overhead.

If fear were a visible thing, Christie was sure she would see it walking up and down the stairs, poking into corners, looking in at doors, trailing its musty garments along the corridors. She waited patiently for whatever was going to happen next. She knew Miss Killigrew was dead and that the rest of them were sure she was dead. Only they were afraid to admit it. Parry had looked so unsurprised when Miss Killigrew had been shouted for, hadn't answered, and couldn't be found. So she was dead, and, presumably, locked up in the dining room with Lawty. What an ill-assorted pair to keep each other company, except that Miss Killigrew had possessed a sense of humor, so if her spirit were anywhere about, it would be amused at the dismay of Lawty's spirit, which most certainly would resent its handsome male body's sharing the same room with such an unattractive female body.

The ash fell off the tip of Christie's cigarette onto her skirt, and she automatically brushed it off. Who, in the whole house, besides Jim and herself, would seem to Parry to have a reason for killing Lawty? Nearly everyone, to her, had some sort of reason, however nebulous, however farfetched. Did Parry think the same? She hoped so.

Someone was coming up the stairs. She stared at the floor, in case it was Jim.

It wasn't.

"Can I share your palm grove for a minute?"

Christie smiled up at Parry and shifted to make room for him.

"Are you enjoying your busman's holiday?" she asked. "Of course you aren't."

"The responsibility," Parry said, "of being snowed up in a house along with a murderer and a murderee, without a hope in hell of being able to hand over the mess to the local authorities before morning, is rather over the odds. To try to keep tabs on everyone in a place of this size is a damn sight too much over the odds. As soon as you're all nicely bottled up together in one room, you escape. God alone knows where everyone's got to now, except that you're here."

"At least that's something," Christie pointed out. "At any rate, you know that at this particular moment I'm behaving quite innocently. What've you done with Miss Killigrew?"

The abruptness of her question would have put him out of his stride, except that he'd been expecting it. As it should now be obvious to the meanest intelligence that Miss Killigrew would scarcely have gone out for a nice walk all by herself in the middle of a snowstorm, it must be quite obvious that something had happened to her. He credited Christie with plenty of intelligence, even though it took rather a curious form.

"As you seem to know so much," he said, "then you ought to know where Miss Killigrew is."

"I don't actually know anything," she answered. "I'm only putting two and two together and trying to make the sum work out right. Lawty's locked in the dining room, and as that's the only room that is locked, I suppose Miss Killigrew's in there as well."

"Why mightn't she be sitting in there reading a book, or knitting?"

"If she is, then I'm really surprised. Miss Killigrew wouldn't calmly sit there reading or knitting, or even just thinking and taking no notice, while Anabel was shouting her head off for her."

"Why not?"

"Because she was devoted to Anabel. She spent all her time trying to keep worry away from her. If she thought Anabel wanted her, she'd have shouted through the keyhole and told her everything was all right."

"I see." Parry did see. Christie's argument was nothing if not logical. He wished she were beyond suspicion, as she would have made a valuable ally. But he was damned if he was going to embark on an alliance with someone who not only had a motive for murder, but was, for all her smallness, quite strong enough to have pitched an unconscious Lawty out of his window. He knocked his pipe out on the edge of one of the brass pots in which reposed the nearest palm. The door of Anabel's sitting room opened, and she and Marigold went slowly down the stairs. Unfortunately, as their backs were toward him, he was unable to see their faces. An assortment of noises, muffled by the thick carpets and unnecessary hangings, filled the corners of the house. The dismally crying wind had died down to an occasional mournful whine.

"I suppose," Christie said, breaking in on his cogitations, "the idea, or rather, your idea, of not saying a word about what's happened to Miss Killigrew is to keep everyone on such tenterhooks that whoever killed her and Lawty'll get in such a state of nerves he'll give himself away."

"Don't you think it's a good idea?" Parry smiled.

"Very. Except that if I'd done it, I've rumbled your game. Only I didn't murder them. I don't know who did," she added firmly.

You're afraid Jim did, Parry said to himself, because he's got such a strong motive. And you're afraid I may think he did.

"By the way," he said slowly, "as you're so observant, you may've spotted something I haven't spotted. I admit it's a bit awkward for you if you have, because some, if not all, of these people're friends of yours. But it's been proved time and time again that the more someone tries to divert suspicion from a guilty person, the more certain the police are to nab their man."

"I'm sure you're much too clever to be deceived like that," Christie said with a simplicity that didn't deceive Parry at all, and which he was sure wasn't meant to deceive him.

"And I'm sure you're much, much too honest and sincere to wish to deceive me," he smirked.

"What can you expect from a braown maouse but a weezy, weezy squeak? Whoever killed Lawty killed Miss Killigrew because he was afraid she knew or had guessed who'd done it."

"You do know all the answers, don't you?" Parry refilled his pipe and stared at it absently. "Though I suppose that's the obvious answer. That's to say if Miss Killigrew has been killed and not just gone for a walk in the snow." He looked at Christie out of the corners of his eyes. "Who or what was she staring at up in Lawty's room?" he shot at her.

"I've been wondering," she said calmly. "Did you notice that too? Of course you did. I honestly don't know. We'd all somehow got wedged together by the dressing table, hadn't we? All but you and Miss Killigrew— Julian, Paul, Marigold, Jim, Cintra, Anabel, me, the seven of us, seven of us all in a row. Her eyes suddenly blinked, stared very hard at something or someone, then shifted a little and stared and stared at something or someone else. I don't know who or what. She had such small eyes, and they were so colorless that one couldn't tell exactly the direction they were staring in. I mean, her upper and lower lids were so tight round her eyes that you couldn't see the white, except at very close quarters, so it wasn't like a huge pair of eyes with the pupils rolling about in the whites. But she was staring, all right. She spotted something."

"What then, my dear Holmes?"

"I told you, I don't know what at, or why."

Parry didn't know either. If he knew at whom or what Miss Killigrew had stared, the murderer would have been securely locked, barred, and bolted into the boiler room long ago. The hall clock struck one. At least five hours more before the first tradesman would call, if any tradesmen was going to brave the snow and call at all. The next complication would be that everyone would start clamoring to go to bed. He hadn't the slightest intention of letting anyone go to bed if he could possibly help it. The more wearied they were, the more likely someone would be to get careless and drop his guard. Besides, why the devil should they go comfortably to bed, even if not to sleep, when he had to prowl about all night, being stifled by the heat?

He sucked at his pipe, realized he hadn't lit it, and that anyway the stem was clogged. Still sucking, he tried to place where they all were in the house. Christie was here beside him, as quiet as the braown maouse she was supposed to so closely resemble. Anabel and Marigold were down-stairs, probably in the bar. Lilly, Ethel, and Marion he had caught sight of fleeing for the kitchen, and he thought he had heard the voice of Robère as they'd opened the door. That left Gaston—or whatever he liked to call himself—Jim, Cintra, Julian Frake, and Paul Livingston. Parry frowned. Like a fool, after he'd seen Christie peering down at him from the first-floor landing, he'd gone into Miss Killigrew's office again for another search for the safe key. He hadn't been in there for more than a minute or two, but during that minute or two anything might have happened.

"Where're the others?" he asked Christie. "Jim, Frake, Livingston, Cintra, and Gaston?"

"I don't know," she said. "I heard them, but I don't know whether they were upstairs or downstairs. Everyone was tearing about, yelling, and then all at once they seemed to vanish." Christie dropped the butt of her cigarette in a palm pot. "Not that it's very remarkable for anyone to vanish in a house conveniently provided with a secret staircase. Except, of course," she added, "that Anabel's always made such a deathly secret of it that it isn't a secret any longer. It's now most unromantically become the back stairs."

Parry gazed at her with admiration. Most people, making such a pronouncement to a police inspector shut up in a house with a murderer, would have delivered this tidbit with an air of either studied and unnatural calm or smug satisfaction. Instead, Christie was half smiling in reminiscent amusement. His admiration changed to exasperation.

"I suppose you wouldn't know why nobody told me there was a ruddy secret staircase in this corpse-ridden place? Where is the damn thing, anyway?"

For the first time, Parry heard her laugh outright, and the sudden blithe sound seemed almost improperly normal in the abnormal atmosphere of Anabel's rococo mansion. She did not, however, answer his question very directly, though her explanation was just as clear to him as if she'd done so, and far more entertaining.

"The house really is old, though you mightn't think it." She looked at him challengingly, as if she expected him not to believe her. "At least, some of it is, so I expect the secret staircase happened by mistake, when bits were added on and pulled down about a hundred years ago, and two walls didn't meet and so they filled the gap up with steps. Or maybe it's even a real secret staircase, part of the old original house. Of course, I never saw it as it was when Anabel took over, but anyhow she couldn't resist having it all done up too, with lights stuck in sort of iron sconces, and a lot of chains and manacles and hooks and old-world thumb screws on the walls."

"Good God," Parry stared, "what for?"

"I think Anabel got rather confused between secret stairs and dungeons. The stairs were terribly secret, and only shown to the chosen few, who were suitably impressed and rather terrified, as Anabel always showed it to them by candlelight, and I must say the effect of the chains and whatnots was pretty dreary. Naturally, the chosen few told everyone else, which wouldn't have mattered except that about two years ago Anabel decided to let some very chosen people indeed into the secret, and when she opened the secret door downstairs and held the candle aloft it all fell rather flat. You see, all the lights were up, and the cook she had then was sitting on the steps in his white apron having a whale of a time with one of the kitchen-maids, half a chicken, and a bottle of beer, and a dog belonging to one of the guests was sitting with them eating the chicken bones." Christie folded her hands neatly in her lap. "I must say, Anabel does have bad luck. Even the secret staircase comes unstuck on her. Still, it's more useful as it is, because a house this size with no back stairs is rather awkward."

To Parry, Christie's story, without any particular beginning and no end, explained fairly satisfactorily why no one had told him a second staircase existed. The secret staircase was now the back stairs; everyone else knew about them, so he ought to as well, and if he didn't, he was a fool. Perhaps he was a fool.

"That was a lovely story," he said, and meant it, wondering what Anabel's reactions would be if she ever discovered how well Christie knew her. "Were you there when the cook and the kitchenmaid were discovered illicitly feasting and flirting?"

"I was in the background. My role was to shudder when the secret was displayed. If you want to know where the doors are, the top one is along the corridor, to the right. You can't have missed that striking reproduction of Venus rising from the waves, surely? There's a perfectly ordinary door-knob on the right of the frame, and the whole thing opens like an ordinary door. The light switch's just inside. The bottom door is that long, gilt mirror opposite the bar near the kitchen. There's a knob on the frame exactly like the one up here, and the light switch is in the same place."

Parry levered himself to his feet and decided he must be getting old. He felt all cramped up.

"Oh, and," Christie said, "if you're going to explore, do be careful. The secret staircase's the dumping place for all the shoes that have to be cleaned, and empty bottles and so on."

"So long as I don't plunge into an oubliette," Parry smiled down at her, "I'll be fairly safe, I hope. I'll leave both doors open and all the lights on. You couldn't lend me a hairpin, could you?"

"I thought your pipe was stuffed up." Christie felt in her bun, pulled out a hairpin as long as a bent skewer, and handed it to him politely. "It's a good thing everyone here's used to, as they say, keeping late hours."

Parry dug at his pipe, mercilessly shaping the hairpin to his own convenience.

"Asking all your questions by delivering them in the form of statements or information seems to be your strong suit, doesn't it? And, correct me if I'm wrong, of course, you do enjoy talking for talking's sake, don't you?"

"So would you, if you never talked."

"You aren't dumb, so what's to stop you from talking?" What the hell, Parry wondered, was her particular trouble?

"To say more than three consecutive words on end at Beechlands, you need a voice like a trombone or a screech like a corn crake, a cast-iron skin of self-assurance or conceit, or—"

"Money talks? D'you enjoy doing all the listening?"

"Yes, thank you very much. I've been listening for twenty-nine years, if you count my infancy when all I could say was goo-goo."

"Ingrowing toenails," Parry said disapprovingly. "Living your life inside you's not only unhealthy, but sometimes dangerous. Surely there must be plenty of people round here who're more or less human?"

"I work for my living," Christie smiled. "I take in other people's typing, so I haven't time to go out much. When I do, I come here."

Parry finally cleared the stem of his pipe, and without thinking what he was doing, threw her hairpin into one of the palm pots. The mystery—if it could be graced by such an important name—of the silent little braown maouse who could be so exceedingly chatty given an appreciative audience was a mystery no longer. The resentful Jim Bridges would probably walk ten miles round rather than come within hailing distance of wherever she lived. The braown maouse, he guessed, would rather perish before she stuck her nose unasked inside the doors of Sloes Farm. So, when she had time, she came to Beechlands, because he came there too, and she might meet him. And, when she did, she scarcely spoke to him, and he openly resented her. Was such restraint admirable, or insane? Why Jim? He was irritatingly full of the things called inhibitions, and even before he'd been boiled in burning oil and patched up, he could never have been a beauty, like Lawty.

"That fond maternal instinct, I take it?" he suggested, incautiously saying his thoughts out loud.

"I think," said Christie agreeably, "that women who talk about fond maternal instincts for men are either being hypocrites or damned insulting. Mind the steps, won't you?"

"Sure," Parry thanked her, thinking that two bodies were bad enough, but a girl who was dying of love for a man who didn't love her was the end of all things. He headed for the striking reproduction of Venus rising from the waves, then stopped and looked round. "By the way, you and Miss Whatnot, or Mrs. Whatever-she-is, Cintra, seem to get on very well, don't you?" Christie's clear eyes inspected him gravely through the palm leaves.

"That's because everyone—at least, the sort of people who meet her here—thinks she's either shooting a line, tight, hysterical, good for any amount of cadged drinks, free seats for film shows, or that it's nice to be able to buck about knowing her."

"I see. Except you." Parry strolled on to the waiting Venus. He longed to ask why Cintra's mouth was always open, but an almost feminine instinct warned him that if he did the answer might be a black eye. As he passed the bottom of the stairs that led to the top floor, he noticed that the lights on the landing above, which he'd switched on when he'd been looking for Miss Killigrew, were out. It only then occurred to him that while he was talking to Christie, entrenched behind Anabel's forest of dusty palms, anyone could have slipped unseen up the unsecret staircase, and, if he moved cautiously enough, on up to the top floor. He stood still and listened, then turned quickly. The noise he had heard was only Christie going into one of the bathrooms. Evidently she shared Jim's passion for washing her hands. Over his head a board creaked twice. There was a crash of breaking crockery. The first-floor corridor lights went out, the hall lights went out, and he was left in pitch darkness.

A voice too terrified to be recognizable wailed in anguish, something that sounded like a mad elephant plunged down the black, unseen stairs, and Parry was overwhelmed by an avalanche of arms and legs, a strong smell of bad whisky. As his head met the floor with a dull thud, his last coherent thought for quite half a minute was that thank God, this body, at any rate, was a live one.

CHAPTER 14

WHETHER the body was clinging round his neck with intent to strangle him or had attached itself for protection, Parry had no idea.

"Let go, damn you," he said, and took a sock at the place he hoped its jaw would be. An unhappy grunt informed him, much to his satisfaction, that his aim had been true. "Who the hell are you? Get off, and put the lights up. What're you playing at? Hide-and-seek in the dark?"

"God almighty," gasped the body, "I never thought the time'd ever come when I'd be glad to see your face around, Parry."

"You can't see it. Get off my stomach before I sock you again, and put the lights on. Otherwise, my dear Albert—"

"Sssht—Gaston," Gaston's voice whispered frantically. "There's some-one after me. I daren't put the lights on. Listen, d'you hear them?"

"Hear what?" Parry asked irritably. "How d'you expect me to hear anything when you're plastered all over me like a door mat? Pst-psting into my ear as if you were a steam engine?"

"What's happened? For God's sake, what's happened?" Dimly, shak-ing with fear, Paul's voice piped from the hall, and then the lights both upstairs and down went on again.

Parry scrambled to his feet, dragging Gaston up with him. His always pasty face was a dreadful shade of gray, and he was quite obviously and genuinely terrified out of his wits. At the far end of the corridor Christie looked out of the bathroom door, a towel in her hands.

"Anything wrong?" she called.

"Nothing at all," Parry answered, "except this lunatic fell down the stairs on top of me."

Christie vanished back into the bathroom, and rubbing the back of his head, Parry leaned over the landing banisters and inspected the inmates of the hall. They were all there: Paul clinging to Marigold, his eyes goggling; Ana-bel, screwing one of her many chiffon handkerchiefs into a ball, looking a hundred years old; Julian, a pair of horn-rimmed spectacles pushed up on his forehead, jabbing a fountain pen at the air as if he were defending himself with it; Lilly, Ethel, Marion, and the chef huddled together in a bunch; Cintra, her mouth even wider open than ever, holding Jim by the elbow.

"N-not another?" Paul whimpered.

Anabel took a deep breath. "Another what? Pull yourself together, Paul. We heard such a crash, Lane—"

So at last it had come to Lane. Soon it would be Lane dear, then Lane darling.

"Only Gaston falling downstairs," he said reassuringly. "He must've fallen against the light switches and put the lights out. Nothing to worry about."

"Oh, yeah?" Gaston muttered through chattering teeth, and Parry kicked him in the shin.

Marigold detached herself from Paul and attached herself to Julian. Anabel, Cintra, and Jim reluctantly headed back to the bar. Lilly, Ethel, Marion, and the chef straggled back to the kitchen, Lilly giving tongue.

"Coming to help me finish my letter?" Julian said to Marigold, and she nodded. They disappeared from sight, and Parry heard the door of the lounge close.

Paul gazed up at Parry in agony. "What about me? You aren't going to leave me all alone? For God's sake, I can't take any more of it! Parry, old boy, you aren't going to leave me here alone to be murdered, for God's sake? I'm all to bits. You know how it is when you've had a shock?" He swayed perilously, clutching for support at nothing. He'd had, Parry decided, not one over the eight, but a good dozen over the eight.

"You can go into the bar," Parry suggested. "Or help Frake and Miss Trent write letters. Or, of course, you could lock yourself up safely in one of the many usual offices and stay there."

"Vulgar," Gaston remarked.

"I didn't start it. Come along, there's a convenient linen room, or whatever it's called, at the far end of the corridor, where I trust we shan't be disturbed."

"You and me both," Gaston agreed with feeling.

There was a key in the lock of the linen room. Parry took it out, pushed Gaston in among the shelves of sheets, towels, and pillow cases, and locked the door from the inside.

"Now then, Albert, what the hell's all this about?"

"Gaston—"

"Very well, just to please you, Gaston. Now, begin at the beginning, if there's anything to begin about. And while you're at it, don't embroider your story with any of your fancy patterns."

Gaston straightened his tie, which was under one ear.

"It was when everyone was looking for Miss Killigrew. And what's happened to her? Not that I like her."

"She's in the dining room, quite safe."

"With Lawty? My God. So she is dead, is she?"

"Go on, and make it brief and to the point, if you can."

"Well, it was like I said. Everyone, and that includes me, was looking for Miss Killigrew, and somehow I found myself on the top floor, alone, so I thought I'd have another look round in the rooms there for her."

"Hoping for a bit of loot? Never mind, go on."

"I was in one of the rooms at the end of the passage, the end farthest away from Lawty's room. The light there's pretty feeble. Anyhow, it was a room no one was using, so I was just going to clear out, and then I heard a noise, just outside the door. First I thought it was the wind, but it wasn't. I don't know anyone who's got hearing like me, I don't suppose anyone but me'd have heard it." Gaston's face, which had slowly resumed its normal pallor, began to turn gray again, and he licked his lips. "I stood quite still and listened. There was someone outside the door, only I couldn't see him, as he must've been pressed against the wall. Jees, Parry, he was waiting for me to come out."

"What did you suppose'd happen when you did come out?"

"Lord alone knows. A cosh on the head, a bullet through my ticker— easy, with a silencer. He didn't move, he waited." Gaston's voice shook, and he dropped it to a hoarse whisper. "These walls've got ears. If I'd known who it was—but I didn't. Might've been a man or a woman, or a bloody ghost. I don't know. Anyway, how he kept so still! Listen, Parry, it was godawful. You know my record, I've never gone in for scrapping or violence, and I hadn't even a pencil on me to crack back at anyone with. Talk about one's flesh crawling—mine crawled like it was covered with lice. I don't know how long it was, it seemed hours, and then I couldn't stick it any more, only I didn't know what to do. The idea came into my head if I could make out someone was in there with me I'd be O.K., but if there'd been someone with me, he'd have talked—we'd have talked. Hell, you've heard the bunch here, yap, yap, yap all the time and no one can get a word in. Then I suddenly thought of the only one that didn't talk. I guess she's a lady, and doesn't speak unless she's spoken to, and then she only says a couple of words. Mark my words, Christie's the best of the bunch that ever came into this dump."

"I'm marking your words," Parry said pleasantly, "and I suggest you might call her Miss Layne."

Gaston looked at him with withering contempt. "What d'you think I am? A common waiter? And anyhow, it shows how much you know about what goes on in the kitchen. Think me and the cook calls them all Mrs. and Miss and Mr.? That's the worst of you policemen who've been to Oxford and Cambridge—oh, all right, Oxford or Cambridge, if you want to be choosy. However, I thought of Christie, so I said in a loud voice, 'Have you done looking at the snowflakes, M'selle Christie?' Then I made a noise like she sometimes makes, kind of mmm, if you know what I mean? Then I said, 'Do you wish for a light, M'selle?' and clicked my lighter on and off, as if I was lighting her cigarette. Then I remembered that sometimes I'd heard her whistle a bit of a song, when there wasn't anyone around, always the same one, as if every time she thought of some particular thing it brought the tune into her head."

Parry raised his eyebrows. He'd never given Albert Cummings credit for such imagination. "So you whistled it?"

"That's right, just like she does. The beginning part; it goes, *'Du bist mein ganzen Herz, und wo du bist, muss ich auch sein.'* Didn't know I could speak *Deutsch* as well as *Français,* did you? It worked all right. There was a kind of scuttling noise, and I knew he'd gone."

"And d'you mean to tell me, you miserable worm, you never took a look to see who it was? You just let him get away without even having one sight of him?"

"That's what I damn well do mean," Gaston said, bursting into a cold sweat. "You don't know how bloody awful it was, up there all alone with the wind making a row like spooks."

"And why," Parry asked, "should anyone be after you?"

Gaston turned grayer than ever and avoided the question by going on with his story as quickly as possible. "How should I know? There's a murderer about, isn't there? O.K. I waited till there was plenty time for him to've hooked it downstairs, and then I went down too and streaked for the bar. Didn't see a soul on the way. They were all in there, barring Christie, that little runt Paul, Jim Bridges, and Frake. Old Frake was having strips torn off him in the kitchen, by the sounds of it."

"Who by, and why?"

"Sounded like he was trying to make Chef understand they wanted some more sandwiches in the bar, only Lilly and Ethel were bawling him out. I'm sure I don't know what the lower classes're coming to nowadays," Gaston sneered. "You should've heard those bloody girls yawping they weren't going to wash up no more plates, and who did he think he was anyway, giving orders in the kitchen, and they were going to give notice, and he could go back in the bar and stuff their notice up— What's that?"

"Mice," Parry said. "Which way did you come down from the top floor? Or rather, from the first floor?"

"Back stairs. Listen, Parry, there's someone outside the door."

Gaston shook like an aspen, his teeth making rattling noises. Parry turned the key softly in the lock and threw the door open. There was no one there, only Christie sitting quietly on the settee along the corridor. All Parry could see of her were her legs in their white knitted stockings. The rest of her was hidden by the palm grove. Who or what, if anything, was she waiting for? he wondered. So *"Du bist mein ganzen Herz"* was her theme song, was it? Presumably Jim was her whole heart, and where he was she must also be. He shut the door and relocked it.

"Pull yourself together and get on with your rambling tale, and for the Lord's sake be a bit briefer."

Gaston looked hurt, or as nearly hurt as it was possible for anyone to look who had eyes like a boiled cod.

"I got behind the bar again, and then Paul came in, and Jim, and then Frake. The old woman was trying to look as if she hadn't got the willies, and I'm telling you the happy party spirit was a flop. The old girl told me to open another magnum, to cheer things up, I suppose."

"Just a minute," Parry interrupted. "Was everything in the bar just as it'd been when you were last in there? Nothing missing that was usually there?"

Gaston's eyes narrowed, and his top lip curled back over his teeth like a frightened animal.

"The ice hammer was gone again. It wasn't there when I went back in the bar. For God's sake, Parry, was that what did them in?"

"I'm asking you questions. Get on with it."

"I wanted a drink bad after what I'd been through, but none of the bastards offered me one. I said to the old girl I'd get some more ice, so I took the ice pail, dumped it outside on the steps, and legged it up the back stairs and then up to the top floor to my room. I didn't want no one to hear me, so I left the bottom door of the back stairs open as I didn't mean to be gone no more than five minutes or so. I had a bottle of whisky that I bought myself—you needn't give me a dirty look, Parry, I tell you, I bought it—in my room, and a tot of whisky was just what I needed. You know my room? It's at the far end of the top-floor passage, a ruddy kennel, that's where I sleep, like I was a dog."

Parry wasn't aware that dogs generally slept in attics, but he remembered the small, low room. He had nearly missed it when he had searched the house for Miss Killigrew, for it was under the roof, a short, narrow stair leading to it. Gaston drew his breath in, his nostrils contracting, and he clutched Parry by the arm.

"I was just having a short one, when I thought I heard something. I looked round, and took a dekko at the steps. Christ, Parry, someone had put the passage lights out, and I knew he was there again, trying to get me. He was down there, just round the corner at the bottom of the steps, waiting for me, only this time it was different."

"Different?"

Gaston's mouth twitched at the corners at the remembrance of what had been to him the ultimate horror.

"I could smell scent—perfume—drifting up strong out of the dark, and there wasn't a sound, just the smell of the scent." Gaston's voice clogged in his throat, and Parry didn't altogether blame him. The combination of the darkness below, the silence, the disembodied perfume drifting on the hot, heavy air, must have been nothing if not unnerving.

"I nearly went off my rocker. Listen, Parry, it wasn't no scent I know, and I'm good on perfumes. That tart Marigold uses stuff called 'La Lune et toi,' the old girl uses Molyneux 111, Cintra uses a scent that's specially made for her and smells of sandalwood, and Christie don't use no scent at all. And the scent I smelt wasn't any of them, it was more like the whole lot of them, Marigold's, the old girl's, and Cintra's, all mixed up together."

"What about those three girls? Lilly and Marion and the other one?" Parry asked.

"Them? The old girl won't let them use scent. Of course, they do when they go out with their boyfriends, but cheap stuff. You know the kind I mean? Eau de jockey Club, or Lily of the Valley, that doesn't smell like any lily or any valley ever invented. No, this stuff, whatever it was, smelt like the ten-guineas-a-drip line, and it was strong, it made me feel sick, and

I was feeling sick enough already—like a gas attack, you could damn nearly see it coming up the steps."

"Don't exaggerate," Parry said. Gaston was an expert liar, but he knew he was not lying now. His terrified story of the scent was so unlikely that it was most certainly true. The very nasty mess took on an air of added nastiness. "And you couldn't place the scent?"

"I told you—it was like the old girl's scent and Marigold's and Cintra's all mixed up."

"I suppose it's too much to ask you to call them Mrs. Adams, Miss Trent, and Miss Norton, or Mrs. Whatever-her-name-is? Elliot, isn't it? And while you're about it to tag either Inspector or Mr. onto my name?"

"I thought you wanted me to be brief?"

"It's a wish near to my heart. Get on with your adventures. You had a swill of whisky, saw the landing, or rather corridor, lights were out, and smelt the perfume. Well? What happened then?"

Gaston dragged at his limp collar as if it were strangling him.

"Nothing happened. Whoever it was simply waited. And he was waiting to do me in, he bloody well was. He nearly killed me with fright as it was. I didn't dare move, my knees were knocking together so much, I couldn't have, anyway," Gaston said frankly. "Only I knew I couldn't stick it much longer without going off my nob. And I could hear him breathing, very soft, but quick, like an animal, and the smell of the scent seemed to be getting stronger. I couldn't stick it no more. I picked up the big china jug and basin off the miserable thing that's supposed to be my washstand, and threw the whole lot down the steps and made a bolt for it. Whoever it was must've been scared by the row and legged it ahead of me, because it must've been him that put the rest of the lights out."

"Or he may've put the lights out, waited till you'd half murdered me, and while you were pounding about on my stomach slipped past and gone down either the back stairs or the main staircase. Blast you," Parry said with feeling, "if you'd kept the thing that goes for your head, I'd have got him. How do all these lights work?"

"This house's like a ruddy booby trap," Gaston complained, "what with the burglar alarms and one thing and another. There's a row of switches in the hall that turns the hall lights, the first-floor corridor lights, and the top-floor corridor lights on and off. Same arrangement on the first floor and the top floor. That's supposed to be convenient. Last to bed can put the lights out from whatever floor they're on. Or put them up, for that matter."

"I see." Parry inspected Gaston's gray and twitching face with interest. "And what is it that you've got that someone else wants so badly? It wouldn't by any chance be the contents of Wing Commander Lawrence's wallet, would it?"

"No, it wouldn't," Gaston snapped. "D'you think if I'd got Lawty's dough I'd still be here? I'd be miles away by now, burglar alarms, snow, and everything, and murders, too. His wallet's empty," he added incautiously.

"And when did you make that interesting discovery?" Parry smiled.

Gaston looked at him out of the corners of his eyes. "I went up to see if the radiator and the lights and so on were all right in his room this afternoon—well, yesterday afternoon. He'd left his wallet on the dressing table, open, and I could see there wasn't nothing in it but a few snaps."

"Very disappointing for you. And, as a matter of fact, he'd stowed it away in a pocket of his dispatch case. I'm going to search you, Albert."

"Gaston. And you won't find a thing."

Parry searched him with painstaking thoroughness. He even made him take off his shoes and socks. He was glad to notice that though Albert Cummings might have a heart and soul as black as ink, his feet were as clean as driven snow. Also his toenails were varnished a delicate shell pink.

"Very pretty," Parry remarked;,and Gaston writhed and gave a ticklish giggle that ill became him. All his pockets disgorged were a silver cigarette case, a very fancy lighter, two handkerchiefs, one clean, one dirty, some odd change, a crumpled pound note, a key with a tag on it that announced it should unlock the cigarette cabinet, a nail file, and a pocket comb.

"What'd I tell you?" Gaston demanded.

"The real question is, what could you tell me if you would? What d'you know or what've you got that's so interesting to someone else? I'm going to escort you back to the bar, for the reason that there's safety in numbers, where you'll kindly keep your eyes and ears open. And listen, if by any chance you should discover where Wing Commander Lawrence's wealth is, you'll tell me. I'm telling you this for the good of your own health. In life you're a mess, but in death you'd be a worse mess. Very much worse. How much money did Lawrence have on him?"

"Plenty," Gaston muttered with a mixture of wistfulness and satisfaction. "I heard him tell the old girl—oh, O.K., Mrs. Adams—he'd cashed a check in town that morning for five hundred. If it was all in his wallet, it must've been in fifties."

"Oh?" Parry unlocked the door. "We'll go down the back stairs, and I'll wait at the bottom while you bring me out a large whisky. Then you'll go back in the bar, and I'll go up and search your room."

Gaston's eyes flickered. "While you're about it, you might bring down the silver pepper pots and saltcellars I took up there to clean. I wouldn't like to think of anyone lifting Mrs. Adams' silver. Maybe that's what whoever it is was after."

"Liar," Parry said agreeably. "Also thief. You'll be lucky if tonight isn't the prelude to another little holiday in one of your homes away from home."

With Gaston slinking nervously beside him, he made for the striking reproduction of Venus. Christie was still occupying the settee in solitary state, nothing of her visible but her legs. Any amount of traffic, Parry decided, so long as it was silent, could have gone backward and forward between the ground floor via the unsecret staircase and the top floor while he was talking to her, without his being any the wiser.

He turned the knob in Venus's frame, found the light switch, and gazed in awe at Anabel's conception of what a secret staircase ought to look like. Christie's description had been remarkably apt. Anabel had certainly got a little confused between secret staircases and dungeons.

CHAPTER 15

IT had stopped snowing, but the trees still thrashed uneasily in the gusts of the north wind. Occasionally one of the upstairs windows rattled as if someone were shaking it.

Refreshed by a double whisky, Parry started up the back stairs, then changed his mind and came down again. Gaston's room could wait for a few more minutes. Whoever had lurked up there had been interested in Gaston himself, not his room. Damn him, Parry thought; if he'd had a gun on him he'd have stuck it in dear Gaston's ribs and kept it there till he confessed what he knew, or what he had, that someone else wanted so badly. The criminal mentality was utterly illogical. The man was terrified out of his wits, but rather than share his tender secret he'd risk his life to keep it to himself. Damn his eyes, Parry repeated to himself.

Frowning, Parry strolled along to the hall. There was only one person in the house who couldn't have waited at the bottom of the steps leading to Gaston's attic, and that was Christie. Unless she had supernatural powers, and could be in two places at once: sitting on the settee under the dusty palms, talking her head off, and waiting in the darkness above, smothered in a mixture of perfumes. Did this solid alibi let her out of the mess? He tried mentally to locate the inmates, where they were and what doing at that moment. By rights, Robère, Ethel, Marion, and Lilly were in the kitchen; Anabel, Cintra, Paul, Jim, and Gaston in the bar; Julian Frake and Marigold in the writing room, not, Parry was sure, writing letters. Christie might be anywhere.

To imagine he could discover the murderer, or, possibly, murderers, single-handed, before morning, was, he finally decided, sheer conceit. The best he could do was to snoop, pick up such crumbs of information as might be useful to the local police, and wander wearily and ceaselessly round and round the house in the hope of preventing further violence. He caught the sneering eye of "The Laughing Cavalier" and thought that next time he went on a holiday he would stuff his pockets with a fingerprint outfit, a magnifying glass, a portable wireless receiving and transmitting set, a pair of knuckle dusters, his Colt .45, and a bunch of lock picks suitable for opening safes.

The radiator under the stairs gurgled at him in derision, and he realized he was sweating. When Gaston had made up the furnace, he must have recklessly flung on half a ton of coke. The heat was getting more and more unbearable. He felt drugged.

"My God, what a bloody awful dump this is!" he said out loud, and pushed open the door of the lounge. It was empty, but the door leading into the writing room was half open, and he heard Marigold's honey voice saying, "Really, Julian, my sweet, I can't believe it. How absurd, darling— What's that? Julian, what's that?"

"Me," Parry said, and trying to look pleasant, invaded Marigold's and Julian's privacy.

Evidently Anabel thought there was something queer about people who actually wanted to, and did, write letters. Anyone who wasted time with pen, ink, and paper could not, in her estimation, be worth bothering very much about. The walls of the writing room were papered a plain, dark brown, the carpet was plain brown, and, except for the frame surrounding the large and rather lugubrious lady who unsuccessfully tried to hide her nakedness with a wisp of chiffon above the fireplace, there was no gilt, no crimson, and no pomp. The remains of a log fire glowed in the grate. The only light came from the standard lamp on the writing table, where Marigold perched gracefully, her silver-sandaled feet cocked up on the edge of Julian's chair.

But for the suddenly guarded flicker in Marigold's green eyes, the faint but sticky smell of the perfume she used, which Gaston said was called *"La Lune et toi,"* and the brief, sudden silence, watchful and questioning, that had greeted Parry's unexpected entry, the scene would have been welcomingly normal.

"I thought you'd deserted us," Marigold said, letting her breath out and slowly lifting her head, so that her hair trickled back behind her shoulders.

"You didn't think anything of the sort," Julian said good-naturedly, and twisted round on his chair so that his back was toward the writing table and Marigold. "She's very highly strung," he added, as if he were responsible for accounting for her emotions.

Parry realized he must have been almost going to sleep standing up and became very wide awake indeed. According to Anabel, Lawty and Marigold had taken one look at each other the day before, though it had been quite platonic, of course. Now, her beloved of a few hours dead and gone, she had returned to the attack of Julian. Parry felt sure the same thing had happened often before. There was a solidity about Julian that lovely strays like Marigold would always return to.

"May I sit down?" he asked.

Julian stared at him and began to laugh. "It's a hotel, open to nonresidents, fully licensed, with French cuisine. Facilities for ridin', 'untin', shootin', and fishin', dogs and children welcome."

"I'm afraid I'm not a dog or a child. I don't know if I even come under the heading of nonresidents. I'm simply an accidental interloper, and I don't suppose I'm at all welcome."

"Of course you are, sweetie." Marigold pointed a silver sandal at a fat armchair, and Parry sat, disliking her more than ever.

Julian clasped his hands over the back of his chair. On the desk behind him lay the scattered sheets of the letter he had been writing, the ink still fresh and pale. By the looks of it, he must have been busily scratching away for a considerable time. Did that, Parry wondered, absolve him from the guilt of lurking for Gaston upstairs? He couldn't possibly have written so many pages between the time Gaston had plunged down in the darkness and the very few minutes that had elapsed before the lights had been turned up again, and he'd appeared in the hall with the rest of them. Parry was sure that with lovely Marigold for company sitting on his desk, he hadn't wasted his time over a letter.

"Come and have a drink, Parry," Julian invited. "You must be all in. I should think you're wishing you'd never set eyes on this place, though I'm exceedingly glad you did. It was an extraordinary coincidence, your walking in here right into the middle of a—"

"Stop it, can't you?" Marigold bit her teeth together. There was a sudden common twang in her voice, harsh and disagreeable. "I've had enough. For God's sake, let's go and have a drink."

"I'm sorry, my sweet." Julian turned and looked up at her, and Parry thought, he's crazy about her. Well, he was the age when men went crazy about lovely, expensive tarts young enough to be their daughters. How old was he? Fifty-six? Marigold would be getting on for thirty, to judge by the care she took over her makeup.

"I don't think I'll have a drink just now, thanks, Frake," he said. "I'll sit here for a bit and take the weight off my feet. You two go along. It might be as well if you all kept together," he added.

Marigold slid off the desk. "What d'you mean? Keep together? Why?"

"Come with your uncle Julian, Marigold." Julian pulled his mouth down and made a warning face at Parry, who ignored it.

"Safety in numbers, Miss Trent."

Rather to Parry's surprise, she didn't burst into a fit of hysterics.

"How delicious," she smiled, her mouth curving. "D'you think Julian and I're going to set about murdering each other if we're left alone? For God's sake, come on, Julian darling, I'm parched." She slid her hand through his arm, and Parry saw her long fingers were moving restlessly, trembling, but whether with some inward excitement or fear, he didn't know.

Julian led her to the door into the lounge, let her go through ahead of him, gently shook off her hand, and came quickly back.

"Just a moment, child," he said to her over his shoulder. "I've forgotten my letter—by mistake, on purpose," he muttered grimly at Parry, collecting the sheets, folding them up, and putting them in his pocket. "I've been wanting to see you alone for a minute. Parry, this is a nightmare. What in God's name's happened to Miss Killigrew? The others seem to be too frightened to even comment on the way she's vanished. It's—it's—" he spluttered, at a loss for the right word, and ended up lamely, "it's preposterous."

"Does she often disappear like this?" Parry asked.

Julian looked at him as if he were quite mad. "Miss Killigrew? Disappear? Like a conjuring trick?"

"I thought perhaps she was given to going for midnight walks. Some people are. It makes them sleep, or so they think."

"Miss Killigrew go for midnight walks?" Julian repeated incredulously. "I don't suppose she's ever been for a midnight walk in her life, even in her heyday, if she ever had one. Besides, it's long after midnight, and who in their senses'd go out for a walk in all this snow? There must be feet of it."

"There's the possibility," Parry suggested, "that she might've taken it into her head, as the phone's broken down, to wade off into the night and get help—there's a policeman at Ditching, or Ditchit, or whatever the place's called."

"Without telling anyone?" Julian looked even more incredulous, more worried. "I admit she's a gutty little woman, but she'd never worry Anabel by going off without a word. Besides, how could she? Anabel said everything's locked up, and the burglar alarms are set. If she'd opened the front door, the place'd have been a bedlam of clanging bells."

"Julian! What the hell're you doing?" Marigold's voice from the lounge was a mixture of impatience and suddenly rising panic.

"Just coming, my sweet. Wait for me, and I'll be right with you. Well, Parry?"

"She might've switched off the burglar alarms, then quietly gone out, thinking no one'd notice she wasn't there. As you remarked, a gutty little woman."

"We can soon find out."

Before Parry could stop him, he pulled aside one of the long, brown velvet curtains that hung inert and heavy over the nearest window, reached up, slipped back the catch, and started to push up the sash.

"God, what's that?" Marigold stumbled into the room, reaching out to Julian, as if her arm could expand like a telescope and grab him, cling onto his safety.

"The bloody window's stuck, damn it," he swore, while the clamor of bells seemed to get louder and louder, filling the whole house. "Parry—"

"Julian! Julian!"

"Parry—"

Smothering a strong desire to laugh and just sit there and let the racket go on forever, Parry went to the rescue. The window descended with a crash. There was a hardly noticeable silence, followed by a renewal of noise in the hall, Paul leading the chorus.

"Oh, God," Julian groaned, "give us strength."

Then Marigold enveloped him like a shining silver cloud, and he half carried, half dragged her away, the sweat standing out under his eyes, which looked, all at once, sagging with an elderly yearning to go to bed, like any human, with a hot water bottle and a book to send him to sleep. As he kicked the door shut behind him, he glanced over his shoulder at Parry, and faintly, above the tumult, Parry was just able to hear his parting remark:

"I'm afraid I'm not as young as I was."

"None of us are, are we?" Parry said to the violently slammed door. "Once I was wheeled round in a perambulator."

There was a small round mirror at one side of the fireplace. He carefully detached the sheet of blotting paper from the blotter Julian had been writing on, and held it up, squinting at the reflection. It showed nothing but a blur; letter after letter, written in different hands at different times, superimposed out of all recognition on the original virginal surface. He folded it up and put it in his emptiest pocket.

Muffled by the shut door, there came the sounds of Julian trying to pacify the mob receding into the distance, presumably the bar. To judge by the incoherence of Paul's gabblings, he was very drunk indeed. Parry did not envy Julian his job. Something, a creeper or a shrub, scratched at one of the windows, a faint, insistent tapping. With a hiss and a thud, a small avalanche of snow slithered off the overladen roof. The wind died down suddenly, so that it seemed unnaturally quiet in the shadowy brown room.

Parry lit a cigarette and watched the blue spiral of smoke rise to the ceiling and disintegrate. Gaston's attic was the next item on the program. Then he must find the ice hammer and the key to the safe. For in the safe, he was sure with a quick flash of conviction, was Lawty's wealth, locked up by Miss Killigrew. Someone besides himself wanted to find the key.

And if anyone had already found it, he might join Lawty and Miss Killigrew in the dining room, unless he was responsible for the two inmates of the temporary mortuary.

Hoo-bloody-rah, he said to his reflection in the mirror. His chin was darkening with nearly twenty hours' growth of black stubble. He wished he had his razor with him, and his toothbrush would not have been amiss. He threw his cigarette in the grate and reluctantly dragged himself away from the temporary haven of the writing room.

CHAPTER 16

"I WANT to talk to you."

Parry suppressed a string of curses. He might have known that he wasn't going to escape so easily. For a moment he wondered if he could pretend he'd gone stone deaf and blind and had neither heard nor seen Cintra sprawling inelegantly in the largest armchair in the lounge, her long, thin legs stretched out in front of her, her gingery, streaked hair in even worse disorder.

"If I don't talk to someone sane, I'll go mad. I think I'm going mad as it is."

If her widely gaping mouth were a sign of insanity, then she had gone mad already, Parry thought, and said, "Oh?" as politely as he could. She flung herself to her feet, jabbing her hands in her pockets, hunching her shoulders, her eyes staring. Then she sat down on one of the radiators, and shot off it again.

"The thing's red-hot," she snarled, and gave a gasp of laughter, "Har-har-har."

"Har-har-har," Parry echoed. "Personally, I always thought it was spelt 'Ha-ha.' However, have it your own way, do. I'll be back again in a few minutes if you want to talk to me." He would like hell.

"No, you won't. You're planning to escape right now and hide till I'm sick of waiting for you. Don't try to fool me, it's a waste of time." She lurched up to him, drawing her upper lip back in a terrifying expression. "Now then, we all know where Lawty is, poor old boy. But where's Miss Killigrew? Where's the ice hammer Lawty was killed with? Where's the key to the safe? If you've got it, I want it. I want to lock my jewelry up. If I lose any more of my stuff, my insurance company won't pay up. A murderer wouldn't be above helping himself to my diamonds. Anabel hasn't got it, she said Miss Killigrew had it. Very well, Miss Killigrew's dead too, isn't she? Isn't she? Go on, tell me. She's dead too, I know she is, poor little devil. And the ice hammer? Also the garden scissors. They're gone too. I wanted to cut my hair and the garden scissors've gone. You might tell me what's going to disappear next, because if it's me, I'd like to write a farewell letter to Max and leave instructions for my funeral, unless my fate is to be cremated in the central heating thing—but then there'd still be my ashes, wouldn't there, Parry?"

"Bones," he said, "most probably."

Cintra's voice was a hoarse, jagged, almost animal noise. She was, heaven knew, no beauty. But suddenly Parry realized that she would be a magnificent actress, that from the screen she would somehow fling her violent personality, alive and vital, at the heads of the audience as if she were there herself, among them. For the violence of her emotions was perfectly natural, born in her. Poor Max, he decided, had married an explosive sort of wife.

"Well?" she said, and hurled a very crumpled cigarette at him.

"I haven't the faintest idea what's going to disappear next," he said with perfect truth. "Unless you open your mouth a bit wider and swallow yourself."

"Oh, my God!" Cintra exclaimed, and put her hands, which were now very dirty, over her mouth. "I've got a sore throat," she groaned through her fingers. "It's my adenoids. No, not adenoids, they're so terrible. Tonsils." A gleam of inspiration came into her eyes. To Parry's relief, she seemed to have forgotten all about Miss Killigrew, the ice hammer, the garden scissors, and the key to the safe. "Tonsils," she repeated speculatively. "It'd cost a lot of money to have my tonsils out, wouldn't it? It's very serious for a grown person to have her tonsils out, isn't it? I don't suppose even Max would be allowed to see me for a few days afterward, would he? What'd it cost? At least five hundred pounds with the surgeon and the nursing home, wouldn't it?"

"Good Lord, no," Parry said, completely dazed. "About one hundred at the very outside."

"Is that all?" Cintra nearly wept. "With complications, it'd surely be a great deal more? I'd have to have at least five hundred, I'd be bound to have complications—I always do. I'd have to reckon on at least five hundred, wouldn't I?"

"How the hell would I know?" Parry tried to shake her off as she gripped his arm with her golden talons. They dug into his flesh, even through the tweed of his jacket. "I'm not a surgeon. Ask a surgeon."

"Listen! There's someone outside the door." She held onto his arm like a vise, whispering croakily. "There's someone there. Listen, Parry—"

"If you'll let go my arm, I'll look," he said impatiently. Patience would be wasted on Cintra, he knew. She didn't expect people to be patient if they weren't, or good-tempered if they were in a rage. "Take your claws out of what you've left of my arm, blast you, Cintra."

She let go of his arm, and quickly, as quietly as he could, he crossed the room and opened the door wide. It was already open a crack. There was no one there. But a pair of gray-flanneled legs was rapidly vanishing up the staircase to the floor above. So Jim had been eavesdropping, had he? What an outfit!

"There isn't anyone there. Come along to the bar and stay there. I'll convoy you."

"I don't want to roast in the bar. Marigold makes me vomit—Julian's a fool."

"I don't care a damn if Marigold makes you vomit, or if Julian's a fool." Parry took Cintra's bony elbow and marched her off. Their progress was a little unsteady, as she kept staggering like a ship in a rough sea.

"Come and have a drink," she invited. "I like you. What's your wife like?"

Parry dragged her down the steps leading to the bar. "How d'you know I'm married?" he asked, levering the bar door half open with his foot.

"Doctors and policemen always are," Cintra said. "They do it on purpose, so that none of their female clients can lead them astray—much. Is yours the usual sort? Plain and homely?"

"She's exceedingly beautiful," Parry said, and almost throwing her into the bar, shut the door behind her.

The mirror-cum-door at the bottom of the back stairs was open, as he had left it. Before anyone else could waylay him, he nipped through and closed it. The stone walls of Anabel's secret pride were painted a dull red, a sinister red like blood, against which the black chains, the black wrought-iron sconces that held the lights, the peculiar old-world oddments meant to represent instruments of torture, looked very black indeed. The general effect, Parry thought, though exceedingly funny, was rather unpleasant.

He half shut his eyes, trying to digest Cintra's ramblings. She had neither adenoids (they were so terrible—terribly unromantic for a film star, presumably) nor tonsils. The tonsils had been an inspiration. Then why was her mouth forever open? To induce some inflammation of the throat or nose, or both, that would necessitate a visit to a nursing home, the attentions of a surgeon, and an operation? If that were so, there was only one obvious conclusion to come to. She had been unfaithful to her husband, had been careless, and was now faced with an illegal operation, for which someone was going to rook her £500, which, as she was probably wildly extravagant, she hadn't got. Cintra would never, he was somehow sure, ask her husband for money to get rid of the evidence of some wild and thoughtless episode, and no woman would relish confessing her forthcomings.

Parry sighed. So Cintra was short of £500, and Lawty, according to Gaston, who ought to know, had arrived with £500 on him. And she wanted the key to the safe. The mess was getting even more of a mess. In idle curiosity, he inspected an enormous black chain, each link nearly six inches long and as thick as a man's thumb. He took hold of the bottom link, instinctively bracing his wrist to bear the weight, and hit himself a violent blow on the nose. It was made of some sort of papier-mâché or plastic and was as light as a feather.

"Damn it and blast it," he swore loudly, and, nearly helpless with irritated amusement, mounted the stairs. The globular Venus still hung open in her frame. At first Parry thought the corridor was empty. Then he saw Christie's straight white legs. She seemed to have permanently taken possession of the settee under the potted palms. She was not, however, alone. Between her and the top of the stairs, Jim stood in an attitude that proclaimed indecision, resentment, distaste, and guilt. He was too far away for Parry to see the expression on his face, but he was sure it was expressionless. Bolting from discovery, he had run headlong into Christie's deliberate or undeliberate ambush, and now he didn't know what to do about it. Neither of them was saying anything. Christie's silence seemed taunting, as if she hoped to goad him into doing something violent.

Hoping they wouldn't hear him, Parry crept on up to the top floor. The deserted corridor had an abandoned look about it, like a woman waiting in vain for a husband or lover who would never come back. Lawty, at any rate, would not return to his favorite room. Parry wondered if Anabel would lock up No. 20 and keep it empty, a sort of shrine to his memory. Or allow the select few to view it as if it were a showplace. He stood still and sniffed. If he hadn't already known where the steps were that led to Gaston's attic, the smell would have guided him. It was overpowering, heavy and sickly. In case some joker put the lights out, he switched on his torch. Its light was feeble, but better than nothing if he were suddenly left in darkness. At the bottom of the steps the jagged pieces of broken washstand crockery were very white against the spilled water that had seeped, a black pool, into the carpet. The remains of the broken jug and basin were not the only objects of interest, however. A large, thick pad of cotton wool lay by the wall, exuding a mixture of fumes that made his head reel. By it, an oil-silk sponge bag, of the kind that is fastened by a zipper, gave forth waves of the same fumes; two pairs of eyebrow tweezers completed the collection.

Parry knelt down, sniffing and staring. No wonder Gaston, the connoisseur of perfumes, had said it wasn't any scent he knew. It wasn't any one particular smell in any case. It was a combination of chloroform fighting for supremacy against a mixture of expensive perfumes; a combination of hospital operating theaters, Anabel, Cintra, lovely Marigold, and a dash of somebody or something else thrown in, Parry supposed, to taste. The net result was quite disgusting. It was sickening, sinister, and certainly calculated to put the fear of God into stouter souls than Gaston's, alone in an attic, with darkness below. Puzzled, sickened by the smell, he crawled backward on his knees and sat down. There had been no smells the first time Gaston was alone in the room at the end of the corridor, while the hunt for Miss Killigrew had been going on and the unknown had waited outside the door. It didn't make sense. Perhaps he'd then been armed with the ice hammer, which Gaston had said was missing from the bar when he'd nerved himself to go down.

Go on, you damn fool, think, Parry goaded himself. He'd handled the ice hammer when he'd been in the bar before the hue and cry for Miss Killigrew broke out. O.K.—work from there. In the general rush for the door, the unknown X might have whipped the ice hammer, stowed it about his or her person, either with a preconceived intention of doing Gaston grievous bodily harm, or because he never knew when it might come in handy. Disturbed in his first attempt on Gaston by the latter's ruse of pretending Christie was in the room with him, he'd fled downstairs to await another opportunity. Then why not, if he'd been armed with the ice hammer the first time, rely on it as a weapon the second time? Either he'd decided it was too damning an article to carry round, and, if he had had it on him, got rid of it, or he'd not had it on him at all, and when he'd first lurked, waiting for Gaston to come out of the empty room, his sole weapon of offense had been his hands. If, on thinking it over, he'd decided hands weren't good enough, he'd been quite right. Though Gaston drooped like a willow, his toenails a delicate pink, he was exceedingly strong and wiry, and, if not valorous or belligerently inclined, would fight like hell in protection of his own precious person.

So where do we go from here? Parry wondered. Maybe X, deciding against the ice hammer, or unable to get hold of it, had had a flash of inspiration, and knowing that somewhere in the house there was chloroform, had devised the scheme of anesthetizing Gaston should the opportunity arise. And it had arisen. His jaded nerves badly in need of a recuperative pick-me-up, Gaston had obligingly done the right thing and ascended to his dog kennel.

Wait a minute, Parry pulled himself up. How would anyone know where he'd really gone? He had left the bar ostensibly to get ice from the kitchen, not to go upstairs. But that was easy—he hadn't come back with the ice. He'd dumped the ice pail on the steps that led to the bar and left the mirror door at the bottom of the unsecret staircase open. Any moderately intelligent person observing these signs and portents might safely assume that Gaston had gone aloft, and, with fell intent, follow. But surely the ice ham-

mer would have been a simpler instrument of offense than the paraphernalia of sponge bags, tweezers, and cotton wool? Sorely puzzled, Parry
decided to drop the ice hammer altogether, to assume that when X had
lurked the first time, he hadn't got it, and for his second attempt, was unable to find it.

With this simplification, the curious puzzle took on a less complicated
form. Dear X, though his or her (damn it, Parry decided, make it his and be
done with it) blunders had been many, though he'd taken risks innumer-
able, must have both a good working brain and imagination. With murder
on his mind, what more natural than to think out other ways of murdering
or disabling one or more of his fellow inmates, if it so pleased him? A good
many hours had passed since Lawty lay in the snow with the blood running
out of his mouth, and any amount of thinking could have been done in that
time. So X, who either possessed chloroform or knew where to find it, and
knew very well that all the women must have bottles of perfume in their
rooms and such things as eyebrow tweezers, and that most people kept
their sponges in sponge bags, had conceived his plan of anesthetizing Gaston, most likely during the half hour or so that had elapsed between the first
and second attempt to do him a mischief. The half hour, Parry thought
wryly, that he'd wasted poking about in Miss Killigrew's office, then set-
tling down in the shade of the palm grove to talk to and be talked at by
Christie while, fifty feet away, Lawty's and Miss Killigrew's murderer must
have crept from room to room making his preparations. Then, with equal
silence and coolness, crept up the stairs to the top floor, put the corridor
lights out, unzipped the sponge bag with the tweezers, lifted out the satu-
rated cotton wool, and stood in the darkness at the bottom of Gaston's
steps—waiting.

Only instead of the quarry descending the steps, the bedroom crockery,
spewing water, had hurtled down into the darkness. Damn Gaston's feeble
nerve, Parry cursed. If he'd had the guts to walk into the trap, the murderer
in their midst would now be discovered. For yet again he'd made one of his
childish mistakes, as idiotic as the shoe prints on Lawty's window sill. Like
the average child, he knew that chloroform in large doses would make anyone unconscious, but apparently it hadn't occurred to him, or he didn't
know, that the pad of cotton wool would have had to be firmly held over
Gaston's face before he passed out, his ears singing, into a black world
unpopulated even by ever curious policemen. One of the tweezers was still
sticking in the corner of the pad. Evidently X's idea had been to hold the
pad by each corner, outstretched, so that Gaston would walk into it, take
one deep breath, and fall down flat. Instead of which, if Gaston had gone
bravely to his doom, he'd have had one smack in the face from the cotton
wool, fought for dear life, yelling blue murder for help. As it was, he'd

simply scared his would-be assailant, and in the ensuing darkness and confusion he'd got clean away.

Still inwardly swearing, Parry got up off his knees. Blunders and risks or no blunders and risks, somebody, male or female after their kind, had killed two people, and so far there wasn't a clue to his identity, and he had nothing to work on but assumptions and surmises, all of which might be, and probably were, quite wrong. As for useful things like fingerprints, the whole house would be smeared with them from top to bottom; the best he could do would be not to add too many of his own to add to the mess. He pulled on his gloves and, avoiding the broken crockery, climbed up to Gaston's attic. The whisky bottle and a tooth tumbler were on the chest of drawers. Gaston was very tidy. His flasks of hair lotion, mouthwash, and lavender water stood in a neat row along with his manicure outfit, his shaving tackle, and a tin of talcum powder. Very sweet and girlish, Parry thought with amusement. Gaston's clothes were just as neatly arranged.

With practiced thoroughness and speed he went through the room; not even a pin in the crack between two floor boards missed him. He found Anabel's best silver salt cellars and pepper and mustard pots stowed away inside the ticking of the hard, kapok-filled mattress, wrapped in tissue paper, with Gaston's usual care. He put the silver back where he'd found it, resisted a strong desire to have a gulp of Gaston's—or Anabel's—whisky, negotiated the steep steps and the jagged bits of china, and collected the anesthetizing outfit, using the tweezers to handle the cotton wool and sponge bag. As he juggled with the tweezers, he thought he heard voices on the floor below, indistinct and far away. The snow wind had got up again, cold, lonely, shrilly whispering. Against the glass of the uncovered window at the end of the corridor flakes of snow settled like swarms of white moths, fluttered a little, and melted on the warm glass.

Holding the sponge bag away from him, he went softly along the corridor and unlocked Lawty's room. It was colder than ever in there. The snow had blown in the open window and lay in a small drift on the royal-blue carpet. The towel he'd put over the shoe prints was still in place; there were nearly three inches of snow covering it, and the two ashtrays looked like cakes iced with white frosting. He dropped the sponge bag and the tweezers in the dirty-clothes basket. His gloves smelled faintly of chloroform, Anabel, Cintra, and Marigold; he took them off and threw them in the basket as well.

Now, he supposed, he'd have to try to solve the problem of how anyone could have sneaked about practically under his and Christie's noses, helping himself to sponge bags, chloroform—and where'd he got the chloroform from, anyhow?—and all the rest of it, then got upstairs, unseen, unheard, with all his paraphernalia. He stared at the dressing table, and the unpleasant idea occurred to him that perhaps Christie'd talked and talked to distract his attention from what was going on, unless the chloroform preparations had been made before then, which was unlikely, as no sponge bag could keep that smell in for long, wherever it was hidden.

Lawty's pigskin gloves lay on a chair. Parry tried them on. If there was anything he wanted to handle that might possibly not have been pawed by everyone else in the house, it was as well to be prepared. The gloves fitted perfectly.

"Thanks, Lawty," he said to the empty room.

CHAPTER 16

CHRISTIE was still on the settee, her legs straight out in front of her, visible only from the knees down. Apparently Jim had some aversion to sharing her seat. He stood a couple of yards away from her, his hands jammed in his pockets, staring at one of the palms as if he were anchored there, an unwilling, resentful prisoner.

Parry was too busy to listen to their conversation, if any. He reached the back stairs, went halfway down them, and, looking at his watch, started up again. Paul's room was directly on the right of the Venus, Cintra's directly on the left.

Marigold lived opposite Cintra. Julian Frake's room was at the far end of the corridor, past the palms, opposite Anabel's suite. The rest of the bedrooms on the first floor were empty. Parry chose Paul's room first, without any particular reason for doing so. Neither Christie nor Jim appeared to hear him. Christie's legs didn't move. Jim went on staring at the palms.

Paul's tastes were as expensive as Lawty's, but far more showy. He went in for a lot of bottles, clothes brushes, talcum powder. A black and yellow silk dressing gown was thrown on the bed, along with a pair of green pajamas. Parry looked at the color scheme and shuddered. The broad glass shelf above the washbasin was interesting and explained how Gaston's bogy had somehow helped himself to Anabel's brand of perfume without going into Anabel's room, when he or she, would have had to pass the settee. For either Paul scented himself with Molyneux 111 or he had brought a bottle down for Anabel as a present. Half empty, a flask labeled "Molyneux 111" reposed on the shelf among bottles holding lavender water, hair lotion, and mouthwash, its new wrappings torn off and carelessly thrown among Paul's sponges and face flannels on the side of the basin. There was no sign anywhere of a sponge bag. Paul, surely, wouldn't allow sponges and face flannels to be packed in his suitcase (somehow Parry felt sure he kept some minion to pack for him), damp and dripping among his clothes? Very well, the sponge bag and the Molyneux 111 had very likely come from Paul's room.

Only two minutes had gone, Parry saw, since he had started from half-way up the back stairs. He looked out in the corridor, then tiptoed to Cintra's door. Christie and Jim gave no sign that they noticed or heard him creeping about. Cintra's bedroom was in chaos. When he'd been in there before he'd been looking for Miss Killigrew and hadn't paid much attention to small details. How in hell, he wondered, would Anabel get the bits of squashed and trampled lipstick out of the carpet? How in hell did Cintra manage to find anything she wanted? Her discarded dinner frock, odd stockings, shoes, sandals, scarves, littered the floor and the bed. The dressing table was a wilderness of upset powder, brushes, combs, hairpins, face creams, and bottles. She appeared to have no jewelry with her at all. The table next the washbasin was cluttered with more bottles; hair-setting lotion, some mess that looked like hair dye, her sandalwood perfume in an oddly shaped flask— Parry stared, and saw what he'd missed before, and someone else hadn't missed when the search for Miss Killigrew was going on: a half-pint medicine bottle with a small chemist's label on it. "Chloroform. Not to be taken internally." And the bottle was empty.

What on earth did she want chloroform for? To put it to the use of anesthetizing either herself or someone else? And lying on the floor by the table was a large package of cotton wool, half unrolled. Another two minutes had gone. He imagined the motions of tearing off a wad of the wool, uncorking the bottle of chloroform, emptying it on the wool, adding some of Cintra's perfume, then—then what? Carrying the smelling, sopping wool into Paul's room? That wouldn't do. First the sponge bag would have been taken, some of the Molyneux poured into it. After that the performance would be continued in Cintra's room. Unless there had been in reality no Molyneux mixed up with the rest of the hell brew, and the sponge bag wasn't Paul's. Cintra, at any rate, had no sponges, only a vigorous-looking luffa with which, no doubt, she savagely attacked her skinny body. The luffa was far too long to go into the oil-silk bag upstairs in Lawty's clothes basket.

Parry suddenly felt so tired he wished he could lie down on Cintra's rumpled bed and go to sleep. Why didn't he leave all this till he could hand it over to the local authorities in the morning? Professional pride, I suppose, he told himself. I'm so clever I think I can clear up two murders and a possible attempt at a third all on my own, like Sherlock Holmes minus Watson.

He let himself out and crossed the corridor to Marigold's temporary home-away-from-home. Christie had raised her voice a little, saying a few words at a time, then waiting for an answer that did not appear to be forthcoming.

Marigold's bedroom was as immaculate as herself, and as highly scented. Everything was exquisite and in perfect order. Her chiffon nightdress, so thin it was almost invisible, lay on the bed. Her sponges, large, fat, luxuriously soft, like Persian cats, were carefully laid on top of a platinum-colored plastic case, in which, Parry supposed, they traveled. Plain oil silk with a zip fastener wouldn't have been good enough for lovely Marigold. Two bottles of her perfume, *"La Lune et toi,"* stood on her dressing table. The largest of the bottles was practically empty.

What about the pincers? One pair might have been Marigold's, one Cintra's, or even, Parry smiled to himself, Paul's. Paul was very fancy, even if he did sweat, make noises when he drank, and was now drunk. Parry looked at his watch and thought it must have stopped. He felt as if he had been poking about for half an hour, but exactly eight minutes had passed since he'd started on his prowlings. He hadn't hurried and his watch hadn't stopped. Whoever had prowled before him through the three rooms could have done the whole job in less than four minutes, if he'd already known where to lay his hands on the necessary items.

He frowned, running his hands through his hair. After all, his investigations hadn't got him much further, except that he'd proved how easily and quickly Gaston's anesthetic must have been to prepare, unseen, unheard. And that was all. He took another look round Marigold's pretty-pretties, and deciding it was time to interrupt Christie's and Jim's tête-à-tête, he went quietly along the corridor and shamelessly listened.

"What the hell're you trying to goad me into doing?" Jim asked, in answer to what goading Parry didn't know.

"Am I goading?" Christie's voice was polite. "I didn't know I was. I was only asking for what particular reason, or reasons, you dislike me most. If I knew, then I could do something about it."

She needed smacking, Parry decided, his sympathies for the moment with Jim. She was damn well trying to goad him into losing his temper to such an extent she'd get a smacking, that attention, Parry supposed, being better than none. Only she didn't seem that type of little hussy; she wasn't a blatant man-chaser, like Marigold. A dim idea of the truth dawned on him—that in some roundabout way she was trying to rid Jim of his tiresome complexes and inhibitions by driving him into such a rage he'd forget about them, for once.

"Do something about what?" Jim was getting incoherent. "I don't give a damn about what or what not you don't or do do about anything. In any case, I don't know you well enough to dislike you."

"That's why you do dislike me. You do know me well enough to resent me. You dislike knowing more about me than anyone else, except, perhaps, Parry."

"Parry?"

"You were listening up on the stairs when Parry was asking me questions outside Anabel's room yesterday evening."

"You *knew* I was listening?"

"Trying not to listen might be a better way of putting it."

Inadvertently, Parry let out a laugh. Jim turned, staring at him, the scars on his face throbbing, and Christie at last moved. She stood up, smiling her small, neat smile round the palms.

"Someone else listening," she said pleasantly.

"How d'you know I wasn't trying not to listen?" Parry asked.

"You can't even think in private in this bloody place," Jim said by way of answer. And Parry thought, that's what he resents so terribly in the girl. He knows she knows the inside of his mind as well as she knows his face. She's invaded his privacy.

"You were listening outside the door of the lounge when I was talking to Cintra Norton, or Mrs. Elliot, whichever she is. You seem to do quite a bit of listening, don't you? In between, of course, washing your hands," Parry pointed out.

Jim flushed, and Christie's eyes widened, a look of dreadful apprehension in them that went as quickly as it came.

"I wanted to see you," Jim said. "Only not with Cintra there. She'd have thrown one of her fits of second sight, and we've had about enough of them for one night. I wanted to tell you that when we all went to look for Miss Killigrew I took this off the bar and pocketed it. Cintra's second sight about it might have put ideas into someone's head. Here, Parry."

Jim pulled his hand out of his pocket, and the gilt ice hammer flashed under the lights.

"Jim—don't!" Christie leaped at him like a small tiger, dragging at his arm, trying to pull the hammer away from him, her head pressed into his chest like a ramrod. The hammer flew out of his hand, landed conveniently at Parry's feet, and he picked it up, watching the one-sided struggle with amusement and curiosity. Christie didn't seem to have noticed she had succeeded in making Jim open his hand, and still fought for possession of the hammer that was not there, while he stood perfectly still, doing no more than trying to push her away from him. Far from having lost his temper, he was perfectly calm and collected. It was Christie who had lost control of herself, her face scarlet, her maddening composure gone.

"Stop it," Jim said; and as she didn't seem to hear him, put his face down to her ear and repeated, "Stop it!" very loudly.

She jerked her head up, hitting the top of it on his chin, breathless and disheveled.

"You fool," she panted. "You fool—why didn't you give it to me?"

"Give what to you? What d'you mean?" Jim stared down at her. "What the hell—"

Her hairpins had fallen out. Parry thought she looked very nice. Her hair was soft and thick, and came only as far as her shoulders. She looked more than nice, he finally decided. If his heart weren't permanently occupied elsewhere, he might have thought of offering it to her in the approved manner.

"D'you think I killed him?" Jim said.

"I—" Christie suddenly remembered Parry, and said, "No, of course not."

"Yes, you did—or do," Parry said. "Did you kill him, Jim?"

"No, I didn't."

"Of course he didn't. You're slipping, Parry." Christie was unruffled again, though she didn't seem aware that her bun had come undone.

"Can you account for everything you've done since this charming night began yesterday?" Parry asked Jim. "Where you were and what doing every minute since you arrived here?"

"I'm not one of those geniuses in books who remember what they had for breakfast exactly a year ago. I couldn't possibly tell you where I've been and what I've been doing every minute for the past dreary eight hours or so, or however long it is. Could I? Where were you at nine in the morning this day last year?"

Parry took out his notebook and flipped the pages over. "At my dentist in Wimpole Street, groaning with agony. You wouldn't like to examine the filling he put in, would you? If I were Lilly, Marion, or Ethel, I'd probably add, so there, yah-boo. Surely Cintra's goings-on about the ice hammer didn't impress you so much you thought it was dangerous to leave it lying about?"

"Yes. I told you, I thought it might put ideas in someone's head, if it hadn't put them there already. So I took it before anything else happened."

Parry raised his eyebrows. "I don't remember I mentioned anything about the ice hammer having been used to kill anyone with."

"I saw you looking at some mark, or something, behind Lawty's ear." Jim glanced quickly at Christie, and then down at the floor.

Good Lord, Parry thought, now he thinks she may have done it, and she thinks he did.

"It's as good a way as any to knock someone unconscious, or even kill him," Jim went on. "And the ice hammer would come in handy to give anyone a tap behind the ear with—obviously, while he was changing for dinner, and then sling him out the window. Anyone tall enough and strong enough could have lifted him up."

"But not someone small like Christie, you mean?" Parry suggested. "It'd make things clearer, perhaps, if you both realize that even my mean intelligence can gather you suspect each other of having had a hand in tonight's performance."

"Why?" Christie looked straight at him.

"Jim knows, now, you had a reason to get your own back on Lawty. There's another reason, too, why you might've wanted to do him harm."

"Oh?" She was all polite interest, though her face had turned very white.

"You must've resented his messing up Jim's life in the way he did."

"I'm the one to've resented that." Jim dug his hands farther down in his pockets. "You've got slightly mixed."

"I'm not in the least mixed," Parry said agreeably, "so figure that one out. D'you know where Miss Killigrew is?"

"I told him," Christie said quickly.

Parry sighed, trying to repress a yawn. "You can now both go down to the bar and stay there along with the inmates."

"I'm glad you didn't say other inmates," she smiled.

"Oh, and by the way," Parry added, "you'll be glad to hear that Gaston thinks you're a lady because you never talk, though you occasionally whistle."

Jim started down the stairs, then stopped and looked over his shoulder. "Come along." He snapped his fingers at her.

"Bow-wow," she murmured, and followed him.

Parry leaned wearily on the top of the banisters and watched them. Jim's back gave the impression that it was prickling with some peculiar emotion. Christie walked lightly, as if she were contented and suddenly happy. Evidently that was the first time Jim had ever called her to come along and snapped his fingers at her as if she were a dog. It didn't take much to please some women, Parry mused.

He sat down on the top step and listened. Presently he heard, very faintly, the sound of a door being opened and then shut—presumably the bar door. The dim mumble of voices from that part of the house was like a swarm of bees buzzing in the distance, muffled by the cloggy heat. The hall radiators still bubbled and hissed. The air felt stale, used up. He thought of the bitter cold, the clean whiteness, and the emptiness outside the house with longing.

The hall clock struck half past three. Another three hours to go before there was a hope in hell of any outsiders turning up. Parry tapped the pane of the hammer on the back of his hand, and wondered if anyone had ever thought of committing suicide by giving himself a crack behind the ear.

CHAPTER 18

ANABEL'S little parties often went on till three and four in the morning, and when they broke up, everyone was still quite fresh and energetic, though the freshness and energy were generally the result of the tonic properties of the Beechlands liquor. It was Anabel's parties that had driven away the more permanent and solid kind of guests, who stayed not for a night or a weekend but for weeks, even months, and paid their bills regularly every week. No one who came down to the country for a rest enjoyed being kept awake till morning, so one by one they departed, never to return again. Not that there was anything wrong with Anabel's parties. Nobody got too drunk, hiccupped, tore his clothes off, or danced on tables, and, as a rule, the jubilations took place only on weekends.

Julian absently stroked Marigold's arm as she dropped half on his knee, half on the chair beside him, and decided that when he had the principal say at Beechlands, things would have to be changed. First the terrible decorations, then a new bar would have to be built onto the end of the house, well away from such guests as wished to sleep at night. He liked parties, but only if they didn't interfere with business. He liked parties very much indeed, even though he was fifty-six. And they amused Marigold, who shone like a bright light in company. But he wasn't enjoying this party at all. Shut up in the smoke-filled, overheated bar, they were like a lot of prisoners waiting for their execution at dawn or mourners at some funeral feast. He slid his hand down Marigold's arm and ran his fingers over her bracelet. It was, he thought, very pretty, and approved his choice of design. She should have another one exactly like it to wear on the other wrist. He glanced up, and catching Christie's eye, smiled at her. She and Jim had come so quietly into the room that he hadn't realized they'd joined the party again.

Not having seen Anabel for the best part of two hours, Christie was horrified at the wreck she presented, though, as wrecks went, she was a very imposing one, still valiantly clinging to her dignity like an exhausted swimmer trying not to go down for the third time. The heat had made the last remains of her complexion run, so that her face was dappled chalk-white and a mauvish red. Christie reached up and turned on the switch of the electric fan over the bar. It whirred to life and began to churn the cigarette smoke about in sluggishly agitated clouds.

"Oh, God," Anabel suddenly croaked, "the night is long."

"What you mean is, darling," Cintra corrected her loudly, "the night is dark and I am far from home, lead Thou me on."

"I don't mean anything of the sort." Anabel flapped at her face with her powder puff, now very bedraggled. She had been sitting in horrible discomfort on the same bar stool, without moving off it, for what seemed like years. She didn't dare move, in case, if she stood up, her legs gave way under her. Besides, perched on high, she felt she was still in a position of command over the others. She was in the peculiar stage of having drunk so much she'd drunk herself sober, except that her sobriety was of the nightmare kind that wasn't quite real. "I said," she repeated, "the night is long, and that is what I mean."

"No, you didn't, darling." Cintra stared up from the floor, where she was crouched over the building of a card house. "You said, 'Oh, God, the night is long.' "

"You said it, anyway," Gaston muttered, poking at the top of the bar with a cloth. His panic had left him for the time being, and he was anxious to escape from the safety of numbers. Only there was Parry to be reckoned with. Parry was nosing round the house, minding other people's business for them.

"What d'you say, Gaston?" Anabel demanded. "Any of your nonsense and out you go."

"I said, you said it."

"Said what?"

"Anabel, why don't you sit in a comfortable chair?" Jim suggested. He wanted to help Cintra build her absurd card house, but he was afraid, if he did, Christie might decide to help too.

"Come along, Anabel, have this chair." Julian gently dislodged Marigold and stood up, wondering if the creaking of his cramped knees was as audible to everyone else as it was to him. "Do get off that awful stool and be comfortable."

"Comfortable?" Anabel pressed her hands to her bosom and closed her eyes. "Comfortable? How can I be comfortable when—after—with Lawty—"

Julian patted her arm soothingly. "My dear, these things do happen sometimes, I suppose, and people do get over them."

Anabel opened her eyes and tried to visualize his money, the security it would bring her, the freedom from worry, but all she could see through a mist that swam in front of her was Julian himself. "You and I, Julian," she muttered, "you and I can—could—" Could what? She tried to think what she wanted to say, a few dignified words of reassurance. Could what? "What's that policeman up to now?" she asked instead. "Using my house like a police station, as if it belonged to him."

"Anabel, my sweet, not a police station, surely?" Marigold swept like a silver flame across the room. "Scotland Yard, don't you mean? Not a police station."

"Same bloody thing," Gaston hissed under his breath.

Cintra tore her tangled hair out of her eyes. Her hands were filthy, her golden talons chipped, as if she'd been down a coal mine. Out of her cavernous mouth came an inarticulate sound of rage, and she clenched her fists and shook them. "Beast! She did it on purpose, trampling all over my card house with her great hoofs!"

"Are you talking to Anabel, Christie, or me?" Marigold asked sweetly.

"You know perfectly well I'm talking to you."

"Did I spoil your little game? So sorry, sweetie. You'll never grow up, will you?"

"I'm adult," Cintra glared, "which is more than you are."

Marigold's eyes narrowed, hard, green slits in her magnolia face.

"Where's Paul?" Christie's voice sounded very cool and polite in the atmosphere of rising tempers, and Cintra suddenly burst into one of her roars of laughter.

"Behold!" she shouted, and crawled on her hands and knees into the only shadowed corner of the room behind the outsize radio. "Paul? Paul? He's had it," she said to Christie over her shoulder. "He couldn't stand up any longer. Paul? Come out of your kennel. Wake up, it's Christmas Day, and your stocking's full of presents.

"Paul, wake up!" Cintra persisted. Slowly Paul's head, his shoulders, and his potbelly rose into view from behind the radio. He had taken off his collar and tie, unbuttoned his waistcoat and the top button of his trousers. His sleep in the corner hadn't done him much good. He was still drunk, and he'd mislaid his aitches in his disordered nightmare.

"What's 'appened?" He tripped over Cintra, staggered into the middle of the room, a shaking finger tracing the weaving clouds of cigarette smoke. "What's it? Anabel, for God's sake, the 'ouse's on fire."

"The house is not on fire, Paul."

"If you can't see all the smoke, then you must be dead, damn, blind drunk, Anabel."

"Shut up, Paul," Jim said, hoping he wouldn't, and half winked at Christie. He felt his face turning red, his old scars throbbing. Now he'd voluntarily let her into his confidence by one twitch of his eyelid. She'd pry into his mind with added curiosity, just to try to find out if he was by nature a winker.

"I won't bloody well shut up," Paul said mulishly. "The 'ouse's on fire and I know why." His voice rose to a terrified howl. "Someone's set the 'ouse on fire because they want to burn up the corpses, and us with them— what's called suppressing the evidence."

Anabel put her hands over her ears, and her insecure world turned black and cold. No one had yet mentioned the word corpse, and in the darkness that engulfed her she saw pictures of blood, putrefaction, coffins.

"Anabel, hold up." Julian put his arm round her. "Can't someone gag that fool Paul?"

Parry, who'd been listening outside the door, opened it.

"Anything wrong?" he asked.

"Give me a hand with Anabel," Julian implored. "She's going to faint."

There was a jug of tepid water on the bar, as stale as the air. Parry poured out a tumblerful and held it to Anabel's sagging mouth. She moaned, sipped it, choking between each sip, and opened her eyes.

"What's the disgusting stuff?" she asked with a feeble attempt at dignity. "It's corked."

"It's water," Parry said, speaking very distinctly, in the hope she'd take in what he was saying. "Out of a tap, presumably. It's supposed to fur up the pipes, but I don't suppose that little drop'll harm you."

"I told you it was corked." Anabel turned her head, with some difficulty, toward Gaston. "How many more times'm I to tell you not to put fur in the water?"

"Oh, my God," Julian cried helplessly. "Why'd you give her water, Parry? It's gone to her head."

"Fatal." Cintra dug her nails into Parry's arm. "Water on top of liquor wakes the fumes up again, especially if you've been at the vodka. Max went to a vodka party last year, and next morning he was so thirsty he drank about a gallon of water and was tight for two days afterward."

"I didn't know Max drank." Marigold raised her fine eyebrows. "How frightful for you, sweetie!"

Cintra let go of Parry's arm, and her chipped talons reached out toward lovely Marigold. Parry waited hopefully for them to engage with the flawless face and tear slices out of it. But Cintra only waved her fingers, as if she were groping for the keys of an invisible piano.

"What a lovely bracelet that is, Marigold," she said calmly. "You ought to wear it more often."

Paul leaned perilously forward, his business instincts fighting against the fumes of everything he'd had to drink. "Cost a lot. How much? Five hundred pounds. I know diamonds when I see them." He pawed at Marigold's wrist, and with a click the bracelet came undone and hung suspended by the thin safety chain, swinging to and fro, glittering. "Six hundred," he amended. "I wouldn't give you six hundred for it, but that's what it cost. Did they rook you that much for it, Julian?"

"I'm never rooked." He bent and snapped the clasp together. "Much," he added, smiling.

Everyone seemed to have forgotten Anabel. Marigold ran the tip of her pink, catlike tongue over her lips. The whirring of the fan sounded very loud. Jim tried not to look at Christie, but he looked at her, and she wasn't looking at him. She was at it again, lapping up the atmosphere, feeding on it. Something's cooking up, Parry thought. Someone in the bar was abnormally tense and had infected the others.

"Can't someone say something?" Paul burst out. "Now what's 'appened?"

"Nothing has happened," Anabel said, trying to focus her eyes on some object that was stable and didn't swing from side to side or up and down.

"Nothing's 'appened?" Paul repeated hysterically. "Nothing's 'appened, when the 'ouse's full of corpses?"

Marigold shook Julian's arm. "Can't we get out of this damn bar?" she almost screamed. "Julian, take me away."

Anabel felt as if she were going to choke. She was sick, frightened. She wanted to cry, not dramatically, but like a child.

"It's safer in 'ere." Paul bumped against Parry. "I want to stay in the bar. Don't let them go away—I don't want no one sneaking up behind me in dark corners."

Marigold drew her breath in. "Then keep out of dark corners," she said in an ugly voice. "Unless you want to have a look round for your aitches."

Nobody laughed. Parry thought that on the whole there was nothing to laugh at. Marigold's dig at Paul was merely unkind.

"By the way," Parry said, trying to attract Anabel's wandering and horrified attention, "I quite forgot to tell you Miss Killigrew gave me the key to the safe."

Anabel drew up her sagging shoulders. "So tiresome if it got lost," she said without interest.

"Very," he agreed, wishing he knew where in hell the safe key was.

"What d'you mean?" Cintra rounded on him, her eyes staring like a mad dog's. "I told you I wanted the safe key an hour ago, so that I could lock my jewelry up. Why didn't you tell me you had it?"

"I hadn't got it then," he said pleasantly, and with perfect truth.

"But you said Miss Killigrew gave it you."

"Well?"

There was a strained, secretive silence. Gaston's Adam's apple jerked up and down as if he were swallowing pills very quickly, one after the other. The sweat ran down Paul's face, and Anabel swayed on her stool. Marigold's fingers moved restlessly on Julian's arm, but whether with fear or some strange excitement, Parry still couldn't decide. Julian's face sagged like an old man's. Only Christie and Jim seemed unmoved. Were their composed exteriors hiding some inward tumult? He hoped that whichever of the party had killed Miss Killigrew was feeling duly panic-stricken, wondering if it were really true she had still been alive an hour ago, and capable of speech.

Cintra was staring at him very oddly, her eyes boring into him. The ice hammer, tucked away inside his jacket, kept poking into his chest. He would have liked to put it back on the bar, in the hope one of them would take it again. But someone might help himself to it without his seeing him, and that was too dangerous. Marigold ran the tip of her pink tongue over her lips again. Evidently none of them wanted to broach the subject of Miss Killigrew in public. If she were really alive, or had been alive an hour ago, then there must be some dreadful reason she hadn't appeared in the flesh among them. If she were dead, murdered, then only a monster could have killed her. And nobody, Parry thought, wanted to admit to a monster in their midst, breathing the same foul air, rubbing shoulders with them. So, when they were all together, shut up in the same room, Miss Killigrew, as a subject of conversation, was taboo. What the eye didn't see the heart didn't grieve over.

The silence began to pall, and he could feel the sweat beginning to trickle down the back of his neck. The murderer could roast till he or she was red-hot, but it seemed rather unfair that the others should roast too, and in any case, Parry didn't want them cooped up forever. At large, roaming about the house, if they wished to roam, something else might happen. And he wanted something else to happen, so long as it wasn't a third death.

"It's terribly hot in here, isn't it?" he suggested, breaking the silence. "There's no reason why you shouldn't go where you please, and, of course, I can't stop you. I need hardly say that you should stay in the house till the local police arrive, and anyway, the burglar alarms would announce anybody's intended departure." He was aware that eight pairs of eyes were staring at him, in their different ways trying to probe his mind. Well, he'd give the party something to think over. He took out his cigarette case and lit the last cigarette in it, slowly, deliberately. "I think I've picked up enough clues now to put your police onto Lawty's killer. I can't prove anything at the moment—I don't travel round with a fingerprint outfit and the rest of the box of tricks when I'm supposed to be on a holiday."

"I can't stand it!" Anabel clutched her head, choking. "I can't stand any more! My nerves're in shreds. Oh, my God, I can't stand it!"

Poor duchess, Parry thought. She looked like a bedraggled old barmaid dressed up in someone else's finery.

"Then lock 'im up, lock 'im up," Paul beseeched Parry. "Lock 'im up before 'e gets another of us." He tottered to the door, tottered back again.

Anabel descended from her stool, clinging to Christie. Parry waited for Cintra to do something dramatic, scream or tear her hair. But she was standing perfectly still, her eyes staring at nothing, her hands stretched out, her face blank.

"I can feel—there's death here—" Her voice was a whisper, flat and emotionless. "There's someone here with death on his hands—I can feel it." She began to move round in a circle, her arms still stretched out. She touched Parry, moved on. "I'm coming closer to him. Wait, I'm coming closer—"

"Damn her!" Marigold shrieked. "The crazy bitch! Julian, Julian!"

Suddenly the bar emptied itself, except for Parry and Cintra.

"Very interesting," he said. "D'you do much of that sort of thing?"

Cintra blinked, nearly shut her mouth, and squeezed her hands round her throat. "Where's everyone?" A tangled lock of hair fell over her face, and she glared through it accusingly.

"You frightened them all away. You were about to expose the murderer. Must you strangle yourself?"

"Ough." She stuffed her hands in her pockets. "You're a first-class liar. Miss Killigrew didn't give you the key to the safe. You haven't a clue the local cops can get a line on. You're hoping to use yourself for bait. And when you get a knife in your back, with your dying breath you'll denounce whoever it was, having nobly sacrificed yourself in the cause of law and order. Don't stick your neck out too far." She shivered and hunched her shoulders. "It's not over yet. There's more to come."

"As you know such a lot, d'you mind telling me why you wanted to lock your jewelry up when you haven't got any jewelry with you? That is, unless you've hidden it under the floor boards of your bedroom, having previously taken up the expensive carpet that's nailed down all round the edge."

"I've got my wedding ring, haven't I?" She waved it under his nose, nearly scratching him. "I never wear gewgaws, except when I'm making a picture that calls for them. I don't like a lot of glitter-glitter like Marigold. Though I know real and false stones when I see them," she said, peering into Parry's eyes. "I'd like to lock up my wedding ring. Someone might cut my hand off as the easiest way of stealing it."

Outside, the branch of a tree began to creak, and the wind sighed past the windows. Cintra pulled back one of the curtains and let it drop again. The brief glimpse of the darkness, the vagrant flocks of snow, made the house feel more shut in, more dangerous than ever.

"You haven't been doing any killing during the night yourself, have you?" Parry asked.

Cintra stumbled toward the door, her feet catching in the edges of the rugs.

"You have to grit your teeth when you kill anyone," she shouted, as if she'd suddenly gone demented. "Grit your teeth and clench your jaws, or whatever it is you do with jaws. Go on, try it and see!" She burst out of the room, then burst in again. "Listen! Parry, listen, listen! The three knocks—"

Parry listened, and felt a slight prickling sensation up his spine.

Like the thump of muffled drums, three dull bangs sounded from the direction of the hall. A pause, then three more bangs, louder, more insistent. And a voice, hollow, sepulchral, called, "Open the door. I'm here, let me out!"

"It's Lawty!" Cintra gasped. "His spirit's come back—he's come to haunt us, with the blood running out of his mouth!"

CHAPTER 19

DRAWN by some morbid, terrified curiosity, the weary inmates of the kitchen fled like a flock of fowl along the corridor. Anything was better than staying where they were, waiting for some fearful ghost to knock three times on the kitchen door.

"Oh, my Gawd, my Gawd," Lilly whimpered, and grabbing onto Gaston who was standing petrified outside the office, his face twisted into a green mask of panic, tried to drag him along with her, her free arm hugging Ethel's waist for support, both physical and moral.

"If you're going to have hysterics, I'll throttle you," Parry said to Cintra. "Come along." He felt as if he'd spent half the night taking her firmly by the arm and pushing her from one place to another; his own arm, he was sure, must be covered with bruises from the many times she'd dug her claws into it. "Probably Paul's locked himself up somewhere and can't get out."

"No," she shuddered. "No."

Parry marched her into the hall and pushed her at Christie. They were all there. None of them locked in anywhere, everyone was present, though not in order. Twelve pairs of eyes stared unblinkingly at the dining-room door. Anabel was swaying backward and forward. In two ticks she'd faint, Parry thought. Marigold's pretty mouth was contorted into a mirthless grin, like a wild cat's. Paul had put the fingers of his right hand in his mouth, and appeared to be gnawing them off. They were all stricken into silence. The usual noises of hysteria Parry had got so used to bursting out at the slightest provocation were missing. The silence, punctuated by the three monotonously repeated knocks on the other side of the dining-room door, and the banshee voice demanding to be let out, was even nastier than if they'd all been shrieking at the tops of their lungs. He unearthed the key to the dining room from his pocket and put it in the lock.

"Stand back and give me air," he said cheerfully, and opened the door.

The lights were still blazing as he'd left them. A thin wail of wind from one of the windows flapped the curtains, making them look like witches' wings, and little flurries of snow blew into the room. The bottom of the middle window was wide open. Lawty's feet, stiff in their black silk socks, were visible for all to behold; so too was the white-shrouded shape of Miss Killigrew, Parry's offering of pale pink roses wilted and scattered. And standing just inside the doorway, with blood running out of its mouth and smeared on its face, an apparition in a dinner jacket and blood-spattered boiled shirt hovered unsteadily. For one mad moment, Parry thought Cintra was right, that Lawty's ghost had risen from his body and come to haunt them. Then he went into the room and shut and locked the door behind him, shutting out the awful, shrill scream that broke the silence, the ponderous thud that announced Anabel had fainted dead away at last.

"Who the hell're you?" he asked the bleeding visitant.

"Eric, or Little by Little," was the bemused reply. "Eric Hammerton, Bart., as they say. Who the hell're you?"

"I'm an inspector of police."

"Inspector of what'd you say? Drains? If it's drains, then that's all to the good. There're a couple of corpses here. Anabel ought to have her drains seen to."

"In the name of the Almighty, pull your socks up," Parry said, losing his temper. "You're drunk as hell. What're you doing here?"

"I came to the party. The party for Lawty—Anabel asked me to yester-day."

After all, one of Anabel's ratting guests had arrived. The permanently pickled baronet had changed his mind.

"How'd you get in here?"

"Through the window, old boy. Turned the latch from outside with my penknife. Front door was locked, and I couldn't find the bell. Thought I'd come in through the window and give the girls and boys a surprise."

"You gave them a surprise, all right," Parry said in grim amusement. "You've probably killed half of them with fright." He shut and latched the open window and opened and shut the other windows in turn. Either the burglar-alarm system had gone wrong or someone had got at the switch, for not even the faintest tinkle came from the clamorous bells.

"Call me Eric, old boy," the fuddled baronet begged. "Everybody does."

"I'll be damned if I'll call you Eric," Parry said. "And considering you mayn't even be who you say you are, I don't even propose to call you Sir Eric. How'd you get all that blood on you?"

"Tripped when I climbed in the window and bashed my mouth on that chair. Mind if I sit down, old boy?"

"My name's Parry. You'd be safer sitting than standing. You don't seem very surprised to've found two dead bodies in here."

"Nothing," the unexpected visitor explained, "surprises me when I'm pickled. I'm damn sorry about little Miss Killigrew, all the same, poor little woman. Besides, I'm used to dead bodies—last war but one—too old for the last one. Who's the other body, poor devil?"

"Wing Commander Lawton Lawrence, or all that remains of him."

"Is that Lawty? I've never met him before, but I saw him once when he was alive."

"When?" Parry prompted. "Where?"

"In town, week before last. I was in one taxi and he was in another, stuck in a traffic block. He was leaning out the window, saying something to his driver, so I saw him, and that's him there on the floor."

"You're wrong, you know. He only arrived in England the day before yesterday, so Anabel told me."

"I may be wrong," Eric agreed. "I was a bit lit up. It looks like the same chap, though."

Parry frowned. If it were true Lawty had arrived some time before he'd told Anabel he'd reached England, or she'd got muddled, then it would be easy enough to check up on the date he'd flown across. Supposing he'd really arrived some days before he went down to Beechlands and had lied to Anabel that he'd only just landed, then he'd have had to lie to the rest of the inmates as well. Why?

"Was he alone?"

"Wh'?" Eric made a violent effort to be intelligent. "Was he alone? So far's I could see."

"Were you alone?"

"Me? No, old boy. Sssh, not a word. No names, no pack drill. She was only lunching with me, anyway. Everything quite all right and above-board." Eric rubbed his beak of a nose, then looked up at Parry. "What'd Lawty and Miss Killigrew die of?"

"They were murdered," Parry said.

"Good God! No wonder you're taking a gloomy view of me. Who did it?"

Parry didn't answer. Someone was knocking at the door softly but urgently, and Jim's voice said, "Parry, are you all right?"

"Yes, thanks," Parry said to the door. "D'you know a chap by the name of Eric Hammerton?"

"Is that Eric?" Jim asked. "Good Lord—Paul's yawping that he's the devil, and Cintra's going on and on that he's Lawty's ghost. There's absolute hell popping, Parry."

"How are you, Jim?" Eric rejoined. He'd had a quick nip from his flask while Parry's back was turned and now felt fit for anything. Eric's flask was his constant companion when he left his home. A lot of people said he took it to bed with him.

"Eric? What the hell're you up to?" Jim asked, his voice muffled by the thick door.

"I came to the party, old boy. I changed my mind—thought it'd be a pity to miss it. Walked all the way up to my neck in snow. How's that for an old crock like me? Tell Anabel I'll be with her when I've had a wash."

"All right."

"What time did you start?" Parry asked. "And why walk? Haven't you a car?"

"Wasn't going to ditch my car in a drift. So I walked. Took me hours, as it's uphill all the way from Watching." Eric looked at his wrist watch. "Started about one o'clock. I couldn't have made the grade at all if I hadn't had my flask with me. And now there's no party."

Parry looked at him speculatively. If he was of the same kind as the rest of Anabel's guests and friends, then there seemed nothing out of the way in starting off to a party at one in the morning, through miles of snow, in a snowstorm. "D'you often do this kind of thing?" he asked.

"Why not?" Eric looked surprised. "If Anabel throws a party it goes on till all hours, and I sleep here."

"I see. What d'you know about Lawty?"

Vaguely, Eric explained he didn't know much about him except what he'd heard. And what he'd heard was no more than Parry knew himself. About the rest of the party he was equally vague. Jim was a nice chap, Christie was a nice little thing, Paul and Julian he'd met only once. He thought Cintra pretty queer and Marigold a peach. Anabel was one of the best, and he knew and cared nothing about Gaston or the rest of the staff. As a source of information he was practically useless. But at any rate, Parry thought with relief, he couldn't have killed Lawty and Miss Killigrew.

"Any idea why someone should have murdered Lawty and Miss Killigrew?"

Eric shook his head. "Burglar?" he suggested. "Might be some lunatic that got in. I must say, old boy, I got a bit of a surprise when I climbed in the window and found the place full of dead bodies. Afraid I disarranged Miss Killigrew's wreath. It's a bloody bad show." Suddenly he sobered up. "Good God, Parry, who'd kill a poor little woman like that? She wouldn't hurt a fly. Lawty might have got into a scrap with somebody and was killed that way."

"There wasn't any scrap," Parry said. He must go and see what had happened to the burglar alarms. Miss Killigrew had said she'd locked the box where the bells and the switch were and then locked the key in the safe. He opened the window Eric had come in by. It had stopped snowing again, and the wind had died down. "Hammerton?"

"Yes, old boy? Do call me Eric, by the way, everyone does."

"Never mind that now. If it's downhill from here to Watching, d'you think you could walk back there now, with a message for me?"

Eric took out his flask, looked at it, unscrewed the top, and drained it. His small, bloodshot blue eyes gleamed brightly out of his gaunt, raw face.

"Walk to town, if you like."

Parry tore a sheet out of his notebook and scribbled, "Duty Officer, Police Station, Watching. Two deaths by violence have occurred at Beechlands Hotel. Please inform chief constable. Help needed as soon as possible. Also ambulance. Lane Parry, Inspector, C.I.D., Scotland Yard." He supposed they'd have the sense to bring up the usual paraphernalia of fingerprint outfits and so on. But help was what he needed—the local police in full force, whatever its full force was, to take over, so that he could get his car out of the ditch and go back to London. He handed the sheet of paper to Eric, who read it owlishly and, folding it up, put it in his pocket.

"I'm to deliver this to the chap that's on duty at the police station, is that the idea?" he asked Parry. "You want the police and the chief constable and the ambulance and the fire brigade, is that it?"

"Not the fire brigade, thanks," Parry smiled. "Haven't you an overcoat of some sort?"

"Funny," Eric puzzled. "I had, but now I haven't." He got up and poked round the dining room. "Here it is. Hell, no it isn't. Must've taken it off on the way here, I got damn hot wading all those miles. Never mind." He began to clamber out of the window, grunting.

"Wait a minute." Parry tried to pull him back. "I'll get you mine."

"Not a bit of it, old boy." With another grunt, he was over the sill and floundering in the snow. He looked up at Parry and grinned. In the streak of light that shone out the window, his face looked old and tired, but his eyes were determined. "Damn sorry about all this. Good-by, old boy, and don't let your braces dingle-dangle. I'll be back with the Black Maria and the fire brigade in no time." He waved, and swaying unsteadily, stumbled away into the white night, the snow up to his knees, undaunted.

"Not the fire brigade," Parry called after him and added, "Thanks, Eric."

He shut the window and latched it. The remaining roses he'd left in the bowl among the tinsel and the dry Christmas holly were still quite fresh. The room smelled more and more strongly of mortuaries and death, a cold cloying smell that not even the heat of the house could instill warmth into. He smoothed the tablecloth over Miss Killigrew, threw the dead roses in a corner, and replaced them with the fresh ones out of the bowl. When he opened the door inch by inch, he could hear voices in the lounge, the pad of footsteps going upstairs and coming down. He slipped into the hall and, as he locked the dining-room door, blessed whoever it was who kept the locks so well oiled. Near him was a screen, gold-embossed; he made its shelter in three long strides. He didn't want anyone to see him go into Miss Killigrew's office and was wondering how he'd make the whole breadth of the hall to the office door in the corridor without discovery when he remembered there was another door that opened into the redout of the reception desk.

Christie's voice, so clear that she might have been standing beside him, said, "Hello, Gaston, coffee?"

Cups rattled on a tray. "Yeah, coffee when the bloo—when it's ready, m'slle. By the orders of madame, in the lounge. And another tray up in her sitting room, for the spooks, I suppose."

"Marigold? Marigold, my sweet?" Julian calling.

Footsteps so soft that they were almost inaudible. The gentle swish of a skirt. Anabel's voice, deep and hoarse with nerves, in the lounge. The snick of a lighter. Then silence. Parry stuck his head round the screen. The hall appeared to be empty. He made a quick, silent dash for the reception desk, swung himself over it, and cautiously opened the door into the office. The room was empty, the lights blazing. The safe was shut. Everything appeared to be untouched, till he looked in the corner near Miss Killigrew's desk and saw that the box of tricks that housed the alarm bells was open, its grille door hanging down, the lever, which was of the fusebox variety, pushed down to "Off." I'll be damned, he said to himself, and pulled on Lawty's gloves.

For hanging in the lock of the burglar-alarm contraption, as if someone had tried to pull it out in a hurry and it had stuck, so he'd left it in a panic, was the key. Like all the keys at Beechlands, it had a tab attached to it by a split ring, neatly printed in, he was sure, Miss Killigrew's writing, "Burglar Alarms," just as the key to the dining room was labeled "Dining Room." Parry pushed the lever back to "On," locked up the box, and put the key in his pocket.

What the hell had happened? Miss Killigrew had said, quite definitely, that she'd locked the burglar alarm key in the safe along with the others. The only conclusion he could come to was that someone was in possession of the safe key, had unlocked the safe, helped himself to whatever he fancied, including the key to the burglar alarms, which he'd put out of action preparatory to either making a getaway through snowdrifts several feet deep, leaving a trail any idiot could follow, or opening a window and dropping the booty—Lawty's £500—out into the all-concealing snow to be collected later, as and when convenient. The latter move, owing to the weather, seemed the most probable. What would I do, under the circumstances? Parry wondered. I know damn well what I'd do. I'd open the safe, spot the burglar alarm key, and before I took anything else I'd make everything ready to hop it or chuck my loot out the window, anything so's it wouldn't be found on me. So I'd unlatch the window by Miss Killigrew's desk, then unlock the burglar alarm box, pull the lever down to "Off," and, ready, as I hope, for all emergencies, go back to the safe.

Parry lifted back one of the curtains, and reaching up, felt the catch of the window. It had been snapped back, and the window had been raised perhaps a quarter of an inch. Silent, but in a violent hurry, he unlocked the grille door behind which the bells and the lever were dimly visible and pulled the lever down again. When he pushed the window up, the snow was a smooth white wave, blown by the wind in a drift against the house. No mark scarred its glittering surface, no one had climbed out, nothing had been dropped out. He shut and latched the window, relocked everything, and stared at the safe. Why leave the key in the door of the burglar alarm box? And like a flash of revealing light he got the answer—the present illegal owner of the safe key, having unlatched the window, unlocked the box, pulled the lever down, and started to raise the window, had been disturbed. What'd be the first thing he'd do? Shut and relock the safe, of course, then try to shut the burglar alarm box. But the key, the bloody key, sticks— anything's better than being caught out, so he leaves it half in, half out the lock and bolts into the corridor. Parry smiled, remembering the almost shocking disturbance of Eric Hammerton's thunderous bangs on the dining-room door, and Gaston, a delicate green in the face, shooting away from near the office when he and Cintra had joined the throng in the hall. He jerked his head round and held his breath. Someone was furtively trying the handle of the door that gave onto the corridor, as if he weren't sure whether he was safe from interruption. Fascinated, Parry watched the handle move, and thankful for the deadening effect of the thick carpet, walked across the room on the tips of his toes and put the lights out. It might be Gaston, it might be anyone. He backed to the other door, the one he'd come in by, and feeling for the handle, slowly opened it, straining his eyes into the darkness, waiting for the crack of light that would announce the stealthy entry of the intruder, ready to duck down and squat on the floor, so that he wouldn't be outlined against the lights behind him. He waited, breathing quietly. Nothing happened except a small sound that might be someone making himself scarce as quickly and silently as possible.

Then a blinding explosion of stars filled his head. Dimly, a thousand miles away, he heard the thud of something heavy falling. He rushed giddily down into a black sea, and the black sea engulfed him.

CHAPTER 20

SLIDING past the office with another trayload of drinks and coffee, Gaston stopped, and the hair on the back of his neck prickled. Someone was inside there, groaning the dim, thick groans of the unconscious. He licked his lips, and the silver coffeepot on the tray rattled. He thought he could hear somebody walking down the stairs. On the first floor a door thudded very softly. So they were wandering about the house, were they? The groaning had stopped. He began to shake with terror. He was an excellent craftsman, but woefully lacking in guts. A few minutes ago the soft pad of feet had scared him; now he thought he heard them again. His imagination, already highly tried during the night, was working overtime, so that he didn't know if the noises he heard were real or whether he imagined them. What a bloody house it was! he thought. Once you were round the corner into the bar corridor, you couldn't see anything that was going on in the hall. A crash of discordant notes on the grand piano in the lounge made him bite his tongue. He couldn't stand it any longer; he had to know who was in the office.

Slopping the coffee and the drinks in his agitation, he put the tray on the floor and slowly opened the door. The office was dark; his mouth dry with fear, he snapped the lights on.

"Gorlmighty," he muttered. So Parry'd got his at last, had he? He lay face downward, his hands bound behind him with one of the curtain tie-backs, the other tieback knotted tightly round his neck. And on the base of his skull was a lump the size of an egg, the skin broken and bloody. Whoever'd trussed him up must have left him for dead, only he wasn't dead. Gaston had often wished he could see Parry swing, but some almost human instinct made him undo the knots of the betassled tiebacks, roll Parry round, and shake him. He'd been gagged with his own handkerchief, which was stuffed in his mouth. Gaston pulled it out and dropped it on the floor. On Miss Killigrew's desk was a vase of disagreeable evergreens. He threw them in a corner and emptied the dirty water on Parry's face.

"Wake up," he said without much sympathy.

Parry grunted, opened one eye, then the other. "Behold," he whispered hoarsely, "our latest good Samaritan."

"Who the hell done that?" Gaston inquired.

Parry worked his jaws, rubbing his neck. His heart thumped like a trip hammer, and jabs of pain radiated from the back of his head. "How the devil should I know?" he said. "You didn't, anyway, otherwise you wouldn't be rescuing me in my dire distress. I suppose the perfect lady or gentleman who attended to me was the same customer who was after you, and's probably still after you." In the distance the discordant, rough hammering on the piano went on with relentless persistence. "The same perfect lady or gentleman who killed Wing Commander Lawrence, unless there's more than one tough round the house."

"Lawty and Killigrew both." Gaston chewed his underlip and grinned. "Fancy you being caught out like that, Inspector, all tied up like a chicken

ready to go in the oven." His eyes swiveled round the floor, and he pointed
with an unsteady finger at the far corner of the room. "What's that? It's got
blood on it. It's the match stand from the reception desk."

"Then why ask what it is?" With some difficulty, and unaided by Gaston, Parry dragged himself to his feet, feeling sick and giddy. The piano
banging stopped suddenly. "Don't paw it about, I've got gloves." He picked
up the large round granite match stand and put it on Miss Killigrew's desk.
It was as big as a polo ball and as heavy as a large flatiron, with a hole on its
top to hold safety matches and its bottom surface flattened so that it didn't
roll about. The fog began to clear from his mind, as if a curtain were suddenly lifted, letting the light in. It was easy to visualize what had happened.
When he'd been standing in the open door, his back to the reception desk,
all his senses concentrated on the other door, waiting for it to open, someone must have crept up behind him, picked the stand off the desk, and
hurled it at his head. After that, he'd simply swung himself over the desk,
just as he'd done himself, tied him up while he was unconscious, and left
him to strangle to death. Had for a mug, he thought ruefully, and was thankful
that if he'd searched him, he hadn't found the ice hammer. He could still
feel it poking uncomfortably into his chest, buttoned up inside his shirt.

"I'm off," Gaston remarked.

"No, you aren't." Parry sat down on Miss Killigrew's desk and, with
his back turned to Gaston, turned out his pockets. Everything was intact.
The pieces of telephone line, the garden scissors, the blotting paper from
the writing room, the neatly labeled keys, "No. 20," "Dining Room," "Gents'
Cloakroom," "Burglar Alarms." His would-be assassin had been after the
safe key he hadn't got, for he'd been searched, all right. His wallet was in
the wrong pocket. Gaston would never make an amateurish mistake like
that. The safe key—there was more in the safe, he was suddenly sure, than
Lawty's £500. Some evidence, some clue. He put the keys and the rest of
the collection back in his pockets.

"I'm off," Gaston repeated, with an air of finality. "The old woman'll
be letting out a howl for the coffee, and when she howls, she howls." He
eyed the key on the inside of the main office door with furtive longing and
edged toward it. "I'd keep your back to the wall," he advised.

"Thanks. And you might chuck that key over to me, will you?"

Gaston handed it over without a murmur.

"Albert? At least, Gaston? I suppose I'm about the only policeman
alive today whose life's been saved by a member of the criminal classes. If
you'll try to answer a few questions as truthfully as you can, I'll forget
about Mrs. Adams' family silver hidden in your remarkably hard-looking
mattress. I might even put it back where it belongs." Parry lowered his
voice. There was no knowing, in this repulsive establishment, who might

be eavesdropping. "What's it you've got someone else wants so badly? The safe key, isn't it? Only he thought I had it."

"I haven't got no safe key." Gaston's mouth twitched. "Use your loaf."

"I'm using it, and if you'd like to add 'at last,' I don't mind. You dropped it in the bar after you'd come back with the sherry, when you couldn't find Miss Killigrew, artfully disguised with a tab printed 'Cigarette Cabinet,' didn't you?" Why in hell didn't I think of that before? Parry silently fumed. He'd even had the thing in his hand when he'd searched Gaston in the linen room. "Someone recognized the key. Who?"

Gaston's Adam's apple jerked convulsively. "I haven't got any key to any safe. If you haven't got it yourself, someone thinks you have."

"I don't know how you got hold of the safe key," Parry went on, ignoring the protestations of innocence, "as I haven't second sight, like Miss Norton—Mrs. Elliot—though no doubt time will tell. Correct me if I'm wrong, but when you and everyone else but Miss—Mrs. Elliot and I'd hooked it out of the bar, you came in here, unlocked the safe, found the key to the burglar alarm box, unlocked it, switched off the current, unlatched the window, and then—then what, Gaston? You were interrupted by three thunderous knocks and the ghostly voice of Sir Eric Hammerton demanding to be let in. Knowing you as well as I alas do, I take it you got in a panic, shut the safe, and tried to relock the burglar-alarm affair. The key stuck, and you hopped it, rather than be caught fiddling round. Later, quite a good bit later, about twenty minutes ago, you returned to the attack."

"I didn't," Gaston glared. "You bloody liar."

"I was in here and heard you. Why'd you scuttle away like a frightened mouse? Did you hear someone lurking round? If so, it was probably the sportsman who went for me. Well?"

"Well what? That crack on the head's made you a bit queer, Parry. You'd better go lie down and sleep it off."

"What'd you take out of the safe besides the key I found?"

An expression that might have been relief contorted Gaston's face. "I don't know nothing at all, nothing, about the key you found in the burglar alarm, d'you get me? And anyhow I haven't got it, you have." He pressed his hands together as if he were going to kneel down and pray. "As God's my witness, I haven't got a thing out of the safe, not on me or stowed away. As God's my witness, I didn't lift so much as an empty envelope—not that I even looked in the safe, how could I when I haven't got the key? Listen, Parry, slit my throat, I don't even know what's in the safe. May God strike me dead and the house fall down on top of me if I'm not telling the truth."

Parry gazed up at the ceiling in some trepidation, waiting for it to crack and descend upon his head in slabs.

"There you are," Gaston shrugged. "And I'm a religious man."

"Then as a saint about to be canonized at any moment, you won't mind my having a look in your pockets?"

"I'm busy, if you aren't."

The door banged in Parry's face. For a minute or two Gaston could wait. He looked at his watch. Half past four. If Eric or Little by Little didn't fall by the wayside he'd be in Watching soon. Help should come, at the latest, by six. He turned the granite match stand round in his gloved hands, tossed it up, and caught it again, and a nasty picture came into his mind of Christie hurling snowballs with the deadly accuracy of a Test Match bowler. There were no keys to any of the drawers in Miss Killigrew's desk, but it was a safe enough hiding place. He pushed the match stand to the back of the top drawer, behind a packet of blank menus. What the devil did Gaston want keys for, he wondered, when he was a professional lock-picker? By that token, where'd he hidden away the implements of his trade? What a mess, what a hopeless tangle! Miss Killigrew'd said the burglar alarms had been fitted after some of the guests had been robbed. The thief, unless some-one else had poached on his preserves, could only have been the *soi-disant* Gaston. Then why had Anabel, if she'd known about his little failing, kept him on, her only precaution being to fit burglar alarms to stop anyone from breaking in—a kind of muddled interpretation of locking the stable door after the horse had gone?

I give it up, Parry thought, feeling the back of his head tenderly. But at any rate he was at least sure now that Gaston had the safe key and that his pleas to the Almighty to strike him dead and fling the house down on top of him if he'd stolen anything out of the safe were fairly genuine. He'd opened the safe, taken the key to the burglar alarms, but nothing else. For if he'd got what he wanted, he wouldn't have returned a second time to finish the job. Now what? Find Gaston, remove him to some secluded corner, search him, and if he hadn't got the key on him, turn the house upside down and find it. Then what? Hang about till the Watching police turned up. The safest move would be to lock everyone and himself up in the same room, but unfortunately they might strongly object to such imprisonment, even in the interests of safety. He couldn't force them, only suggest. The law's an ass, he thought venomously.

The office was stuffy and airless. He opened the door into the corridor and took in lungfuls of even stuffier air, leaning his head against the door-jamb.

"Oh, Lane?"

He pulled himself together with a jerk. He'd been on the point of going to sleep, like a worn-out horse dozing between the shafts.

"Yes, Miss Trent?"

She stood looking at him, a little breathless, smiling a phony wistful smile. "We are formal, aren't we?" she said, still wistful. "Everyone calls me Marigold. This isn't Scotland Yard, sweetie."

Bitch, Parry thought briefly, and smiled back at her. She'd changed out of her lovely silver frock into an even more lovely silver garment suitable for bedrooms and boyfriends.

She might just as well have had on nothing at all. The sleeves flowed from her like wings, the skirt flowed round her on the floor like a transparent waterfall. Quite transparent.

"Yes?" he said. "D'you want me? Want to speak to me?" He hurriedly corrected himself in case she misunderstood him.

She went on looking exquisitely wistful and little-girlish. But at the back of her eyes Parry saw a flicker of fear, and something that was almost guilt, and waited for what was going to happen next. She pulled back one of her sleeves, and unclasping her diamond bracelet, slipped it off her wrist.

"I thought it'd be safer to lock this up." Marigold glanced quickly over her shoulder. "Don't you think so, sweetie?"

"Frightened someone'll rob you? I don't think anyone will so long as you're wearing it."

Her eyes snapped. "I think it'd be better to put it in the safe. Oh, and I quite forgot, Anabel wanted to see you at once, she wants to know what Eric was doing. Where is he, Lane?"

"He went home. He thought it'd be more tactful, under the circumstances."

"Straight home?" Marigold asked; and Parry wondered why she was so anxious to know whether Eric had lingered or not.

"Not very straight."

"Listen—Anabel's calling. Sweetie, do go and see her before she has more hysterics and nervous breakdowns." Marigold came closer to him, and he tried not to look as bilious as he felt. *"La Lune et toi"* emanated from her in overpowering whiffs, mixed with other smells—grease paint, powder, bath salts. Brothels and third-rate film studios. Her blood-red fingernails ran up and down his jacket. "Do hurry, Lane. I'll lock my bracelet up and bring the key straight back to you."

So here was another one who wanted to get at the safe. Parry resisted an almost overwhelming impulse to bring his knee up with a jerk and crack lovely Marigold in her no doubt lovely stomach. She was breathing right into his face, her curving mouth only about six inches from his. He wondered if she knew her breath smelled of stale liquor.

"I—I didn't—know—" She drew her breath in, which gave Parry a short respite, and spoke in small gasps. "I never knew—a policeman who was a—gentleman before."

"Before what?"

Lovely Marigold licked her lower lip, temporarily floored, and pressed herself closer. She was shaking all over in her effort to persuade him to give her the key he hadn't got. The tremors ran up and down her body as if she were electrified, and she was frightened too. "Lane," she whispered. "Oh, Lane. My God, what's that?" She flung herself at him, nearly knocking him over, her arms round his neck in a stranglehold.

"Let go," he said sharply. Mixed up with her hair, her arms, her floating sleeves, he couldn't locate where the sudden crash had come from and the animal screams of pain and fear. "Stop hugging me, I'm not one of your boyfriends." He tried to push her away from him and over her shoulder saw Cintra dart round the corner, her mouth gaping at him; the three terrified faces of Lilly, Ethel, and Marion bursting out of the kitchen like jack-in-the-boxes; Julian hurrying in Cintra's wake; then Christie, white in the face, but unruffled.

"Marigold!" Julian's eyes were horrified. "Darling, what's happened to you? My sweet, are you hurt?"

Thankfully, Parry pushed her backward into his arms, and Cintra let out one of her extraordinary roars of laughter, "Har-har-har!"

"Cintra!" Julian begged. "Please! Marigold, my darling, what's happened?"

"She was trying to seduce Parry," Cintra bawled, and threw her arms round Christie's shoulders. "Oh, Lord, how funny! All dressed up to seduce, mid nearly nuddings on—"

"Parry? Is anything wrong?"

"What?" Pushing his way past Julian and Marigold, Parry looked over his shoulder and saw Jim had joined the party.

"Of course there's something wrong," he said, losing his patience. "What a damn silly question! One of the inmates appears to've fallen down the back stairs."

CHAPTER 21

THE mirror that camouflaged the bottom door of the unsecret staircase was fogged over by the steamy, used-up air that drifted out of the bar.

"Sounds like a pig being stuck," Jim said.

Parry opened the door. The stairs were in darkness, and out of the darkness a white blot uttered its demon cries at him. He groped for the light switch and the old-world illuminations sprang to life. Sprawled in an untidy heap on the bottom steps, Gaston stared wildly up at him, gave a final shriek, and burst into an incoherent babble of words.

"What?" Parry said. "I can't understand a thing you're saying. What in hell've you been doing? Can't you stand up?" He reached down and tried to hoist Gaston onto his feet, but he appeared to be immovable.

"No!" Gaston's babblings rose to a feminine squeal, and he clasped Parry round the waist, pawing at him. "My legs—my legs!"

"Give me a hand." Parry jerked his head at Jim. "And tell those people to clear out—not that they'll take any notice. I'll lift his top half, and you get his legs from under him."

To the accompaniment of renewed screams of pain, they staggered across to the bar and laid Gaston on the floor.

"Good God," Jim said, "has he bust both his legs?"

"He's sprained his right ankle, by the look of it, and busted his left leg below the knee. There's some brandy on the bar. Pour out a stiff tot and bring it here." Parry tried to arrange his ideas in some sort of order. "Then chivvy those people back to their lairs and see if you can find anything I can make some temporary splints out of—and some large handkerchiefs or dishcloths."

"All right."

There was one thing about Jim Bridges, Parry thought, and that was he neither argued nor dithered.

"Gawd," Gaston moaned, and let go a string of oaths that weren't at all in keeping with his ladylike appearance.

"What happened?" Parry asked.

Gaston drained the last drop of brandy out of the glass and pulled Parry closer to him. "I'd been up to my dog kennel," he whispered. "I was coming down again, and just as I got two steps down the back stairs, I heard someone behind me breathing—it was him again. Christ, it was horrible—so I jumped."

"You mean you took a flying leap into space?"

"I didn't touch nothing till I hit the bottom."

"Any idea who it was?"

"Not a clue." Gaston laid back and groaned, the sweat trickling down his chin. "I put the lights out before I started down the stairs, as I didn't want no one to see me."

Parry poured him out another brandy and heartlessly searched him. Everything he'd had on him in the linen room was still on him, except the key labeled "Cigarette Cabinet."

"Cached the safe key, have you? Where? In your dog kennel?"

A sly grin distorted Gaston's face. After the two large brandies on top of the several pulls of whisky he'd had, he was getting on for drunk. "You can turn the whole house upside down, take up the bloody floors, pull the furniture to bits, if you like. I don't know nothing about no safe key—only the key to the cigarettes, and you'll find that on top of the cabinet in the hall." His eyes half shut, and he began to moan and mutter.

Parry stood up and listened, then went very quietly to the door. Footsteps came cautiously down the back stairs, paused as though their owner were anxious, then came on.

"Well, Lord?"

Robère stood poised on the bottom step, his hand on the looking-glass door.

"Yes, sir?" His face turned red, then white.

"Where've you been?"

"Up to my room. I've been having a sleep, if you want to know. Excuse me—"

Parry watched him hurry into the kitchen, and raised his eyebrows. He'd forgotten about Robert Lord in all the noise and violence, and now he had suddenly resurrected himself as another suspect. Faint but clear, the hall clock struck five. Parry rubbed his eyes, blinking. He was so tired that he had an illusion the lights weren't so bright as they had been.

"These were all I could find that might do for makeshift splints."

Parry looked round. Jim came slowly down the corridor, struggling with an armful of umbrellas and two pieces of wood, which looked as if they had been ripped out of a bookcase.

"How many legs d'you think Gaston's got?" Parry laughed. "Haven't you brought anything to tie him up with?"

Jim dropped his burden in the bar. "The Layne girl's bringing some glass cloths, or something, from the linen room." He moved his shoulders impatiently, as though Christie were clinging onto his back, an unwanted burden. "No business of hers," he added under his breath, and leaned over Gaston. "How's the face on the barroom floor? Want some more brandy poured into it?"

Gaston groaned and nodded. "Make it a stiff one this time."

"My God, he's had half a pint, neat, already," Parry said. "I'm going to help myself to a whisky. I'll pay for it when the party's over." He drank a large tot, straight, and as it went down inside him, he began to feel more amiably disposed toward his companions.

"Where the hell's that girl got to?" Jim's voice was suddenly tight, not with irritation and resentment, but with sudden anxiety. "Christie!" He pulled the door open and nearly walked on her. "Where've you been?"

"Paul collared me." Christie laid the neat pile of glass cloths on the floor beside the umbrellas. "I think he must've been at Anabel's gin, because he was crying. Poor Gaston, you are in a mess, aren't you? You must've taken an awful toss." She knelt down and rolled up her sleeves, and Jim stared helplessly at her. "Now, if someone'll hold this leg straight—

you can scream as much as you like, Gaston, only not too loud."

"Efficiency personified," Jim said ungraciously, and squatting on the floor took hold of Gaston's left foot.

"Everybody gone upstairs?" Parry asked.

"So far's I know," Christie said without looking round.

Gaston shrieked.

"I'll leave you to it for a moment. You know your first aid, all right, don't you?" Parry said.

"No. But I typed a book for someone once, a very dull one about first aid in the home."

"You're bloody well killing me!" Gaston howled.

Parry left them to it and scouted along to the hall. The cigarette cabinet was under the stairs, a red-lacquered monstrosity made even more monstrous by its gilt and silver embellishments. He felt on top of it, and his fingers touched a key. It was a small, impractical bit of workmanship, with a simple ward that was dwarfed by the ornamental gilded and silvered bow. The tab attached to it was neatly printed, "Cigarette Cabinet," and when he tried it in the flimsy lock, the glass door opened. So that was that. He helped himself to a packet of Players, thankfully lit one, relocked the door, and put the key back where he'd found it. He had no doubt it was always kept there and had been there all night. The key to the safe, which Gaston had so artfully disguised, had been a sturdy steel affair with a curiously complicated ward.

Damn me for a mug, Parry rebuked himself. It would have been the easiest thing in the world for Gaston to get hold of a tab, print "Cigarette Cabinet" on it, and substitute it for the tab on the key to the safe. I hope they torture him, he thought vindictively. Gaston's cries had dwindled to a clogged mumble, like a giant cat purring in the distance, getting fainter and fainter.

He yawned and rubbed his eyes again. It was as if a mist had come between them and the lights. The brilliant glare of the chandelier that hung in the middle of the hall seemed veiled. The patches of light and shadow blurred. The high ceiling, much too high, like all the ceilings in the house, was a shadowy vault; and away in the corner near the main door the sneer on the face of "The Laughing Cavalier" had faded. Was he going blind? he wondered. Or was the whisky he'd had in the bar hooch? The background of noises that had accompanied the long, unpleasant night, muffled voices shut in behind closed doors, sudden outbursts of overwrought nerves, shrieks, bangs, had faded like "The Laughing Cavalier's" face. There was something aghast about the silence, as though everyone in the house, and the house itself, were holding their breaths in anticipation of something horrible to come—the crowning horror of a night of horrors.

Parry stepped back into the middle of the hall and stared up at the landing balcony above him. Very slowly, Anabel's sitting-room door was opening, a dim, gradually enlarging oblong of ghostly light, which filled and emptied again with the shadowy outlines of figures. Five faces looked down at him: Paul's despairing, as if he'd given up all hope of further life, Julian's anxious, pouches under his eyes, Cintra's haggard with emotion, Marigold's stiff with fear—and Anabel's a majestic, powdered mask, a martyr facing the flames of the stake, the final destruction, the end of all things. Swaying a little unsteadily, she raised one hand and pointed down at Parry, and he thought, the old girl's quite tipsy, and waited for what was coming next.

"The lights," she croaked. "The lights are going out. My electric plant has been left unattended. In less than an hour we shall be left in darkness, groping blindly—" She clutched onto Paul for support, and he temporarily disappeared from view behind the landing rails. "Groping blindly—groping—"

"Haven't you any candles?" Parry called up at her.

"What's a candle? But a little flame in the darkness, flickering for an instant before it is puffed out. Just as our lives—" Anabel broke off, groping in confusion for words. "As our lives are—"

Parry stuffed his hands in his pockets and made an encouraging noise in his throat. What the devil was that in his right pocket mixed up with the keys? He felt it with his fingers, at first puzzled, till he realized that while she'd been pawing him about, lovely Marigold had used him as a dumping place for her diamond bracelet.

Anabel's bosom heaved, and she leaned perilously over the landing balustrade, which creaked under her weight. "Lane, for God's sake," she moaned, her speech about candles forgotten. "It's in the dark ghosts walk. What's that? Look!"

"It's only me," Christie said. "It's all right, Anabel. I found an old hurricane lamp in the kitchen." She held it up, swinging it, so that its feeble light bobbed about like a poltergeist.

"Stop it!" Marigold's voice was shrill with a mixture of panic and rage. "You did it on purpose, sneaking round the corner pretending to be Lawty's ghost—trying to frighten m—you've been at it all night—in the bar, with the ice hammer, knocking—"

The lights died, then brightened again, uncertainly, like someone struggling through his first public speech. Christie put the hurricane lamp on the floor and looked thoughtfully up at Marigold.

"Shut up, before I give you a sock in the jaw and make you," she said in her neat, tidy voice, very pleasantly.

Parry was getting used to Cintra's opened mouth. It seemed part of her, as her extravagant mannerisms, her lurching walk, her wildly shouted comments were part of her. So it was almost a shock when she shut it, for it seemed to accentuate the incredulously gaping mouths on either side of her, Marigold's mouth the widest open of the four.

Sensation, Parry thought, and wasn't in the least surprised when Anabel burst into tears. When she had felt in the mood, she'd whistled up a braown maouse and behold, the braown maouse had turned out to be a viper that had just insulted one of her guests, the girlfriend of her financial hopes.

"I'm sorry, Anabel," Christie said. "I don't think any of us are quite ourselves."

"I trust not," Parry said under his breath, and remembered that the helpless Gaston was alone in the bar with Jim.

CHAPTER 22

THE lights grew slowly dimmer. Suspicion lurked in every dark corner, and fear. Everybody suspected everybody else. Parry wondered if he was suspect too. It was obvious Gaston couldn't be moved. He was in a bad enough way already, without jolting him about. He was breathing thickly, his eyes shut, his pasty skin mottled with purple patches. Parry looked covertly at Jim. One of the many ways of finishing people off was to give them an overdose of neat liquor.

"Why'd you give him more brandy?"

"He asked for it—dulls the pain, anyway."

"His stomach'll be skinned," Parry said. "However, that's your responsibility. Christie—Miss Layne—seems to've made a good job of strapping him up."

"Yes."

"Most efficient." ·

"Yes."

"Ever seen her sock anyone in the jaw?"

"No."

"Well, you perhaps will before daylight." Parry threw his cigarette end into one of the overloaded ashtrays. What now? Gaston couldn't be left alone, nor could he be left in the sole charge of Jim, who might just as well be the murderer as anyone else in the house, except Lilly, Ethel, and Marion." I'll be back in a minute," he said. "I'm only going as far as the kitchen."

The three girls stared at him in terror, as if he'd come to slit their throats. On the table three candles burned in three tin candlesticks, and Robert Lord tussled with a dilapidated lamp, slopping paraffin on the floor.

"I think," Parry suggested, "it'd be more cheerful for you in the bar. Take your candles along and keep Gaston company."

"That creeping snake!" Marion snorted in her nose.

"He can't creep now," Parry soothed her. "His legs're broken. Come along."

To his relief, they came along, scuttling nervously down the corridor holding their candles, like three wise virgins, followed by the chef, who had given up the lamp as a bad job.

"My Gawd," Lilly squeaked. "Look at him—he's dead."

"Gaston's not dead." How long, Parry wondered, would he be able to go on keeping his temper?

Gaston opened his eyes, and a look of disdain came over his face. The company, evidently, wasn't to his liking. But he said nothing, and shut his eyes again. The girls huddled in a corner by the bar like frightened sheep. Robère planted himself on a high stool and rested his head in his hands. They presented a forlorn and depressing spectacle. The flames of the three candles wavered and jumped in the draft from the electric fan, which was revolving slower and slower. Parry switched it off. The more power that was saved, the longer the current would hold out. He switched off all the lights in the room but one, and Ethel began to whimper.

"Anabel's going on the main next month," Jim volunteered, "if there ever is a next month."

"Where's the plant?" Parry asked.

"Down in the old stables, about a quarter mile from the house. Hilden, the head gardener, is supposed to look after it. It has to be filled up with petrol every morning early, and again about eight in the evening. Probably Hilden took one look at the snow and skipped it. His cottage's some way off."

"Who sees to the central heating furnace?"

"Hilden," Jim answered.

It wouldn't be long now before the house was lightless but for the candles and Christie's hurricane lantern. The red glow of the filament in the globe of the lamp Parry'd left on was visible. It certainly wouldn't be long.

"I'll be back. I'm going to rake out some more candles."

Parry switched off all the corridor lights but one, and gloom descended like a forbidding twilight before total darkness. The kitchen gave an illusion of being brighter than it really was. The polished aluminum pots and pans, the polished range, the white glazed tiling reflected back the dull glow of the overhead lights. There were a few loose candles on the table and an unopened packet. There didn't seem to be any more candlesticks. In the rest of the house, anything that might possibly hold a candle was already provided with a sham electric horror, either gilded or silvered, with blobs of imitation wax running down it. There were, however, plenty of empty glass jam jars in the kitchen cupboards. He stood them in rows on the table, fifteen of them, and planted each one with a candle, secured in a pool of its own wax. The effect, when they were all lit, was enchanting. He switched the lights out, and the four walls receded, as if they were trying to escape from the homely illuminations. The next thing was to place the jam jars in strategical positions, preferably on top of cupboards, where they couldn't be got at easily. That was the trouble with candles—they could so quickly be blown out, not so quickly relighted.

Knives, he suddenly thought, and opened the table drawer. It was full of knives. Carving knives, bread knives, two meat choppers, all of them a direct invitation to murder. He whistled silently, looking round for a hiding place no one would be likely to think of, then collected the knives, the choppers, a hammer that was lying on one of the shelves, two heavy rolling pins, an antiquated flatiron, and stowed the lot away in one of the ovens in the range.

If only, he thought, he could persuade Anabel, Cintra, Marigold, Christie, Julian, and Paul to join the party in the bar and stay there till rescue came, it would save further alarms and violence. But it was unlikely that they'd let themselves be persuaded to do anything they didn't want to do. Dear God, he groaned, feeling not at all pious, would the drunken Eric do his stuff? Sister Anne, Sister Anne, is there anybody coming? I see a cloud of dust, but it is only a flock of sheep. He pressed his nose against the uncurtained window. Not even a solitary flake of falling snow disturbed the emptiness of the dark early morning.

He found a packet of matches in one of the cupboards, and as he stuffed as many boxes as he could find room for in his already overfilled pockets, he remembered Marigold's bracelet. It looked even more lovely by candle-light. None of the diamonds was large, but the setting, the design, the craftsmanship, and the purity of the stones that went to make the gracious pattern of true-lover's knots, miniature flowers, and curlicues proclaimed that Julian didn't stint his money on his girlfriend. The kitchen door gave a well-oiled groan, and he looked up quickly.

"It's only me," Christie smiled at him. "I left the hurricane lamp with Anabel. I was going to get more candles." She leaned against the table so that the light shone up on her face, and for the first time Parry noticed how deadly tired she looked. "They look pretty, don't they? Like Christmas when one was small, and everything was enchanted. Parry, the lights'll be dead in a few minutes. The house was like those caves in Tom Sawyer when I came downstairs. Paul and Anabel've just had the most awful row. Poor Paul kept on and on about the house being unlucky and doomed, and not touching it with the end of a broom handle, and Anabel threw that big silver cigarette box at him. I hope she doesn't remember in the morning."

"Why?"

"Why? Because it'd be so mortifying if she realized she'd let her dignity and poise slip."

"It's slipped a bit already, surely?" Parry suggested, amused. "Everyone's reverting to normal, including yourself. You'll be quite human soon."

"That's Marigold's bracelet." Christie held out her hand, and he dropped the shining circle into it.

"It must have fallen off," he lied glibly. "I just found it in the corridor. What's the subtle fascination diamonds have for women, above all other stones?" He was wasting time, letting his curiosity lead him down bypaths. "D'you like diamonds?"

"I like real diamonds, though I've never had any."

There was a small, glass-topped tray on the table. Christie slipped the bracelet over her knuckles and drew it across the glass.

"Now you've ruined one of Anabel's trays," Parry said. "You've scratched it right across."

She stared down at the tray and the thin scratches very deep and straight, turned the bracelet in her hands, feeling it, and handed it back to him. "Don't lose that. They're real diamonds."

Something in the tone of her voice startled him. It was as though she were trying to convey some information to him without actually speaking the words.

"What d'you mean? Of course they're real diamonds. Why shouldn't they be? I can't imagine Marigold accepting paste with a sweet smile."

"Marigold can smile very sweetly even if she's not feeling sweet."

"Listen to me, Christie. Two people in this house have been killed. There've been more attempts at violence as well. D'you know that?"

"I thought Gaston fell downstairs."

Parry ignored that. "Someone had a crack at me, only it didn't come off."

"I saw the lump on the back of your head—we all did—and the blood on your neck." She laughed suddenly. "Now you know what this household's like. Everyone thought you'd had a few in the bar and slipped and caught your head a crack. Anabel said we mustn't notice as you're a policeman."

"You don't seem very surprised somebody tried to bump me off as well, do you?"

"I'm past being surprised at anything. I think it takes a lot to surprise me, in any case. But I'm sorry—does it hurt?"

Her calm acceptance of the fact he'd been nearly murdered didn't seem natural. Then he realized she was thinking of something else. Her eyes were looking right past him.

"What's biting you?" Parry asked. "Something is. If there's anything you know, then you'd better tell me. There's such a thing as being an accessory. Have a cigarette? I stole these, which ought to give them an added flavor."

"Thanks." She lit the cigarette from one of the candles, staring into the flame. "Parry? It's a little difficult, you see. It must be obvious, now, I loathe Marigold. I couldn't stand her any longer—she's such a hypocrite. That was the second time in the night I lost my head, wasn't it?"

"Ingrowing toenails have to come out sometime. What about Marigold?"

"Nothing about Marigold herself." Christie hesitated. "I'm prejudiced against her, and that makes it all the more awkward." Parry waited patiently, wishing she'd say what she had to say and be done with it. "It's that bracelet," she went on at last. "Julian sent it to her for Christmas. He didn't come down himself. She wore it all the time for a few days, I know that, because Anabel had the goodwill, merrie, merrie Christmas and New Year spirit, and kept ringing me up and asking me to come and join in the fun. A day or two after Christmas, when I was washing my hands in one of the bathrooms, I found Marigold's bracelet lying on the shelf—I suppose she'd taken it off to wash and forgotten to put it on again. I don't know why, but I started to scratch with it on the looking glass over the basin."

"Yes, and? It didn't scratch, I suppose? Is that it?"

"That's it," Christie agreed. "It only made feeble little scratches that I could rub off with my finger. And Marigold came in and caught me at it. After that, she didn't wear the bracelet much."

"Did she say anything?"

"The usual little braown-maouse remark, that's all."

"I see. And your theory is that the bracelet Julian sent Marigold for Christmas was a very good imitation, this one is real, and so there're two bracelets in existence?"

"Yes."

"Maybe you're right." He wasn't going to tell her of Marigold's eagerness to get at the safe, or that she'd landed him with the damn bracelet. "But it's perfectly feasible. Julian may have sent her an imitation for Christmas to see if she liked the design, and when she did, sent her along the real McCoy. Very often a bit of jewelry with a unique design has a duplicate in paste. A lot of women keep their real stuff at the bank, and wear the imitation. Has she been wearing the bracelet—the real or the phony, you wouldn't know unless you examined it—the last couple of weeks?"

"This is the first time Anabel's sent for me for about ten days."

"I see. Any idea how long Julian's known the girl?"

"I don't know. Julian's been coming here on and off for a long time. Marigold came down for the first time before Christmas."

"The Pantons sent her down?" Parry grinned. "Anabel's very old friends?"

"Very, very old," Christie said seriously. "They were here for a week last summer, so of course they're very old friends indeed." She gave a smothered gasp of laughter, and putting three of the illuminated jam jars onto the little glass-topped tray, hooked the kitchen door open with her foot. "I think Julian knows the Pantons. Probably he suggested to them they might suggest to Marigold it'd be nice for her down here. I suppose that'd look better."

"I don't know why. It's pretty obvious what the situation is. Where're you going?"

"To rescue Anabel with lights." She looked out into the corridor. "Parry, be quick. The current's died. Where's Jim?"

"In the bar with Gaston and the servants." He watched her flit along the dark corridor. She looked like some sort of will-o'-the-wisp, and he had an odd idea that she was suddenly terribly frightened, and didn't blame her. To be shut up in a huge, lonely snowbound house with two dead bodies, a murderer, no lights but a hurricane lamp and a total of eighteen candles, till sunrise at about eight o'clock, wasn't particularly pleasant.

He loaded the rest of the jam jars onto a large copper tray. On either side of the bar door was a gilt bracket on which sat potbellied gilt cherubs. Parry put the tray down on the floor. There'd have to be a light in the corridor. There ought to be a light in every corridor, on every landing, in every room in the house, but as he was unable to perform a loaves-and-fishes miracle, more than half the house would have to be in darkness. He reached up, whipped one of the cupids off its perch, and dumped it on the floor. In the mood he was in, he felt like trampling on it; the candle in its jam jar made a far more pleasant decoration for the bracket. The bar door was shut. He opened it and looked in. The three maidens were still in a huddle, their faces hollow in the candlelight. Robère had evidently helped himself to several drinks and stared owlishly at Parry as if he weren't sure who he was. Gaston snored thickly, half awake, half asleep, breathing out fumes of brandy.

"Everything under control?" Parry asked, and stopped short. Jim Bridges was missing. "Where's Mr. Bridges?"

"Went to wash his hands," Lilly said in a voice clogged with sleep and terror. "There was blood on them!" Her voice rose to a squeak, and she burst into tears. "Dripping with blood! His nose started bleeding—"

Parry banged the door, shutting in Lilly's howls, and began to swear loudly. Still swearing, he picked up the tray, deposited a candle in the office, another in the hall, and another on the reception desk. Then he went up the stairs, the jars rattling and clinking. How had Jim found his way upstairs in the dark? Or wasn't he upstairs? "Bridges?" Parry shouted, and the door of the bathroom at the end of the corridor opened.

"Yes?" A thin pencil of light from a pocket torch wavered along the floor. "I was washing my hands," Jim said. "Now what's wrong?"

"You were dripping with blood, so I'm told," Parry said.

"My nose started bleeding and I couldn't find my wipe."

"In fact, any excuse for another wash. Go back to the bar and stay in the bar." Parry knew that he had no authority to order anyone to do anything but hoped the unargumentative young man would do as he was told.

"I'll be damned if I'll die of suffocation in the bar so that you can have a busman's holiday. Aren't two dead bodies enough for one night?" The old scars on Jim's face began to show bluely, and he mopped his nose with a bloody towel. "My God, you're a fine detective—shut up in a house all night and half the morning with a murderer and can't find him."

"Or her?" Parry suggested pleasantly.

"What her?" Jim flapped the towel as if he were cracking a whip. "Lilly? Why don't you arrest Lilly? Or Marion? Or the other one, whatever her name is? Born murderers, you can see that by their faces."

If everything hadn't been getting nastier and nastier, Parry would have enjoyed Jim's display of perfectly ordinary temper and nerves. He appeared to have succeeded, where Christie had failed, in making the erstwhile able seaman quite human. They were all reverting to normal, their various facades peeling off in layers. Parry wondered what, by the time help arrived, he'd have reverted to himself. It was half past five. Had Eric Hammerton fallen into a snowdrift, or was he now warming his feet in front of the inevitably smoky fire that seemed part of the year-in, year-out complement of country police stations?

"Well?" Jim screwed the towel into a ball and threw it on a chair.

"Not very well, I think," Parry said. "Do you?"

"Like hell I do. I suppose you sent Eric for the local cops? What a hope in hell! He'll drop in for the night at Effie's and stay there."

"May I ask who Effie is?" Parry rested the tray on the top of the banisters. "The countryside seems more densely populated than I thought."

Jim sat down on the settee in Anabel's palm grove and vanished into shadow except for his feet, which were dimly visible in the candlelight.

"The Countess Delamonte, relict of the late phony Count Delamonte." His voice was suddenly pleasant and faintly amused. "Effie's small, round, and comfortable. Eric says she's cuddly, which I don't doubt. She's fiftyish, blondish, and she giggles really rather nicely."

"She sounds quite normal," Parry said, wishing Effie were there, giggling nicely and being round and comfortable. "So you don't want to take refuge in the bar?"

"No."

Parry transferred the tray to a table with legs that were both bowlegged and knock-kneed, like some sort of deformed animal. He couldn't spare more than two candles for the first-floor corridor and landing. He put one opposite the striking Venus, one on top of a tallboy, the other next Julian's bedroom door on a high, carved stand that seemed to be of no possible use for anything.

"This electric-light plant." He addressed Jim's feet from a distance. "It appears to be an antiquated contraption? Don't the accumulators hold the juice unless the engine's working?"

"They ought to. But they don't. It's one of the two plants Noah took into the ark. Like Paul, it's 'ad it. The thing's got to work the refrigerator as well as the lights."

Parry looked speculatively at the feet. "Would you mind turning your pockets out? It's not idle curiosity."

Much to his surprise, Jim got up and emptied the contents of his jacket and trousers pockets onto the tray among the jam jars. Two pencils, an eraser, some loose change, a penknife, a broken rubber band, a screwed-up receipt, and a lot of fluff.

"Thanks," Parry said.

"I don't mind a reasonable request. But I'm not going to suffocate in the bar with those three girls sniveling in a corner."

"Then you'd better sit with the others in Anabel's room."

"No, thanks."

Blast him, Parry thought, and knocking on Anabel's sitting-room door, went in. For a hair-raising second, he thought that she, Julian, Paul, Cintra, and Marigold were dead and that Christie'd killed them in some fiendish and uncanny manner. Anabel lay in her armchair, rigid, her feet out in front of her, her head thrown back. Cintra sprawled flat on the floor, her mouth sagging open, her eyes shut, a look of excruciating agony on her face. Marigold lay on the sofa, across Julian's legs, and Julian was doubled up over her. Paul appeared to have been stricken while saying his prayers, on his knees, his face against a chair.

He looked at Christie, who was standing with her back against the wall, and she looked back at him.

"They are not dead, they only sleep," she said. "It's the gin, I think."

"In that case, they'd better wake up." In the dim light of the three candles and the hurricane lamp, the sleepers looked like figures in some macabre painting, the effect stressed by the still-life group on the low, round gilt table in the middle of the room—a gin bottle, a brandy bottle, glasses, ash-trays, empty coffee cups, and the three candles. "I think they'd be safer awake."

Anabel groaned, unstiffened, and opened her eyes.

"I am not asleep," she said. "When I've guests for dinner, I'm not in the custom of going to sleep."

"It'll be breakfast time soon," Parry said.

One by one they sighed, yawned, moaned, and began to move. Cintra sat bolt upright and shuddered. "It's going to happen again!" she cried in an agonized voice. "Someone's taken all my chloroform—every drop, gallons of it, enough to put a regiment under." She drew her breath in and put her hands over her mouth. "The chloroform I use to paint my—my tonsils with."

"It's all right, Cintra, it's all right," Julian said wearily. "Marigold, my sweet, you'll get cramp."

Paul rolled round so that he was sitting on the floor facing the room. His sleep, crouched on his knees, had miraculously restored him his aitches. "Anabel? Anabel? You get out of here—you get out of Beechlands. It's doomed—I wouldn't touch it with the end of a broom handle."

"Shut up!" Marigold held her hands over her ears. "Julian, strangle that devil, damn him."

"Marigold, darling—"

Parry raised his voice. There was only one way to make himself heard, and that was to shout. "If you will, I'd like you all to go down to the bar and join the others."

"What others?" Anabel demanded with a slight return of her old dignity.

"Gaston and the staff," Parry explained as loudly as he could.

"I refuse to sit in the bar with the servants." Anabel pressed her lips together. "I refuse." She tried to emphasize her meaning by thumping the arm of her chair, but missed it. "I am not the housekeeper that I should sit with the servants."

"Oh, God, give me strength," Parry said. "Of course you aren't the housekeeper, but it won't kill you to sit for half an hour with the staff, surely?"

"I am not afraid of death. I shall stay here."

"Oh, Lord, poor Parry," Julian sympathized. "I don't think you'll move her."

To his dismay, Parry saw that Paul had struggled onto his knees and was trying to crawl across the room to him.

"Lend me your car," he choked tearfully. "I'll tip your driver."

Hopeless, Parry thought. He'd never move them. As for politely asking them if they would very much mind, as a favor, and only, of course, if they wanted to, to turn their pockets and evening bags out for his inspection, that seemed more hopeless still, at the moment anyhow.

"You'd better look after Paul," he said to Christie. "He needs it." Anything to keep as many of them as possible occupied.

Marigold and Julian clung together, occupied in each other. With any luck Paul would attach himself to Christie like a leech. That left Cintra and Anabel as odd men out—apart from Jim, who'd donated himself a roving license. "Mrs. Adams? I do wish you'd keep your eye on Mrs.—Miss—Cintra. She seems to be in pain."

Anabel lifted her chin off her bosom, and her eyes wandered helplessly over the dim, untidy room, the pool of light on the dried-blood-colored carpet, the red brocade curtains, now black in the shadows, and the mist of cigarette smoke, which had turned from blue to gray.

"Tell Gaston to show Sir Eric Hammerton up and put some more champagne on the ice."

"But—" Parry began, and gave it up and, mentally, spiritually, and physically exhausted, somehow got out of the room before anyone could stop him. Anabel ought to've added, he thought, "And let the party commence."

Jim had gone. The six remaining candles burned in their jam jars on the tray, their flames motionless, straight, golden wisps. The candle he had put on the tallboy seemed miles away. Down below, the hall was a deep, black well, its darkness accentuated by the feeble pin point of the solitary little light. The radiators had stopped hissing and bubbling. It was like being in a church, a baroque-rococo nightmare that had strayed from some far-off, uncongenial setting to an even more uncongenial setting in an alien country, the candles lit in preparation for some strange ceremony, the worshipers unaccountably vanished.

CHAPTER 23

SOMETHING, a kind of pendulum, was swinging backward and forward inside Anabel's head. When she was able to half open her eyes another pendulum swung backward and forward in front of them, so that she caught only occasional momentary glimpses of the people in the room with her. One minute they were there, the next minute they weren't. She wanted to ask them why they kept getting up, going out of the room, and coming back again. And why, suddenly, they didn't make any noise at all, and then their voices flooded at her, at first in a mumble, then rising to a roar like an airplane engine. Then not a sound, except the singing in her head.

What had happened? What was happening? Eric had arrived for Lawty's party after all, and Gaston was just showing him up and putting more champagne on the ice for dinner. It would be a good party. She'd make a small speech, very touching, to welcome Lawty home. Then Lawty would tell everyone to stand up and drink her health, because she was a darling and so good to them all. She'd catch Julian's eye, and he'd wink secretly at her, raise his glass, and drink a silent toast to their new business partnership. At last the red carpet would be paid for. The butcher wouldn't dare cheek her any more, or the grocer in Watching persist. They'd grovel. That horrible little man in that horrid little brown car wouldn't thrust himself on her ever again, with bits of blue paper. She'd be able to go back to the dress shop in St. Edwards that had refused to let her buy anything else unless she paid cash for it. She'd sweep in, they'd "Yes, madam" and "No, madam" her, she'd turn the whole shop upside down and then sweep out because nothing they had was good enough for her. She'd build a squash-rackets court, have a golf course laid out in the grounds, and the best tennis courts in England would be at Beechlands. Then the swimming pool, covered and heated so that it could be swum in in winter, would be an added attraction. The best people in London would fill the place, smart people, with titles and a lot of money, who'd be her great friends. You've done damn well, Anabel, considering what you started from, pulling bar handles in pa's pub in Stepney, but there, you can't keep a real lady down.

"Anabel? Are you all right?"

"What? Who's that? Christie? Of course I'm all right."

Anabel hoped no one saw her lips trembling. She could feel them trembling and quivering. Lawty was dead, Miss Killigrew gone too. Gaston wasn't showing Eric up, there was no party. Paul was right; the place was doomed, haunted. No wonder he wouldn't touch it with a broom handle. Julian'd never put even a penny in the business now. She was done for, and she loved Beechlands more than anything else in the world. And somewhere, poking about in the house, a policeman was looking for a murderer. She pushed her eyes open with her fingers and sat up. This was her house and she was the hostess, whatever happened.

"Had a nice sleep?" Julian asked.

"Very nice," Anabel agreed rather stiffly. "You must all be so tired, poor darlings. Paul, wouldn't you be more comfortable if you sat on a chair?"

"I can't fall off the floor," he explained and Cintra howled.

"Sweetie, are you in pain?" Marigold was all kindly concern. "You look awful, quite a hundred."

"What a lovely housecoat that is, Marigold!" Anabel almost shouted, feeling that she could die from the effort of raising her voice. "It's most becoming. Paris?"

"Folies Bergères," Cintra flared. "Back row of les girls."

"Cintra!" Anabel was shocked to the core that she should have drawn attention to the fact that was obvious to everyone, Marigold's semi-nakedness.

Julian reddened with sudden anger. He was an even-tempered man, but he wasn't going to have Marigold insulted. Rather unhappily, he wished, at the same time, she'd kept some nontransparent underclothes on. "You aren't being funny, Cintra, and I didn't know you had a dirty mind."

"I haven't," Cintra snarled at him. "Marigold's got a dirty mind. Her costume's pornographic, an aphrodisiac in your honor, or anyone else's, so long as he wears long pants."

Julian dragged his tired body off the sofa. "I suppose you're tight, Cintra—we've all had a bit much—but if you don't apologize to Marigold, now, immediately, I'll borrow a walking stick and lay it across your stern till you do apologize."

"I won't apologize for speaking the truth." Cintra was as tall as Julian; she pushed her face at him as if she were going to bite him.

"Silence!" Anabel's stays creaked as she somehow got to her feet, but she stood fairly steadily. "I won't have things like that said in my house. And at such a time—a house of death, a tragedy—"

"Well," Paul blinked owlishly, "you can see everything Marigold's got, so what?"

Marigold drew her lips back from her teeth. "You bloody revolting little sap. What gives you any right to make that stinking remark about me?" she spat.

"If you were a decent woman, living a decent life with your husband and bringing up your children, nobody'd be able to make remarks about you. At least, nobody could say they saw you sitting naked on a sofa with your body showing to a roomful of people." Paul relieved himself of this sentiment with remarkable composure.

"Damn you!" Marigold stormed. "Julian, hit him!"

"You're impossible." Tears began to run down Anabel's face, making crooked furrows on her cheeks. "Horrible! How dare you, Paul? Cintra, you ought to be ashamed—and in front of Christie—" Her wrath was righteous, genuine. She'd never heard such words used before at Beechlands. Marigold and Julian mightn't be married—how could they be when Julian had an elderly wife who wouldn't divorce him?—but theirs was a romance. Now Cintra had torn the veil away. "Leave the room," she gulped, addressing no one in particular.

Cintra pushed her hair out of her eyes, and grabbing Christie by the hand, hauled her into the corridor. "Come along," she muttered. "Come along." They stared down the dark tunnel of the passage. The two candles were like stars in a moonless sky: they didn't make the surrounding night any lighter. Now that the radiators were cooling down, the air had a dank feel about it, musty and used up and chill. The house seemed very empty, and suddenly silent.

"There won't be any light in your room," Christie said.

"I'll take one of the jam pots. I've a new battery in my night light, too."

They crept along the corridor. Cintra kept looking over her shoulder, and her fingers dug into the palm of Christie's hand. "I feel as if someone were coming behind me, someone invisible." She lifted the candle off the tallboy and pulled Christie into her room.

The electric night light, a frosted glass cone sprouting from the round battery case, gave a pale, greenish glow that was far from cheerful. The squashed lipstick on the carpet looked like clots of blood. Christie picked up a stocking and hung it over the back of a chair.

"Christie?"

"Yes?"

"I think I'm going off my head." Cintra clutched it, as if she were afraid it would fall off her shoulders. "How can I explain about the chloroform? How? How?" She began to prowl round the room, tripping over sandals, shoes, bumping into the chairs. "My God, what'll I do? I wish I hadn't had that last drink. Five hundred pounds, five hundred pounds." She dragged the words out as if they hurt. "If only Max didn't think I was perfect. I wish I'd never come down here. Christie? What d'you think Parry suspects? I suppose he suspects everyone and everything, and that includes me. He'll ferret—" She poked among the clutter on the dressing table, found a very bright-red lipstick, and slashed her mouth with it. "When they let us out of the house, can I come and stay with you?"

"Of course." Christie looked at her feet, at her sensible shoes, her knitted stockings, then at Cintra's golden sandals lying upside down on the floor, their thin heels pointing at the ceiling. What would happen if she suddenly appeared in nylons, in sheer silk, an evening frock like Marigold's, and with her eyelashes made up with black blobs on the end of each lash, like Cintra, who, lavish in everything, recklessly smeared the contents of every pot, case, and bottle she possessed on her face, then got her hands dirty, and without caring messed up the whole effect. "Of course," she repeated. "I'd love you to come and stay, though people might think it rather suspicious."

Cintra turned round and stared at the palely illuminated oval of Christie's face. "Suspicious? Christie, why suspicious?"

"It wouldn't be—what's the word I want?—in keeping," Christie smiled. "Cintra Norton and the braown maouse. Everyone'd think you were hiding behind my ordinariness."

Cintra threw the lipstick back on the dressing table. She was furious, almost incoherent. "D'you mean these awful people've given you some sort of inferiority complex, or whatever the blasted disease's called? Or what? What is it?"

Christie picked out the lipstick Cintra had discarded, carefully made up her mouth, and smeared her eyelids with blue eye shadow, greasy, out of a small pot that had cigarette ash flicked into it. "They'd think you were trying to prove how innocent you are by going all rural, helping with the washing up and so on, basking in the reflected glory of my dun-colored aura. And don't you see that none of us may be allowed to leave Beechlands? If we are, then you must go straight back to Max, or get him to come down here. The police'll want to know about the chloroform. If you don't tell them the truth, then you'll be in the soup, so Max'll have to know anyway."

Cintra clenched her fists, swaying backward and forward. "It's like a sort of nightmare. Christie?"

"Yes?"

"Anabel's cuckoo thinking Parry had a secret booze-up in the bar and fell down and whacked his head. Someone must've sneaked up behind him and tried to knock him out."

"He told me somebody went for him. He didn't say who—probably he doesn't know."

"My God." Cintra put her hands over her eyes. "Suppose he gets murdered too? Christie? You ask him for the key to the safe—say Anabel wants you to get something out for her."

"But darling, don't you see that now Lawty's dead—"

"What's that? Be quiet, there's someone outside the door."

They stood and listened. The silence was fearful, empty, and yet as if it were possessed of a goblin body that listened outside the door, enjoying their sudden horror, waiting for them in the corridor in company with ghosts.

"What was that noise?" Cintra's voice was like a sigh, a wisp of wind.

"Your own heart thudding." But it wasn't, Christie was sure. She'd heard that small snapping noise before during the night, but now she heard it again she couldn't place it. "I'll look." She didn't want to look. It was worse than making herself look at Lawty's body, much worse, for she'd got over her horror of dead bodies at last. She went slowly to the door on tiptoe.

"In the name of heaven!" Cintra dragged her back. "You look like—I don't know—not like you. Wipe your face. Here, I'll do it for you." She scrubbed Christie's face with a crumpled handkerchief, smearing the lipstick and the blue eye shadow. "You mustn't do that again, ever—as if you were touting for custom at midnight in Jermyn Street."

"You see? Now you see why a braown maouse I am, and a braown maouse I'm fated to remain."

"D'you want to look like Marigold in a drink-and-dance dive? You haven't seen her and her kind when they're on the warpath in town. I have, lots of them, all the same." Cintra wailed in anguish, prodding the handkerchief into Christie's eyes. "You're too pretty. Don't you know that? What d'you think Marigold looks like early mornings without her makeup?"

"I've never seen lovely Marigold without her makeup after a night in London. I—" Christie stared at Cintra's enraged face. "I'll be back in a minute. Lock your door and don't let anyone in but me or Parry. I'll have to take the candle."

"But—"

Christie shut the door behind her. The candle at the other end of the corridor had gone out and she was in pitch darkness except for her glowing jam jar. "Parry?" she called cautiously, and heard footsteps, very wary, above her on the top floor.

"Hello? Yes?"

Now what did Christie want? Parry wondered. He was not feeling inclined for long conversations. After an exhaustive search of Gaston's attic and the rest of the top floor he had failed to find the safe key, and his temper was frayed. He had, however, helped himself to two electric torches, one from the chef's room, the other from Miss Killigrew's. He leaned over the top of the stairs. There was nothing to be seen of Christie, only the faint reflection of candlelight two flights down.

"Yes?" he answered. "Are you there? What's the matter?"

"I've just thought of something." Her voice was muffled and sounded a long way off. "It mayn't have anything to do with Lawty being murdered, but I thought it might give you some sort of line. Are you coming down? Parry, about ten or so days ago Marigold—"

"Yes? Come up here. Christie?"

The faint glow of light vanished, and there was a small thud. Parry switched on both torches and ran down the stairs. The corridor was black. In the light of one of the torches, the jam jar, its candle out, lay on the floor, as if it had been dropped there, or thrown. There wasn't a sign of Christie. He picked up the jar, relighted the candle, and put it on the tallboy.

"Christie?" he called.

There was no answer. He called again. Cintra's bedroom door banged open, and she gaped at him, blinking in the miniature twin searchlights.

"What's happened? Where's Christie? What was that bump?"

"One of the jam jars fell down," he said, cursing the thick carpets, the curtains, and the hangings, which so effectually muffled noises.

"It didn't. Christie had that one."

Parry evaded her outstretched hands and went into her room. He thought she'd make an outcry when he looked under the bed, into the cupboards, but she didn't, and it worried him. The inmates were more normal when they were screeching their heads off.

"When d'you last see her?"

"A minute ago—two minutes. We were in here. She suddenly said she'd be back in a moment, and that I was to lock the door and not let anyone in but her or you. I don't know what it was, but I heard a noise. I think Christie heard it too."

"What sort of noise?" There seemed no end to Cintra's moods. Was this the real woman or not? Quiet, sensible, her mannerisms, except for her open mouth, discarded.

"I don't know. Christie said it was my own heart bumping. Maybe she was right. She's right about most things except wasting her doglike devotion on Jim. I like him, but what's the good of loving a man who's always trying to run away from you? Or maybe she sees something in him no one else does. She sees inside people, she doesn't take anyone as she finds them. Why do people boast that they take other people as they find them? As if there were virtue in the casual acceptance of face values. Everybody but me accepts her at her face value—the braown maouse. A braown maouse shut up in a cage manufactured for her by a lot of people who don't know her, and her own cockeyed sense of humor."

"She's escaped tonight," Parry frowned. "In more ways than one. Where the hell is she?"

Cintra suddenly exploded out of her mood of quietness. "Why ask me? Find her—come on."

"By all means," he agreed dryly and taking a firm hold of her bony elbow raced her out of the room and along the corridor. "Very likely she's in with Anabel." Somehow he was sure she wasn't and when he opened the door of Anabel's sitting room, he found he was right.

"She's not here," Cintra whispered.

"Stay here and keep an eye on them." Parry pushed her in, and she staggered across the floor and nearly fell over Paul. "Anyone been out of the room lately?"

"All of them," Anabel croaked, her eyes half open. "In and out, backward and forward, backward and forward. Oh, God, the night is long."

As Parry didn't know about her two pendulums, which were now working again, this news rather bewildered him. "I see," he said, and beating a hurried retreat, shut the door firmly on the gloomy party. The jam jar he'd put on the stand outside Julian's door had gone. There wasn't time to look for it now; he had to find Christie. He called her, very softly, and listened. All he could hear were noises that sounded as though Cintra was waking up Paul. He peered into the dark cavern of the hall, then went along the corridor, found the handle on the bulging Venus's frame, very quietly opened the door, and shone a torch down the steep flight of the unsecret staircase.

"This is too much," he exploded, losing his temper. "Damn and blast it, another body."

The huddled shoulders below him moved, and the body of Jim Bridges turned its head and stared into the light.

"What the devil's wrong now? Can't I sleep in peace?"

"No," Parry said irritably. "Get up. I thought you were dead."

"Sorry I can't oblige." Jim smiled crookedly. "Would you like me to provide another body for you to use your professional talent on?"

"Perhaps you've already been so thoughtful. If so, where've you put it? At the moment I'm looking for the person of Christie Layne."

Jim staggered stiffly to his feet, his face gray, his scars suddenly showing painfully. "Is that your idea of a good joke?"

"No, is it yours?"

"No, damn you," Jim said. "It isn't."

CHAPTER 24

IF the preceding happenings had been fantastic, there had at least been something to show for them. Two dead bodies, a sprained ankle, a broken leg, not to mention an almost broken skull—all visible, tangible things, however wrapped in mystery. But in Christie's disappearance, so complete, leaving no trace behind her, there was a gruesome smack of the macabre. She had gone, just as if she might have walked out the door into the snow. The burglar alarms were switched on, but, Parry realized, the bells wouldn't ring now the current had died, and he wondered if anyone else had realized the same fact. The doors to the outside world were still locked, and the windows latched. Had someone quietly let her out one of the ground-floor windows and relatched it after she'd gone? He couldn't suggest it to anyone, in case none of them had tumbled to it that the way to freedom, even temporary, was wide open.

But when he and Jim shone the torches out of the windows, through the plate-glass doors, there wasn't the trace of a footprint. Even Eric's foundering tracks, after another fall of snow, were visible only as blurred, indistinct potholes when Parry hung out the window of the lounge and shone his light along the side of the house. She wasn't in any of the rooms or hidden in any cupboard. She wasn't in the boiler room, or roasting in the furnace, which had died to a sickly glow.

With the help of a chair balanced on a table, and a leg up from Jim, Parry wedged himself through the small, unpractical trap that appeared to be the only means of entry into the spider-ridden, dusty space under the roof, a cat's cradle of tie beams, struts, purlins, and rafters, from which dangled the black, clotted remains of ancient cobwebs. She wasn't up there. He poked corners, shifted the wooden covers off the water tanks, and peered into their depths. He ought to've been up there before, he thought, damning himself. After all, he hadn't searched the house properly the first time. He swung himself through the trap and hung by his hands till Jim guided his feet onto the chair. His hair was full of cobwebs, he was filthy dirty, and his bashed head ached almost unbearably. The candles he'd put along the corridor were half burned out, and there was a smell of hot wax that mercifully drowned the remains of the smell of chloroform and perfumes.

"Damn queer," he said, thinking it was far more than damn queer.

"D'you realize anyone can get out of the house?" Jim rammed his hands into his trousers pockets, staring at the floor. "Now the juice's petered out, the alarm bells won't ring."

"I've realized that, thanks. In case no one else has, you might keep your mouth shut. If anyone can get out of the house, anyone can get in. Hammerton unlatched the dining-room window with his knife."

Jim looked up quickly. "Why didn't the bells go off when he did?"

Parry ignored the question. "Come on downstairs. We're not doing any good up here. Is there anywhere we haven't looked?"

"No." Jim followed him down the gloomy, dark staircase to the hall. "I suppose you can't help not being able to be in twenty places at once, but this puts the lid on it." He turned up the collar of his jacket. He'd forgotten his overcoat, still hanging on the radiator under "The Laughing Cavalier." "I'm going home, and I'm going to ring up the Watching police. I told you Eric'd never be able to pass Effie's without going in. That's where he is now. Snoring. Effie's got a feather bed. I'm off."

"Just a moment," Parry said. "You had as good, if not a far better, reason than anyone else in the house for murdering Lawty."

"Are you suggesting I killed Christie? Killed her and ate her?"

"Why not? You appear to dislike her. You even dislike being in the same room with her—or should I say disliked, in the past tense? You don't want to talk to her and you seem to resent her existence."

Jim's face turned a dull red, and one corner of his jaw began to twitch. He was trembling with a kind of nervous anger, but his voice was calm. "I don't dislike her. I've met her on and off for years, but I hardly know her. She's—she dissects people down to their guts, I realized that last night, and poses as a braown maouse. Or did." He began to get incoherent. "She's come out in the open. I don't want to know anything about her. I'm damned if I want the intimacy of sharing in her privacy—I mean, her private life. I didn't ask her to dig into my mind, and I'm damned if I want to dig into hers—going round with her hair hanging down, looking so—Oh, to hell with you."

"Prig," Parry said briefly. "You're so eaten up with your own bloody inhibitions, or whatever you'd like to call them, you won't even admit the obvious."

"Obvious what?"

"That minus the hairpins and the prim and tidy expression she's very pretty." Parry half shut his eyes ruminatively. "More than pretty. Delectable."

"Then why the hell don't you find her and go to bed with her?" Jim's calm voice rose to a shout. "There're plenty of beds in the house, and Anabel'll think it quite right and proper, and you wouldn't be seducing her, damn you!"

Hoity-toity, Parry thought, and with considerable satisfaction heard Jim fall down the steps leading to the bar as he fled precipitously. He was welcome to the company of Gaston, moaning on the floor, the three girls asleep on each other's shoulders, looking not at all beautiful, and Robère slouched over the bar, his head on his arms, among the unappetizing remains of the last rounds. Now what? he wondered. It took a lot to surprise Parry, but Christie's disappearance dumfounded him. Paul's insistence that the place was haunted, fated, and doomed seemed suddenly less ridiculous. The house felt haunted and doomed in all conscience, an echoeless cave of perpetual darkness, relieved only by the ghost lights of departed souls. Wake up, Parry told himself. One minor mystery, anyhow, had been solved. The potted candle that had vanished from outside Julian's bedroom, he'd found in Marigold's room on the dressing table when he and Jim had looked for Christie.

A gust of wind cried sadly at the main door, then wailed on its way and was gone. This wouldn't do. Parry was damned if he was going to carry any more keys, but the ground-floor rooms must be locked in case someone decided to go home or make a bolt for it. If Jim had realized the alarms were now out of commission, the rest of them might have realized it as well. Fortunately, every door on the ground floor was provided with a species of door mat. They looked, to Parry's overstrained imagination, as if they'd been constructed out of scalps torn from the heads of screaming Negroes, then dyed in their own blood for Anabel's special pleasure. Moving cautiously, he locked all the rooms that had windows to the outside and were not already locked and put the key to each door under its mat. Except that it would have been exceeding his duty, which he'd already exceeded, he would have locked the bar and its occupants up as well.

It seemed useless to start looking for Christie all over again. What a mess, what a nasty, unpleasant mess it all was! he thought, wandering back to the hall. If only Miss Killigrew could come to life or speak to him from wherever she was. Miss Killigrew knew who'd killed Lawty

"Parry?"

He looked up quickly. Groping at the banisters for support, Cintra felt her way down the stairs, her eyes screwed up, trying to see, feeling for each step with her feet.

"Well?" he said. "Not that anything could be well in this home-away-from-home. Well, what is it?"

She made the rest of the stairs with a rush, floundering at him, and began to gobble hoarsely.

"What?" he complained. "Can't you possibly enunciate properly? You're an actress, so you ought to know how."

She opened her mouth wider and cleared her throat.

"I said, I've looked for Christie too. Everywhere. Parry, what's happened? The others don't seem to realize. They haven't missed her at all. It's horrible, appalling—I mean, to vanish and not be missed."

"You know she's missing, I know she's missing. So does Jim Bridges."

"You miss her because you know she's missing." Cintra dragged at the top of her slacks, and something split.

Parry looked at her, into her staring eyes. "Tell me about the chloroform. Enough chloroform is as good as a lethal feast. You had plenty of it, to judge by the size of the bottle."

Cintra drew her breath in and made a choking noise. "It was to paint my throat, my tonsils. It kills the pain. I got it on a doctor's prescription. You can prove that, if you want to." She glared at him in defiance. "I spill things, so he let me have as much as I wanted." Suddenly she began to laugh, and her loud "Har-har-har" sounded almost indecent in the darkness-filled house. "I spill things because I'm as shortsighted as an owl. Max knows that, anyhow. Go on, tell Marigold—she'd love it."

"Tonsils," Parry said irritably, "my boot. Where's the chloroform now?"

"I don't know," she shivered, and flung her hands out. "Parry, I keep feeling the feel of someone who's killed. I feel it coming near, the vibrations, and then they go, as if they'd been deliberately controlled, held in at leash. Sometimes they escape, but before I can grasp them, they're dragged back again. What's that?"

"Nothing," Parry said firmly. "Go on about your vibrations. You don't carry a radar or anything like that round with you, do you?"

"Be quiet." She snatched one of the torches from him and pointed the beam upward. A hand, white against the dark rail of the landing balcony, slithered slowly along the polished mahogany, giving a horrible impression that there was no body attached to it. A wandering hand, with a life of its own, creeping round the house upon its lawful or unlawful occasions.

The beam of the torch began to jerk and waver in time to Cintra's shudderings and suddenly the candle in the jam jar Parry had allocated to the hall fell sideways and went out in a sizzle of running wax and black, oily smoke.

"Who the hell's that up there?" Parry called, his voice sharp. "If you start screaming, Cintra, I'll gag you. I'll go and see who's playing the fool now."

"No," she gulped. "No—"

The hand stopped its eerie wandering, and slowly the top of a head, then the forehead, and finally the whole of Paul Livingston's face reared itself above the rail, his eyes glittering in the torch's light, bemused and frightened.

"Paul!" Cintra cried, and laughed hysterically.

"What the devil're you doing?" Parry asked, wondering how long Paul had been creeping about up there, listening and watching.

Paul's mouth opened and a noise like a strangled sob came out of it. "I'm trying to stand up, Anabel's bloody liquor's gone to my knees. I was looking for Christie and Cintra." His head wobbled, and with a groan he heaved himself upright. "I won't stay alone with— I don't want to be alone with her. Why'd you leave me, Cintra?" He tottered toward the head of the stairs and came down them sideways like a crab, leaning his chest on the banisters, and fell on Cintra hungrily. "Anabel's gone off her head, she's walking up and down like a tiger, saying her father was an admiral and her mother the daughter of a lord."

So, Parry thought, Anabel, despairing of Julian's financial aid, was now trying to impress Paul, after throwing the cigarette box at him.

"Sweetie, Anabel's father *was* a lord high admiral, and her mother a duchess in her own right." Cintra pushed Paul at a bloated sofa, where he collapsed, while she sprawled on the floor at his feet. "Anabel's late husband was the youngest son of an earl, and she's related to all the titled gentry of England."

Cintra was in full swing. Parry reckoned she would thus occupy herself and Paul for quite a time. He ran up the stairs and listened, then tapped on Anabel's door and went in. She had changed her evening dress for a garment he supposed would be called a wrapper. It was constructed of thick, blood-red silk, and draped her like a theatrical Roman toga. Despite her blotched face, she looked more imposing than ever, and she had either sobered up or had so many more drinks that she had temporarily sloughed off her despondency.

"All alone?" Parry asked unnecessarily.

"Lane dear, how lovely of you!" She reached out her hand in a gracious gesture, a hostess welcoming an honored guest, an old friend. "I wondered where you'd got to. They've all deserted me, though God knows I'm glad to be alone with my sorrow."

Marvelous, Parry silently congratulated her. "One doesn't always want to be surrounded by people, even if they're old friends," he said, tuning in to her mood. "Solitude of mind and body is sometimes necessary."

Anabel pressed her hand on her bosom and gave a slight lurch to starboard. "I believe you're someone who understands me. Have a drink?"

"Thanks," he said gratefully. "I will. Shall I help myself?"

Anabel inclined her head and steadied herself against the mantelpiece. "Where the hell's that little runt Paul got to?" She flipped her face with an enormous mauve powder puff. "Not that I'm not very fond of Paul," she added hurriedly. "Very fond indeed. He has great qualities."

And lots of dough, too, Parry imagined. "But rather tactless," he said, "to go on harping all the time on the place being doomed to ill luck." The brandy was good, though he wished it had been whisky. Apparently the whisky supply in Anabel's room had run out.

Anabel sank into an armchair with extraordinary dignity, considering she had to sit down because her knees had suddenly given way.

"Paul's so temperamental." Her voice was uncertain. "Things—things do happen in any house."

"In the best regulated of families," Parry agreed, and exploded his latest mine. "I suppose you know Christie Layne's vanished completely?"

Anabel didn't seem to hear. "I shall have to dismiss Hilden tomorrow. Really, letting the lights go out! As for Gaston, falling down and breaking half his bones, it's his own fault. At my whisky again, I suppose. And Robère—he'll have to go too. Can you imagine it, my dear? He hasn't been near me to take the orders for tomorrow—today."

"Can you suggest any place in the house," Parry almost shouted, irritated beyond words, "that I haven't looked in, where Christie Layne's body might be hidden?"

"What?" Slowly, aghast, Anabel turned her black eyes on him. "Her *body?* Christie?"

"Her body, dead or alive. She's gone, vanished, disappeared."

"My God," Anabel began to tremble. "Another? A third? Here, in my house?" Tears came into her eyes. "And Beechlands has always had such a spotless reputation—and now a third. Oh, God! Now Paul will never— Who killed her?"

All she cares about is her ruddy hotel, Parry thought, annoyance rising in him. All that Christie's disappearance meant to her was another blot on the Beechlands escutcheon, already well provided, he felt sure, with a maze of bend sinisters. He gulped the remains of his drink and put the glass down. "And such a charming girl," he said acidly.

"Charming," Anabel echoed. "So sweet. Such a pity she's got no clothes sense. Oh, God." She put her hands over her eyes and burst into tears. "Oh,

God damn it." She struggled to her feet, the red toga swaying as she moved, ruby where the candlelight caught the folds, like rivulets of blood pouring from her shoulders. "What'll I do without her? I could tell her things—she always listened—she didn't tell other people. How can I ever hold my head up again? Go on, arrest someone and stop all this."

She turned her back, so that Parry didn't see the rest of her emotions, whatever they might be. He felt suddenly highly suspicious of her. Behind her outbursts, there always seemed to lurk an unconscious wariness.

"I can't arrest anyone without a warrant," he pointed out, thinking that if he knew who the murderer was he'd sneak up behind him and bash him on the head with a bottle and take the consequences. "Besides, even if I had a warrant, I couldn't arrest anyone. This isn't my stamping ground."

"Oh, God, the night is long," Anabel moaned. Walking on tiptoe, Parry sneaked out of the room and shut the door silently behind him. He lit a cigarette, and leaning over the top of the stairs, flashed Miss Killigrew's efficient torch into the hall. Cintra and Paul had gone. For a moment he was puzzled that they'd stayed there at all in the darkness, till he remembered that Cintra hadn't given him back the second torch. He listened. Evidently the door of the bar was shut. All he could hear was a faint murmur along the corridor to his left. Paul with Cintra in her room? Julian with Marigold in her room? He turned his head. Anabel's door was opening, and she appeared, holding the hurricane lamp on high. She looked like a rococo edition of the Statue of Liberty.

"I quite forgot." She paused, half shutting her eyes, as if she'd forgotten what she'd forgotten. "I quite forgot—the bar takings. The bar takings, in the till, Lane. I must put them in the safe." She held her hand out, and it was shaking.

So she was after the safe key too, was she? "I thought of that," Parry lied unblushingly. "I've locked them up already."

"But I must count them." She drew herself up, so that her bust seemed to tower over him, and with her free hand she drew her flowing draperies round her. "The money must be counted and banked."

He looked at her ruminatively, pulling his lower lip. "Not now, my dear Anabel," he said. "Not till your local police come along and take over."

As she backed into her room and shut the door with a thud, defeated, the back of Parry's neck prickled. There was one place in the house he hadn't searched for Christie. The safe was large. She was small.

The hall clock chimed six.

CHAPTER 25

HE'D never stay the course, Julian thought wearily. It wasn't any good kidding himself that he could keep up with Marigold's endless vitality, her capacity for drawing the life out of him till he felt like a sucked orange. Tonight—this morning—had proved, cruelly, that when he'd told Parry he wasn't as young as he had been, it was nothing more than the truth. Suddenly he wanted to put his head in his hands and cry. But he smiled at Marigold's reflection in the dressing-table mirror as she sat on the gilt stool and brushed and brushed her platinum hair till it shone and glittered. She'd got her second, her tenth wind, and from her emanated an almost terrifying aliveness. Rather to Julian's relief, she'd felt cold and changed, yet again, into a soft white wool housecoat, mercifully not transparent, which had absurd great pockets made of white fox. In the light of the nearly burned-out candle she looked like some decoration off a Christmas tree or as if she should be enshrined on a snow topped mountain, sparkling in the moonlight. Nothing, he thought, that his money could buy her was good enough.

"Marigold? D'you know I'm getting old?"

She turned slowly round and got up, stretching her arms above her head, then went and stood beside him, her hip   pressing against his shoulder.

"Why d'you perch on the end of the bed? Why don't you lie on it? Sweetie, you'll never grow old. You'll always be—"for once Marigold searched for a word and found the right one—"always be immaculate." Her pink tongue touched her lower lip, then disappeared again. "Why didn't you wring that bloody bitch Cintra's scraggy neck?"

Julian sighed and looked up at her. "Darling, only words like pearls ought to fall from your lovely lips."

"What in hell d'you mean?" She stepped away from him, her   eyes glinting. "Really, sweetie—"

"What I mean is," he said firmly, "I wish you'd cut out a few of the 'bloodies' and the 'bitches.' You can say what you like when you're alone, my sweet, but it doesn't sound too good in front of people like Parry, a stranger."

"What's Parry got to do with me?" She began to shake, and J u l i a n reached out and took her hand, trying to pull her near him again.

"Nothing," he comforted her. "Darling, don't be upset. I simply took Parry as an example of someone who's a stranger. It's all right—all right. Go to bed, and try and get some sleep. It must be six or more."

"I don't want to go to bed." She jerked her hand out of his and sat down on the dressing-table stool. "Julian darling, give me a cigarette. I'm sorry I'm so temperamental."

He held out his platinum case to her, but it was empty. "I've some more in my room." He snapped the case shut and got off the end of the bed.

"Don't leave me, for God's sake." Marigold's voice was shrill. "I won't be left alone to be murdered—I've got a cigarette—I've got some somewhere." She pulled open one of the dressing-table drawers, feverishly scrabbling her long nails among chiffon handkerchiefs, gloves, nylons. "I've got one, I've got one." She flicked her lighter on.

"Your nerves're in shreds," Julian said gently. "My poor darling."

"Oh, Christ!" She ground the newly lit cigarette out in the ashtray, screwing it into shreds of paper and tobacco. If she looked in the mirror she'd see Lawty's face, his eyes glassy, his mouth and chin clotted with blood and the white shroud with the pink roses soft against it. "Julian!"

He put his arms round her and lifted her to her feet, holding her to his chest. "It's all right, it's all right," he soothed. "I'll take you back to town tomorrow." That was to say, he thought gloomily, if they weren't all kept there by the police. "We'll go back to town and forget it—get away from this damn snow. I'll take you to the south of France. You'd like that, wouldn't you? Marigold, it'll be our first winter together in the sun, with the blue sea and the blue sky."

"I'm sick of the Riviera." She stopped trembling and bent her head back, letting her hair trickle behind her ears. "Sweetie, Algiers?"

"Oh?" It hadn't occurred to Julian that any of his predecessors had done her so well as to take her to the south of France. He stared over her shoulder at the candle. He'd taken plenty of attractive young women to Nice, to Cannes, to Monte, to Cap d'Antibes, in his time, but none of them had meant anything. No one had meant anything at all till he'd run into Marigold last spring. He'd quite literally run into her; they'd met head on rounding the corner of the Ritz, going in opposite directions, and he'd trodden on her foot. And she was sick of the south of France. She was sick of it as she'd been there before. He said, "Oh?" again, feeling hollow, and ran his hands along her wrists. "What've you done with your bracelet?"

"My—oh, my bracelet?" She drooped her head forward, so that her hair brushed his chin. "Parry and I locked it up in the safe, and my clips. Hours ago."

Parry got up off his hands and knees and removed his right ear from the keyhole of Marigold's door. Now, he decided, was the exact moment for him to make his entrance. Enter, upstage, Inspector Lane Parry, C.I.D., Scotland Yard. He hadn't heard much the two of them had said till Marigold had raised her voice. Feeling very stiff, he tapped on the door, opened it, and went in. They whipped round, staring, expectant, holding hands as if for mutual protection.

"You did say come in, didn't you?" he asked, trying to look as innocent and amiable as he didn't feel. "Isn't this your bracelet, Miss Trent?" He fished it out of his pocket and swung it round one finger.

"I thought you and Marigold locked it in the safe?" Julian's question was more a flat statement than a question.

"So we did." Marigold let go of his hand and transferred her charm to Parry, breathing into his face. This time her breath smelled of *"La Lune et toi."* She's rehearsed this, just in case, he thought.

"We didn't lock anything in the safe. I found this in my pocket, where, I take it, you popped it skillfully. You ought to go in for professional pocket-picking, Miss Trent."

"Oh, Julian, darling!" Lovely Marigold spun round on one heel, and with a naughty-little-girl gesture, leaned her head against his cheek. "Of course we didn't lock anything in the safe. I suddenly found my bracelet must have come unclasped and slipped off my wrist. I couldn't find it anywhere, and I was too scared to tell you. I thought—I knew it'd turn up. I d-didn't want to worry you. Where'd you find it, Lane?" She looked back at Parry over her shoulders, sweetly smiling.

"In my pocket," he said.

"Then someone picked it up and dropped it in your pocket." Julian patted Marigold's arm. "Considering everything, a practical joke in rather bad taste."

"That cow Cintra." Marigold drew her lips back. "Sweetie, for God's sake let's go down to the bar and have a drink."

"Good idea," Parry agreed. "You'll have company there. Gaston, Lilly, Ethel, Marion, the cook, and, presumably, Cintra and Paul, perhaps Bridges as well. Don't you want your bracelet?"

Julian smiled wanly. "I think now it really had better be locked in the safe. You look done to a turn, Parry. Why don't you have a shut-eye in my room for half an hour? Or put your feet up on Marigold's bed, if you like the color of her eiderdown better than mine? Personally, I do. The bulging purple horror I'm supposed to sleep under reminds me of lying in state."

"Oh?" Parry laughed pleasantly. Julian was talking at random. Any moment dear Julian was going to suggest he'd lock the bracelet up in the safe himself. He waited expectantly.

"Have a quiet kip, old boy. If you'll give me the key I'll nip down and lock the pretty-pretty up and bring the key back to you. Not that my elderly legs feel like nipping. Marigold, stay here and I'll be back and take you down to the bar." Julian's hand was only fairly steady as he held it out for the safe key and the gleaming diamond circlet.

"No—no, Julian. I'll come with you." Marigold's fingers twitched in the odd way Parry'd noticed before. "But it doesn't really matter. I'll put it on."

She was tensed up, taut as a fiddle string, as if she vibrated, giving out a note so high it wasn't audible to human ears. Parry, ever sensitive, knew she'd infected Julian. Most appropriately dramatic. If he hadn't been so dead tired, he would have been entertained by the scene. The dim, golden candle end, doused by Marigold's urgent silver flame, the contrast of dark, shadowed corners, the white expanse of Julian's shirt front in his black dinner jacket, his lined face contrasting with Marigold's smooth skin, the whole atmosphere of the room clogged with various emotions. It was a pity Cintra wasn't there, in a glassy-eyed trance, to complete the picture.

"I think, on the whole," Parry remarked, "that till this business is cleared up, valuables'd be better in the safe. I'll lock the thing up. If you like, I'll give you a receipt."

"In God's name, what for?" Julian relaxed, though he looked anxiously at Marigold. "Lock it up, by all means. It's safer, my sweet." He put his hand through her arm. "That catch isn't too good."

"Do what you like with my possessions, do." She gave Parry an angry stare, and turned her eyes away quickly. "Anything else of mine you'd like to help yourself to, Lane *dear?"*

"Oh, Marigold, darling—" Julian groaned. "Really, darling—"

Parry pushed the door open wide with his foot. "It's cold up here," he said. Marigold hesitated, then hugging Julian's arm, ventured into the corridor. They were like two doomed souls descending to the bottomless pit, Parry thought, lighting them down the stairs with the torch. On the midway landing he stopped. "It's an appalling thing about Christie Layne, isn't it?"

"Our little braown maouse," Marigold smiled.

"Christie?" Julian gripped the banister with his free hand. "In the name of heaven, Parry, what's happened? Is anything wrong?"

"She's gone. Not home. Vanished completely. Didn't you notice she wasn't around?"

"No," Marigold said impatiently.

"B-but she—" Julian was aghast, his horror and surprise as complete as Christie's disappearance. "It's impossible. Haven't you looked for her? Of course you must've. Why didn't you tell me before? She can't have vanished, pft, like that?"

"She has," Parry said, "and the bar's calling you."

Julian blundered down the rest of the stairs, dragging Marigold down with him. "I thought she was with Cintra. She went with Cintra. I mean, out of Anabel's room."

"Then Cintra's cut the little bore's throat, and that's about the only sane thing she's ever done."

"Marigold, darling, you're overwrought, you don't know what you're saying—I'm not surprised. Parry, what a ghastly thing! She must've gone home, got fed up, and went home to bed."

"She hasn't."

They navigated the hall and its obstructions, groping after the beam of the torch. Except for the faint reflection from the candle on the reception desk in its alcove, the hall was black. Parry hoped Marigold would fall down the steps to the bar corridor, but she didn't. The candle on the gilt bracket where the cherub had sat was holding bravely, nearly half of it still intact. Parry opened the bar door and was engulfed in a humid, invisible cloud of smells that made him wonder how anyone could stay in the room with them. He stood aside for Marigold and Julian, and as they passed him Julian whispered, "If I can settle Marigold down, I'll give you a hand looking for Christie."

"Thanks." Parry half shut the door, and putting his eye to the crack, inspected the inmates. Some thoughtful person had provided Gaston with two hot-water bottles and covered his middle with Jim's overcoat. He was awake, but to judge by the congested dimness of his eyes, still anesthetized by his earlier libations. Beside him, Cintra and Paul sat cross-legged on the floor, shooting dice. Cintra played for Gaston. Round them, sixpences, shillings, and half crowns were carelessly scattered, looking like pimples growing on the crimson faces of the rugs. Cintra was breathing hoarsely through her open mouth, while she shamelessly cheated on Gaston's behalf. Evidently Paul found the company congenial, for he looked quite happy, and every now and then tried to pinch Cintra's arm. Lilly, Ethel, and Marion were still in a huddle, asleep. They contributed to the general smell by smelling as if they needed baths. The three candles smelled of grease, and as Marigold, ignoring the common herd, draped herself on a high gilt stool, *"La Lune et toi"* struggled for supremacy. Behind the bar Julian opened another bottle of champagne. It frothed sluggishly when he let the cork fly. The ice had long since melted in the icebox; the champagne was lukewarm.

Anabel must still be in her room. She hadn't joined her guests to celebrate the dawn. Nor was Jim enjoying the company of the party, and uneasily Parry realized Robert Lord was missing as well. What'd happen, he wondered, if he tore the ice hammer from his suffering bosom and flung it into the room? He backed away from the door and cannoned into a solid, human body.

"Where the hell've you been, Lord?" he asked.

"To the lavatory, upstairs. I'm human, if no one else is."

"In the dark?"

"Miss Norton lent me her torch, if you got to know. Pretty decent of her, seeing it's my torch. 'Scuse me."

The door thudded in Parry's face. He felt like a reproduction of "Love Locked Out," unwilling companion to "The Laughing Cavalier." At any rate, for the time being he'd got them all back into the bar, with the exception of Jim and Anabel. He opened the door of the unsecret staircase and flashed a light upward. It didn't surprise him to find Jim sitting halfway up the steep flight of steps.

"Go to hell," Jim said curtly.

"I think I'm there already. Anyhow, it can't be worse than this place. What the devil've you got there?" Parry's eyebrows shot up.

"From the boiler room. The thing for raking out the furnace." Jim twisted the blackened iron cinder rake round in his hands. "If you must know, I've been trying to force the safe open, in case Christie—"

So he wanted to get at the safe as well? Only Paul, the three maidens, and Lord didn't appear to be interested in the safe. "Why didn't you ask me for the key?"

"Because I know damn well you haven't got it."

"Then who has?"

"You ruddy fool!" Jim began to splutter with irritation. "If I knew who had it, or where it is, I'd get it, wouldn't I? Go to hell," he repeated.

Parry pulled the door to behind him and started up the stairs. "Take up your bed and walk. You're going to escort Anabel in state down to the bar, where, I hope, you'll keep her. Up you go. And give me your weapon. I might need it."

"Cold feet?" Jim handed the L-shaped rake over. "I might need it too, mightn't I?"

Parry didn't answer. He was suddenly grateful for the feel of the solid weight of iron. He prodded Jim in the small of the back. "I take it you didn't succeed in forcing the safe?"

"All I succeeded in doing was to get my hands filthy and scratch the safe. It must be made of solid steel."

"Safes generally are," Parry said, "and you were committing an illegal act. Lucky for you it didn't entirely come off."

The Venus swung shut behind them. Their feet padded along the corridor. Jim knocked on Anabel's door and opened it. She sat on a stiff gilt chair, staring at the door in horrified fascination, a bird mesmerized by a snake.

"Good Lord," Jim said, "what on earth's the matter, Anabel?"

She's drunk all over again, Parry thought, then changed his mind. She was frightened into what seemed like complete paralysis. She'd sobered up and realized she was all alone. "It's all right," he reassured her. "We've come to take you down to the bar. You can't leave your guests, you know."

"Poor old Anabel," Jim muttered, and raised his voice. "It's O.K., Anabel, it's only us."

"He's going to shoot me." As though it were weighted by a ten-ton anchor, she raised one hand and pointed at the cinder rake.

"I've been making up the boiler," Parry shouted, and nearly bit his tongue off. He'd forgotten about the independent house telephones. The unexpected shrilling of the bell went through his painful head like a knife. "Yes?" He picked up the receiver, and Robère's voice quacked in his ear. "Of course Mrs. Adams's all right. Why shouldn't she be?" Thoughtfully he put the receiver back. "Your guests're waiting for you in the bar," he said to Anabel, not quite truthfully. "By the way, has your cook-chef been up here lately?"

The seed of practical, everyday things fell on the fertile soil of Anabel's mind and took root.

"Chef? Been up here?" she repeated, arranging her words carefully. "He has not been up here. He hasn't even asked me what the orders are. He can go back to France."

"Pimlico or Balham," Jim said out of the corner of his mouth. With a heave he got Anabel to her feet and with some difficulty steered her across the room to the door.

Parry listened to their unsteady progress till he could hear it no longer. He waited for a couple of minutes, then plugged in to the bar on the little switchboard. In a few seconds Julian's voice answered, sounding surprised. "Hello?"

"Parry here. Everybody present and in order?"

"Yes, old man. I'm just mixing a drink for Anabel."

She'll get alcoholic poisoning, Parry thought. "Why'd the chef ring through to her?"

"I think he's tight, or's got nerves, or something."

"Then you'd better keep your eye on him. Hello?" Julian's voice was replaced by Marigold's, clear and cool. Marigold's voice suggested that sweetie should come down and have a drink.

"Like hell sweetie'll come down and have a drink," he said to the telephone, as he put the receiver back. "You make sweetie vomit."

He contemplated the switchboard absently, then picked up the receiver again. By the sound of the scuffle, dim and far away, confused by a background of gabbling voices, Marigold must have snatched the telephone from someone else.

"Is that you, my sweet?" Parry inquired in a sugary voice. "What were you doing ten—eleven days ago?"

The only answer was a gasp, and the line went dead. Well, what had lovely Marigold been doing a week before last? Murdering someone? Gold-digging? Prospecting? If someone had murdered her instead of Lawty and Miss Killigrew, his sympathy would have been with the murderer, not the

victim. He pulled back Anabel's heavy brocade curtains. For a moment he
thought he saw a light blink, golden in the darkness. It must have been his
imagination, for when he opened the window and hung out, breathing in
the sharp air, there was no light anywhere. Or in his mind either, he thought
glumly, and banging the window down, latched it, shutting himself in again
with his uncongenial companions.

CHAPTER 26

THERE was, perhaps, another half hour of life in the candles. Not more.
The winter dawn, even with all the curtains pulled back, would never be
able to fight its way into the house against the deep reds, golds, and blues,
the complications of paneling and embossed wallpapers, or penetrate the
dark corridors and furtive corners of Anabel's beleaguered mansion. Like a
cat burglar trying to break into an impregnable fortress, the pale light before sunrise would be repulsed by the blank eyes of gilt cupids, the darkly
leering lips of "The Laughing Cavalier," the two eternal sleepers in the
dining room. The homely fires in Anabel's room and the writing room had
died natural deaths. The rest of the horrible fireplaces were filled with sham
logs, unpleasantly encrusted with some kind of red metal foil, intended to
represent the glowing embers of the ever welcoming hearth.

The vagrant snow wind had died down, and outside the house it was
very quiet and still, the trees a pattern of black and snow-decked white
against the lightening sky. It was still dark, but now the darkness was pen-
etrable.

Parry sat at Miss Killigrew's office desk and stared at the safe. Unlike
the darkness, it was quite impenetrable. The only effect the cinder rake had
made on its implacable steel was to add some more scratches to the ones
already made by Jim. He had turned down the idea that Christie, gagged,
bound in the appropriate dramatic manner, could be hidden inside the safe.
It simply wasn't possible that anyone could have killed or stunned her,
carried her down to the office, and stowed her away right under his nose. It
was the other secrets he was sure the safe held he wanted to look at. And
without the key, the secrets would remain secrets.

Wearily he tried to tick off in his mind the many problems and red
herrings that bestrewed his way. Gaston had once had the safe key. Now he
hadn't got it, or rather it wasn't hidden on him. It didn't appear to be anywhere in the house, though of course it must be. On the other hand, the key
that had been disguised with the cigarette cabinet label mightn't have been
the safe key at all. If Gaston had his tools with him, artfully hidden in some

very secret place, he could have opened the safe with a lock pick. Unfortunately no one could make Gaston talk if he didn't want to. Third-degree methods weren't lawful in England. I'd like to twist the bastard's broken leg, Parry thought, relishing the fancy. Gaston could be threatened with the charge of withholding information, theft of salt cellars and mustard and pepper pots, contempt of court, hindering the police, and a hundred and one other sins. But by that time, if he chose to open his mouth, it might be too late.

For Parry had an odd, unreasonable, illogical feeling that by the time the local police arrived, opened up the house, and took statements and fingerprints, any scent there might be would have faded. There were too many clues, all confusing the main issue. Too many people had motives, however farfetched, for murder. Everybody in the house had behaved in a highly suspicious and abnormal manner, except Lilly, Ethel, and Marion, who, under the circumstances, had behaved very normally indeed. Apart from the three girls they were all suspect, even Christie, who had vanished. Cintra's forever open mouth was nothing if not suspicious—it was connected with chloroform, the chloroform was connected with the murderer, the murderer was connected with Gaston, Gaston was connected with the safe, and inside the safe, as well as Lawty's £500, was what?

"Hell," he muttered, cursing Eric Hammerton, who, instead of delivering his message to the Watching police station, was now, no doubt, hogging it in either Effie's feather bed or his own. The safe might already have been looted. Everything was likely, nothing unlikely in this ghastly house. If only he could look into Miss Killigrew's dead eyes and see what she'd seen in Lawty's room—Lawty always had that room, he liked the view— inside the safe Christie smiled politely, tidily—Miss Killigrew stood at the bottom of the steps that led to the main door, pointing— "The view really is lovely in summer." It snowed pink roses—they came down very softly, lighting on Miss Killigrew's stringy gray hair, on her stumpy, outstretched arm, and burst into small, clear golden flames.

Parry felt for the cinder rake as something hit him a blow on the forehead. He had fallen asleep. His head had flopped forward onto a paper weight that anchored some envelopes. Now his head would ache in front as well as at the back. He hadn't inspected the paper weight carefully before. It must have been, he was sure, Miss Killigrew's personal possession: a round glass ball, inside it a miniature church with a red roof and a pointed red spire. When he shook it, snowflakes rose and gyrated in a cloud, then fell gently down on the church. How often had Miss Killigrew, in some rare private moment, made sure no one was about, then created snowstorms? And the Lord said—no, Miss Killigrew said—let there be snow, and there was snow.

He stood up, stretching himself stiffly, tucked the cinder rake under his arm, and dragged his weary feet to the door. Someone was coming unsteadily along the corridor, feet shuffling on the thick carpet, stopping, coming on, feeling their way. Two heavy bumps and a groan announced he'd fallen up the steps. A cigarette lighter snicked, heavy, labored breathing approached slowly.

"Peep-bo," Parry said, putting his head round the door and switching on the torch.

The lighter fell out of Paul's nerveless hands, and he trod on it. "For God's sake, what's that?" He hugged his stomach as if he were afraid it would drop off.

"It's me. Or rather, it is I," Parry said as pleasantly as he could. "Were you looking for anyone or anything?"

Paul gazed beseechingly at the torch, unable to take his eyes off it. "None of them'll take any notice, not even Cintra. Where's Christie? I'm damned if I'll get lost in the dark alone."

"Stomach worrying you? I know how it is, the shock. I'm afraid Christie's vanished. Disappeared."

Paul swallowed convulsively. He appeared to have forgotten about his stomach. "Again? Another? Is that what Cintra's going on about, staring in a glass of water, crystal-gazing or something, trying to find someone? My God, she's mad's a cut snake. I wouldn't touch this place with a broom handle. Anabel's had it." He looked over his shoulder, listening. "You're a policeman, so for God's sake get me out of here before I'm the next. I tell you, this place's had it, it's doomed, haunted. If you don't get me out, I'll be the next."

"Next what?" Parry asked brutally.

"You know." Paul pressed his hands together. He didn't want to say corpse. "You know, the next—I'd pay anything to get out, Parry. I can't stand it in the bar. Anabel keeps getting me in a corner and telling me about some legacy that's coming to her from Australia, only it's held up. Legacy, my fanny. Julian's through, so she's trying to get me to put money up. Listen here, lend me your car, old boy—"

"Certainly, if you can walk half a league, half a league onward, or rather backward, through the snow and haul it out of a snowdrift. It's a rather large-size SS, so on the whole I think you'd be better off in the bar hearing about Anabel's legacy. Or you could get Cintra to tell your fortune. You don't want the key to the safe, by any chance, do you?"

"No, I don't." Paul looked at Parry out of the corner of his eyes. "So don't lay traps for me. And anyway, I don't think you've got the key to the safe."

"Oh, you don't, don't you?" Unable to think of a more appropriate answer, Parry took Paul's arm, turned him round, and began to steer him back to the bar, lighting their progress with Miss Killigrew's torch, which was beginning to get very dim. Paul, drunk, superstitious, was no fly paper. And Julian was no longer a rival for the hand of Anabel in partnership. There weren't any rivals. "Was Lawty interested in the hotel business?" he asked.

"Seems like he was interested in anything." Paul stopped and regarded the half-open door of the bar in fear and repulsion. "For God's sake don't leave me," he whispered. "My stomach—"

"Damn your stomach. Hail and farewell." Without compunction, Parry pushed the hapless man into the room and quietly shut the door. The mutter of voices rose to a jagged, exclamatory crescendo, then died to an undertone punctuated by recognizable voices. "Sweetie, you ought to be a lavatory attendant." "Oh, Marigold darling, please—" "Cease groaning, Albert." A long, surprised pause. So Anabel knew Gaston was Albert? "Who's Albert, duckie? Anabel, d'you mean Albert or Gaston? Don't tell me Gaston's baptismal name's Albert? Albert? Poor devil, he's passed out. Where's some water?" "Cintra dear, I never mentioned anyone called Albert." "Jim, prop the Prince Consort's head up." "Julian—" "I tell you this house is—"

Doomed, Parry supposed. They'd feel fairly doomed when the candles gave their last flare-up in a gout of oily smoke, then died a smelly death in pools of blackened wax, and they had to huddle in the gloom, waiting for sunrise, knowing that one of them was a murderer. Pursued by a vagrant idea, he lit himself back to the hall, groped up the stairs and into Anabel's sitting room. The fire had gone out, but it was still warm, and the smell of the warm wood ashes seemed to clear the air of its taint of brandy and gin fumes, humanity, perfumes, and sex gone stale. The hurricane lantern burned with an uneven flame. To save the last of the candles, he blew them out, and the jam jars looked like jam jars again, rather dirty, as if they'd been debauched. In a round silver box he found some biscuits. He ate the lot, pushing one after another into his mouth till he nearly choked. The others had drunk so much that they were nourished, he supposed, by the fruit of grapes, by malt and juniper berries. There was a little coffee, now cold, left in the silver pot, and one unused cup. He laced the coffee with brandy and drank it in a couple of gulps. It tasted exceedingly nasty.

If anyone wanted to come in, he could damn well knock. He locked the door and methodically started to go through all Anabel's papers. In the sham Buhl desk in her sitting room were bills and more bills. She didn't owe hundreds, but thousands—at least five thousand. There were a few receipts, some sheets of paper covered with figures, a lot of returned checks, but no checkbook, no checkbook stubs. The returned checks were filled in by typewriter, signed by Anabel, in a huge untidy scrawl, the A's printed in capital letters. There were no papers in her bedroom at all, no letters, not even a book. But in her sitting room a lacquered stand with shelves was packed with newspapers, illustrated papers, and catalogues. *Vogue, The Tatler, The Sphere* were all well thumbed. The daily newspapers were neatly folded, uncrumpled, as if they'd never been touched. They dated back to two weeks ago, arranged in their proper sequence. Evidently Anabel lived in a world of her own and took not the slightest interest in what went on in the world without.

He put the hurricane lamp on top of the stand, unfolded each paper in turn, running his eyes up and down the columns. Yesterday's Sunday papers he ignored, and Saturday's. He worked back by degrees through Friday, Thursday, Wednesday, till he'd got to the beginning of the week. The Sunday before last, Saturday week, Friday week, Thursday week—woman found dying in hedge, another airmail crash in France. To hell with it, Parry swore. Routine inquiries would have to be made, and they would be the business of whoever was put in charge of the case. Eric, as a witness to what he thought he'd seen in London, when he was a bit lit, wasn't reliable. The routine inquiries might take a day or so. There were more airlines than one, more shipping lines. There were more ways of getting into England than traveling by a direct route. There were hundreds of hotels all over England and such tricks as giving false names.

Parry folded the papers up again, arranging them in their right order. A twelve-day-old *Daily Telegraph* escaped from the bundle as he was pushing it back on the shelf, scattering its pages on the floor. Damn and blast the thing. He put the pages together, fumble-handed from lack of sleep and irritation. Page one, page three—at the bottom of page three, a few lines in very small print leaped at him, as if they'd been printed in letters of fire. "Yesterday's arrivals by the South Atlantic Air Packet Service included Sir Henry Cullen, O.B.E., M. Serge Lavinsky, and . . ."

CHAPTER 27

THE bar, Jim thought, presented the appearance of some ghastly *tableau vivant,* though Anabel was the only one of the party who showed any signs of life. The others might have been dead. Anabel stumbled backward and forward, muttering incoherently about legacies and Australian uncles, her draperies catching on ashtrays and glasses. From time to time an ashtray or a glass was swept to the floor and either broke or rolled away unheeded into a corner. She didn't seem to notice the havoc she was causing, and Jim wished she would sit down. To refuse to be beaten was admirable, but when it was obvious she'd lost her battle for Beechlands, what was the use of pretending she hadn't? For Paul, whom she was trying to impress, took no notice of her at all. He crouched on a small gilt chair, immovable, as if he were tied to it, his bloodshot eyes staring at the floor.

Hunched over her glass of water, Cintra might have been asleep or awake, or dead and stuffed. She looked like someone steaming her chest with Friar's Balsam except that she hadn't a towel over her head. Packed into the same armchair, the only comfortable one in the bar, Marigold and Julian slept. Marigold had somehow arranged herself so that she was half on top of him, half twined round him, like a boa constrictor crushing its next meal to death. Lilly, Ethel, and Marion, huddled together for warmth and safety, dozed uneasily with their mouths open, dim figures that had faded into the background of shadows as the candles burned down. Laid out on the floor, Gaston gave an illusion of being dead, except that now and then his eyelids twitched and he made a gurgling noise in his throat. A sudden odd idea came into Jim's head that no one had properly examined him to see if his leg was really broken. But what the hell did it matter, anyhow? Nothing mattered compared to the fact that there were two dead bodies in the dining room, and Christie had vanished. He wondered what would happen if he pulled back the curtains and in a loud voice said, "Behold the dawn!" They wouldn't like that. Sunrise would mean the arrival of policemen with fingerprint outfits and inquiring minds, a procession removing the dead bodies, reporters gathering like blow flies.

Behold the dawn, Jim Bridges. If the police let you go, then you can wade through the snow back to Sloes Farm, cold and fireless and lonely, sit down at your bloody drawing board, and finish those plans for the new St. Edwards Town Hall, not forgetting the courtroom and the dock, the lavatories and the washrooms, the police station at the back, the tidy rows of nice, neat cells . . . . Without any warning, Cintra suddenly came to life, flung herself across the room at the radio, banged back the lid, and turned on the switch that set the records going. It won't work, you idiot, Jim thought dully; there's no current. But a slow, uncertain scratching started, accompanied by scarcely audible wailing moans that rose and fell till they resolved themselves into a phantom voice sobbing, *"Du bist mein ganzen Herz,"* horribly out of tune. His heart contracted and he felt as if he were going to choke. Above him the one light Parry had left switched on was glowing faintly, a pale, watery drop of blood that quivered as if it were going to detach itself from the ceiling and fall on him. *". . . und wo du bist, muss' ich auch sein."*

He stumbled out of the room, groping in his pocket for his torch. Little points of light dotted the darkness of the hall, like cats' eyes. He bolted up the stairs and along the corridor. That was Christie's theme song. He'd heard her whistling it very softly when she hadn't noticed he was there, and he'd sneaked away. Now he was running away from her again, from her haunting little ghost. He blundered against a door, opened it, and found himself in the linen room with its tiers of slatted shelves reaching nearly to the ceiling, the top shelf so high it had to be provided with a stepladder. The blankets were on the top shelf, long, rolled-up woolen sausages, comfortingly plump. He was bitterly cold, his teeth chattering. He wanted to hide, to get away from those damned people. They weren't human. They'd forgotten Christie had disappeared, or they simply didn't care. He clawed his way up the ladder and dropped his torch. In the darkness he burrowed under a blanket, pulling it round his head, shutting out the world.

Parry let himself out of the bathroom at the other end of the corridor and leaned over the landing balustrade. After washing his face and hands and the lump on the back of his head, he felt more awake. Lawty'd arrived in England twelve days ago. So what? He contemplated the hall thoughtfully. The effect of the slowly brightening bulbs was strange and somehow disconcerting. They were alight, but gave no light, and they seemed to throb as if they beat time to the engine a quarter of a mile away, which Hilden, conscience-stricken, must have turned out to attend to. Oh, God, he agreed with Anabel wryly, the night is long. He'd pulled back most of the curtains, and the gray ghost of the morning crept through the windows and the main door to be consumed by the shadows that lurked for it. The chairs in the hall were faintly visible. They had a sad air as if they'd waited for years for someone to sit on them and would forever wait. It was all inexpressibly dismal, cold, and musty. He stood there minute after minute listening for noises, for the furtive pad of footsteps, till the gray light began to turn a soft blue as if an iridescent blue mist had drifted into the house, making it for a short time beautiful. *L'heure bleu*—those enchanted moments that come sometimes before sunrise and after sunset. The dust on the banisters was blue, the film of dust on the furniture of the hall was blue, like the bloom on a plum. All the candles had guttered out and there was a smell of burned wicks. He went softly down the stairs and thought, I ought to've put a candle in the dining room for Miss Killigrew; she'd have enjoyed the effect of candlelight on pink roses. He had no definite idea where he was going till he heard an outbreak of voices in the bar and whipped into the office and locked both doors.

The desk lamp burned faintly, and as he hadn't pulled back the office curtains, it might still have been the middle of the night. He stared at the safe, wishing his eyes could bore through it, and idly dug in his stuffed pockets. Marigold's bracelet had wound itself round one of the keys; it ought to be wrapped up in a bit of paper in case it got damaged. He hooked his finger round it and laid it on the desk, its sparkling curlicues and delicate flowers caught in the wards of a key that had never been in his pocket before, a stout steel key labeled "Cigarette Cabinet." I'll be damned, Parry said to himself. No wonder dear Albert had said he could turn the whole house upside down, take the bloody floor boards up, and pull the furniture to bits, if he liked. Evidently, after his plunge down the back stairs, Gaston had decided the safe key was too dangerous a possession, and had got rid of it in the neatest possible way, by slipping it in his pocket while he and Jim were trying to lift the damaged hero. I'll be damned, Parry repeated to himself. Very likely Gaston had had hopes he could pick his pocket when things got safer, and if he didn't get the opportunity, at least he couldn't be accused of stealing the key.

Parry disentangled Marigold's bauble. The key slid easily into the lock of the safe, but when he turned it, nothing happened. He went on turning it. At the fourth turn there was a click and the door swung open. There was no time to be choosy. He swept the contents of the two shelves, a black enamel dispatch-box, a sealed envelope—"The Property of Wing Commander Lawrence"—some folders of papers, a small cardboard box, and the keys of the outside doors, into Miss Killigrew's sensible wastepaper basket. The key wouldn't turn to the left. He pulled it out of the lock, slammed the door, and it snapped shut. The office was no place to examine his finds. It was too near the bar. The lounge, the writing room were both vulnerable, so were all the rooms on the first floor. Only in Lawty's room would he be safe from interruption, as no one was likely to go up to the cold and loneliness of the top floor.

The light in the hall had turned from blue to a sickly grayish yellow, which made everything look hideous, vulgar, and disenchanted. One of the chairs was now occupied. His feet planted close together, Paul sat bolt upright, his hands holding the carved arms tightly, a curious expression on his face of watchfulness.

"Enjoying some solitude?" Parry asked.

"No." Paul pressed his feet on the floor. "Anabel went up to her room," he added, as if that explained his presence.

"I see."

"No, you don't."

Parry shrugged and went on his way. It was more important to investigate what had been in the safe than to hang about keeping an eye on Paul or anyone else. The stairs were patches of light and shadow, striped like a tiger, but the top corridor was so dark he had to grope for Lawty's door, feeling along the wall with his free hand. But the room, when he unlocked it, was full of a hard, cold reflection from the snow that almost eclipsed the dressing-table lamp. The snow that had blown in the window still lay unmelted on the rich blue carpet; the room had a lonely deserted air as though Lawty's clothes and possessions had been lying there untouched, forgotten, for years. A few hours ago his personality seemed to have filled the place, now there was nothing of the living Lawty left, just the cold and the untidiness, the sickly smell of the chloroform and the perfumes in the clothes basket.

Parry pulled on Lawty's gloves and turned Miss Killigrew's wastepaper basket out on the bed. The holders held nothing of interest, only papers and accounts to do with the hotel. The black dispatch box was adamantly locked; he put it on the floor, jumped on it with the full force of his heels, and the lock sprang. Inside it, rolled in chamois leather, were the implements of Gaston's trade, oiled and shining. Thinking they were his savings or his dear old mother's trinkets, Miss Killigrew must often have obligingly shut the delicate lock picks, the files, the beautifully cast tools up into the safe, then handed over the box when Gaston wanted to put some more hard-earned tips into it, or have a look at Mother's lockets. How damn funny, Parry thought, feeling immensely cheered, and opened the small cardboard box. It held a round white leather case, and in the case was a replica of lovely Marigold's diamond bracelet. When they were seen together, side by side, in the hard white light, it was obvious that the one that had been in the safe was an imitation—almost perfect, but still, an imitation. Christie had been right, but were the two bracelets evidence? If so, against whom, and why? He slit Lawty's bulging foolscap envelope open. He had no right to open it at all, any more than he'd had any right to open the safe.

There was more light by the window. He shook the envelope onto the dressing table. Secured by a rubber band were ten fifty-pound bank notes, Lawty's £500, all intact, and a new checkbook with not a check taken out of it. Nix, Parry muttered. The only other thing in the envelope was a fat leather case, rather larger than a note case, stuffed with letters and bits of paper. He shuffled them through, starting at the top, just as they came. Three letters signed Yvonne, the first written while she was still married to Jim, the ink faded, the second dated two years back, the third, the only one in an envelope, was postmarked Rio, just over a year ago. They were love letters, extravagant, stupid; and the third one, full of protestations of undying adoration, didn't ring true. That was all of Yvonne. Either she hadn't been a great letter writer, or her other letters were not so affectionate. There was a gap between her last letter and the rest of the collection of nearly six months. The spring must have got into Lawty's blood, for last spring he seemed to have started on an endless series of affairs that had started in Buenos Aires, proceeded in swift stages as far north as Mexico, then made the return journey in a roundabout way via the Bahamas back to where they'd started. The history of Lawty's temporary fancies, if they'd ever been fancies, was told in scribbled notes, long letters, in both English and Spanish; and there were hotel bills, always a double room, receipts for various presents—cigarette cases, bits of jewelry—all most carefully made out in Lawty's name.

Parry half shut his eyes, trying to conjure up the real Lawty, not the reckless hero of the last war who'd never got further than wing commander, but the man who had taken Jim Bridges' wife away, the only one he'd loved enough to marry. Out of all his apparently endless string of girl-friends he'd picked Yvonne Bridges as his wife, and she'd let him down, hurt his pride, taken the stuffing out of his strong, handsome self. He must have kept those three letters of hers, the pick of the bunch, to prove how she loved him. And when she didn't want him any more, when she'd finally finished with him, he'd started again on affair after affair, collecting one woman after another as he'd done before he married Yvonne, keeping these souvenirs of them, their letters, the receipts for the presents he'd given them, the hotel bills. Why? Parry thought he knew why. Lawty'd been so hurt he had to have proof positive to prove to himself he still had the same fascination for women, the same gift for making them fall for him. Was that why Christie'd said so gently, "Poor Lawty"? Had she guessed his vulnerability while she'd sat there in the bar being ignored by him? Parry felt a quick sympathy for the rake lying dead in the dining room who'd so disgracefully taken Jim's wife away from him, only to lose her to some South American joe, fated to have as his last roommate Miss Killigrew.

There were three more bits of paper at the bottom of the pile, clean, new. A receipted bill for a single room at the Royal Flying Club for the night of January 7, another receipted bill for a stay of two nights at the Grand Palace in Piccadilly, a double room for Wing Commander and Mrs. Lawrence from January 8 till the tenth. Parry's eyebrows rose. The third slip of paper was another receipt dated January 9—received from Wing Commander Lawton Lawrence, with thanks, £500 paid by cash.

The room suddenly turned pale gold, and Parry squinted, dazzled. The first slice of the sun, thin as a paring from a sovereign, was up over the far-off white horizon, warm on his face. There was dust on the backs of Lawty's brushes, on his cigarette case, on the mirror. Without thinking what he had been doing, Parry had drawn wavy lines on one of Lawty's handkerchiefs that lay on the dressing table neatly folded. The lines stood out clear and blue against the white, and he remembered that it wasn't just now he'd done his doodling, but hours ago. His pen was in his pocket. He frowned, recapturing words, incidents, details he'd noticed and packed away in his mind, lightly touching the edge of the mirror, the brocade dressing-table cover, the lamp, without seeing them. With a thud the lamp fell on the floor and went out, and as he picked it up, fumbling with his gloved hands, he had a split-second illusion that Miss Killigrew was standing by the door staring at him. He must be going mad. People didn't come back from the dead. Or had she? Had he conjured up her ghost? The brass door handle glittered, trembling in the early sunshine, and he realized he'd left the cinder rake downstairs and forgotten to lock the door. For very slowly the handle was turning, as if someone were trying it to see if the room was still shut up. So gently it might have been moved only by a small draft, a breath of air, the door began to open. A hand wrapped in a handkerchief crept round the lock, feeling for a key. The door opened wider, wider still.

"For someone," Parry said with icy calm, "who's committed two murders and attempted two more, you look damned immaculate, Frake."

CHAPTER 28

MARIGOLD'S clothes sense was so acute it took the place of her conscience, pricking her violently when by mistake she wore the wrong rig. Half the sun was above the horizon, therefore her lovely white wool garment with its white fox pockets was no longer suitable. She picked through her cupboard, with some annoyance wondering where Julian had got to. She'd wanted more cigarettes. He'd left the bar to go to his bedroom and get some and never returned. So she'd gone upstairs herself and there wasn't a sign of him. Now the damn sun was rising, the day was here, and she'd have to change. She chose a pair of white corduroy slacks that had a jacket to match them, a bright red shirt, and red sandals. The effect was very gay, just the thing for breakfast on a snowy morning in a country house, though she wasn't accustomed to having her breakfast anywhere but in bed. She looked at herself in the mirror and remembered the snow last night, and the red of Lawty's blood running out of his mouth onto it—Lawty and Julian, Lawty and Julian, and the two bracelets, the damned locked safe and the key Parry wouldn't give her. How dared Julian palm off a fake on her? But she'd made a joke of it to Lawty, and when they'd passed Cartier's he'd said, "Come along in and we'll see if they've got the same thing in real diamonds." They had, and he'd bought it for her, he'd even paid cash. She ought to've thrown Julian's fake away, but she didn't. It was worth money, and next day when she went back to Beechlands she'd put the phony one in a cardboard box and had Miss Killigrew lock it in the safe.

Suppose Julian found out? Julian would take plenty from her, but not open infidelity, and that's what the second bracelet would mean to him:

infidelity with a man who gave her diamonds in place of his paste. She began to tremble all over. Why had Eric turned up? She must keep Eric away from Julian. She'd only meant to go to town on the eighth for the day, just to have lunch with Eric. He was an old bore, but he had money, so she said she'd lunch with him at the Savoy, sssh, just for a lark, keep it a secret, the silly old fool. It was after lunch it had happened, when their taxi was stuck in a block in Trafalgar Square. Eric was talking about some repulsive place in India, she'd been bored, and she'd looked out of the window next her and seen him in the next taxi, leaning out, shouting directions to his driver. She caught one word, Fortnum's, and made Eric drop her there, summarily dismissing him with thanks for the lunch. For she'd recognized Lawty, though she'd never met him. He'd been one of her heartthrobs, her pinup boys, when she was much younger. He was handsome, exciting, reckless. She ran him to earth with a pile of ties on the counter in front of him. She was wearing her silver foxes, but no hat, so that her hair flowed round her white neck like a platinum waterfall. She said, "Hello, where in the world have you been all this time?" He said, "Hullo," smiling, showing his white teeth, holding a case bulging with notes, looking rather like Clark Gable when Clark Gable was thirty-seven. Shyly she said, "I don't believe you remember me, do you?" And he forgot about the ties. He put his hand under her elbow and walked her out into Piccadilly. She seemed to hear his voice again, "If I'd ever met you before I'd never've forgotten you. What's your name, beautiful? Marigold? Get in that taxi and we'll go along to my club and I'll pay my bill. I only pulled in yesterday—day after tomorrow I'm going up north for a few days—"

Till then he'd done her proud. He seemed to be lined with money, hard cash. She rang up Anabel and told her she was staying in town for a day or two, as an aunt of hers was ill. They hadn't gone anywhere near the places they might be likely to meet Julian. She told Lawty about him, old, mean, jealous, potbellied, bald, a donor of phony diamonds. But Lawty'd been more interested in talking about the coincidence of their both knowing Anabel and Beechlands. When he was drunk he harped and harped on the coincidence, saying Beechlands was mixed up with his fate. When he was in that mood it had taken a lot of coaxing to get him out of it. He said a lot of odd things, awful things about women that fascinated her, because he seemed to consider her different from the others, in some way unique, which, of course, she knew she was. She supposed he had one hell of a hangover when, about four in the morning of their last night, he'd waked up, put the light on, stared at her almost with loathing, and said there was only one woman in the world who meant anything to him, and that was his wife. But when he woke up again about midday he'd forgotten all about the one woman. He promised to come down to Beechlands in a week or ten days, and not to tell Anabel they'd met—as if she'd be likely to—otherwise the old girl'd be offended if she found out he'd been in England the best part of two weeks without letting her know. So he'd say he'd only arrived the day before, and they'd meet as strangers.

And Lawty'd been as good as his word, he'd come down, disastrously, on the same day as Julian. Lovely Marigold bit her teeth together. Julian had a lot to worry about. Lawty was dead. Maybe it was just as well. Julian was her bread and butter, the rock of strength in the stormy sea, always a safe port in a storm. He was good-tempered, and she'd got him just where she wanted him, under her thumb. If that bloody old wife of his he hadn't seen for years would only die or divorce him, then she'd marry him and find another Lawty to keep hidden safely in the background to amuse herself with. On the whole, things had turned out for the best. Lawty'd never have run in double harness with Julian. She stopped trembling, though her fingers still twitched with the excitement she always felt when she was afraid of being found out. Methodically collecting the South American cigarettes Lawty'd given her in town, which she'd hidden at the back of her drawer, she rolled them up in paper, put them in her washbasin, and tried to set them alight. If Julian came in she could say she was burning old face tissues—only they wouldn't burn. They just smelled strong and heady, but they wouldn't burn. They smelled of Lawty, as if he were lolling on the bed behind her smoking, filling his lungs, letting the ash drop on the floor. In frantic haste she searched for her lighter fuel, poured it recklessly into the basin, and struck a match.

In her sitting room, Anabel inspected herself in the big mirror over the fireplace. She decided she looked like hell. Worn down with worry and a sleepless night, she'd made the enormous effort of redoing her face and her hair and changing into suitable raiment for the occasion. Her mind was too confused to place the occasion in a conventional category, such as a party, a funeral, a wedding, or even, she shuddered, a death in the house when everybody cried appropriately and the blinds were pulled down. But it was an occasion, all right, horrible and frightening. So she had dressed herself for it in black, for in black, she thought, no one could ever go wrong. Her best black tailor-made and her black satin blouse were still unpaid for, but they looked distinguished and suitable. The thought of breakfast made her feel violently sick, but there were her guests to think of. As a rule most of them had breakfast in their rooms, but this morning they would all sit together in the dining room. Then she remembered the dining room was occupied and nearly fainted. Shivering, she forced herself to leave the haven of her room.

The house was like an icebox. Hilden would have to go, only she owed Hilden his wages for two weeks. No sounds came from the kitchen. The dust lay thick everywhere, and golden motes of dust gyrated in the long beam of sunshine that cut the hall in half like a searchlight. Monotonously the motes turned and twisted, rose and fell. The hall clock must have stopped; she hadn't heard it strike for the last two hours. The silence of the house was ominous, as if it presaged a renewed outbreak of trouble. She stood at the top of the stairs, listening, and out of the beam of sunlight below, Paul's head appeared as if he had been swimming underwater and had risen to the surface for air

"Owp!" Anabel gasped, disagreeably startled, and her heart missed a beat.

"There's a smell of burning, Anabel," Paul said, "and I'm not drunk now or playing the fool. I've been watching your door in case anyone tried to have a crack at you, only nobody didn't except those three sluts and the chef." He wobbled unsteadily up the stairs till he was on the step below her. "They tried to make the grade to your room to give you notice, only I stopped them. Stopped them going up, at least. Nothing'll stop them going out of here directly they get the chance, and they're a good riddance. That cook's tight as a newt, tighter'n I was. He's broken in the kitchen door and the four of 'em're in there in a huddle. What you want's a good French chef, Anabel."

"Robère is French," Anabel said coldly.

"Nuts." Paul picked at his right ear with a match, twisting it round and round as though he were trying to bore into his brain. "Lord's a damn French name, isn't it?"

"Lore, not Lord. Lore, pronounced in the French way. What's that smell?"

"I told you, burning." He made the top step, breathing heavily. "An hour ago I'd have said it was the murderer burning up the evidence. But not now. Anabel, I've been sitting in the hall watching and waiting. Julian didn't see me when he went up. He looked at your door, stopped and listened, and then sneaked away. I guess I know where he is, and I guess I know where Parry is, and I guess—"

"Be quiet," Anabel silenced him in a stricken whisper. "Listen, my God, listen—a bell, car engines, coming along the drive. It's the police, Paul, it's the police, they're here—"

"Damn good thing, too."

"Anabel? Anabel?" Cintra's door burst open and she flew along the corridor, her hands waving in front of her. "There's a whole armored division arrived. There's a snowplow first, then a fire engine, and an ambulance and two cars—one of the cars is full of policemen. I think Eric's driving the other one. What's that smell? Look, Anabel, there's smoke coming under Marigold's door!"

"I told you so," Paul said triumphantly. He took Anabel's arm and propelled her in Cintra's wake. Wisps of smoke drifted round their feet, and the smell of burning grew stronger. Cintra rattled Marigold's door handle, but the door was locked.

"Open up," she shouted, hammering on the panels. "Open up, you fool! We'll have to break the door down. Come on, when I say three, throw your shoulders against the door. One-two-three!"

Anabel held aloof, but Paul and Cintra flung themselves at the door with enthusiasm. Nothing happened except that Paul slipped and fell down cursing.

"Now again. Get up, Paul, for God's sake, and stop rolling about like a dog. Anabel darling, this isn't the time for dignity." Cintra looked over her shoulder and her mouth dropped open even wider. "What on earth're you doing in the linen room, Jim?"

"Having a sleep." He ran his hands through his disheveled hair and disentangled his shoulders from the blanket that hung round them. "Or rather I was having a sleep till you woke me up. What in hell's happening?" He kicked the blanket back into the linen room, turned to shut the door, and stood paralyzed. A pair of white knitted legs appeared dangling from the top shelf, and seemed to grow longer and longer. With a whoop and a whirling of blankets Christie descended to the floor and sat there, blinking sleepily.

"Why didn't someone wake me up?" she asked, yawning. "What's happened? What's the time? Why, it's daylight. I wanted to tell Parry that ten or twelve days ago Marigold—"

Jim dragged her to her feet, pushing Cintra on one side. "How long've you been up there on that shelf?" he demanded, his face working.

"Don't know," Christie smiled vaguely. "I've been asleep."

"So've I." Jim almost threw her into Cintra's outstretched arms and coughed as another wisp of smoke oozed from under Marigold's door. "The damn house's on fire." He tried the handle, shook it, raised his foot, and brought his heel down on the lock. The door slammed inward, letting out a dark gray acrid cloud from which lovely Marigold appeared like a genie, and Anabel screamed shrilly.

For Marigold's white corduroy suit was scorched and dripping with water, her platinum hair was matted on her head in burned strands, some short, some long, like a skullcap from which her face seemed to spring forward, a mask with green glass eyes that rolled from side to side as if they were operated by wires.

"Har-har-har!" Cintra bawled, hugging Christie's shoulders. "Once she was young and beautiful, and nobody called her cow, her face was as fair as a lily, but look at the bl—"

"Julian!" Marigold screamed. "Julian, helpl"

Parry stopped for a moment on his way down from the top floor, and took in the confused scene with a quick look. "Oh, no, you don't." He tightened his grip on Julian Frake's arm. "Escape me never. Come along. You'd all better go into Anabel's sitting room," he ordered the bewildered group. "And stay there," he added, hurrying Julian away.

Downstairs the main door shook under repeated knocks for admission. The beleaguered fortress was falling.

"Oh, my God," Anabel wailed, and fell backward into the arms of her depleted garrison.

CHAPTER 29

THE tumult and shouting had died. Refreshed by tots of Anabel's rum, the driver of the snowplow, the firemen, the ambulance men, Dr. Blake, the sergeant, and the two constables from Watching had departed, taking with them Lawty and Miss Killigrew, still fated to be companions, the morphine-injected Gaston, and, immaculate as ever, wedged between the sergeant and one of the constables, Julian Frake. At the last moment, her head swathed in a sea-green turban, wrapped in her silver foxes, Marigold had flung herself and a suitcase into the back of Dr. Blake's car and demanded to be taken to hospital, shaking her scorched hands under his nose as proof that go she must. Parry had let her go, with instructions to the doctor to have her put to bed and her clothes taken away. Later on, the police would want a few words with lovely Marigold.

Now the drive in front of the house was deserted but for Eric's big gray saloon, parked in the rutted, sparkling snow. Nothing remained to show that during the night two people had died violent deaths, except a few drops of Lawty's blood on the dining-room carpet and the waterlogged wreckage of Marigold's bedroom, after her successful efforts to burn the cigarettes Lawty'd given her. In Anabel's sitting room, the remaining members of the party drank cup after cup of black coffee, and ravenously consumed the sandwiches reluctantly made by Robère, while they waited for Parry to enlighten them.

"Oh, go on, tell us." Cintra spilled half a cup of coffee over her slacks. "He confessed in the true dramatic manner? Julian did—why?"

"I think he suffered from some delusion that my heart'd be touched, or that by admitting everything he'd do himself some good." His soul sighed within him. He wanted nothing better than to get off to Watching with Eric, write out a report, hand the case over to the Watching police and the chief constable, who hoped, so the sergeant had said, to reach Watching by eleven o'clock, snowdrifts permitting, then have his car extricated from the ditch and go back to town. "I hope I can read my own shorthand. And, by the way, before I try, there're one or two things I'm rather curious to know. None of you need tell me a thing if you don't want to. I'm not in charge of this business, thank God, and none of you is bound to answer. In fact," he added hopefully, "you can kick me straight out."

Nobody answered. Evidently they didn't want to kick him out. That was rather too much to hope for, he thought with regret." We shall only be too glad," Anabel announced untruthfully, "to give you all the help we can."

"Thanks so much. Sir Eric?"

"Call me Eric, old boy, everybody does." He sat up and rubbed his red-rimmed eyes, yawning. "What's it, old boy?"

"It was the Trent woman, wasn't it, who was with you in your taxi when you saw, or thought you saw, Lawty in the next taxi when you were in town?"

"Matter of fact, it was." Eric squinted sheepishly down his nose. "Nothing in it, though. Just took her to lunch. She asked me to drop her at Fortnum's. Funny, now I come to think of it, I believe what Lawty was shouting at his driver was something about Fortnum's."

"Very funny," Parry agreed dryly. "Thanks for telling me."

"I don't see anything funny to laugh at," Paul burst out. "There I was, trying to put Julian against investing his dough in Beechlands by making out the place was unlucky and full of ghosts, till I frightened myself so much I believed it. My God, the liquor I drank to pull myself together, and that only made it worse. I've got the damnedest awful thick head all for nothing—how was I to know Julian was out of the running before he even started? But I guessed he'd done it when he went upstairs and didn't come down. Anabel, you were sucking up to a murderer. It'd serve you right if I changed my mind and didn't put a cent in this place or haul you off the rocks."

"Paul—darling!" Tears of unutterable relief filled Anabel's eyes and overflowed down her cheeks. "How was I to know? I mean, all your broom handles, and so on?"

"I wasn't darling a short time ago," he grumbled, and absently reached for Christie's hand.

Thank the Lord poor old Anabel's rescued, Parry thought, and hoped that between them they'd make the ghastly place pay. "By the way, were you all, that is, all but Anabel and Eric, lurking up in the dark in Lawty's room for the reasons you said you were?"

"Of course we were." Christie looked steadily at him, then smiled her tidy smile. "It was queer no one but me thought of telling you Marigold'd spent three nights in London ten days ago, and then I didn't finish telling you. You see, I suddenly remembered about it when I was with Cintra in her room. Only I was almost afraid to go and find you. There was someone there, I mean in the corridor. I heard a little sort of click that I knew I'd heard before. I know what it was now, it was Julian opening and shutting his watch. I wish I'd realized then. When I went out in the corridor and called you, I heard someone creeping up behind me, so I dropped my candle and bolted very quietly. Somehow I missed Cintra's door, because the corridor was quite dark, and went in the linen room. I didn't want to be murdered before I could tell you about Marigold, so I felt for the ladder, nipped up to the top shelf, and hid under the blankets at the back of the shelf. Only I must've been so tired I went straight to sleep, because I don't remember anything else till the noise of the banging on Marigold's door woke me up."

"I trust you slept well?" Parry inquired, and catching sight of Jim nearly laughed. He was scarlet in the face, and his hands shook. "Jim and I looked in the linen room for you. Evidently we didn't probe the blankets thoroughly enough."

"Fancy," Anabel said in a vague voice, her mind drifting in roseate clouds of high finance. "But Jim was in there with you, Christie dear. Weren't you, Jim dear? You said you were having a sleep too."

"Why the hell doesn't someone say that now of course I'll have to marry her?" At last Jim's armor of reserve and complexes gave way with a crack. "How the devil should I've known she was there? The shelves're so broad you could share them with ten gorillas and be none the wiser."

"Thank you so much," Christie said sweetly.

"I didn't say you were a gorilla. I said ten gorillas—I mean, I didn't say you were a gorilla. I didn't even say anything about brown mice. If you want to pretend you're a gorilla, then go ahead, only don't expect me to pretend I'm one too, because I'm not. If you must marry a gorilla, then go along to the London Zoo and pick one."

"Har-har-har!" Cintra yelled, then caught Parry's eye and put her hand over her mouth.

"Well?" he encouraged her. "Or'd you rather not tell anyone about your chloroform?"

She groaned through her fingers. "It'll come out anyway if I don't. Won't it? It will, won't it? Anyway, sweet Marigold isn't here. I've got pyorrhea. I didn't tell Max. I couldn't, it's so—so unromantic. My teeth wobble, that's why I don't dare shut my mouth, I'm afraid they'd fall out, bang, bang, bang, or shoot forward like rabbit teeth. God knows, I'm no beauty, but I could look worse. I thought if I came down here for a bit of country air they might get better, but they haven't. They hurt like hell, so my dentist gave me a prescription for chloroform, a big bottle because I spill everything. It stops the pain for a few hours, the chloroform does, only now it's all gone. Then three days ago I got a letter from my dentist saying there's some marvelous new system of sticking new teeth right into one's jaw or something like that—you know, no plates, or teeth grinning at you in the tooth tumbler, or rather, grinning at Max. Only the operation costs five hundred pounds, and I haven't got five hundred pounds. At least, I've got it in the bank, of course, or wherever one's money lives. Only you see I'm so extravagant I make Max look after everything, and if I want more than a hundred pounds I always tell him what it's for. How could I tell him I wanted five hundred pounds because I've got to have all my teeth out and new ones stuck in?"

"Just tell him?" Christie suggested.

"I'll have to, now." Cintra tore the top off one of her nails. "And now I'm at it I might just as well tell the lot. I'm no good at lying. I used to know Lawty very well, just as a good friend. I asked him, yesterday, if he'd lend me five hundred pounds just for the time being. He said sure, he'd make out a check. But he must've forgotten. I went up to his room before we all met in the bar before dinner. He wasn't there, and there wasn't a sign of a check, or even a checkbook. That's why I really went up to his room when you found us all shivering in the dark there, Parry. I though he might've made out a check before he died. And that's why I wanted the key to the safe, I thought there might be a check there for me. I'd forgotten a check was no good when a person was dead. There, now you all know. Why don't you laugh?"

"There's nothing to laugh at," Anabel remarked. "Poor darling. I must say I did wonder why you were going on so queerly. Of course, dear, you're always high-spirited, but not quite so, quite so—"

"Nuts?" Cintra grinned.

"Nonsense, dear." Anabel's mouth went dry. Was Parry going to ask her why she'd wanted the key to the safe? She'd have to stick to her story of locking up the bar takings. Not she to confess that she'd had her mind on helping herself to Lawty's £500, only as a temporary loan, of course, to keep the wolf from the door. She smiled fondly, if a little wanly, at Paul, and cleared her throat. "And now, Lane dear," she begged Parry, wishing he hadn't quite such a knowing look in his tired eyes, "do tell us all about everything—I mean, that dreadful man's horrible confession."

"Did you like mine?" Cintra asked.

"Very much indeed," Parry said. "I was just trying to think of some way we could account to the Watching police for your chloroform, leaving out the teeth. I'm glad your ever open mouth's accounted for. I'd an unreasonable idea that it somehow had something to do with the night's happenings. Via the chloroform, it had."

"Good thing I didn't forget the fire brigade, wasn't it?" Eric's eyes were slowly closing. "All the way to Watching I kept reminding myself, fire brigade, fire brigade, fire brigade—" His chin dropped on his chest; he began to snore.

The room was slowly growing warmer, as down below in the boiler room a repentant Hilden stoked the furnace. Five pairs of eyes fixed themselves expectantly on Parry, and commending his patience to the Almighty, he flipped open his notebook.

CHAPTER 30

"I CAN'T read my ghastly shorthand word for word. I'll have to give you a condensation, if that's possible, and stick to the essentials. You can imagine the details for yourselves, especially Frake's infatuation for the Trent woman."

"Of course, Lane dear." Anabel powdered her face, trying to hide her anxiety. At all costs she must placate Lane dear. He was charming, of course, but he was a policeman; all policemen, she knew, could make things nasty even for their friends if they felt like it. It would be too dreadful if he started asking her questions about Gaston.

"Well, here goes." Parry tried to sound as if he were enjoying himself. "Let's see. 'In the bar before dinner I heard Lawrence say something to Marigold that convinced me they'd met before and knew each other too intimately. When Lawrence announced he was going to throw himself out the window, I decided that out the window he should go. I'd noticed Christie fiddling with the ice hammer, and that gave me the idea. I slipped it in my pocket when we all went to change. I changed very quickly, went up to Lawrence's room, and asked him for the loan of a collar stud. I said how beautiful the snow looked, and he leaned out the window. I cracked him behind the ear with the hammer, and he fell with his chest on the sill. I thought it better to put out the dressing-table light, in case anyone might be outside the house. I found the switch was broken, but that by twisting the top of the lamp one could put the light on and off-some kind of short, I suppose. I lifted Lawrence under the knees, tipped him out, put the lamp on again, and ran down to my room, just in time for Cintra's snowballing party. When you turned up—' "

"Who?" Cintra demanded.

"Me. 'When you turned up I made sure you couldn't ring the police. When you and Jim were in the dining room, and Miss Killigrew was in her

office, I escaped from the others and went into the men's lavatory, intend-
ing to tear the phone wire down—but someone had left the garden scissors
in there, so I cut the wire in sections and put them and the scissors in the
cistern. Previously to this, by the way, I had put the ice hammer back on the
bar.' "

"I took the garden scissors to clean my nails before dinner," Jim said.
"I must've forgotten them."

"You did. Where was I? 'Then I thought I'd make the suicide theory
more convincing. I'd forgotten Lawrence hadn't been wearing shoes when
he was found, and I didn't know the pane of the hammer would have left a
mark behind his ear. I managed to evade the rest of the party and went up to
Lawrence's room again. I put the lights out, and using my lighter to see by,
smoothed the snow on the window sill and made prints on it with his evening
shoes.' You all know what happened next," Parry said. "Except Eric, and I
don't see why anyone should wake him up and tell him. But in case you've
forgotten, Frake put the dressing-table lamp on when Cintra called for light,
and when Paul knocked the lamp over and it went out, it was Frake who
picked it up and turned it on again. That put paid to poor Miss Killigrew.
She must've known the lamp was broken, and that unless Frake'd been in
the room before and handled the lamp, he wouldn't've been able to turn it
on with such unfumbling ease. She had the misfortune to stare first at the
lamp, then very pointedly at Frake, so he killed her."

"How?" Christie asked, horrified.

"He lured her to the boiler-room door and killed her just as I thought he
did. Then he joined Marigold in her bedroom, gave her the money to pay
her bar chits, and went down to the bar as if nothing'd happened. I found
Miss Killigrew's body and carried it to the dining room. That was a nasty
shock for Frake when Gaston went to stoke the furnace and didn't find the
body, but he had an iron control over his nerves." Parry turned over two
more pages of his notebook, longing for a bath, breakfast, bed. "To get on
with the abridged edition of Frake's statement: 'When Gaston went to look
for Miss Killigrew with the sherry, and came back saying he couldn't find
her, he dropped some things out of his pocket. Among them I recognized
the safe key, which I know well. I'd wondered why there were no letters or
papers in Lawrence's room, and it then occurred to me they might be locked
in the safe. I wanted to know if there might be some letter from Marigold to
him, and when we all left the bar to look for Miss Killigrew I determined to
get the safe key. Unfortunately, the ice hammer had gone off the bar, so I
had to go empty-handed. Eventually I found myself on the top floor, alone
with Gaston, who was poking about in one of the rooms. I stood outside the
door and waited for him to come out. I was going to punch him in the jaw.
Then I realized that Christie was in there with him, so I hurriedly went

downstairs to the kitchen, where I had an argument with Chef about more sandwiches.' "

"But I wasn't with Gaston," Christie puzzled, and turned faintly pink when Parry explained Gaston's neat deception. "Do go on," she said hurriedly.

"Certainly. 'Later on, Gaston came downstairs, then left the bar to fetch more ice. The ice hammer was still missing, but by that time I'd thought of another way to knock him out. I said I was going to write letters, helped myself to a drink, which I took with me, left the bar, and closed the door after me. The empty ice pail was on the steps, and the door of the back stairs was open. I therefore concluded Gaston had gone up to his room, and followed. I drank my drink, put the empty glass in my pocket, and stood at the top of the back stairs listening. You'—that's me," Parry explained patiently, " 'you and Christie were on the settee, but I chanced my luck you wouldn't see or hear me.'"

"See or hear what?" Jim asked.

"Frake." Parry lit a cigarette, which tasted of old hay, and described Julian Frake's movements, the same as he'd later repeated more or less accurately himself, except that Julian had taken far less time, for he'd noticed and remembered all the paraphernalia he needed while the hunt for Miss Killigrew had been going on. Then the patient wait on the top floor, in the dark corridor, and the unexpected bombardment of bedroom crockery.

"What happened then?" Cintra's eyes looked as if they were going to explode out of her head.

"We'll go back to Frake's statement. "I dropped everything, bolted for the stairs, put all the lights out, and more by good luck than anything else avoided running into you'—that's me—'and somehow found the hall and the door of the lounge. I went into the writing room, threw a letter I'd written in the train on one of the desks, put my empty tumbler beside it, and was out in the hall again, waving my pen, by the time the lights went up.' "

"How clever of him," Anabel remarked vaguely. "Do continue, dear."

"Oh, hell," Parry muttered. "The next item on the program is Marigold's bracelet. 'At Christmas I gave Marigold a very lovely bracelet in paste. I had just given her her silver foxes, and owing to a business deal I had just embarked on, I didn't feel inclined to pay for diamonds. I knew I could get her the same design in diamonds, and intended to do so this month, and have a second ornament made to match it, also in real diamonds. When Paul looked at her bracelet and admired the quality of the diamonds, I realized that was not the present I'd given her. Lawrence, no doubt, had gone one better than me. This made me even more determined to open the safe. I wanted more proof that I'd been justified in putting Lawrence out of the way, and little Miss Killigrew as well.' "

"Ough, ough, ough!" Cintra exclaimed. "The foul beast."

"Very foul," Parry agreed. "Now I'll try to cut the rest of the far too long story short. If you remember, I implied Miss Killigrew'd given me the key. That made me Frake's next target. I was trying to draw the badger, and made a fool of myself. All too conveniently for Frake, I stood in the office door with my back to the reception desk, forgetting my vulnerability. Frake happened along, I didn't hear him, he picked up that round granite match stand off the desk, threw it at the back of my head, and stunned me. Then he trussed me up in the office, searched me, didn't find the key, and left me there to strangle to death."

"And why didn't you, Lane dear?" Anabel inquired, coming out of a dream of yet more new carpets, gilt cherubs, and bric-a-brac.

"Gaston came to my rescue." Parry gave dear Albert his due. "After which he got nerves, thought he heard somebody stalking him, and jumped down the back stairs. When Jim and I were lifting him, he slipped the safe key into my pocket—I suppose the thought of it was too dangerous to carry round any longer. And, by the way, he found the key among the coke in the boiler room. It must've shot out of Miss Killigrew's pocket. He put a new tab on it marked 'Cigarette Cabinet.' Very cute of him. Almost too cute."

"But you haven't said if there was really anyone creeping up behind me when I bolted for the linen room," Christie said. "Was there? Was it Julian?"

"It was. He assured me he was only going to say boo and startle you so that you'd forget what it was you wanted to say about Marigold. He was most puzzled at the way you apparently vanished into thin air."

"Startle her to death, I take it?" Jim looked inquiringly at Parry with grim eyes. "The bastard! Sorry, Anabel."

"What, dear?" Anabel pulled herself up with a jerk. Any moment Parry would ask her about Gaston. Somehow she must head him off. She treated him to one of her high-society smiles, offering him another cigarette. "And now," she tempted him, "you must tell us all about how you were so clever. I mean, how you discovered Julian—Mr. Frake, that is—was the murderer."

"Is it really necessary?" he asked, beginning to lever himself out of his chair.

"After all I've gone through," Paul insisted, "it damn well is."

Parry gritted his teeth, wishing he could bat them all over the head with one of the empty bottles that still graced the disheveled table. "One," he began, talking very quickly, "I knew it was murder because of the mark of the ice hammer behind Lawty's ear, the ridiculous mistake of the shoe prints on his window sill, and the cut phone line. Two, Anabel'd told me that Lawty and Marigold had been carrying on a flirtation ever since Lawty'd arrived in the morning, though they'd never met before. Three, Frake was in love with the woman. Four, jealousy is one of the biggest motives for murder. Five, Frake was the only person in the house who could be jealous over Marigold. Six, Christie put me on to the two bracelets, the real and the imitation. Seven, Frake's immaculate calmness—or comparative calmness— was almost too good to be true. Eight, I gathered that ten days or so ago Marigold had been up to something. Nine, it occurred to me Lawty might've arrived in England before he said he did. Ten, I found this was the case when I read over Anabel's old newspapers—Lawty'd arrived nearly two weeks ago, on, I think, the seventh. Eleven, that as this was so, Frake might've guessed it and put two and two together. What's that add up to?"

"Sixty-six," Paul said, with remarkable promptness, considering his hangover.

"By way of conclusions, I meant. However, thanks for the lightning calculations." Would they let him go now? Parry wondered. No, they wouldn't. They were staring at him, still expectant. "All I had to go on was surmise. Miss Killigrew'd spotted the murderer up in Lawty's room. I saw her staring, so did Christie. Miss Killigrew'd been on the right track, so she was killed. Anyhow, at long last I found the safe key in my pocket and was able to open the safe. I shoveled everything in it into Miss Killigrew's wastepaper basket and took it upstairs to Lawty's room. Among other things I found Trent's paste bracelet, Lawty's five hundred pounds, a receipted hotel bill from the Grand Palace—a double room for Wing Commander and Mrs. Lawrence from January eighth till January tenth—and a receipt for a diamond bracelet bought on the ninth. I still had no proof, only sur- mise. Miss Killigrew had the proof. Then I realized that hours earlier I must've scribbled on one of Lawty's handkerchiefs with my pen, clear, blue lines that still looked quite fresh—and when I'd gone into the writing room after Gaston's experience with the chloroform, and found Frake and Trent there, Frake's letter looked so freshly written I had come to the wrong conclusion it was freshly written, that he'd been in the writing room while Gaston was upstairs."

Paul delved in his breast pocket and wagged his pen. "And all the time he'd written the letter coming down in the train, with one of these—only needs refilling once a year, any color ink you like, dries at once, stays looking fresh forever—well, nearly forever. And you and he had the same make of writing implement—same as mine, only mine's filled with violet. Very nice, too."

"Got an interest in them?" Parry inquired, and wasn't very surprised when Paul said he had.

"Oh, do go on." Cintra scratched her head as if she were a dog.

Parry filled his aching lungs. "I was thinking over the pens and some- how knocked over the dressing-table lamp. It went out, and I couldn't put it on again till quite by mistake I turned the top of the thing and it functioned.

That's what Miss Killigrew spotted. It needed practice and the knack of it to put the light on and off without fumbling. Frake didn't fumble. I'd just seen daylight when he walked in on me, and that was that. He was pretty good at sneaking up behind people, but not so hot face to face."

"Now I come to think of it," Anabel pondered, "yesterday morning Miss Killigrew told me the lamp had gone wrong. I told Lawty, and he said it didn't matter. I'm sure you did your best, dear," she comforted Parry, inclining her head graciously.

For which crushing summary of my night's involuntary sleuthing you shall pay, he thought. "Can I have a word with you alone—quite alone?" he added, as Christie showed signs of lingering with intent to protect.

The door shut with a slam as the banished audience departed. With considerable difficulty Anabel stood up and faced what she knew must at last be coming to her. "You needn't tell me," she moaned. "It's about Gaston, isn't it? I can only throw myself on your mercy and kindness." She swayed dangerously, as if she were about to put her plea into practice. "I discovered he wasn't honest when some of my guests' jewelry disappeared. I taxed him, and he said if I called the police he'd tell. So I had burglar alarms fitted, just to please the guests. Then my gold bracelet disappeared, and things kept disappearing. Again he said if I told, he'd tell. How he found out, I don't know—I mean, found out my secret. By mistake he let out his real name, and who he was, but even then he had this hold over me. Not that I wasn't always on my dignity with him."

"Don't you think you'd be safer sitting down?" Parry suggested. "You seem a bit unsteady."

"I always take it standing up," said Anabel, and collapsed backward into her chair. "Now you—you too know my secret."

"That you can't read or write except when it comes to figures and signing your name? I guessed Albert had something on you. I got him alone before he was carted off and squeezed it out of him."

"Oh, what'm I to do?" Anabel wrung her hands as if she were rubbing in skin lotion. "No Miss Killigrew to read everything and answer it. I've always had somebody. The late Mr. Adams, then—well, later on I had secretaries. What're you going to do?"

"I handed Albert and his tool kit, which, by the way, was locked in the safe, over to the Watching police. They can do what they like with him. I suppose he'll get a stretch if they can prove his kit is really his. That's all. You can swear you'd no idea he was a criminal. Your silverware is hidden in his bed. If it'll make you any happier, Anabel, I'll promise you not to divulge your grisly secret."

The door half opened. Paul regarded her through puffed lids, and plunging a finger in his right ear, twisted it round and round. "I'm going to bed.

So'd you better too. I'll get back to town by the evening train and buy up a good chef and a decent staff. When I come back I'll bring my solicitor with me, and we'll fix things. You'll have to manage as best you can till then. I've given Christie enough money to carry on with. She and Jim'll hold on for you till I get back or send you down a secretary, or receptionist, or whatever you like to call her. And Anabel, I wish you'd pull your socks up and learn to read and write. 'By."

Anabel stared at the closed door, her mouth open. "I never told him," she muttered hoarsely. "I never told Christie or Jim or anyone at all." Slumping back in her chair, she shut her eyes, breathing heavily. At first Parry thought she'd fainted. Then he realized she was asleep. He pulled at his lip, amused. Poor old Anabel, how many peopled rumbled her game? he wondered. But nothing mattered to him now, for at last he could escape. He tiptoed into the corridor and looked down at the hall. It was blessedly empty. No one waited to pounce on him with more confessions. He ran down the stairs and made the main door without discovery. Out in the snow and the sunshine, Eric sat behind the wheel of his car, talking through the window with Christie and Jim. Christie had screwed up her bun with a quill pen, which gave her an air of festivity.

He took a deep breath, cast a last look of loathing at "The Laughing Cavalier," bolted down the steps, and got into the car beside Eric. "We're off," he announced. "Good-by, Christie, good-by, Jim." A hoarse shout came from the hall door, and he dug his elbow into Eric's ribs. "Step on it," he urged.

Too late, Eric fumbled for the starter. Her mouth hidden by a woolen scarf, trailing a mink coat and a bulging suitcase, Cintra threw herself into the back of the car. The case burst open, and Parry swore under his breath.

"I'm coming too," she panted. "There's a train to town from Watching in about an hour. I want to go home. I want to go back to Max, teeth and all, and be damned to them. Good-by, Christie darling. Look after her, Jim. Good-by, Anabel."

The car lurched forward, skidding in the snow. As it rounded the bend of the drive, Parry craned his head out of the window. The immensely tall gray-stone house seemed to be staring back at him without interest or regret at his departure. Christie and Jim waved from the top of the steps. Then Jim took her elbow. They turned and went in the door. Parry glanced cautiously at Cintra. Surrounded by the jumbled contents of her case, she dozed peacefully. Her hair, in the sunlight, was an even stranger color. The scarf had fallen off, and for the second time he saw her with her mouth shut. Asleep, unrestless, she looked twenty years younger, and, somehow, vulnerable. He reached back and pulled her mink coat over her knees.

"Watching, old boy?" Eric asked. "The pubs'll just be opening up.

How'd you enjoy your dinner party?"

"I didn't enjoy it at all. They forgot to give me any dinner," Parry said with feeling.

THE END

Inspector Parry also appears in
Murder at Shots Hall
(0-915230-55-0)
also published by
The Rue Morgue Press